AN M-Y BOOKS PAPERBACK

© Copyright 2006 Kevin Saunders

A CIP catalogue record for this title is
available from the British Library

ISBN 978-0-955606465

Published by
M-Y Books Ltd

Cover design and typesetting by Rockfish Creative Consultancy,
19-21 Bull Plain, Hertford SG14 1DX
rockfish.eu

Kevin Saunders
kev@kevsaunders.co.uk
myspace.com/kevsaunders

(BIG)

TO JIM

I'VE BEEN TRYING TO THINK OF SOMETHING CLEVER TO SAY. BUT I'VE USED UP ALL MY CLEVER SHIT IN THIS BOOK.

WOTCHA!

by Kevin Saunders

PUNK ROCK RULES!

LOVE (LITTLE)

Kev

For my dad, Ken Saunders, who wouldn't have been too keen on
the language, sex, drugs and rock 'n' roll that pepper these pages but
would have got the jokes and the point. And it's for my mum, Greta,
Helen, Christine, Graham and all my friends - without whom I could
easily have ended up like the people in this story.
Of course I still might.

Thanks to:

Jonathan Miller at M-Y Books
Simon, Heidi, Matt and Dan at Rockfish for design and typesetting
Charly Rogers and Nell Bacon for insight, support and advice
Mark and Fabienne Evans and Mark Daniels
for unrelenting back-up generally
Cliona Healey, who I think will be a great writer one day
Everyone at Hertford Marquee

'*Wotcha*' – a contraction of the 15th century English greeting:
'what chere be with you?'

Watcher n – a person who watches or observes somebody or something.
A voyeur.

'It is necessary only for the good man
to do nothing for evil to triumph.'
Edmund Burke. English Philosopher & Irish Politician

'A little learning is a dangerous thing; drink deep, or taste
not the Pierian spring: there shallow draughts intoxicate the brain,
and drinking largely sobers us again.'
Alexander Pope. 1709

'When you blame yourself, you learn from it. If you blame
someone else, you don't learn nothing, cause hey,
it's not your fault, it's his fault, over there.'
Joe Strummer

1

Saturday 28th June 1969. 2.25pm. Norfolk

Their father's moonwalk strides in his battered suede fell boots and tucked-in tweed leave his wife and kids trailing disconsolately behind him. The brisk pre-breakfast constitutional hasn't been as advertised and has taken in a good five-mile stretch of featureless grey coastline shrouded in drizzle and mist and untroubled by anything so distracting as drama. Damp and cold, the two Raines kids grizzle and whinge and clap mittened hands together to stoke circulation.

'Honestly, Erich,' mutters Rosa, 'if we'd wanted to get cold and wet we could've walked along the beach at home.'

'Oh show some spirit woman.'

She tuts, puts her head down and quickens her pace.

Her husband stops.

'Look,' he calls after her, uncharacteristically sympathetic, 'If you want to get warmed up, why don't you take the kids to that café over there.'

'Not the Spazz Café!' pipes up Bart. The last time they visited the misty-windowed greasy spoon with aspirations to tea-room status it was mobbed out with a party of children with Downs Syndrome and their carers and the boy had to be dragged outside when he parroted at them all the abusive names he got called at school.

'If they'll have us back in there after your performance last time,' his mother sighs as she turns towards the café, tugging her two kids by the toggles of their quilted anoraks.

'I'll just go and check on the beach hut and...' Erich begins, but the wind takes his words away and his family trudge off oblivious.

The last of a fifty-strong regiment of salt-scoured beach huts in varying degrees of disrepair, whose faded paint in pale blues, hospital pale green and greying whites hangs off their cracked boards like dead sunburnt skin, the Raines hut is among the most dilapidated. The concreted promenade, bounded by a weather-rounded sea wall, disintegrates where it reaches his hut. It is now the last of the line after a stormy winter weakened the half-hearted bluff that tried and failed to tower over the seafront and a landslide engulfed the four huts at the end.

Luckily no one had been around. Well, not that lucky. There's never anyone around.

Nevertheless, Raines can't help looking over his shoulder as he wrestles with the rusty padlocks and finally wrenches open the uncooperative door, whose hinges complain bitterly at the disturbance. He winces as the dank air's mix of rotten seaweed, salt and wet wood hits his nostrils. The exterior door leads into what you'd call a sun deck in warmer climes – now shuttered and sealed with triple folded, glued and tacked polythene sheeting, its sand-scratched surface repelling light more effectively than it resists the storms and spume. Another set of three padlocks secures the inner door, which leads to a doubly dank, windowless interior. He lights a guttering hurricane lantern, then the gas stove, fills the kettle from a Tupperware flask and begins unpacking his rucksack full of provisions: a child-size sleeping bag, a teddy bear still in its packaging, several bags of crisps and sweets and a pile of books. *The Secret Seven. The Famous Five. Swallows and Amazons. We Didn't Mean to Go to Sea.* Sipping a cup of tea, he lights the paraffin heater, zips up his cagoule and steps out to survey the deserted beach.

2

Sunday 29th June 1969. 8.04pm. Norfolk

Her swimming costume clings clammily to her chicken flesh. That's what her brother always calls her: *Chicken*. The big bully. Just a couple of years older and thinks he's Long John Silver with his toy telescope and his little inflatable dinghy. That's why she'd steeled herself and jumped into the thing – little more than a lilo really.

While their parents dozed under the picnic blanket behind their stripy windbreak, the two children had padded across the sand to the drainage outflow, then paddled along the shallow channel that teased into existence a micro delta on the vast expanse of flat sand.

'To boldly go where no man has gone before!' Simon had trumpeted once they were out of parental earshot, that precious plastic telescope of his clamped to one eye. But there was nothing to see through it – apart from the last yob gulls, wheeling above them and squawking like the last pissheads reeling round the pub at closing time. Ahead of them was nothing but endless pearl-grey air and the distant, cast iron-grey delineation of sea from sky, which was where the sun was going to settle for the night, presumably extinguished with an explosive hiss and a storm of steam to cool and rest in the icy depths till the morning shift. In the meantime the full moon had clocked in early to oversee the territory with its modest, yet power-saving nightlight, the friendly face of a lesser god basking in Apollo's reflected glory.

'Look – the moon's huge tonight,' Susan says.

'Full moon – happens once a month. Big deal,' comes Simon's world-wise and weary retort.

'But how does the moon get bigger and smaller like that?'

Simon tuts with exasperation.

'Girls just don't know anything do they!'

'Well how does it?'

'It just does OK!' he snaps, making a mental note to look that up.

Susan pouts and huddles down in the dinghy – which is awash with water, but at least its sausage-like walls afford some shelter from the abrasive, salty wind that seems to be sandblasting away whole layers of protective and warming skin.

Simon paddles and paddles and seems to get nowhere. Reaching the now blazing flatline horizon is like following a star (which, in a way they are): it never gets any closer. As the sun sinks immeasurably yet inexorably into the sea, the lack of light, as much as the plummeting temperature, chills Susan to the bone and her sand-encrusted swimsuit chafes painfully in places that she doesn't yet know are private.

'Where are we going?' she moans.

And predictably big brother scorns her, revelling in the wisdom of his thirteen years.

'To explore you idiot!'

'I wanna go back.'

'Well you can't. This is a mission. You can't just abort the mission. What if Armstrong, Aldrin and Collins just gave up? What then?'

'Who?'

'You really, *really* don't know anything about anything do you,' he huffs with a self-importance that's failing to convince even himself in the failing light and overpowering wind.

So, relenting a little, he explains that in less than two weeks the Apollo 11 mission will be hurtling through that twinkling dome above them towards the moon and that this is a historic moment; one that everyone should witness.

'We'll be able to see it live on telly – but I want to see if I can see them coming back, once they're in Earth orbit,' he lectures.

'Are they landing tonight then?' Susan enquires, perking up as she envisages the rocket speeding into the moon's friendly pockmarked face like a needle lancing a boil.

'No, silly. They don't launch till the sixteenth of next month – and then it takes about four days to travel a quarter of a million miles – even in a rocket. Our mission tonight is to reconnoitre...' He sees the perplexity on her face. 'I mean check out some places where we can get a good view of the sky through the telescope without interference from light pollution. And before you ask – that's stuff like streetlights and cars and houses that shine so much light that you can't see past it. You know – when you're outside the house in the dark and they have the lights on you can see everything...'

'And they can't see you!' Susan interjects with a look of wonder.

'Yes! Maybe you're not such a complete girl after all!' Simon says, favouring his little sister with a rare proud and affectionate beam.

'I'm still cold and frightened Simon. I think we should go back.'

Her brother casts a seafarer's eye in a 360 degree sweep. The sun has sunk all too suddenly and only a faintly pink ribbon of light separates the crow black, sloe black, beach shop dinghy bobbing, kiddie-drowning sea from the heavy, jewelled and still descending stage curtain of sky. The sun, star of the day's show, isn't coming back for any encores now. Not till morning.

'Well if you're frightened, I'll take you back,' Simon says, failing to disguise the panic that's taken him by the shoulders and shakes them as if to wake him.

'I'll just take a butcher's through the scope and then I'll get rowing,' he goes on and then is silenced by the staccato woodpeckering of Susan's teeth.

'Here, take this,' he says, summoning courage from her fear, taking off his anorak and tucking it round her.

'But you'll freeze,' she protests feebly.

'I'll keep warm by paddling,' he reassures her bravely.

Susan snuggles under the quilted coat, kindling and corralling her tiny body's warmth till her blood creeps back towards her skin with a message from her heart that she's safe to sleep with her heroic brother rowing her home. And, rocked and rolled and lulled by the rhythmic swell beneath their delicate little wobbling, bobbing, buoyant blob, she floats off.

★   ★   ★

'That's a nice telescope!' a kindly voice rumbles, inches from her ear.

Susan sleepily opens her eyes, rubs them and winces as their encrustation of salt grinds against her dry sclera. The sun, though not exactly hot, is fiercely bright and half-heartedly warming – enough to make the sloshing brine in the dinghy warm as a bath that's cooled after you've dozed off. Susan reaches out blindly, helplessly, for a hot tap that isn't there.

'Daddy,' she starts, then focuses on the pitted slab of grey face that looms over her, eclipsing the sun.

It's the man in the moon, she thinks, as the cratered, flat and otherwise featureless face swims into focus. But then, it can't be. The face isn't round. It's oblong. No – *rectangle.* That's what Simon says. Only kids say oblong. It's a rectangle. And grey. A bit like granny's gravestone. Not nice, anyway. And it's got horrid grey bristles - like the hairs on pork scratchings.

Susan sits up – and the little boat folds in the middle and dirty brown water swooshes in and swamps her. Now up to her tiny eight-year-old waist in icy water, she cries.

'Simon! Where's Simon?'

'Who's Simon?' the man says, gently but not gently - like Daddy when he's trying not to be angry.

'My brother!'

'Ah – he must be the Captain of your little ship then! And the owner of this fine telescope, I imagine.'

Susan nods.

'Well I don't know where he is. I found you all alone, washed up ashore like Robinson Crusoe.'

'Who?'

The man sighs.

'Never mind. I think your Captain may have been lost at sea my dear.'

Susan brightens.

'Oh no. Not Simon. He knows everything about boats and exploring and pirates and everything. I bet he swam ashore to find Mummy and Daddy and he's coming back with them to get me. With crisps and chocolate probably.'

'And pemmican, I expect,' the man chuckles, like gravel in a can.

'That's a big bird that eats millions of fish all at once!' Susan boasts.

'No – that's a pelican. Pemmican is a dried... Well, never mind. Let's get you dried off and warm!'

The man's strong hands – which look nearly as strong as her daddy's – scoop her out of her puddled lump of plastic and gently set her down on the sand. Susan looks around. It's a beach. But not the one she left. Where's the little teas and snacks hut where the nice lady gives her free packets of crisps? Always with the little blue sachet of salt in them and not those silly new flavours. Where's the old wrecked rowing boat, ribcage clutching at the sky like a dinosaur skeleton, that Simon says will be their very own ship once he's collected enough driftwood to repair it? And where's the red and green striped windbreak behind which Mummy and Daddy curl up under blankets and sip coffee from their flask and listen to the radio?

The man kneels on the sand and wraps a big towel round her. It warms her. But it smells funny. She doesn't like it.

'Where are my Mummy and Daddy?'

The man says nothing. But stands, picks up Simon's toy telescope and casts his magnified gaze slowly and carefully along the infinite-looking sweep of this unfamiliar beach.

'Simon must be bringing them,' she says confidently. 'They won't be long.'

'There's no one here. No one,' he says quietly. 'I'm sorry, child, but you seem to be lost.'

Tears well up, lapping at the rims of her eyes like the dissipated waves at her feet.

'I'm not. Simon's King of the waves. He's my brother!' she states defiantly.

The rock-face seems to soften a little.

'Well, I'm sure he is. Specially if he's the owner of a fine telescope like this. But we can't have you catching cold here can we! '

Susan shrugs. Then a shiver provides his answer.

'See! You're freezing. Tell you what, I'll take you somewhere nice and warm and then we'll see about finding your Captain and your Mummy and Daddy. How about that?'

With a final scan of the barren beach, Susan acquiesces with a petulant shrug and is swept up, swaddled in the smelly towel and carried across the footsuckingly swampy sands towards a distant row of dilapidated and deserted beach huts. Once upon a time they'd been jollied up in brightly painted red, blue and green and pink and yellow stripes. Now they were faded, jaded, their emptiness full of the sadness of happiness spoiled.

The man opens up a door and leads Susan inside. It smells horrible. Like her granddad's bedroom. But it's warm and the man sits her down and gives her crisps and chocolate and a cup of cocoa before going out again to find her mummy and daddy and Simon. He even has the very book she's just started reading. So she cuddles up under the smelly blankets, sips her cocoa and waits for him to bring her family back.

She finishes *Swallows and Amazons* long before she hears the clink and click of keys in the padlocks. She's been crying and crying and crying for hours and as hard as she tries, she can't stop when the man comes back. Before he's closed the door behind him and painstakingly slid across all the bolts, she hears the voice of another little girl,

'Daddy, I can hear someone crying.'

'Don't be silly Daisy – it's just the seagulls,' the man's voice booms as the closing padlocks clunk home.

3

July 20th 1969. The Eyelid Incident

'A small step for man. A giant leap for mankind,' crackles Neil Armstrong through a storm of static, the blizzard of blips on the knackered black and white set merging into drifts of moon dust. Daisy Raines sits cross-legged and upright the way they teach at Sunday School, transfixed by this historic moment, cat-green eyes wide to absorb every fleeting electron of evidence that man has escaped; he's shed his earthly bonds and hurtled outwards towards the stars.

⋆ ⋆ ⋆

Bart Raines's room's like a miniature planetarium, the walls, ceiling and floor painted glossy black and pinpricked with silver self-adhesive stars – from the same stationer's bulk pack he bought to stick over bad essay marks and forge false fatherly approval. Swirling distant galaxies are depicted with swathes of multicoloured glitter liberally hurled at carefully painted spirals of modelling cement. From the light fitting with a dim red bulb that represents the sun in the centre of the orrery, hang painted ping pong, golf and tennis balls together with painstakingly painted Airfix models of the Lunar and Command modules, dramatically out of scale with the Mother of Pearl bead moon they orbit. Bart's telescope, his pride and joy and conduit to a better place, sits priapically on its tripod, poking its one enquiring eye out of the window. The Raines had finally bought it for Bart for his ninth birthday after a laboured discussion about the rights and wrongs of Galileo's treatment at the hands of the Catholic Church and agreed upon after the kitchen table conclave concluded that, as strict Methodists, they needn't see a Catholic excommunication as any sort of precedent. They'd approved of the orrery, despite its part in their son's fascination with Godless science, because it symbolised Descartes' clockwork universe, which was clearly fashioned in six days by the ultimate clockmaker. Not that they rationalised it quite like that. But clockwork worked. Clockwork was trustworthy technology; the stuff the universe was made of. Not like Newton and Einstein's science, which desecrated the Lord's creation.

Otherwise unaware of Descartes version of things – or indeed anyone else's, Erich Raines continues to view his son's scientific obsessions as a veiled affront to God. The door opens a crack, spilling light from the landing onto the bed, where Bart dozes and drools into the centrefold of a magazine displaying the entire Apollo 11 mission in graphics, charts and moon maps as lurid and glossy and exciting as porn.

Disregarding his *MISSION CONTROL - ENTER AT YOUR PERIL* plaque, Daisy gingerly pushes the door open wider, just to the brink of the creaking point she's subtly marked in white chalk on the black glossed floor just next to Orion the Hunter's bollocks – on which she treads with a smile. Flitting, light as moonshine and nearly as strong, across to the window, she freezes as the apple tree, whose leaves nestle in through the window frame, shakes in a sudden breeze and sheds fruit onto the lean-to's roof with a salvo of thuds like distant guns. Satisfied that no one's stirred, Daisy takes the end of the telescope ticklingly gently in hand, scrabbles among plastic rocket parts and tiny enamel paint pots and picks up a tube of glue, which she squeezes, suppressing a gasp of delight as she spurts a gob of translucent cement onto the eyepiece. Beaming with glee, she leans back to check that her handiwork isn't visible and places a hand on the old school desk behind her. It squelches. And stinks like Death. She squawks in horror and swivels. Her hand's plunged into the splayed belly of one of Bart's 'scientific' experiments: a still-warm tortoiseshell cat, pinned out and splayed like a spatchcock chicken, fur flayed and intestines sprawled. Jaw open in mid–miaow, the unfortunate feline's clouded eyes seem to stare accusingly into Daisy's and she flinches from their hazy gaze. To the right of its head is pinned its heart. On the left, what looks like its liver is bayoneted by a scalpel. Bart stirs. Daisy gags and, with a hand held to her mouth and the other holding her nose, slips silently out of the door, pulls it shut behind her with a shiver and reels down the stairs to resume her place in front of the telly's warming glow.

★   ★   ★

Her reverie is only partially resumed as the astronauts hop and skip and leap and bound in the boundless freedom of lunar gravity. The opening front door grinds and grates and sends Daisy plunging down to Earth. Erich Raines's shadow eclipses the light and falls over her as he reaches for the television - as does a sudden gloom when the full moon that beams through the screen suddenly dwindles with a clunk and click to a tiny white dot.

'Oh Dad,' Daisy sighs, crestfallen but resigned. 'Please may I watch a little more? Pleeease?'

Raines senior glares over his glasses and looms over her.

'Absolutely not. I've told you before and I'll tell you again. If the good Lord had intended us to fly he'd have given us wings,' he preaches as if to a far bigger and greater audience than the little girl looking up at him.

'But it's the Apollo moon landing...'

'Exactly – this whole sacrilegious venture is named after a pagan god. The Roman god of the sun – too close to which they're trying to fly on wings of wax. Does this not tell you something, child? These people are godless. They build empires just as the Romans did, they flout the laws of God and Nature and soon their decadence and pride will bring them to ruin – just like the Roman empire.'

Daisy gazes at the carpet, whose swirling, almost fractal, patterns are refracted and kaleidoscoped by the tears in her eyes to form whirling galaxies full of planets that don't revolve around her father and his bible bashing bunch of zealots.

'Where's the pansy?'

'Frankenstein's in his laboratory, where d'you think,' Daisy snaps with instant regret as the hand of God smites her down with a hefty slap. Erich leaves her sprawled in tears on the floor and strides towards the staircase.

'And don't think I haven't noticed you're not wearing your school uniform.'

He turns at the foot of the stairs and awaits a response. Daisy raises her heavy head like she's lifting a hundredweight.

'Sorry, Father. I shall put it on straight away.'

Erich nods and allows her a rationed smile.

'Good girl. You know how much those uniforms cost. You must get as much wear out of them as possible before you grow out of them. It's only common sense.'

'Yes, Dad. Only common sense.'

Daisy gives it a few seconds before following up the stairs and darting quickly into her room. Dropping her jeans and hauling off her T-shirt, she picks up the training bra her father bought her recently and struggles behind her back to hook it together, still unpractised in the art. The familiar creak of Bart's door pinpoints in her mind her father's precise position. She freezes, breathing fast but shallow, straining to hear...

★   ★   ★

Perched on a stool at the window amidst avalanches of astronomical magazines and rockfalls of weighty scientific tomes, the brittle scree shucked off by his precious mountain of precocious knowledge, Bart's glued to the eyepiece of his telescope, scouring the skies for a glimpse of the slow shooting star that's Collins's fragile orbiting tin can.

'Pansy!' booms the figure silhouetted in the doorframe.

'Just a minute, Dad – I think I've spotted the Command Module! It's like a shooting star but slower... It's fantastic and...'

'Come away from that thing now. It's for the appreciation of God's creation and Heavens – not the blasphemies of heathen.'

'OK, Dad. Just let me...'

★   ★   ★

Holding her bedroom door open a crack, Daisy trembles as she eavesdrops on voices venting through two doors half ajar and a carpet-muffled corridor landing.

'No – I won't let you "just" anything Bartholomew. You're spending far too much time looking at what you shouldn't.'

'But Dad, this is fascinating... I just can't tear myself away...'

'Oh can't you!'

Daisy cringes at the thump, thump, thump of the three paternal paces it takes to cross several galaxies and send the model solar system clickety-clacking as if in a solar wind.

'Well I'll tear you away from the damnable thing!'

The scream transcends the landing's muffler and resounds round the house.

'My eyes! My eyes! My eyes!!' Bart's scream shrinks with each reiteration of his agony to a whisper.

'Stop fussing, Pansy boy. Will you never be a man?'

'My EYE!!!'

Daisy slumps terrified to her knees, her back slamming her bedroom door shut.

Silence. Her speeding heart marks time for the countdown to the blast-off. Ten, nine, eight, seven, six... BANG!

The door explodes prematurely, sending the little girl bowling across the room. She hits the side of her bed and lays dazed, her still unhooked and titless training bra hanging loose from her equally titless breast, her eyes squeezed shut with all the strength her facial muscles can deliver. But a veil of thin skin can't save her from this sight. The light that fills the room as her father hits the switch bleeds bright red through her clamped eyelids. A huge, and hugely strong, hand takes her whole face easily in its grip, while another scrabbles at her eyes until they're prised open.

Bart's face oscillates inches before hers, held by a hinge hand and swinging from the floppy top of his short back and sides. The wash of red bleeds out of her field of vision and somehow floods into her brother's pain-wracked countenance. Another hand snatches at her hair and effortlessly wrenches her to her feet, shoving her tear-wet face against Bart's. But the sheen of wetness that shimmers on his face isn't tears. It's blood – seeping in tiny pulsing waves from the top of a lidless eye and dripping onto Orion's belt on the floor. Bart stares through an enlarged socket, a gory target, red circling white circling blue with a black heart circled in blood. The telescope's eyepiece, now blinking with its own ragged, blood and Airfix glue-mascara'd lid, is thrust at her own eyes. Her father's roar, her brother's screams, the tearing at her scalp as she's swung round the room by her hair and the pounding of her own blood in her ears all combine in a dreadful crescendo that only abates as she slumps in a faint to the floor.

★   ★   ★

'Now, finish putting on your uniform and perhaps you won't be punished too severely for what you've done to the pansy.'

The words filter through long after their meaning does. In an inverted Pavlovian response to her father's edict, Daisy's clutching at the bra with one hand and dragging her school skirt up over her knees while Erich salivates. As she edges up onto her bed and hunkers up her hips to

15

get the too-tight skirt over them, two ominously gentle hands take hold of her feet, slide up her calves and tenderly roll down her white socks.

'Now – I think you're old enough for grown-up stockings, don't you?'

She opens her eyes to find Erich kneeling by the bed dangling a cellophane-wrapped and cardboard-mounted rectangular package between a quivering thumb and forefinger. He rips it open and strips away the silky diaphanous contents from their sleek backing, rolls one up and inserts a hand into its opening like he's fucking it gently.

'You're about to be a woman now Daisy. And for women life is pain – you can blame Eve for that!'

His fingers thrust to the puckered tip of the stocking, flex and spread, slip the rolled nylon over Daisy's right foot and slowly pull and ease and tease the new skin over hers, like he's flaying her in reverse. With the right leg sheathed, and the stocking's black lace top underlining the V of wispy seedling pubic hair and cutting across her thighs to form a W, Daisy blinks away tears and raises her other leg automatically.

'No. Not the left leg. Not the left. Not the left. The left is sinistre. It comes from sin. This is right. Just right.'

At the door, blood and tears seeping from the right eye, just tears from the left, his mouth strung with elastic snot, Bart watches, eyes wide open, yet unable to take it all in. He closes his eyes; shuts it out as he has so many times before. But this time one eye won't close. It makes him see. Forces him to see too much as it always will from now on.

A shriek so horrible the sound's almost visible – almost touchable. It pierces the stifling silence, then is deadened. Through the eye that can't not see, Bart watches as his father yanks free the knot on his pyjamas' cord, lets the trousers slip to the floor, then sweeps them up, bundles them tight and clamps them to Daisy's face to smother her kittenish mewls of pain. Bart closes one eye. Tries the other. Again and again. But still he can see, so he turns, walks to his room, closes the door and sinks onto his bed, reaching for the headphones dangling from the record player. Before he can get the music on to drown it, a whimper penetrates his sanctuary. He drops the headphones and hauls himself shakily to his feet. Shuffling noiselessly to the door he kneels, levers up a carefully cut section of floorboard and dips in a hand, which comes out clutching three padlocks. These he clicks into place on clumsily nailed metal straps across the door jamb before wedging a chair under the doorknob. After a final security check, Bart slowly removes his clothes, pulls out a pornographic magazine from the cache under the floorboards and settles naked on a chair next to his dissected cat and his half-assembled crystal radio set with one hand clutching his telescope.

4

'Smith is Going to be a Plumber'

'No way. Not in a million years am I going back to that place. Not for all the coke in Colombia, beer in Belgium or tea in China!' I shouted in the general direction of my mobile phone.

'A thousand quid's a thousand quid though,' cajoled Jimmy, alarmed at the prospect of losing out on his cut. 'It's not as if you don't need it.'

'A thousand quid's eight hundred quid actually,' I retorted haughtily, 'after you've got your grubby mitts on it.'

'Have a little think…' my so-called agent began just as I hit the red and cut him off.

★   ★   ★

Although I wasn't exactly on my uppers, royalty cheques could no longer be relied upon to keep me in the rock 'n' roll lifestyle I'd been accustomed to – which was a bit of a downer. I'd become addicted to the annual financial shot in the arm I still enjoyed thanks to the apparently endless yuletide appeal of a little ditty I'd written fifteen years earlier, which generally covered the mortgage, the booze and the obligatory coke habit. But it didn't run to the luxuries – like my fifteen-year-old lad's school fees. It had only been a couple of years ago that his mother had bothered to tell me I was a dad. And only then because she was in prison and he was being taken into care. Rather than be a grown-up and interrupt my latest world tour, I'd taken him out of th local boys' grammar and the equally atavistic care home he'd been dumped in and palmed him off on an obscenely expensive private college.

So there I was – as Jimmy knew I would be. Back at the old school. Lured by a quick thousand quid for a snip of a ribbon and a snappy speech to open the new science block, I was unfashionably early, nervous as hell, mooching around the labyrinthine corridors and sneaking a cigarette in one of the dingy classrooms in the school's oldest wing.

Till recently I'd been flying just about high enough to escape the nearly ineluctable pull of my personal Big Bang's source and the gravity of the etiolated memories that stalked its ageless gloom. But now my downward spiral conspired to bring me back into Hartham Grammar's orbit – and I didn't like it one fucking bit.

I'd been invited to officiate at the open day in my capacity as 'Rock Star Winston Smith', the only 'famous' old boy close enough to the Z List to accept the paltry fee on offer. But it wasn't just the dosh that brought me back to my smelly old alma mater. It was an excuse to sniff around and decide whether my own boy should be subjected once more to its archaic regime now I could no longer afford the posh, progressive version. The rock 'n' roll rebel in me told me in no uncertain terms to blank it: ignore the invitation like I'd persistently and deliberately ignored the Rugby Club dances, the old boys' reunions and the jolly hockey sticks emailed approaches of half-remembered names who'd summoned me up through the medium of Friends Reunited. I say ignored. But that's not quite true. I rarely did. I slagged them off; I cursed them and I binned them and I eventually snubbed them. But I never ignored them. So it seems that hate really is closer to love than indifference. I hated it. Hate it still. Still can't manage indifference.

Question now was whether I really, truly, honestly believed that creaking, reeking place fucked me up.

My depressingly middle-aged mind was telling me maybe not. What if I ruined the little fucker by leaving him at posey, arty Dartington? Not that I could afford to. What if he had nothing to rebel against?

No pricks to kick against? What if he turned out bland and beige and old for his age? Then again, the private school would certainly be the antithesis of the church children's home I'd found him in, which was the sort that kept its charges on the strait and narrow by terrorising them with hellfire and brimstone; where God created the world in six days and evolution was anathema. It certainly wouldn't have been my natural selection. But then wasn't that me hoping to create a clone – a mini-me? A procreative ego-trip like that of every other parent hollering on the rugby sidelines, enforcing the right attitudes and angles, bigotries and prejudices, only to watch their re-run selves kick them in the balls and kick them into touch.

My boy Joe… He was named after Strummer (the front man of The Clash in case you didn't know), or so his mother had informed me after dropping her fifteen years overdue bombshell, presumably in an attempt to pique my interest. What if he rebelled against my Johnson's biker boots and tatty leather and recreated himself in pinstripes? Could I handle it? Nope. I hadn't even met him yet – let alone told him that a change was on the cards. As far as he knew I was some mysterious philanthropist who'd funded his posh schooling through a made-up trust fund.

Of course they'd brightened the place up since my day. A bit. Gone were the fly-filled fluorescent lights, which used to flicker, flash and glimmer with a harsh light that made even hot summer days feel cold. Modern paint gave the room a far friendlier atmosphere than the cold lavatorial pale greens and cheerless creams that provided the canvas for our handprints, scribbles and ink pellet art. But basically it felt the same because of the smell that still pervaded the place. A smell you don't dispel by changing your brand of disinfectant, paint or polish - the odour of aged adolescence, coagulated in the air, permeating the bricks and mortarboards and gowns and cold concrete floors. From skirting board to chair rail, the walls were still clad in the rich green glossy tiles I remembered. The ones you associate with Victorian Gents' public toilets and the unsavoury purposes to which they tend to be put. Such as the 'bogwashing' of new boys that I'd endured one sunny September morning in 1972 – a ritual that involves dragging the unfortunate victim kicking and screaming to a toilet stall, ramming his head down the usually un-flushed and shitty bowl and flushing...

Water frothing and gurgling in my ears and the back of my throat as a tiny, gently disintegrating turd flutters and flaps in front of my eyes. Strong hands clutch the scruff of my neck and haul me up, up, up to the spluttering, retching and hawking safety of the piss-stinking toilet stall. The gaggle of predators flocks off, squawking and cackling like gulls as I sit dripping in a puddle of shit-flecked piss and disinfectant and rub my weeping eyes...

I shuddered at the memory, as if I was still shaking off that vile toilet water. That charming little episode, I was sure, explained my lasting fear of putting my head under water – and my trigger-happy vomit reflex whenever the smell of shit or its associated disinfectants infected my nostrils. I hoped it wouldn't happen to my son - whoever he was - the unspeakable cruelty I'd seen; the savagery of adolescent boys turning on anyone different, dehumanising him and massacring his otherness with Gestapo efficiency... Absently, I trailed a finger across an ancient desk, across its prehistoric cave-paintings in turquoise ink of imagined female nudes and crudely gouged names of football clubs and long-forgotten rock groups. And then I spotted his name: BRAINS IS A COCKSUCKER. I shook my head and shuddered again like a dog fresh out of a river, but this time failed to shake off the memories... Suddenly though, a familiar sound shifted the theme of my reminiscence, if not its time-frame:

'Smith! How's the plumbing?' boomed a rich, thick, deep brown voice like English grammar school gravy, with a touch of ancient Indian spice, the air of eccentricity made complete by the offbeat clump, click and drag of that shiny orthopaedic boot.

I could see him before I swivelled. A tall gangling black man in a white Graham Greene character suit with gleaming pate and the habitual

hunch of the too tall. I turned and my memory's image shrank. Mr Patel
wasn't particularly small – but he was no Meadowlark Lemon. His five-
foot-ten was coiled into five-foot-six by that goofy foot and curly spine.
But the eyes had shed none of their customary daily-bred contempt.

'Not actually a plumber actually sir.'

Shit. I called the bastard 'sir'.

'Not a plumber! Not a plumber!' he mused, looking past me at
something I couldn't see.

'No. Not a plumber. A musician,' I mumbled, instantly pissed off
with the deference to which I'd reverted robotically.

'Play the pipes do you?'

'No sir.'

Shit. Did it again!

'Actually I sing and play guitar in a rock group... Airstrip One - you
probably won't have heard of us...'

'I'm sure I won't,' he pronounced, dismissing my fame and fortune
and talent and years of dues-paying in a single breath.

'Aren't you a bit old for that?' he boomed.

'Probably – but it's a living. I'm quite famous actually,' I tried,
pointlessly, to impress him. 'And rich.'

'Hmmmm. Can't do simultaneous equations though can you!'

'No, but I can do a simultaneous live TV broadcast and webcast to
thirty nations!' came my resentful riposte.

'I'm sorry Smith, you appear to be speaking in a foreign tongue,' he
ad glibbed at me, leaning, like a colonial diplomat singularly lacking in
the skills of diplomacy, on his walking stick, the ornate silver handle of
which glinted at me between his bony knuckles.

I spun on one biker-booted foot and, with Jackie Chan's élan, kicked
the stick away and sent him crashing in a pile of wizened clickety-
clacking bones onto unfriendly shiny tiles. The glare of his bald and
shiny skull met that of the flawless floor and my steel toecap crunched
sickeningly into the delicately thin cranium and spilled his blood and
brains. Well, in my mind, anyway.

What I really did was try to justify my existence – as much to myself as to him – by pointing out my name on the ornate 'roll of honour' that listed the school's most prominent alumni. It was pleasing to note that I'd only been superseded in celebrity terms by one pro footballer – and since he'd just done a Gary Glitter, my status as 'most famous' – as opposed to notorious - old boy was intact. It also explained why I, not he, had been invited to do the honours. Nevertheless, I was surprised to have been asked - especially after all the tabloids had gleefully and graphically covered my spectacular fall from grace only the week before. Irritatingly, the plaque listed my date of birth as 1960 – which was true but wrong. All my biogs, blogs and press releases clearly stated that I was a sprightly thirty-nine, not forty-four, and surely their vote outweighed this crusty old plaque and my dog-eared birth certificate. I resolved to see if they'd agree to change it. Purely in the interest of consistency, you understand.

'Not a plumber, eh,' was Patel's only murmured comment as he clicked and scraped away.

★   ★   ★

Old Patel has a lot to answer for in my book. Maybe I should explain this plumbing thing, such depths does it plumb…

I was crap at Maths. No – that's not quite true. I was lazy at Maths. At primary school I'd been something of a child prodigy in every subject but I lost the plot in the transition from progressive primary to regressive secondary education. And Patel's eccentric and confrontational approach to classroom discipline compounded the problem. Learning by rote was alien and, like a small child, my constant refrain was 'Why?'.

'Yours, Mr Smith, is not to reason why!' Patel would snap as the board rubber hurtled towards my head with unerring accuracy. I'd gaze at his illegible chalked scrawls on the blackboard searching for the meaning that had never eluded me before.

'Smith, gentlemen, is going to be a plumber,' he announced, one depressingly memorable day, of which I was to be relentlessly reminded.

I rarely managed to duck that board rubber – so I started ducking maths lessons instead in favour of the geometric exercises afforded by the local snooker club. There I managed, I'm kind of proud to say, to mis-spend the mis-spending of my youth by failing even to learn to play snooker, billiards or pool. Instead I played the jukebox. Then, in the early Seventies, it was Bowie *(Life on Mars)* and Bolan *(Get It On)* and Dave and Ansell Collins *(Double Barrel)* that got me saving for a crappy electric guitar from Mum's even crappier mail order catalogue. And, in terms of my career success, theirs was the lesson that made me the man I am.

My memory led me down the dimly lit pale green corridor that dipped under the grand main stairs and along a trail of ancient pipes as wonky and crap-encrusted as those that wobble so animatedly outside tube train windows into the underworld of the Sixth Form Common Room. A mysterious netherworld to us juniors, glimpsed only though grimy windows that leaked cold air in and pompous progressive rock out, this was the major advantage of staying on for the sixth form. It was a haven from the strictures of school discipline where masters rarely ventured – and when they did it was usually with an air of diffidence and fish–out–of–waterness in which we revelled.

Under low sagging ceilings precariously propped by steel uprights and rivet-studded steel crossbeams slouched an equally saggy, and in places decidedly soggy, extended family of armchairs and sofas, lining the walls and cowering under their cushions as if scared the ceiling would finally fall.

The only other furnishing was a regiment of lockers plastered with rock band stickers that peeled like sunburnt skin awaiting use by some future archaeologist to plot the definitive history of progressive rock music. Other than a poorly executed mural of Superman hurtling across the New York skyline with a giant spurting cock and hairy balls scrawled in black marker over his famous pants, the only decor was the inexplicably garish orange, blue and red paint on the pipes that criss-crossed the ceiling so that if you lay on your back in the middle of the room it was a London Underground Tube map. And it reeked of tobacco smoke – with a slight whiff of marijuana. The former was tolerated, if officially banned on school premises. The latter, obviously, was taboo. No one ever got caught, though, thanks to a state-of-the-art communications system comprising alarms and alerts that had been installed during some earlier, more civilised era. At strategic intervals along the passageways leading from the main staircase down into sixth form territory were placed six-inch iron bars purloined from the metalwork shop decades ago. These were tucked out of sight behind the pipe and secured with a chain, their precise position indicated by an Amen Corner or Pink Floyd or Grateful Dead sticker. Every sixth former knew the drill and his duty. Should a master be spotted, the diligent sentinel would tap one of a menu of Morse-like codes on the pipe. This would be clearly audible inside the common room, and fags, spliffs, porn mags and cocks could be stubbed, stashed and secreted well before said master came through the door. The codes were simple enough. For Mr Montgomery, the English master, one tapped out a percussive approximation of the Monty Python's Flying Circus theme tune. For Mr Richards, the Music master, it was the Stones' *Honky Tonk Women*. For Miss Jackson the History teacher – it was a Rod Stewart track. I forget which. But anyway it was some Melody Maker-reading smart arse's reference to Rod the Mod's former life in Python Lee Jackson. Not that smart though – because invariably our two Python references got transposed and the unperturbed reaction to an alert for the timid Miss Jackson would prove inappropriate for the entrance of the imperious and usually furious 'Monty' Montgomery. For Patel, the code was more subtle: the percussive, cash register-ringing opening to Pink Floyd's *Money,* from *Dark Side of the Moon,* which, when you thought about it, was uncannily like the funky groove his orthopaedic boot, steel wing tips and cane made as he clomp-scraped across the clanging concrete floors.

In the end, though, the tradition was dying and fewer and fewer new sixth formers took the trouble to learn the codes (Philistines!). That was when one Bart Raines (AKA Brains) suggested an all-round alert signal. A simple SOS in Morse was rejected on the grounds that the masters would instantly recognise it – and if they didn't, the ancient World War 1 veteran janitor, who taught the code to his troop of army cadets, certainly would. The solution was an inversion of the alphabet whereby A meant Z and vice versa and so on all the way through. Not exactly the stuff of Bletchley Park and the Enigma code but then the stakes were only as high as the Head Master's skip and hippety-hop in his run-up to your six of his fairly impressive best.

So it went like this:
A B C D E F G H I J K L M N O P Q R S T U V W X Y Z
Z Y X W V U T S R Q P O N M L K J I H G F E D C B A
So 'SOS' (or ... – – – ...) became 'HMH and so on.

And because the message was the Morse alphabet reversed, some shining wit called it *Remorse Code*.

★   ★   ★

One wet Wednesday afternoon those of us too lazy or lightweight to join the rugger buggers in the mud and rain – about thirty – sat gazing gloomily out of the common room windows waiting for the deluge to let-up long enough for a dash to the snooker club. It wasn't having any of it – and some bright spark suggested a game of 'Off-Ground He', in which you're 'IT' if touched by the person who's currently 'IT' and you're 'OUT' if you touch the ground.

The sofas and armchairs were strategically placed according to their degree of elasticity and bounce. The newer, foam rubber and plastic models were understrung with tough rubber banding, which offered excellent trampolining properties, while the older horsehair stuffed versions were only good for breaking the fall. On the count of three, we'd all literally spring into action and ape-hang, dangle, swing and swoop from pipe to pipe, sofa to sofa, armchair to armchair — and, in retrospect, the whooping and hollering, grunting and groaning must have sounded like that of a troop of gibbons.

That wet afternoon was no different from countless others. Except that it was about to get a lot wetter.

I was hanging from the biggest, and therefore safest, pipe, which spanned the room widthways. Brains, the bespectacled victim of parents for whom seventies fashion was anathema, was 'IT' and therefore in feeble pursuit. It was unlikely that he'd follow along this dauntingly long span of pipe — hence my cocky demeanour, swinging lazily in the middle, defying the pain in my arms with a devil may care grin. But then Masterson minced in - a nasty, duplicitous little bastard. He fixed me with an evil grin, strolled over to my intended landing point and casually slid it on its coasters a few feet beyond any hope of leaping. The sod left me hanging and made sure I saw how much he enjoyed it — a future copper if ever I saw one. The pain knifed down my arms and stabbed my shoulders. I grinned. But I couldn't bear it. Any second now I would have to admit defeat and I'd hit the ground and they'd all be running from me like I was a disease. Like I was Raines. I hung in there. I sweated. And the sweat trickled down my face while the other apes hollered and guffawed. Then the rivulets became rivers; became ridiculous.

It wasn't sweat. The pipe creaked and leaked a little more and then gushed, the torrent of ice-cold water using my writhing body as a conduit for a few seconds before it cracked open and spewed forth like a shaken Champagne bottle. The fall hurt quite a bit — but at least the pain, if not the humiliation, was dulled by my ice-cold shower. Just as I was smiling weakly in acknowledgment of the good-natured and inevitable piss-taking, shivering violently and thanking my lucky stars it hadn't been a soil pipe, I found that I was in the shit after all when a familiar voice chilled me much, much more.

'Mr Smith – I'm glad to see that we already have a gentleman on the premises with the requisite skills and aptitudes for just such an emergency.'

'Sir...' I stammered through teeth clacking like an industrial mincing machine.

'Mr Smith – thank you. I have every confidence in your abilities. However, I shall be examining the arithmetic of your invoice very, very closely.'

Behind him, still clinging desperately to the yawing, spouting pipe in the forlorn hope he'd not been noticed, Raines screwed up agonised piggy eyes behind misted NHS glasses (this was before Sting made them cool – and before Thatcher made them extinct).

'Mr Raines – what have I told you about hanging around in the Common Room when you should be correcting your dangling participles.'

Having demonstrated the acuity of the eye-in-the-back-of-the-head with which all teachers of a certain age are issued, Patel turned his front-head gaze on the swinging boy, flicked out his middle finger like a stiletto and jabbed Bart right in the dangling participles with mild disgust as if prodding roadkill to see if it were alive.

With that he turned back to his audience of sixth-formers, still freeze-framed in the shot where he'd entered stage left, raised a declamatory hand, threw back his head 'Friends, Romans, Countrymen' stylee and boomed,

'Smith, gentlemen...' The pause was punctuated with perfect comedy timing by a lavatorial gurgle and plop. '...Is going to be a plumber!'

★　　★　　★

Scenting danger in these long-repressed corridors of memory, my trusty ego led me up into the light-filled, glittering glass halls of the new science block. Here, it knew, I was safe from memories of *that thing* – and from facing Bart Raines. I, on the other hand, wasn't so sure. Preparing for my imminent public appearance, I checked my reflection in the expanse of mirror glass, hauling the threadbare and shiny-kneed trousers of my least-fucked black Armani suit over the hillock of my beer gut and spiking my equally threadbare hair with spit and fingers. But I saw someone else. Someone I really didn't want to see; whose piggy bespectacled eyes I'd ignored peering out of the old school photograph next to the 'roll of honour'.

Of course it wasn't him. It wasn't the image of Bart Raines I saw – it was *me*. It was just that after twenty or more years' so-called rebellion my man-in-black image was almost identical to the Hartham Grammar school uniform – particularly as styled by Bart Raines's purityrannical parents. All I lacked was the specs, the embroidered badge and the hacked, sheared and smeared-down fifties hairstyle. This was the fear I hadn't admitted to myself till now; the real reason I'd never ventured back here before now. I was afraid of meeting Bart Raines again – or, more accurately, of facing my shame.

I don't think I can bring myself to tell you about the thing that happened to him. Not yet.

But I will.

Soon.

I think.

5

Daisy Raines – Summer '76

In my game, you could say that academic success was, well, academic. But I still crave the respectability of the educated; still can't resist flaunting my second-class degree from a second-class university as evidence - no, proof - that I'm no dumb-ass rocker. I went back from time to time to the torture of those Maths lessons – usually in the spring term, when hay fever and looming exam conscience tickled and pricked me. I'd creep in and sit at the back and try to shrink myself small enough to hide behind the textbook I stood on my desk like a shield. Once in a while that propped-up book deflected the assault of the flying board rubber (or *torchon* as the French master, who was just as board-rubber-happy as Patel would translate gleefully as he hurled said projectile: *'le torchon qui vol!'*). But it was no defence against the onslaught of humiliation. With sadistic glee, my Mathematics master had passed on my personal catchphrase to the French teacher.

'Messieurs! Smith,' the vicious fucker would pronounce solemnly, 'va être plombier!'

Not the worst insult imaginable, I grant you. But one I wasn't allowed to forget for a very long time – regardless of the excellence or otherwise of my academic performance. That early plumberism, as I came to think of those witless pronouncements, was delivered sometime in the fourth form. By the time I reached the sixth and swapped the school uniform for sports jacket and slacks in even worse taste, the plumberisms had gone away and I could concentrate on being me – or more specifically on working on the 'me' becoming an 'us' with my new-found muse.

I was secretly in love with Daisy, the delicately innocent waif whose green eyes sparkled at me through the school bus windows as her brother mounted the step every afternoon and the coach rumbled away in a cloud of diesel fumes. I couldn't tell my sidekick Bart that I had the hots for his sister. Two years my junior, she was way too young for a man of my nearly seventeen-year-old maturity; too innocent.

Like so much in my life though, even then – my crush was doomed to crash. After *'the thing'*, to which we never really referred, and its repercussions, I was no longer welcome in the Raines household. In fact my parents forbade my going there. Even before it happened, I'd never enjoyed going home with Bart for 'tea'; would never have gone without my ulterior motive. The house smelt of dogshit, damp and death and so did their terrifying tyrant dad. So my ever-efficient gag reflex ensured I couldn't ever swallow a bite of a soggy sandwich or a sip of lukewarm recycled and thrice re-used teabag tea. All I did was sneak longing looks at the elfin vision at the end of the table and pretend I had no time for her. And she did likewise – except I had a feeling she wasn't pretending.

★　　　★　　　★

Daisy Raines didn't have much time for school either. So school didn't have much time for her – and what it did expend on her was measured out in hour-long presences after the school day's end as punishment for her absence within school hours. Daisy's long term strategy – the term in question being the Summer Term of 1976 – was to build upon her achievements and receive the ultimate truants' accolade: suspension from school. The irony of this punishment, which didn't so much fit the crime as make it compulsory, seemed to have escaped Mrs Heacock, the Headmistress. Indeed Daisy had high hopes that a penal system based on the same homeopathic and utterly ineffective principle would soon be introduced to discipline those caught using, possessing or selling cigarettes, drugs and alcohol.

The punishment, like the school, the crap it failed to teach and the witless wimps who gave and got it, was useless. The uniform, on the other hand, was far from useless – that was something her father had inadvertently taught her and which she intended to use against him and everyone else.

Build a bonfire, build a bonfire, put the teachers on the top. Put the prefects in the middle and burn the fucking lot, Daisy scribbled, five lines at a time using five biros Sellotaped parallel and perpendicular to a ruler (the ineffectual student History teacher who'd placed her in this particular detention with a sentence of a thousand lines had neglected to specify what those lines should say).

'Raines, I just don't know what to do with you, I really don't,' Benjamin *'Call Me Benjamin Girls'* Biddle, her Year Tutor and, nominally, French and Art Master had sighed in exasperation muddied by his unacknowledged (by him anyway) lust for her and his much-mocked insistence that he was 'more an older brother than a figure of authority'. He certainly wasn't the latter – and the flares, flowing locks and hippy beard he still wore in devout faith that 'Punk' was just a safety-pinned rip and snarl in Rock's rich tapestry made sure none of the hip contingent would see him as the former. Well, not in a good way. 'Ben with the silent "T"' they called him – although Daisy's precocious PAYDAR (and GAYDAR – not that anyone had yet coined the word) told her the rumours weren't true.

'You're a bright girl – but it seems to me that you simply refuse to use what you've got up there.'

Daisy raised a knowing eyebrow, throwing back her arms behind a flyblown beehive of barely tamed raven-black hair so that her breasts strained against the crisp white cotton of her regulation shirt. Biddle's beady eyes oscillated for a nanosecond then his head dipped, eyes swivelling sideways and beak dipping behind his report book. Ruffled and birdlike, he flicked pages mechanically, head tilting to one side, then the other, then bobbing up with a quiet cluck.

Apparently forgetting that Daisy had said nothing in reply, he went on.

'I mean, what's the point of my trying to teach you if you simply refuse to learn?'

'None,' Daisy replied brightly. 'I'm glad you finally see things my way.'

Camouflaging embarrassment with a wobbly smile, in turn dismissed by a standard issue frown, Biddle buried his beak back in his book and brooded.

'Come on, Daisy. I'm trying to help you here. Can't you meet me halfway?'

'OK, fire away.'

She shifted in her seat – actually his seat. He'd sat her down in his pleasantly Bohemian study, in his pleasantly old and comfortable leather-upholstered swivel chair and pulled up a bony wooden classroom one for himself, which he'd swivelled and straddled, slapping down on it with folded arms and chin resting on the back. Which had the effect of framing the tent at the front of his trousers. To be fair, at the start of their little *tête à tête* this could well have been one of those unfortunate trouser folds that contain nothing but sweaty air and suggestion. By this time though, Daisy was pretty sure it housed something more substantial and she aimed to make it more so. Not for any particular reason other than the discomfiture that grew with it.

'Well, since it's my subject, let's talk about French.'

'D'accord.'

'Very good, Daisy. Trouble is, as far as I can see, the only words of French you've assimilated in five years are *d'accord and merde.*'

'Ce n'est pas vrai.'

'You see, Daisy, I would like to help you get a decent result in your 'O' Levels – because I think you have it in you. In fact I'd like to see you sitting 'A' Levels too... With some effort, you could go further... But it takes two, Daisy. I can't do it on my own.'

'Not what I've heard,' Daisy muttered, shifting on her seat with a leathery squeak and crossing her legs slowly so that her standard issue but subtly customised skirt crackled with static against her decidedly non-standard fishnet tights as it rode slightly higher up her thigh.

'I'll ignore that. I know what the girls say – and it isn't true.'

'I know. I can see that.'

Biddle jumped to his feet, turning away and gazing at a Degas print on the wall – then self-consciously sidestepped to bring a Landseer stag hunt scene into view.

'Who killed Bambi?' Daisy muttered as she gazed out of the window at the clock on the school chapel. Three minutes to five. As if drawing inspiration from the painting, Biddle inhaled deeply and paced up and down – the intended impression of steely resolve hampered by the limited space between teetering piles of exercise and text books, faded and dated exhibition stands and sideways-stacked clip-frames of his charcoaled nudes and fuzzy black and white photographic *oeuvre*.

'I suspect you feel that we - the school, I mean - have failed to challenge you.'

Daisy shrugged, impassive, but nodded; permission to go on.

'So I'm going to try and put that right.'

A raised eyebrow disconcerted him – but he persevered.

'You have, currently...' He consulted his notes. 'Fifteen impending detentions. Now,' he announced as he pounced on his backward chair and thrust his trouser tent back into its frame and rocked forward so that what he imagined was his piercingly intelligent, gentle yet strangely powerful gaze would transfix her, 'I have a proposition for you, Miss Raines, that will cancel out all those detentions and get you back on the road to the glittering spires of academe!'

His steely gaze became alloyed, softened with success as Daisy's hardface melted in the warmth of an incipient new understanding. All she'd needed was a guy like Ben to reach out to her; to show her someone cared; to show her she was valued. This was what teaching was about. Drawing out the goodness and talent in young people, giving them inspiration and making them friends and confidantes.

'Can you really do that Ben?' she whispered hammily and cheesily, not even bothering to act.

'Yes I can – if you're willing to work with me,' he Tony Blaired, suffused with renewed confidence and pride in his work. 'What I'm suggesting is that I have a word with Mrs Heacock and convert your fifteen detentions to just ten hour-long sessions with me...'

'Will you take that long then Ben?' Daisy Barbara Windsored coquettishly.

Ignoring her, Biddle biddled on.

'...In which we shall speak only French, but will be discussing topics such as Maths, History and Geography – that way I propose to help you get through your 'O' Levels in each of those subjects.'

'Will we not be doing practical Biology? Or sexual Chemistry?' she brazened with a subtle leg shift, which generated thousands of galvanising volts that weren't all static.

'Of course not... If you're not going to take this seriously I...'

'I'm serious. Really. Vraiement.'

'Now that's better.'

'Mais vous voulez dire, "ça c'est plus bien", n'est-ce pas?'

'Very good Daisy. Alors, maintenant nous parlons seulement en français, oui?'

'Oui Monsieur. Mais je ne connais pas beaucoup de mots. J'ai oublié beaucoup.'

Biddle smiled. *Now we're getting somewhere,* he smugged to himself.

'Ce n'est pas un problème. Simplement, nous parlerons de quelque chose que tu connais bien! Qu'est ce que tu veux discuter?'

'Soixante-neuf. Ménage a trois. La bête avec deux dos. I've heard about you people that advertise French lessons. Will you be expecting me to use your cane on you or are you a "Dom"?'

'Get out!' Biddle squawked.

Daisy bounced girlishly to her feet and flounced to the door, halting in its frame to blow Biddle a kiss.

'I shall be talking to your father about this young lady.'

'Good idea – he'll be able to give you plenty of pointers!'

It had been her dad, after all, who'd unintentionally taught her that her school uniform had its uses.

6

Back on the A List

'Rich? Rich. Come on wake up you old sod!'

'I'm not asleep. I'm thinking.'

George's graceful curves swam above my eyes, silhouetted but leaking dazzling laser-like shafts of concentrated disinfectant sunlight that scoured through interesting clefts and cracks in her fabulous outline. As her pneumatic form floated lazily into three dimensions – as my eyes began to adjust to the glare – I saw stars, all of them lucky, and counted them, every shimmering evanescent one of them till they faded, as all lucky stars do. This was more like it!

She straddled the sun lounger, raised both hands to her head and tousled and tossed her dreadlocks, raining saltwater onto my chest – so cold on my superheated skin I was surprised it didn't sizzle.

'Hi George,' I rasped.

And she launched into a torrential report on the events she'd packed into the two hours we'd been apart.

'We've got VIP passes to a reception for Bowie on some yacht at seven and then there's the Geffen party and we should be able to make it to the Velvet Revolver gig for midnight. I've got us All Areas passes and the guys are really keen to meet you...'

She curled down to kiss me, her breasts dripping on my chest like they were lactating brine. I put up a silencing hand.

'Hang on... Thought this was supposed to be a holiday.'

'Come on. It'll be fun!'

Clocking my clear lack of enthusiasm, she pouted in that schoolgirl manner that had first hooked me, her pretty, tanned face clouding with exaggerated disappointment.

'New thong?' I evaded.

'Ooh you noticed! How do I look?'

I craned my neck, squinted and pretended to appraise her silhouetted form.

'Absolutely George-ish as always!'

'That won't get you off the hook you know...'

'All right babe,' I murmured and, with a hefty pelvic thrust, sent her tumbling onto the sand.

'That's my rock 'n' roll hero,' she cooed as she flicked encrusted damp sand off taut shiny skin. 'And by the way, I bumped into an old friend of yours!'

I groaned. Not another one. The crossness you had to bear as a famous rock star was that every cunt you ever met was suddenly an old bosom buddy, rather than someone who'd laughed at your early musical efforts, stolen your girlfriends, beaten you up or nicked your fags.

'No, Georgie!'

'Oh but you have to. He's going to be at the Bowie thing – and I promised you'd be there to meet him. He was really chuffed!'

'No!'

That coquettish, simpering, hideously appealing schoolgirl smile.

'What's his name?'

'I forget.'

'Well then...'

'You can't let him down.'

'I won't be – *you* will! I'm not going to this Bowie thing and that's the end of it. And put your tits away!'

★　　★　　★

Two weeks on from my inaugural appearance as a Z-List school/fête/supermarket-opening, ribbon cutting ex-celeb, I was back in what I'd come to think of as my own world. As usual I was no more at home here than there. I was - am - as much of a shrinking, flapping fish out of water in this star-spangled sea as in Hartham's small pool. More sharks in this one though.

Miraculously, just as I had resigned myself to a future of dwindling fame, demotion to the bottom of the rock 'n' roll barrel and a subsistence based on the odd Japanese gig or eighties nostalgia package tours with other has-beens, also-rans and could've-beens, my agent-cum-manager Jimmy Gold announced a substantial back-catalogue publishing offer from some new outfit with massive financial backing for intellectual property investments. To my amazement, he told me it would make me financially secure for life — as long as I curbed some of my more expensive excesses. I was in a Denmark Street-bound cab quicker than you could say 'don't look a gift horse in the mouth' and in a matter of days the deal was, apparently, all but signed and sealed. 'Just a matter of dotting the "i's" and crossing the "t's",' Jimmy grinned, the impending big fat twenty percent lighting up his eyes. It's amazing how the prospect of a major cash injection gets the old heart pumping, the creative muscles primed and the appetite for excess whetted. Full of the old self-confidence that only fame and a soon-to-be fat bank account can endow, I was more than happy to accept when Jimmy informed me that my new publishers were keen for me to show my face at Midem (the big Music Biz event) in Cannes for a high profile press launch of our new deal.

When the tickets arrived by courier the very next day, I found that I'd been promoted back to first class calibre, travel-wise, and better than first-class hotel-wise. Last time I'd been at Midem it had been a humbling experience involving long walks from a mediocre back-street *pension* to the bar of the Gray D'Albion or the Cannes Carlton, where I'd make the acquaintance of the bar staff, make like a resident, hold court with press and posers and network with the new rock royalty as they swanned and swooned up and down La Croisette. Now I was back where I belonged with a penthouse suite at the Gray D'Albion and a virtually unlimited room service tab. Not that I stayed grateful or appreciative for long...

★   ★   ★

'MIDEM. Modem, more like,' I mused sourly the moment I was back in the plush penthouse suite. I had a point though. These industry beanfeasts are a painfully slow and noisy way of networking these days; all chatter and whine and very little action – outmoded by always-on broadband connections. It takes so long to get the picture, to make the scene – and when it finally downloads, it's pixellated by all the powder and fizz. God what a long way I'd come since my wide-eyed debut appearance at this music biz Mecca. And I'm alluding, by the way, to the cheesy seventies Bingo-cum-discotheque meat racks – not the Holy place of Islam. I certainly didn't need to bolster my image or ego by being seen at Bowie's party – or anyone else's.

7

The Daisy Chain - 2005

So, Bowie was looking cool. Well, obviously ('Hi Dave,' I breezed. 'Hi... Er... Mate. Good to see you,' he bluffed). I, however, wasn't (looking cool, I mean). The Thin White Duke's teeth were looking very American — neat and glaring against the decidedly un-White Dukish tan. I couldn't help wondering if he'd had any other work done. The bastard looked way too good for a man pushing sixty and almost twenty - Oh all right, fifteen - years my senior. I wondered too, whether my new benefactors' marketing budget might run to a few nips and tucks for yours truly. Just to keep me in the rock-star running you understand... Then I wondered whether Raines had ever had that eye sorted out. I hoped so — more for myself than for him. It was that lidless eye's shaming, blaming gaze that still haunted me. That wasn't 'the thing' though. The 'eyelid incident' wasn't it. But it had a lot to do with it because it made him a victim — and it was the stigma that showed, no *forebode,* the suffering to which neither he nor I could ever really close our eyes.

Five grand it had cost me - or rather my mysterious 'publisher' - to re-join the international jetsam set. Five thousand smackers to wallow in a sea of shit alongside hundreds of other moneyed wallowers — all tanned or stained deep brown by their bathing in the sun and shite. And all I could think about was that awful thing at school. Who else would fly to Cannes only to spend every dozing moment dwelling on that? Me. And only me.

Knackered after a hard day's sunbathing and hoping to obliterate the memories that kept stalking me, I'd done a bit more charlie than was wise so early in the day and had been forced to offset the resulting jitters with several powerful *Cuba Libres*. And it was all very nice – you know the kind of thing. Well, maybe you don't. I keep forgetting how few people ever get to attend these highly exclusive 'A List' parties. You're not missing much. Honest. Frankly, I'd forgotten about this 'old mate' I was supposed to meet. I was sceptical because I'd still be in touch with anyone important enough to be invited to David Bowie's album launch party. Surely I would. I'd been ranting at a thousand miles per hour to various arseholes, schmucks, fuckwits, schmoozers, losers and groovers, none of whom noticed because they'd all had a head start on the Bolivian march. And I was just gagging on a canapé, inadvisably accepted from a proffered platter just after a voluptuously snot-crackling, literally shit-stirring toot out of some vile young whippersnapper rock star's vial, when someone tapped on my shoulder.

'Hello mate!'

This bloody sun. The bloke was an outline. Couldn't see a thing. Till George slid between us and wrapped her arms round my neck and, in the shade of her locks, I made out a face that looked vaguely familiar.

Taking his hand and shaking it in time-honoured fashion, I stalled for time, mentally scanning the half-remembered pages of the trade rags – Billboard and Music Week, the gossip and paparazzi crap of HELLO and OK… Nothing. Not a clue.

'Great to see you,' I bullshitted, again in time-honoured music biz style.

He smiled – a bit too suavely for my liking. And he was making way too much of an impression on George, who was simpering at him like he was Bowie... Or me, in fact.

'Don't remember me do you, Rich?'

That bloody Hot Chocolate song kicked in on a repeat loop – the curse of the music obsessive: *You don't remember me do you? You don't remember me do you? You don't remember me do you? You don't remember me do you? You don't remember me do you?*

'Er... Yeah, course I...'

I shifted a step, as one star to another, putting the sun to one side so that it delineated features you could almost describe as handsome yet somehow didn't quite make it. He was wearing a pair of opaque shades that were a bit too big to be cool – a bit old school.

'Bart. Bart Raines. From school?' he stated quietly – almost accusingly.

You could almost hear my hard drive whirring and clicking as I processed this information. This did not compute. The filename supplied did not correspond with the data my scanners were inputting.

'Cigarette?'

I nodded and took a Marlboro from the pack he shook at me – and a light from an ancient Zippo. The clang of which, as it shut, rang some distant bell.

'Keep the pack – they'll only find it if I take it home.'

Click click buzz bang! There was the data my processor had been missing. The file opened, clear on my mind's graphic user interface. Bart's dad used to beat the living shit out of him if he caught him with cigarettes. It was much, much worse when he caught him once with a fag – but that's another story.

So I always got to take the pack home after school. He paid for my nicotine habit for the last two years of my secondary education. I owed him. And for a hell of a lot more than the cigarettes. The shame inflamed my face, burning deeper than my sunburn. At least back at the school I'd been ready, if reluctant to face him. But here? Now? How?

'Bart. Brains! B.Raines! Bloody hell,' I blurted. 'I mean, bloody hell!'

'Bloody hell indeed,' he replied with a smirk, the 'indeed' confirming his identity like he'd uttered some secret agent codeword. Only former grammar school boys used the word 'indeed' like that – with all its pomposity and none of its mocking. He removed the shades and his unremittingly baleful one-eyed glare fell on me, its effect undiminished by more than two decades. Evidently he'd eschewed the delights of cosmetic surgery then.

'So what you doing here?' I stammered as I struggled to reconcile this cosmopolitan man of the world with the piggy-eyed geek I'd befriended, defended then betrayed at school.

'Just swanning around.'

Invoked by 'swan', the words 'ugly' and 'duckling' came irresistibly to mind. Depressingly, my unruly and securely insecure mind had decided to cast him in the 'swan' role.

'Good place to do it,' I said.

'Yeah, not bad, Cannes. I'm moored here for a few days but I'm actually based in Barcelona these days.'

'You've got a boat?' I enquired trying to appear unimpressed.

'Indeed. You're on it in fact.'

For some reason I looked at my feet.

'Wow – nice boat!' I blurted.

'I think ship is the word actually.'

'Yes – of course... Great place Barcelona. Love it. You in the Port Olympic?'

'Yes – handy for all the restaurants and so on.'

'So you were resurrected then!' I ventured, 'After the, um, crucifixion...'

There. I'd actually said it.

Bart laughed, a rumbling from deep within a broad and well-muscled chest.

'Oh yes! In more ways than one.'

I'm going to have to explain the *thing,* the 'crucifixion' now; his 'goalgotha'...

8

Goalgotha

OK. Here we go. Here's 'the thing' I can't face. How I let him down. Why I hate myself. And, I assume, why he must hate me.

It's the end of Summer Term 1977 at Hartham Grammar. Exams over. Some leaving; some waiting for 'O' level results and maybe staying on. All in freedom fever, imagining someone cares that we're not in classes that teachers don't want to teach and that only exist on a timetable. Planned rebellion, allowed for in the schedule, expected and anticipated. I'm in the cool dappled shade of the bushes by the swimming pool, hiding from the heat with Dom and Dave and smoking pot. Others are on the sports field not doing any sport. The rugby boys are playing unseasonable rugby like they do on any other Wednesday afternoon. Cricketers click and clop on the heat-hazed table.

So we sit wondering whether this is really hash we've scored, or whether we've made a hash of scoring yet again.

'Feel anything?'

'I dunno.'

'Nor do I.'

'Can you hear that wailing noise though?'

'No.'

'Hang on – maybe I can.'

'I'm a bit scared.'

'So am I.'

'Is it supposed to make you feel like this?'

'I dunno. Thought you were meant to feel all dreamy...' I begin.

That chilling distant scream pierces the sodden air and seems to unsettle the shimmering haze. Three faces, eyes wide with apprehension, poke out of the privet as the cricketers freeze-frame for a moment, glance in the direction of the sound and turn back to their game. A hundred yards to our left a cluster of fifth formers whoops and hollers, fags in mouths in a school-leavers' gesture of defiance. A large ragged object, unidentifiable with the sun's glare behind it, hangs limply from the rugby goalposts' giant 'H'. We crawl along the edge of the shrubbery, clinging to exposed roots as anchors on the steep slope, communicating earnestly with the sign language gleaned and thoroughly misunderstood from a million war films. My head pops up mole-like into the light and I wince and shrink back as a pair of giant cherry red eight-hole Doc Martin boots stomps down inches from my face. Their owner sparks up a No 6 and flings the still-lit match into the greenery with practised James Deanery, where it trickles from leaf to leaf with a tiny smoke trail like a downed Spitfire and lands on my head with a crackle of ignition and that death-smell of burning hair. My panicked yelp pricks up the ears of the Cherry Red owner. He swivels, squats and sneers and his famous 'bouncing' sole squeaks down on my hand. Like an echo, a girlish squeak sneaks out of my mouth.

'Hello, hello, what've we got here!'

A strong hand fucks into the bushes and pulls back, dragging my head by the hair, my body straining pointlessly to elongate behind it cartoon style, then plopping out like a strained shit, complete with small traces of blood as the thorns try to hold me back.

The rest of Cherry Red's pack catches the smell of fear and follows the spoor down the well-worn shortcut round the bottom of the wooded area and crawl up behind our foxhole baying, if not exactly for blood, at least for the humiliation of their quarry.

'Come here little boys,' shrieks one of them, his high-pitched screaming faux camp ruined by a late-breaking voice that cracks from tenor to falsetto and back.

Dom shoots out from cover and darts rabbit-like for the border hedge, through which he ducks and dives onto the road outside the school – out into the safety of neutral territory. Dave's not so lucky. His Marc Bolan corkscrew hair's what snares him. And, like me, he's dragged head first onto the dog-end-strewn and balding edge of the sports field.

We're hauled roughly to our feet and frogmarched like condemned prisoners towards the bare patch at the foot of the goal and the ragged audience of baying boys, school ties wrapped round heads bandana style, faces striped with mud. William Golding has a lot to answer for. Flung to the ground, Dave and I go foetal as if that will protect us from the kicking. It takes a few moments to realise that few are bothering to put the boot in; after a few desultory nudges, they lose interest. I uncoil and flinchingly raise my head. Now the object on the nets is identified. It's Bart. Crucified. Naked but for his saggy grey Y-fronts, his old-school school uniform torn to ribbons, some of which have been used to tie his wrists to one end of the crossbar and ankles to one upright several feet off the ground. Two tar-spattered ladders nicked from the janitor's shed stand sentry at either side as if waiting for the order to take him down. On Bart's head is a crown – not of thorns, but a cardboard one, vaguely familiar from some school Gilbert & Sullivan production. The animal wailing that spooked us in our placebo pot daze hasn't stopped – it's just shrivelled to an insistent low moan punctuated by occasional yelps as branches torn off bushes prod and poke at his sallow flesh, pokers stoking his pain whenever its flames ebb to embers. Tethered at the extremities, his body's switching all its strength into the movable parts – a torso writhing, wrenching and bucking helplessly, hopelessly; the headless chicken reflex of a living body on the cusp of becoming a carcass. Apparently forgotten for the moment, Dave and I are both on our knees. I catch his tear-filled eye and mine brim over. As I finally force myself to look up into Bart's wretched face, it twists grotesquely – too far, so far his spinal cord must snap under the torsion. Maybe that's what he's doing - wringing his own neck to make his escape.

Cruelly, the sun joins in the fun, suddenly throwing its harsh spotlight on a face grotesquely panto-damed and clowned with powder paint rouge, eye shadow and lipstick, now sliding down his cheeks and throat in a filthy rivulet delta of tears and snot. One eye is screwed shut, the strain pulsating in temple and jaw like his blood's bubbling. The other, of course, simply stares balefully — a broadband, always-on connection pouring unprocessable, unbearable visual data inexorably into a hard drive that can't take any more. Nor can mine, come to that. As my image joins the torrential datastream, his Bluetooth snags my output and his other eye flutters into a flurry of single lens reflex snapshots, making up for the other's blink shortage.

'Rich!!!!' he howls, the anguish tempered with hope.

'Rich...Richard...' With each repetition of my name, it shrinks in his throat until it's no longer a name — just a prayer in tongues, uttered in a forlorn faith that the power exists to deliver him.

It doesn't.

Attempting a brave face I stand. So does Dave. I try to catch his eye — enlist him somehow in some comic book SAS rescue. But his head droops, and his fluffy pillow of hair flops over his face like a slow motion car crash bag. Without tearing their eager eyes from the spectacle, the bodies in a loose arc in front of this Goalgotha automatically or instinctively form a circle around me, leaving Dave outside; ignored, irrelevant. Two hands parting his locks like curtains, he peers through at me and, with an apologetic shrug, sheepishly slopes off, slowly at first, then picking up his pace and finally diving headlong into the cover of the shrubbery. Bart's still muttering my name like a mantra.

Eyelids dam my tears. I damn my tears. The dam and damnation burst and instantly wash away my half-arsed mask of defiance.

'Gonna protect your little Jewboy bum chum now are you Smith?'

It's Michael Burroughs. One of those faux public school types who take the term 'rugger bugger' too literally; who somehow manage to make their homosexual proclivities acceptable to what the Americans call 'Jocks' by combining it with a sadistic machismo and disdain for women that fits perfectly with their Max Boyce mindset. Because sex for him is rape. OK he hasn't actually raped anyone. Yet. Maybe never will. But like a paedophile who only looks at other people's pictures of violation, he's a criminal waiting for the crime.

'Fuck off Burroughs!' I grate, wittily.

He slaps me. Yes *slaps!* His cronies titter. I spit in his face. Everything goes black and red and I'm an embryo in a womb that's trying to abort me, curled tight in the spasming grip of ten bodies, their limbs tangling, trying to kick and punch and knee me but mostly cancelling one another out. I try to kick against the pricks but there's no space to swing in and as more and more of them yell 'bundle!' and pile on top, the blackness gets blacker.

And then there is light. At least I think there is. A plethora of redness suffuses my clotting plasma screen and I shake my head to adjust the vertical hold. And the live coverage resumes, Bart's mantra picks up its groove and the automatic focus delivers a depressingly vivid shot of way too many sneering and snarling faces. On the up side, a couple of the wolves have turned distinctly sheepish – they may have lost their enthusiasm for the pack, but they're never going to leave the flock. Gestapo in the making. Or policemen at least. They've backed off. Given me space. Warily I get to my feet, then bend and rest hands on knees, lifting my head to survey them slowly, one by one. Like Steve McQueen in The Great Escape, mocking the Nazis even in defeat; winning the defeat.

I wish.

Burroughs steps forward, his cohorts peeling aside to make way with sickening deference.

'Jew lover. Jewboy.'

'Oscar Wilde eat your fucking heart out,' I trot out a well-rehearsed off-the-peg riposte.

'Another queer,' rebounds his sneer.

'Like you – and your shining wit!' I'm briefly glad for my private practice sessions at appearing sharp. 'Oh dear, I seem to have slipped into Spoonerisms again.'

Burroughs' face clouds for a nanosecond, juggling consonants.

'Cocky cunt,' he hisses.

'Which? Can't have both,' I snap back. 'Well maybe you can!'

'Oh dear. Jewboy's really pushing his luck now boys.' He places hands theatrically on hips.

'Anyway,' I pipe up, suddenly too reedily for comfort, 'I'm not Jewish – as if that matters.'

'But your pathetic little roundhead prick tells a different story – the rugby pavilion showers reveal all hidden shame!'

What? This sentence, this life sentence, is loaded with a meaning that's beyond my ken. I really don't understand.

'Anyway, who cares. Leave Bart alone!' Not my coolest or wittiest ejaculation.

'Make me!' Not his either.

'Wanker!' In my defence, there are times when it's appropriate to sum up your argument in as concise a fashion as possible. Paraphrasing Orwell – never use a long word when a short one will do. This in mind, I have a rethink and edit it down to a pithy one syllable.

'Cunt!'

'Go on then. You reckon you're so hard. Get the fucker down!' he challenges.

Bart's muttering dies in his throat. Silence. A cricket ball clops on willow a million miles away across a two-hundred yard space, where life, impossibly, seems to be carrying on undisturbed. Behind me, the sploosh and splash of junior boys dive-bombing the pool like giggling rain filters through the bushes that are my Swiss border. Following them comes the explosion; the boom of Mr Llewellyn the Sports Master's voice: 'No bombing. No running! No shouting!'

I can't help turning towards the sound of sanctuary. But Burroughs extends a long arm and puts a Larry Grayson finger gently against my lips.

'You heard the man. No shouting,' he intones with a softness that suggests the opposite.

'So, what's it to be, Mr Smith? Are you man enough to get your pet yiddo down off the cross?'

'The aitch, surely,' I mutter.

But again my seeping eyes betray my brave face. I avoid Burroughs' line of sight and home in on Bart's Cyclops gaze, still beseeching me. His right shoulder is curled round towards his left; as if he's trying to shuck off the attached arm. Sunlight gleams off white skin that's stretched tight over bones that seem about to break through and I can't tell whether the red streams converging in the concave pit of his inverted chest are of blood or powder paint. Burroughs follows my gaze. Bart's somehow got his mouth against the rags of his shirt that bind his left wrist. He's gnawing at them. They're working loose. I seize my chance, barge Burroughs aside and leap at the wire. Bart's left hand comes free. I grab his bare right foot. The left is still sensibly shod – the missing shoe full of piss five feet beneath. Scrabbling at the shreds of trouser leg that tie the ankle I only pull the knots tighter. Bloody boy scouts.

Phut. The familiar sound of an airgun discharging is indistinguishable from the pain the pellet inflicts as it thwacks into the tender flesh behind my knee. *Phut.* Another hits my back. A cackle of gleeful laughter from Burroughs prompts a carnival of carnivorous gaiety from his sidekicks.

I run.

'I love a moving target,' Burroughs bellows, levelling the rifle at me as I dive for cover just like Dave before me and run and run and run and run as pellets whipcrack into the foliage behind me.

'Richaaaaaaaaaaaaaard!' Bart's final appeal rings out loud and clear – yet the cricket clicks and clops regardless and a polite flourish of applause flutters through the heat like pigeons taking flight.

'But then again,' I can still hear Burroughs chuckle, Dick Dastardly style, presumably rubbing his hands together in anticipation, 'a still one's a lot easier.'

Phut. I seem to be the only person in the world for whom Bart's shriek is deafening.

'Stop wriggling Jewboy. Take your punishment like a Christian and it will all be over sooner! Did he kiss you ever? Your Judas? Jewboy?'

Phut. Shriek

Phut. Shriek.

Phut. Silence.

*   *   *

Jewboy. A word my dad's generation would use disparagingly about Jews and anyone else who could be labelled as different; the sort of ostensibly benign racism that is and always will be oxymoronic by definition but which then was so ingrained, almost written in DNA, that it wasn't moronic like it obviously is now. What I mean is, Dad didn't mean it. *Judas.* Another name you could never give to a kid; a name forever branded bad. And that's me. Richard 'Judas' Smith. If only I could change it.

9

Like Trousers Like Brain

It was the Summer of '77; the Queen's Silver Jubilee, when the entire nation had street parties and sang *God Save The Queen* while The Sex Pistols sang their own, more anthemic, song of the same title on a boat cruising down the Thames until their inevitable arrest:

God save the Queen
She ain't no human being
They made you a moron
Potential H bomb…

It was the year the suburbs caught on to Punk — at least some of us in the suburbs. The year when suddenly there appeared a clear divide between those with long hair and those with short; those with flares and those with straights or pegs. You may laugh — but what Joe Strummer said then was true: *like trousers, like brain*. You were either on board or you weren't. None of us were real. Not really. Not hardline. I certainly wasn't — but although I was just a 'plastic punk' I was galvanised by that jolt of possibility. The power of the possible; the realisation that you could — can — be who you want to be. Enough, anyway, to finally get my hands on the cheap sunburst Stratocaster copy that I'd been yearning for. And that was the point.

'A number of boys,' intoned the Headmaster at assembly one morning, 'have been found with bloodstains on their shirt collars having foolishly attempted to pierce their ears, or those of others, with needles and safety pins.'

I wasn't among them. Way too squeamish. I glanced along the ranks of uniforms and saw intermittent scarlet splashes screaming rebellion against their navy and grey backgrounds – and wished I'd bled with the other little bleeders.

'This kind of behaviour,' Doctor Wallace continued, 'is what one would expect of secondary - not grammar - school boys – and I and all of my staff are appalled to find our boys sinking to this kind of primitivism. A number of you have already been given detentions and I do not expect to see any recurrence of this revolting behaviour. I'm aware of the facetious comments in the sixth form magazine to the effect that since this obscene ritual is not specifically proscribed by the school rules it should go without punishment. This is, of course, absurd. The school rules are designed to provide a code of conduct to which all of us should adhere. It does not attempt to legislate for every conceivable idiocy that stupid boys might perpetrate. It does not, for example, prohibit specifically the riding of a motorcycle down the back corridor – but leaves it to your own supposedly intelligent minds to discern whether or not this would be a good idea. I think I can trust you all to conclude that it would be as irresponsible as this fad for self-mutilation.'

★   ★   ★

Next day's school assembly looked like a Tarantino movie. Blood all over the shop.

As the senior prefects carried away the wreckage of Simon Dunstan's Yamaha FS1E and the ambulance men stretchered its bloody rider out of the shattered glass door at the end of the back corridor, the rest of us stepped over the impressively expansive pool of his blood and shuffled into the Main Hall.

Tony Morecambe made a killing selling nicked safety pins. Then made another selling lint antiseptic wipes and TCP. White collars dripped red on the left hand side of every pupil over fifteen like we were ranks of wounded soldiers lined up for medals. You just had to do it. But I didn't. Brains did though.

The weird thing was that he'd been bullied for the last five years because he had the misfortune to have parents who were the Home Counties equivalent of the Amish. While the rest of us had haircuts modelled on the likes of David Cassidy and David Essex at worst and at best David Bowie, he had a 'short back and sides'. Until Punk's razor blade cut out the sartorial crap, we wore flares, Oxford Bags, Birmingham Bags with pockets by the knees that made you look like an ape and platform shoes that made you look a clown. Because he was forced to, he wore classic drainpipe black trousers, skinny ties, fluffy home-knitted V-necked jumpers and blazers with narrow lapels. In short, he was a fashion statement years ahead of (or behind) his time. If only he'd known!

But he didn't know. Nor did I. And more to the point, nor did anyone else.

He was cruelly and relentlessly bullied – at home and at school. As the ever helpful Mr Patel once witheringly pointed out,

'Young Raines, perhaps you would suffer less at the hands of your comrades were you not to insist on covering yourself each morning with glue and running through a jumble sale!'

And I did what I could to defend him. I wish I could say that I did it out of pure altruism. I can't. I can say that I'm a sympathetic type; that I do my best to be as decent as I can – and that I abhor bullying in all its forms. I did rush to his rescue on more than a few occasions and fought off or simply intimidated his oppressors – and of that I'm proud. But then, after a while, he felt the need to buy my protection. I wasn't selling it – but when he bought the cigarettes I stood between him and the older boys who were trying to take them off him. When they tried to take his dinner money or his packed lunch, I punched them. When they laughed at him, I took them on. So he kept rewarding me. He didn't need to – but still he did. He couldn't take the cigarettes home to what he called 'The Reichstag' because they'd either be ripped off or found by his fearsome father, Erich, or *Reich* behind his back. So he'd buy ten fags, we'd smoke four and I'd get the rest. Then it was twenty fags – and more for me to take home. Then it was dope or booze – and the same happened again. He was paying me to protect him – and that cheapened what I'd previously done only because it was right.

★   ★   ★

A football game of sorts is ricocheting around a narrow five-foot corridor between the red brick school wall and the grey stone one buttressing a long grassy bank. Sides are chosen – and fiercely disputed. Blazers discarded on tarmac and grass; 'goalies'-cum-lookouts, fifty yards apart smoke cigarettes and keep watch as well as goals and the poorest players get abused. Particularly Raines. Scapegoat for every other crap player. We're fourth years: fourteen to fifteen years old.

The abuse is water off a schmuck's back to Bart. Until Hunt strolls along looking for easy prey. Ostensibly a hippy, he's seriously short on peace and love. Hunt's in the Upper Sixth – three years older. Ancient. Scarily old. He shaves. He's A MAN and he swaggers through our game, confident that we'll all move out of his way – and we do. Except for Bart, who's been told in no uncertain terms that he'll get a kicking if he deserts his goal (lookout) post. Hunt singles him out from the herd like a lion chasing antelopes and BANG – the Hunt hits his prey. Bart goes down. The antelopes disperse, whinnying and pretending not to be glad they weren't the one. Hunt punches Bart. Bart just looks bewildered; resigned. This is what he's used to. Hunt smashes his glasses. One of Bart's eyes blinks through his soon-to-be-hip NHS specs.

The other gazes wide open and innocent. Like Bambi. (Who killed Bambi?). Hunt wears glasses too – thick as bottles. But he doesn't have any empathy with his quarry, even though he's the Bart in his own age group. He's hurting because it happens to him. So I have to stop it. He's on top of Bart as if he's going to bite his neck – but actually he's banging his head on the ground. Bart's impassive.

Defiantly impassive.

'Hunt – rhyming slang I assume?' he grunts through his pain.

Crunch of fragile bone against tarmac. Again and again.

Blood pools around his head.

'You're still a cunt,' he whispers with a smile before his eyes close and he seems to die.

I push the circled and crowing audience aside and leap a thousand feet onto Hunt's back. My fists and feet work robotically. No technique, no martial art, just righteous rage. And I tear the hunter from his game and rip hunks of hair from his head and globs of blood from his face. I take his greasy carrot hair in both hands and pummel his face on my knee, then grind his bloodied head against the ground and smash my fists again and again into his groin.

'You cunt' I scream in a spray of spit that glistens and mingles with a grazed hachure of blood, sweat and tears on his cheeks.

Suddenly the roar of super-pumped blood in my ears ebbs away – so does the baying of my audience. Silence, broken only by Hunt's – and my own – stertorous breathing, which sounds exactly like we're fucking, not fighting.

'Hunt!' Mr Patel's evidently unperturbed voice penetrates the hum in my head. 'Stop bullying Smith.'

My head snaps round like a furiously feeding dog's and even the usually imperious Patel fails to stop my slavering for blood. And he doesn't intervene. He watches. Looks at his watch. He turns to the circle of onlookers.

'Fine day for sport isn't it chaps!

So I keep punching and pummelling. If I relent for a second, give him the slightest respite he'll fight back and win. Keep on keeping on. Keep on... Until the referee says stop.

A strong hand grips my shoulder and effortlessly lifts me away from Hunt, my prey. I flop and drop. The referee speaks and he has my ear.

'Gentlemen – this chap is not one of you. He is a thug.'

I look up and he winks at me. He winks at me! He winks AT ME!

'Not you Smith. Him,' he booms, taking Hunt by an ear and dragging him, now doubly humiliated, in the direction of the Headmaster's study where the canes are kept.

★   ★   ★

I'm on my monthly pilgrimage to the Kings Road, where I generally hang around timidly in the Great Gear market and wish I could afford the 'Destroy' and 'Anarchy' T-shirts on offer in Seditionaries up at the World's End. Not that I have the nerve to venture into the hallowed portals of Punk's Nativity where Adam Ant and Rotten, Jordan, Vicious and Siouxie lounge and leer and sneer - at once thrilling and terrifying.

I leave home dressed in innocuous flared jeans and jumbo-collared shirt and head off towards the station - then, when Mum closes the front door, I shimmy round the back to retrieve a carrier bag I've stashed in the garden shed. With minutes to spare before the London train leaves, I dash into a shit-spattered cubicle in the Gents at the station, strip off and put on the black pinstriped suit I've bought from Oxfam, razored into shreds and safety-pinned back together. My Woolworths plain black plimsolls, just weeks ago the epitome of uncool, are suddenly hipper than hip – a stroke of sartorial luck. Emerging from my dressing room, I pull out a plastic bottle of warm water, in which I've created a saturated sugar solution (hair gel has yet to be invented). This I plaster on my hair, ruffling and tweaking it into tousled spikes just as the clatter and rumble of the train stirs into action the dozily waiting pigeon passengers on the platform. Anxious to avoid being spotted in my new guise by anyone who knows my parents, I wait till the last has boarded and, and as the train creaks into motion, make a dash for the door of the last, usually empty, carriage.

As arranged, Bart hops on a stop later at the arse-end-of-nowhere station at the arse end of town, looking every inch the punk in his tight black drainpipes, skinny black tie, George Orwell haircut, baggy Vee-neck jumper and the Roy Orbison shades that hide his lidless eye. I'm impressed. We're going to fit right in up the Kings Road. But then, with a conjuror's flourish, he whips out a carrier bag from under his threadbare sports jacket and rummages, finally pulling out a hideous hippyshit shirt and a pair of purple loons.

'Managed to keep these hidden from my dad!' he exclaims gleefully. 'I've never ever worn a pair of flares – not in my whole life,' he goes on as he drops his trousers and the train's sudden lurch sends him tumbling in a trouser tangle along the aisle.

'Whoops a daisy,' he blurts, entirely and endearingly irony-free as he tugs up the flares and starts pulling on the paisley.

'Thing is Bart,' I start, meaning to point out his accidentally, and very ironically, inherited hipness in his parentally imposed get-up. But the joy that shines from his face stops me as he takes off his sunglasses and sways up and down the space between the seats like a drunk air steward.

'What d'you reckon?'

'You look great mate,' I murmur, noting the huge bruise that's appeared on his chest since yesterday. 'You'll knock 'em dead... But you...'

But my words are drowned by the rattling roar of the train as it hurtles through a tunnel, which drops us both into a silence that lingers long after we've emerged into the light. Bart's perma-gaze surveys the landscape's transition from rural to urban, measured in railtrack rhythm as green fields are steadily sullied by industrial estates, rubbish dumps and swathes of litter and grafitti. The beam that lit his face has dimmed. I think I know why.

It's got worse – the bullying. Much worse. If only he wasn't so compliant – or maybe if he was more defiant. Or less? I don't know. Why does he have to be so weird? Why do I have to take him with me? I'm going to look an idiot...

★   ★   ★

We're cowering in a doorway just yards from *Seditionaries* when I spot Johnny Rotten, hunched and bandy in his bondage trousers as he slips into the door, his laser glare shrivelling onlookers over the top of his tiny black sunglasses. I nudge Bart – who follows my awed gaze and shrugs.

'Weirdo.'

'It's Rotten you idiot,' I whisper excitedly.

'Who?'

I explain. Bart's not impressed. Never heard the Pistols – he dares not get caught with a copy of *Never Mind the Bollocks*. A pop record more subversive than the IRA. One that my parents allowed in the house on sufferance – and for possession of which a cousin of mine had recently been curfewed.

'Let's go in. He might talk to us!' Bart urges, suddenly suffused with punk rock fever.

I shake my head.

'We can't. It's not done. He'll hate us,' I whine, incapable of breaking the bad news that Bart's hideous outfit will make us laughing stocks – and maybe even punchbags.

So we walk away, me trying on a sneer for size, Bart shaming me with his constant pointing and staring at the endless procession of ripped, strapped, rubbered and leathered, porno punks that glower and gimp for the cameras of GEE SHUCKS WOW American tourists.

And then comes the epiphany – the King's Road to Damascus. As the two of us step humbly aside to make way for a swaggering and spitting posse of punks that hobbles slowly past, their progress impeded

60

but their pedigree paraded by the cripplingly tight straps that bind their legs together. Three of them are chained together at the ankles – a sneering parody of a three-legged race.

Sandwiched and shackled between two heroin-thin, flame haired and sallow-skinned Sid Vicious clones, is a tender, succulent and tasty girl with a fucked-up black beehive and thickly mascara'd lashes spidering out of the top and bottom of her wrap-around shades. Her slinky hips are encased in shiny black rubber – but apart from a ripped and safety-pinned black bra her top half's bare. Not Hollywood nude. Stark. Harsh. Real. Naked. Dirty! Sexy! Her junkie-white porcelain skin stretches tight as a drum over a concave belly bearing a four-inch tattoo: *I'M MEAT. EAT ME.*

I catch myself touching my stiffening dick through my trouser pocket and, cringing, glance at Bart. For a second, I've lost him – then look down. He's sunk to the ground, kneeling as if in prayer to this goddess, not just one as usual, but both eyes, open wide, pupils dilated like black holes sucking her inexorably in. Time stretches and stops ticking. I kneel next to him just as his hand shoots out and clutches at her chained ankle. I grab at his arm, only knowing, as he doesn't, that looking's wanted, provoked, expected – but touching isn't. Too late. Her stilettoed thigh boot clicks on the concrete, lifts and stamps down on Bart's fingers.

He doesn't even say 'ouch'. One eye blinks bewilderedly while the other sucks it all in.

'Oi – no need for...' I protest without much conviction.

Her plum-painted and voluptuous lips curl from a sneer to a smile and back again and then she spits in my face. Not viciously. Slowly. Lasciviously. Lovely. Dirty. Her lower lip backs off from a pout and quivers as saliva pools in the lagoon bounded by her white cliff of overbite. Darkly laughing, the gaze beneath the opaque shades fixes on mine, which she draws up to meet hers like she's got my eyes hooked on fishing line. The spit bubbles and dribbles from the jutting lower lip and slowly, bit by bit, drips onto my waiting, fateful face.

'Wanker,' she giggles, not unkindly, as her chain gang pigeon-steps onward in the direction of Acme Attractions.

I kneel on the cold pavement for a couple of years as the goddess-gob drools slowly down my cheek and leaks gently into the corner of my still-open mouth. Automatically my tongue darts out lizard style and laps it up. Bart's lapping it up too – but it's no longer Ms. MEAT who's snaring his eye. It's one particular member of her retinue, also chained between two others. But where his cohorts strain against self-imposed bondage, one punk in an exact replica of Rotten's outfit on Top of the Pops struggles in a much more heroic and real way. Clearly a Thalidomide victim, he has no arms to be bound and the straps and ragged sleeves of his cheesecloth *DESTROY* shirt hang loose, while two flipper-like hands protrude from specially torn tears at either shoulder. Comprising just three inchoate fingers, curled and clamped together and reddened by the cold winter breeze, they look like frosted pink tulips sprouting where arms should have.

'Rich! Look!!' Bart urges. 'It's *me!*'

And it is. This bloke's sporting spectacles identical to Bart's. What's more he's got a short back and sides just like Bart's – except that it's dyed iridescent purple. His frail frame tortuously twisted as an embryo by the notorious drug his mother must've taken, he lurches and limps along with one scapula jutting proud from his hunched back like a nascent angel's wing. He's Richard III! He's Rotten! Validated, endorsed, promoted to coolness by the values sweeping in on the New Wave's spitting spume, he's a Geek God.

'That could be me!' Bart enthuses.

I nod in agreement – and excitement. It seems that everything – anything – is possible now. If Bart can be re-invented as a punk rock icon, I can do anything. Anything at all! As the mad parade shuffles into the distance, we tear away our adoring gaze and without consultation, as if by telepathy, head as one down into the lurid depths of the Great Gear Market. A hangover from hippiedom, this funky and slightly frightening flea market is an ultraviolet cornucopia of punk paraphernalia, interspersed by limp and neglected stalls draped with kaftans, loons, dippy chicks and other flotsam and jetsam beached by the New Wave. As the Pistols' *God Save the Queen* blares out with its nihilistic *NO FUTURE* refrain, Bart and I suddenly appreciate the deep irony of the whole thing. There IS a future! In a hairdressers' stall fenced off – or, more accurately, caged - by coarse matt-black painted trelliswork, leather-clad denizens of this underworld ply their trade, dying nouveau punks' hair all the colours of a Dayglo rainbow.

'Come on – let's get our hair done!' Bart shouts, grabbing my arm and hauling me towards the scary but spellbinding witch women within.

'You're joking – you seen what it costs!' I stab a finger at the scrawled price list Sellotaped to the trellis cage. Five quid a haircut's a lot of dosh for someone who earns slightly less than that for a twelve-hour Saturday on the local market.

'Da daaa!' he fanfares, pulling a wad of fivers from his pocket.

'Where the fuck?' I begin, then clock his sheepish smile.

'You've nicked that from your dad haven't you?' I chide.

He nods.

'He'll kill you.'

Bart nods again – more gravely this time.

'But he can only kill me once. So I might as well be killed for a hair-do as for a robbery!'

He steps towards the gum-chewing hairdresser, who's wearing a leather bra, biker jacket, leather mini skirt and stockings that look like they've been through a shredder. About the same age as us – sixteen – she drips precocious world-weariness and, when she spots us timidly approaching, something else, which I eventually identify as contempt just as the shower attachment descends over my face in black-taloned hands like it's the anaesthetic mask before surgery. I semi-swoon as her strong, deft fingers massage my scalp and then I doze to the clickety-click of her scissors.

*   *   *

A right bastard of a disease, Hepatitis. A word of advice − never swallow a stranger's spit unless you're actually snogging. At least then it would be worth it! It's bad enough that I feel so shit − but the nurses keep taking the piss, mainly based on the nauseating contrast between my brand new bright yellow skin and equally brand new bright blue hair. In the flickering fluorescent lights of the hospital ward, the ranks of patients' faces look grey and deathly − except for one, other than myself. I've been here two long drawn-out miserable days suffering from the contagion of the punk Goddess. Bart's just arrived and his colour scheme's more attractive than mine. Complimenting his parrot-turquoise short back and sides complete with spiky top is an all-over body tattoo in lurid shades of blue-black and purple, edged with gentle gradient tints of yellow. Evidently his dad hasn't killed him − well not quite. The broken jaw works well with the new punk image, the wires and bolts protruding from bruised and flaky skin out-bondage-ing the best of them. But so comprehensively has Raines Senior covered his son's body with bruises that I wonder whether he kept a diagram of the human body along with a checklist, lest he leave any significant expanse of skin unbeaten, or any part of Bart's spirit unbroken. Apparently it wasn't so much the hair, or the nicking that made him snap − and start snapping bones. It was the second-hand Avon Les Paul copy that Bart bought for thirty stolen quid from some smackhead desperate for a fix. 'Instrument of the devil' apparently. Well, I think smugly to myself, he does have all the best music!

10

The Geek Shall Inherit the Earth

'This poached salmon's delicious!' I grunted through a mouthful, waving my fork at Bart. Georgie mutely concurred with a Galloping Gourmet smirk.

'That's because it was prepared by a poached chef!' our host breezed proudly with a flourish of a linen napkin in the direction of the white-hatted culinary genius sweating over an elaborate barbecue gismo and growling orders to his minions (and mignons) in guttural French.

'I headhunted him from The Ivy actually!' he went on, raising a hand to shield his eyes from the sun.

Georgie shifted in her seat with a winsome arse wiggle, placing herself between our host and the glare so that it set the filigree stray ends of her locks on fire. I fully expected to hear them crackle.

'That better?' she asked, one hand girlishly tapping Bart's white linen-sheathed knee with a sort of tentative complicity.

'Thanks,' he nodded. And as just one lens of his shades rapidly yet imperceptibly shed its opacity and revealed a lidded, but fast shutter-speed eye, he failed to disguise its careful appraisal – no, analysis, input, filing and storing - of her every backlit curve. The other eye, presumably, remained unseeable but all-seeing. If Georgie noticed the odd lenses, she gave no sign of it – but then, cosmopolitan socialite that she was, she wouldn't. The sunglasses turned in my direction and again both were black; implacable. Bart raised his glass to me. I nodded and with difficulty squeezed out a reluctant smile that was sucked immediately back like the last gob of toothpaste in the tube.

'Sacre bleu!'

The exclamation cracked the tense meniscus of our pool of silence. Three heads turned with desultory interest as an angler on the jetty wrestled with a sizeable fish, his rod quivering, arching and bucking under the strain as a flashing explosion of silver broke the water. Then, *snap* – the line gave way with an audible *twang*. As if choreographed, the three of us turned our heads back to the table between us as the man sank to his knees and hurled his rod to the ground. His cursing and the laughter of his *copains* grew louder over there, but to us were muffled by our cushioned exclusivity.

'So, Bart,' Georgie chirped brightly in her best cocktail party networking fashion, 'what is it you do to afford a big fuck-off boat like this?'

'Ship,' he muttered. 'It's a ship.'

'Sorry – ship!' she rallied, body language writing an essay about being a mere girl who really doesn't know the difference.

'Can you explain the difference between a yacht and a boat and a ship and... Oh I don't know...' she tailed off in certain knowledge that he would. And at length. And he did.

'May I?' he smarmed in my direction. Sea, sun and money had dimmed and blunted the edges of that old grammar school irony like pebbled glass shards on the beach. I nodded in kind.

Bart stood up and extended an atavistic arm, which Georgie daintily took as they P G Wodehoused their way aft, Georgie's free arm trailing along glinting brass rails and subtly tossing a wanker sign or wanking a tosser sign in my direction. I returned the gesture, pointlessly.

I rocked back in my chair, rolling my eyes up to squint at the sun barbecuing me through a criss-cross grille of clattering and twanging yacht rigging.

Georgie's cooing and wowing and reallying and goshing came across the soupy air in lazy waves, then ripples that drowned in the gentle slop of oily water on fibreglass hulls, which lulled me into a doze. Seconds or hours later their voices preceded their flipflopflapping as they completed the tour of the ship with a final lap.

'But although I got my start in the eighties with some nifty bits of software, it was my hardware that really cracked it!' reedy shreds of Bart's *curriculum vitae* scraped at the soft shell of my daze.

'Hardware?'

'It started with webcams and applications that accelerated dial-up connections to broadband speeds – and then I saw the future in personal security apps and then started www.winker.com... Our motto is "The Geek Shall Inherit the Earth",' he chuckled.

'You've lost me...'

'Basically, I was among the first to realise that with always-on broadband connections, anyone can have their own private surveillance system – not just in their house. Worldwide.'

'And that's it?'

'In a nutshell. Always have one eye on what's going on, that's me. '

He winked with the eye that could. Which didn't work. It was a blink.

'Bet you don't miss a thing.'

He'd missed the missing of his wink though.

'Not a nanosecond.'

'Richard's a rock star you know. He's Stone, Winston Smith – from Airstrip One.'

I smiled. *That's my girl.*

'How could I not! A Stone broke one these days, I hear...'

I winced at this. Then, to my relief, a squawk of seagulls and a rigging-rattling warm squall blew their words out to sea for a welcome interval before they came wafting back.

'...but in the end it was my dad buying the farm that bought the boat.'

'*Ship,* surely!' Georgie chided.

'Yes. Ship,' he chuckled.

So old Raines senior had shuffled off the mortal coil he'd always despised so deeply. I wondered what he'd died of. Boredom probably.

Or burst a blood vessel in self-righteous rage. Strange I hadn't heard. Or maybe not, considering the little contact I'd had with the old home town till recently.

Another warm windy *woof* swept round me like Neptune farted, filling my ears and spattering pleasantly icy droplets on my upturned face. It subsided but no chit-chat took its place. Georgie did. She *crumped* down on her seat, swiped up a champagne glass, set it noisily down, grabbed the champagne bottle from its ice bucket and chug-a-lugged with a vengeance. A prod in the chest. A where-the-fuck-were-you look. Arms folded protectively over breasts. Long legs crossed with a sudden demureness at odds with her thonged almost-nakedness. She stared out to sea like a cabin boy in the crow's nest. And then the lecherous smirk on Bart's face told me everything as he s-wanked immaculately in his tailored white linen towards us and resumed his seat.

Now our pool of tranquillity was no longer just a harbour. It was a stagnant lagoon. And it stank - of the rotten history that hung in the air between Bart and me. A steward in too-tight, too-white, too-short shorts minced into view out of nowhere proffering a silver salver of tapas. Georgie turned up her nose at all of it — even at her tortilla and chorizo fave. So did I.

'Named after jam jar lids,' I commented, sneering at the pretension of the presentation.

'What is?' Georgie feigned interest.

'Tapas. Means lids. Lumps of food covering your wine glass to keep the flies out. Lorca will be turning in his grave.'

'Why?'

'Tapas on fucking silver platters.'

'If you say so. But why Lorca?'

'Only Spanish poet I can think of.'

'Good enough. You…'

The shape of 'wanker' was just forming on her lips when the wake of another slick white Sunseeker full of smug leisured fun-seekers rocked our boat, sending the ice bucket shooting like a puck into Georgie's barely covered breasts, the ice tumbling and trickling down her cleavage into her lap. Which made her jump – obviously. As she squawked to her feet, the bucket clattered onto the polished deck and her ice-hardened nipples snagged Bart's eye. Forgetting himself for a moment, he whipped off his sunglasses and that unblinking lens swivelled mechanically to input this voluptuous image. And in doing so it met mine – and held its gaze for a moment, then flinched.

'Jacques, clear up this fucking mess!' he barked, springing up as if twanging off the pole that vaulted his trousers and disappearing down the steps to the lounge area. So it wasn't only boys that took his fancy.

The chef stabbed an insolent traffic finger at Bart's back – but sullenly began sweeping up the ice anyway while Georgie and I looked on dumbly. What little convivial warmth we'd kindled had just gone cold, as if a cloud had covered the sun. But it hadn't. For a winter day, even in Cannes, it was stupidly hot; the sky Hollywood blue as if they'd arranged the weather especially for MIDEM. They probably had.

After one of those slack elastic moments that clocks can't measure, a cabin boy – Algerian, at a guess. Thirteen going on thirty-five – popped a head out of a hatch at the bow.

'Monsieur Raines apologises, but he has a headache and has had to retire. He has asked me to say "Mi barca, su barca". You are very welcome to stay aboard as long as you like – and I have been instructed to provide you with anything at all that you require.'

'Thank you very much,' I murmured, bunging him a crisp five Euro note, the unfurling of which sprang a little snow flurry onto the table top. He licked his lips. Brazenly, I licked a finger and dabbed up the smattering of dandruffy white particles as he looked on hungrily. This boy wouldn't turn his nose up at a bit of sniff. Made me wonder how Bart's always sordid tastes had evolved.

As one, Georgie and I shivered in a non-existent chill breeze and, with a jerk of the head in the direction of the jetty, she beckoned and shuddered. It was definitely a shudder now and not a shiver.

'Out of here?' I mouthed.

She nodded and skipped across the gangplank, landing with a barefoot thud and hopping up and down on the jetty's oven-hot concrete. As we walked hurriedly away, the sun was so bright it hummed in our ears and thrummed off the asphalt. Glancing furtively back to see if our departure had been noticed, we zigzagged from one shrinking shard of shade to the next, seeking cool places for hot feet to step, hurrying toward the insistent distant thud of decadent-to-dead disco from the neon and wicker bars that huddled, whored and danced round the wave-lapped fringes of the enclosed marina, their brazen facades facing the sleek status symbols that rocked gently in its embrace and their backs very deliberately turned on anyone outside the jetty set. They were like pole dancers, only swaying for money in the shimmering light round the lasciviously jutting poles provided by hundreds of flag-flying masts.

11

Saturday 6th November 1976. 10.50pm. Hartham-On-Sea

'Do I have to?' Stephen whines at his father's back.

'I thought we said,' comes the exasperated reply, 'that if you got your bloody death trap Chopper bike, against my better judgement, that you'd earn it by walking the mutt every evening before you go to bed.'

'I know but – the werewolf...'

'Stephen, it's the nineteen seventies. Trust me – there's no such thing,' the voice rebounds from the windowpanes through which his dad surveys his kingdom without ever, it seems, turning round. 'You're thirteen now. You really must learn that everything in life has to be earned. The world doesn't...'

'...Owe me a living,' Stephen chimes in, turning to the door and opening it, resigned to his father's inevitable intransigence.

'Brandy! Walkies!' he calls unenthusiastically and in a nanosecond the boisterous bundle of six-month-old retriever pup comes bowling out of the front door.

At least Brandy will protect me, he thinks as he shuffles out of the neatly manicured *cul de sac* and onto the muddy path that leads to the little bridge and the impenetrable blackness of the woods that crowd in on the ever more overgrown footpath that meanders to the beach via Mimram Crescent as if it's as reluctant to go there as Stephen is.

He crosses the bridge, pausing to gob laddishly into the oily black trickle a few feet underfoot. Brandy cocks his leg. Stephen tugs at the lead.

'Not here, Brandy. Come on boy,' he urges, but too late.

The dog's steaming spurt chuckles into the stream below. Stephen shivers and suddenly feels the need to piss too.

Leaning on the rusty iron rail he looks skyward in the way blokes learn to while pissing in public toilets – and that's what reminds him why tonight, especially, he didn't want to do 'walkies'. It's full moon. Worse than that, it's a fuller, fatter, more sinisterly grinning moon than usual. And now, following the time-honoured route his dad always treads on dog-walking exercises, and to whose routine he still insists his son should adhere, he has to walk past the werewolf house; the one where no flickering telly lights up the windows; the one whose garden is untended and whose windows are almost always dark like the eyes of a corpse; the one where the dogs inside howl every time it's full moon. Of course that's all it is. Just pet dogs starved of affection, company or even food. That's why everyone at school called it the house of the werewolf. Just the dogs. And their horrible, sickening howling. And the fact that the man of the house has that oblong, granite-face with its permafrosted frown that looks like it can extinguish the sun - like maybe he's a vampire or a werewolf or a ghoul or something equally horrible.

'Brandy! Brandy! Here boy!'

But the dog has trotted on ahead. Lighting a cigarette he's nicked from his father's pack and dangling it from his lips as if it were a talisman, Stephen follows. Brandy is pissing nonchalantly against the werewolf house's unhinged gate, ears cocked as he tunes in to something Stephen can't quite catch; something soft or distant enough to be drowned by the far away drone of the odd passing car and the ghostly whisper of a breeze in the trees or the hissing sea. Probably the latter – the tide seems unusually high tonight.

'What is it boy?' he whispers, kneeling next to his best friend and hugging him as if it were the dog that needed moral support.

And now he hears what Brandy hears.

The blood-curdling howl of an animal in anguish. Or a werewolf.

'Don't worry son,' says a deep, resonant voice out of nowhere. It's just my dogs. Would you like to see them?'

12

Greed is God

It's 1985. The summer of Live Aid vs 'Greed is Good', Geldof vs Thatcher – and the contagious notion that rock 'n' roll can change the world has re-infected me with a feverish need to succeed. In an effort to scrape up the money for some recording time for yet another fresh set of demos, I'm temping as an envelope stuffer on a self-defeating £1.75 an hour. Passing my lunch hour in the politely muted hum of a riverside pub popular with business lunchers, I'm scribbling half-formed lyric ideas on beermats and looking oh so poetic when the buzz lulls to a hush punctuated metronomically by the clickety-clack of an incongruous pair of skyscraper-heeled *fuck me* shoes trailed by a yappy white Scottish Terrier. Following the wavy line of seamed and seamy stockings up to a belt-short black dress overslung by a studded belt and a cascade of crow-black curls, my gaze is caught by wild green eyes caged by heavily mascara'd lashes. If I had a proper notebook I'd bury my head in it. It's hard to hide behind a beermat.

'What do you mean you don't take Amex?' she shrills at the quailing barmaid, huffily riffling through a wad of twenties and throwing one on the bar before teetering to a table with a Bloody Mary. Perched on a stool, she rummages in a capacious handbag, whips out a pack of gold-tipped Sobrani Black Russian, fires one up and surveys the room balefully.

A gaggle of cheap suits giggles.

'How much love?' comes the catcall, followed by a wolf-whistle.

'More than you can afford babe,' she purrs with as much unction as gumption.

The wolf-whistler's instantly sheepish and turns back to his flock to avoid her coolly appraising gaze. Straining at its leash, the little dog growls. As one, the sheep regain their canines and growl back. The Scottie snaps. Lashing out and catching the tiny mutt's jaw with a glancing blow, a grey slip-on slips off, ricochets off the ceiling and plops into the top of the precious pint I've been spinning out for the last hour. The dog yelps and retreats, circling its owner's stool and binding her at the ankles with its lead. I stand, indignant, holding up the tainted pint in one hand and the sopping shoe in the other.

'Gimme my fucking shoe back!' says the wedge haircut in a shiny grey suit, one grey shoe and one white sock.

'Buy me a new pint,' I reply.

Six shiny suits stand up. Six identical blonde highlighted haircuts flop over spotty faces. Six barely broken voices chorus: 'Fuck off!'

I stand my ground. Then hit it as several fists fly in my direction and a few connect. The hooker (as politically correct and non-judgmental as I am, that's what I've decided she is) stands — and even as my nose explodes in a gush of blood I can't help looking up and clocking a Sharon Stone glimpse of commando crotch. It's only a glimpse because she hasn't realised she's hogtied (no — dog tied) by the studded leather tether and as she takes a meant-to-be-menacing step towards our now mutual enemies she crashes to the flagstoned floor, taking her table, her glass and a load of empties with her. Her shopping bag-size handbag spews its contents: a litre bottle of vodka, which cracks and cocktails with the thick rusty Bloody Mary and my thin scarlet blood in a fast-filling puddle, followed by a cascade of high denomination banknotes, not bundled or wadded but loose. And they get a lot looser as the draught from the open door catches them and whisks away those not soaked and bogged down. They fly skittishly out of the windows and flutter down around the outside tables, sending ostensibly sensible citizens into a flurry of greed as they gather up this money from Heaven or manna from Mammon. The landlord, a big fat, gruff, but usually friendly enough ex-copper, flips up the bar flap to intervene. I grin with satisfaction. Now the little shits are gonna get it! But it's the arse over tit woman whom he addresses with a doorward jerk of a podgy thumb.

'You. Out. And don't come back.'

She struggles to her feet. So do I.

'That's out of order Terry,' I protest. 'It's not fair!'

'Life's not fair son,' he mutters. 'Don't want her sort in here.'

I kneel in the puddle in front of her splayed knees like a midwife before a stirruped mother-to-be and gently untangle the leather thong that binds her ankles. In doing so I can't help feeling a certain frisson, which is intensified by her ineffably obscene wink.

'Thanks darling,' she breathes as I help her to her feet and she totters leaning on my shoulder to the door. Sitting her down at a bench outside I go back to retrieve the bag and its contents. Terry's fat frame fills the door, holding out the bag, which I snatch and walk huffily away towards the girl, who's holding out a hand daintily.

'Gotta pay for it these days have you!' he leers.

'Come on Sir Galahad,' she mutters. 'Don't know about you but I need a drink.'

'I can't. I've got to work.'

'So take the afternoon off.'

'Can't afford it.'

'What they pay you?'

'One seventy-five an hour.'

'A princely sum for a knight in shining armour. Here y'are.'

She produces a sodden fifty pound note and stuffs it into my jeans pocket, her hand lingering a fraction of a second longer than necessary.

'What...'

'I'm paying you to drink with me... Not fuck me,' she states as if it's the most natural thing in the world – and in her world, I guess, it probably is.

'I can't accept this,' I protest without much conviction.

'Yes you can,' she says as she jumps to her feet, taking me by the hand and dragging me away. 'By the way, my name's Daisy.'

'Rich.'

'Evidently in name only,' she purrs.

★   ★   ★

Half a litre of vodka and numerous dabs of speed later we're in the local park and I think I'm in love. Or at least in lust with her sun-starved pallor, whose glistening is incongruously demure as she shrinks back and back from the glare into the shade of a bush. It's as if the sun's trying to spotlight her so the distant pram-pushers that skirt the gated playground full of shrieks and whines can whisk their kids away from her seductive corruption (but maybe that's just my woozy imagination). My heart goes rushing out to her, driven by the amphetamine engine.

'This is a giggle isn't it darling,' she declares with a sigh.

I smile.

'A giggle with my gigolo!' she cackles, witchy green eyes twinkling yet appraising over the top of her Raybans.

Propped on one elbow, shirt open, stomach held heroically and tiringly in, and squinting at the sky, I look down, twiddle some grass, light a fag. She reaches out and lightly takes my fingers in hers. Filigree blue deltas flow from arterial rivers under the translucent white of the heartbreakingly tender folds of skin in the crook of her arm. But the impossibly soft melted marble is speckled by tiny red blotches. She catches me looking.

'Want some?'

She's holding up a little wrap between thumb and forefinger, unfolds it and shows me the light brown powder.

'Smack. No. Don't do smack,' I blurt, betraying my small town alarm.

'Mind if I do?'

I shrug. The cosy complicity we've cooked up goes cold. Or is it

77

just the cloud that discreetly covers the sun for her as she lays out her tackle with an efficiency more often seen in a military weapons drill, then cooks up her brown-bubbling stew over a Zippo in a tiny silver spoon. Matter-of-factly wrenching on the tourniquet she's wrapped round an almost indiscernible tripe-white bicep, she stabs the needle into unblemished nacreous flesh without a flinch. I cringe. She laughs. I cringe again.

'You don't remember me do you?'

I blink dumbly as Errol Brown shrieks the same words in my head in the outro of Hot Chocolate's *It Started With A Kiss: You don't remember me do you!* You don't remember me do you!

'Obviously you don't. You were at school with my brother.'

Evidently I still have a big question mark printed on my forehead.

'Bart Raines. You were his fucking hero. All we ever heard was Rich this and Richard that... I know more about you than I know about my brother!'

Now the sordid jacking up is over, the cloud lets the sun get a look in – and I'm enlightened. Daisy Raines! Bart's shrinking violet sister, my former muse, who'd run away from home at the age of fifteen and rarely been heard of since as far as I knew. So the rumours were true. She'd gone off and got hooked on heroin and ended up walking the streets. But the Gothic beauty smirking darkly at me didn't fit the identikit. Could this preternaturally pearly translucence, these acres of nacre, really be a deathly pallor? Because if Daisy walked any streets, she did it in designer clothes and the streets had W1 postcodes: Park Lane, Bond Street, Berkeley Square.

'Before you ask – yes it's all true,' she laughs, amused by my bemusement. 'I'm a whore.'

I can't think of a suitable response.

'You're shocked,' she teases, prodding me gently in the chest.

'No – I'm... All right I'm a bit shocked,' I confessed with a rueful grin. 'I mean, I heard that you'd run away from home – and someone said you were working in a hostess bar... But...'

'That was nearly ten years ago. I've gone a bit upmarket since then.'

13

Gift Horses

'He touched me,' Georgie hissed incredulously in response to my enquiringly raised eyebrows as we sank into cushioned wicker in a bar beamed in from Harlow.

'You mean.'

'She nodded, legs parting and snapping shut under her sarong with sudden schoolgirl shame.

'Cheeky fucker,' I whistled.

Snake strike suddenly, her face was up against mine.

'Not fucking "cheeky" you cunt (I loved the way she said 'cunt' – with the 't' perfectly enunciated. So posh yet so dirty). Fucking filthy. A fucking sexual assault!'

She recoiled from the rewound memory flash and uncoiled back into her seat as the enormity of the incident registered on my face.

'Fucking hell,' I muttered.

'Fucking hell infuckingdeed! I feel dirty...'

'Back to the hotel room then?' I leered.

One refreshingly icy spritzer facial shower later her thong-sarong combo swished out into the sun, leaving me mopping up.

★　　★　　★

'You told them?' Raines debriefed the boy, literally and metaphorically, his focus panning slowly up from his groin across the flat plain of his belly, to zoom in on flickering eyes.

'Oui monsieur Bart. *Mi barca, su barca,*' I said. But they wanted to leave. I'm sorry...' he broke off.

'Don't be sorry — that's just what was supposed to happen,' his owner/employer beamed, handing the kid back his pants.

'Now, be off with you — take the rest of the day off and do whatever you little poofters do with your spare time. I'm going out on a hot date!'

Raines slapped the lad heartily on the arse and as if impelled by the impact he scuttled off down the gangplank and disappeared into the rattling forest of masts, rigging and fluttering pennant leaves.

★   ★   ★

My cab drew up at the rank outside Hotel Gray D'Albion four taxis back from Georgie's — but my attempt to catch her up was stymied by a gaggle of Japanese fans wielding autograph books. I *sorried* and *excusez-moi'd* my way through them — needlessly as it turned out because Bowie strolled up behind me and I was forgotten in a paparazzi flash. Feeling my sunburnt face re-redden, I loped, casually as I could while holding my belly in, up the steps into the vestibule that still felt as imperious and *who-the-fuck-are-you?* as it ever did. A similar theme was evident back in our penthouse suite, where Georgie looked up from her *iBook*, impassively registered my return and carried on tapping away at draft fifty-thousand or whatever of her screenplay *Rock 'n' Droll* — a romcom about a rock star who's too PC to do any of that groupie stuff and refuses to accept repeated offers of sexual favours. Or something like that. Autobiographical on her part. Frighteningly biographical on mine. And, from the little I'd bothered to peruse, altogether too graphical, period. But, hey, I was only a dumb-ass rock singer — what did I know?

This was the project that was going to propel Georgie into a high-flying movie-writing career that would equal or better my own success.

Obviously I supported her in her ambition. Even more obviously I fucking resented it. I was on the way out – and everyone knew it. I was pushing forty for Christ's sake (as far as they knew). She was a genuine twenty-five (as far as I knew) and on the way *in,* and it was my mission – one I was obliged to accept or self-destruct – to open the doors for her. The idea was that we'd do some networking (brown-nosing) at MIDEM and get our tongue muscles pumped and primed for a major onslaught of arse licking at the Cannes Film Festival. Trouble was, Georgie had an inflated impression of my influence. What power I had was in the music industry. I mean at least my latest stroke of luck proved I could still get a decent advance out of a major music publisher. In the movie world, on the other hand, I was pretty sure no one would buy me a pint, let alone be swayed into stumping up for an unknown writer's first feature script. In this refreshing new flush of success, though, I couldn't quite bring myself to admit this to Georgie – and instead encouraged her to work on her magnum opus just as she supported me in my so-far unsuccessful attempts to write a new album, whose working title was *Gift Horses.*

'I'm sorry,' I grinned sheepishly.

She looked up and her gentle frown evaporated, leaving a lovely smile.

'S'alright. Sorry I walked...'

'How's it going?'

'In the two minutes since I sat down – nowhere. In fact nowhere, period.'

'We're in Cannes, not LA,' I anti-Yanked with a grin.

'Fuck off. *Full stop!* Happy?'

'Maybe,' I ventured, 'rewrites aren't the answer.'

Silence. I gritted my teeth and persevered.

'Maybe, as a writer, as an artist, you'd do better to move on. Start a new project...'

I ducked for shelter as if there'd been a blaring klaxon glare raid warning. But no glare. Just a wan stare.

'You think it's crap,' she accused, less forcefully than anticipated.

'No – I think it's a story about us; about *me*... And it's a good one... But ten years ago, when I was hot...'

'I didn't know you ten years ago.'

'I know... Of course. But ten years ago everyone wanted to know about me. No one gives a flying fuck now – least till the new album comes out.'

'It's a romantic comedy though. Could be about anyone.'

'It could if the people reading it didn't know it was about me – and you. About us.'

'So?' she asked, now apparently genuinely interested.

'So – maybe your connection with me is doing the script harm rather than good.'

OK – so I thought it was crap. OK, so I didn't want her story screwing up my imminent 'comeback'. OK so I wasn't exactly keen on the idea of the 'real' private me becoming some goofy stereotype played by Ben Stiller in a gross-out comedy (because that's where it was going, despite her loftier aspirations, which were more along the lines of *Brief Encounter* set in a rock 'n' roll context. Some fucking hopes).

She stopped typing. Clearly, I had to expand on that.

'Maybe you should write what you *don't* know – present a script that's nothing to do with us?'

'How do you mean?'

I struggled. Gurned. Grimaced.

'Well, I dunno... Spend some time finding your own vision...You know, one that doesn't include me...'

Presumably that was what she was looking for when she stormed out of the door.

★   ★   ★

I tried the obvious places. I knew she'd shun the hip joints, the *meeja* and Hollywood hangouts that were apparently chewing her up and spitting her out. And especially the kind of swanky with a silent 's' boat parties and press receptions where she'd be likely to bump into the appalling Raines. No, feeling low, my Georgie would shun the highlife and go for the lowlife; the ducking dives where we usually scored gear and got wankered and wasted away from prying eyes and wagging tongues – or at least those that spoke English.

I hit the speed dial on my mobile.

'Hi. Georgie here. I'm either switched off or in an orgy. Leave a message!'

I trawled three or four bars full of bottom feeders and finally scored a Henry of charlie at Luca's, an African joint I favoured for its *souk*-style soft cushions, hanging carpets, tented drapes and high-price harem of hardbody whores. The eponymous host twinkled his gold-capped, diamond studded teeth at me (never saw the point of that – an expensive way of making your teeth look fucked up), plied me with free Champagne and, with a regally camp wave of the hand, set in train a parade of almost certainly under-age girls, regimented by categories of body type, ethnicity, skin tone, breast size and so on. A tempting offer. But that Joe Strummer righteousness button went off in my head as per fucking usual (Uncle Joe has a lot to answer for with his relentless integrity) and I declined each girl in turn with what I hoped was a rueful smile that said, 'You're lovely – nothing personal but I really mustn't'.

Then Luca brought out the trannies – and I went through the same routine. When the teenage boys came out, I gave up and excused myself in my inelegant French.

'Je vous remercie, mais tout ceci, ce n'est pas nécessaire parce que j'ai une très belle fille, celle qui je cherche maintenant.'

Luca nodded gravely – that man-to-man complicitous sympathy that's merely allowing you to pretend it's not going to happen. But actually it wasn't. When you've had your fifteen minutes as a major rock star you can get blasé about offers of sexual favours and free pharmaceuticals. I'd seen it all, done the drugs and given the groupies and the whores the brush off – well mostly. Tonight, I'd scored some gear. And that was all I needed to score. Unless I failed to find her. In which case, maybe later, if I found myself in a vengeful mood. But actually, probably not even then. What would be the point if there were nothing better, sexier, lovelier on offer than the woman I'd got, was about to lose and from whom I compulsively fenced myself off for reasons I'd never understand or want to.

'Ah, oui – cherchez la femme, n'est-ce pas!'

'Non – je cherche MA femme, la mienne!' I insisted.

He smiled. Inscrutable – maybe he'd seen her and was keeping schtum.

'Tu connais ma fille, Georgie, oui?' I continued.

He nodded.

'Est-ce qu'elle était ici ce soir?'

He shook his head.

'Je regrette, Monsieur Stone, mais non. Vous êtes sûr que vous ne voulez pas une de ces belles fillettes-ci ce soir?'

'No. Merci, mon ami. Au revoir.'

It was with a certain smugness that I clambered up the wonky steps towards the fuzzy twilit streets. *Vive la résistance!* I'd resisted and pissed on a parade of temptation and persevered on my Georgie hunt.

'Alors, peut être plus tard?' Luca's columbine cooing trailed after me (if I'd owned a gun I'd have reached for it right then).

'Peut-être,' I mumbled. And *peut être* that was true.

★　　★　　★

Twelve bars and a lot of blues later I found her. Irritatingly, she was in the fucking hotel bar. Exactly where I wouldn't have looked. When I reeled into the revolving doors and did a double spin I trusted that my star status still held enough sway (that being the operative word) for the ponced-up bellhops to greet me with indulgent smiles and steadying hands rather than the old heave-ho. Reassuringly that hope was justified.

My faith in Georgie's integrity wasn't. Disappointingly, she wasn't crying into her Martini. Much more disappointingly, she was laughing her *had-a-few-lines-and-drinks-and-given-up-on-the-Notting-Hillbilly-Ladbroke-Groove-and-admitting-my-pseudo-aristocratic-trustafarian-background* tinkling, sphincter-wrinkling laugh. Possibly the most annoying sound known to mankind, that cut-glass titter sliced through the smokily smug fug and sobered me up in a shot. In a flash (literally – the paparazzi never rest), my swivelling eyes screwed themselves in to tight focus on her lovely brown back as convulsions of glee threw her head back and sent her long locks tossing and writhing hydra-style. And then I saw her companion, and his unwavering, un-stare-downable eye locked on mine. Bart deliberately raised a hand, pointing to me. And Georgie's face followed like it was physically lifted, like he was pegging her on a washing line between me and him.

I did my usual sheepish shrug and fell fast and gravity-drawn down the taut line from my standing to their sitting, knocking aside anything in my beeline and landing ignominiously at Georgie and Bart's feet.

'Pisshead,' Georgie said, not as unkindly as I'd expected.

'Hello old boy,' boomed Bart in exactly the non-ironic Tory (as in short for self-congratulatory) middle England speak that gets my goat, raises my hackles and makes me say things like:

'Fuck off you cunt.'

Which is exactly what I said. Although, with due deference to the fame and importance of the other people in the room, all of whom were much more famous than I was, I followed through with a concise explanation of my grievance.

'You stuck your filthy hand up my girlfriend's cunt and now you're taking her on a date!'

Generally speaking, in any confrontational situation, of which there had been many over the years, I was the one who could rely on my trusty bodyguards to get me out of any major violence ensuing from something I said. I had of course forgotten that I was no longer in the personal security league. And that Bart was.

I think it was on the first consonant of the word 'cunt' that a fist the size of a small car connected with my jaw and dropped me to the floor. On the 'f' of 'filthy', the same giant hand snared my hair and pulled me to my feet. And on the 'd' of 'date' I sagged carpetward again as Georgie Uma Thurmaned my attacker with incredibly sexy efficiency.

The hotel's security people hovered, robotically awaiting instructions from their Madonna-style headsets and whispering into their lapel mikes, presumably checking which of the troublemakers spent most on their black Amex. It wasn't going to be me.

It was bad enough that I'd been rescued by my girlfriend. Naturally it got worse. Because she was seized in a nanosecond by the big fisted fucker and two more of Bart's musclemen. That left me unseized – but depressingly seized-up and gripped with sheer fear. Which my former protégé noted with a casual chuckle and an interval he clearly enjoyed before calling them off like they were trained dogs.

'That'll do,' he smirked.

They released their grip on Georgie instantly and she sprung away from them as if elastic. Thank God, it was back to me she twanged. I was still flat on my back – literally and metaphorically. The three stooges grinned down at me, their height, my lowness and my drunkenness amplifying the perspective scarily. Their heads were skyscraper high and their fists Neanderthal low. Following the trail from a giant set of knuckles up a depressingly muscular arm I slowly focused on a face that seemed familiar somehow. Adjusting the angle by thirty degrees, my binocular vision met Bart's telescope – and I was looking through the wrong end. Switching back, I got it.

'Hello Burroughs. Long time no see! Still a fucking bully then. Not surprised this is...'

★   ★   ★

Apparently Bart had his people (including Burroughs, whose knuckles looked grazed like they'd been dragging heavily on the ground, but actually had been beaten up by my face with its lethally sharp cheekbones and chiselled jaw) take me and Georgie to a private hospital and then, once back at the Gray D'Albion, got one of his more presentable people to negotiate my discreet and unphotographed entry through a back door. I was damaged – but it didn't hurt really. If you've ever done any real fighting you'll know that. The adrenalin makes it almost painless – that and the sensible precaution of a load of nasally administered anaesthetic beforehand. Thus numbed, I didn't get round to wondering why Raines had chosen to employ his schoolday Nemesis and place his bullying on professional level. Once ensconced in those crisp Egyptian cotton sheets, my bruised and bloodied brow soothed and mopped by Georgie's hand with a sopping wet ice-cold flannel, I wondered aloud.

'Must be Bart's way of getting revenge.'

Georgie looked blank. Of course she would. We might have skipped lightly over our teenage years in one of those heavily Bowdlerised personal histories you rose-tint with hindsight and wishful thinking in the first flush of love. But in the skipping I was almost certain I'd hopped in a skittish, jittering heartbeat over what happened to Bart. Or if I hadn't, I wouldn't have owned up to the bit where I walked away and never saw him again till now; when I backed down and sloped off at the height of his calvary when I should have been charging towards him like the cavalry.

A question quivered on her lips – but died there instantly, its death knell the ring of the phone. I picked it up.

'Wotcha! Check your email,' a depressingly familiar voice chuckled and hung up. So I did. I hung up and got in touch with my hang-ups – which took a while.

With Georgie looking over my shoulder, I clicked the attachment.

'Here we go again,' I thought as I waited for another of those *ha-ha-aren't-we-crazy-because-we-forward-mildly-provocative-but-unfunny-*

crap Powerpoint self-executing (I wish) documents. That annoyingly small Quicktime screen popped up on the totally-compatible-with-everything-honestly-Mac. Naturally the 'movie' wouldn't open. So we forwarded the email to the PC provided by the hotel, which wouldn't open a Mac-formatted email. So we gave up. And we made up. And we went to bed. And everything was all right with my world – until I couldn't do *it* because of all the drink and the coke and the worry and the bruises and beating and my imminent nobodiness and the terrible unmanliness of it all and I cried and sobbed and then puked.

★   ★   ★

Morning prised open my crusty eyes sometime late in the afternoon and the slopping sweat-pool I'd puddled up buoyed me up out of bed with startling rapidity. Georgie was up, about, slinky as a cat and teasing a mouse round her mat as usual. Trailing a sodden sheet, one-bollock-naked and half-toga'd, I hobbled across the reprovingly clean and gleaming expanse of polished floor to see what she was watching.

It was a round brown blob. With brilliant light intermittently, but rhythmically, lasering round its periphery. It was like a tape loop. Actually it was a taped boob. Specifically it was Georgie's left tit. Then the right one. That got my attention. The unblinking lens trailed from one pneumatically compact brown breast to the other, zooming in on Mediterranean Sea-chilled nipples before trailing lasciviously down a taut tanned belly past a tattoo that said 'Rich' to the irresistible groove of my own Eurovision thong contest winner. The star of the next scene was rather more resistible. It was me. Being comprehensively beaten. It was our holiday video in the third person. So it wasn't ours. It was his.

'I'll kill him,' I stated, surprising myself with my lack of conviction.

'How the fuck...' was Georgie's more apposite comment.

I slumped on a chair. Lit a fag.

'He watches. And dissects,' I spoke as the nicotine crystallised dissolved thoughts. 'And he uses it as power. Like his telescope,' I elucidated dimly.

'Yeah – that makes shitloads of sense,' carped the light of my life, clearly unenlightened.

The Quicktime movie Quicktimed away over and over in that blurry area of your peripheral vision. Apparently women's peripheral vision's wider than men's. Seems right, because it wasn't me that threw the PC monitor across the room to crash rather spectacularly on the equally spectacularly shiny floor and buzz, tinkle and fizzle out like a dying animal.

'Georgie, don't worry about it. He's just a rich flash bastard. I used to like him but...'

'The bastard that's paying for my film!'

Talk about 'words like flame-throwers'.

'He's what?'

'You heard.'

'Fuck.'

I'm nothing if not concise.

Georgie, on the other hand was something. Really something. But concise she wasn't.

So here are the edited highlights of the breakdown the love of my life fired at me in staccato bursts interspersed with information whose relevance could never be discerned by a man.

It was two hours - or maybe days - later as we lay in chastely conciliatory spoons on the bed that I finally got the lowdown – 'low' and 'down' suddenly becoming especially apposite.

'He phoned to apologise...' she started.

'He sexually assaulted you and you gave him your number? Nice,' I snorted, the white line on the bedside table shooting straight to the paranoia button and getting my dander up, if nothing else.

'No you idiot – that was before...'

'This was when he tried to buy you by buying your script?'

'It was business – he invests in movies all the time,' she snapped unconvincingly.

'Yeah *right,*' I Noo Yoiked.

She jumped to her feet, crossed her arms, compressing her goose-bumped breasts, shivered and stepped gingerly to the balcony, where she opened up to the sun like a flower.

'Well so I thought,' she said to a wheeling seagull as it passed, which squawked with laughter.

'Even he doesn't believe it!' I jibed gently, and was relieved when her response was to turn back to me, the sun having warmed her mood.

'I'm such a dumb-ass sometimes,'

'No comment babe.'

'But so are you.'

I had no argument with that.

'So why...' I began.

'Because, you arse, you were being a jerk and he called and was very charming and kind of gentlemanly... Old fashioned...'

I harumphed.

'Your shite in armour!'

She gave me the 'Paddington Stare' that said shut the fuck up. So I did.

'And he said he'd wine me and dine me...'

'And fuck you?'

'Shut up... And discuss the budget for the film and... Introduce me to some important movie people...'

'And fuck you?'

'Who,' she persevered through pursed lips, 'are looking for low budget vehicles and who'd like to meet me...'

'And fuck you?'

'And fuck *you!*' she parried, a bit too keenly for my liking. 'You won't consider, even for one nanosecond, the possibility that someone might actually think my work's worth investing in will you!'

'Well I might if he'd actually read it. You telling me he read a

120-page screenplay in the half hour you two spent getting all shipmatey?'

Her face clouded – a storm gathering.

'Fuck you,' she thundered.

'Where've I heard that before?' I mused, ducking a chunky glass ashtray. Having rained so comprehensively on her parade, I knew it would be a while before the sunshine broke through.

Anyway, he'd sent a Limo. Which took her to a tender. Which whisked her offshore to his yacht – sorry, *ship*. Where a big fuck-off chopper throbbed cockily on the helipad, waiting to beam her up to some super-exclusive *eaterie*. Where he'd try and woo her with his more than sizeable wad – presumably before shooting it in one of his boat's sumptuous boudoir-cabins. Stupidly, I expressed this theory to Georgie.

'And you think I'd have just fucked him because he asked? Like I had no say in this supposed seduction?' she retorted angrily.

'Well, going by his latest form he doesn't feel the need to ask!'

'You're calling me a whore!'

'No, I...'

'You are! You're calling me a tart who'd screw someone just cos they're loaded!'

That hurt. It pricked ten years' worth of ballooning insecurity.

'Well you screwed *me*,' I ejaculated, instantly regretting the outburst and simultaneously feeling nostalgic about other regrettable ejaculations.

'Jesus Christ, you really do think that!' she hissed.

To be more accurate, she'd repeatedly tried to screw me and I'd repeatedly refused, convinced that she was a starfucker (and I said as much); that all she was after was another notch on the bedpost or a score out of ten in the reporter's notebook I assumed she stashed in her Prada bag. I finally decided I'd been wrong and she wasn't (after a notch, I mean). So when eventually, inevitably, I capitulated, I ascribed my reticence to Strummeresque ethics rather than the HIV dread induced by the recent death of one of my rock star chums. Or, more fundamentally, the dread of being found out as just as crappy or even more so than the next man or the last. Amazingly she went for it.

That was then.

This was now.

And she went for me with a Bruce Lee chop, which I ducked with agility born of experience, practice and consummate cowardice.

★   ★   ★

To be fair to yours truly (something I always strive to be), the 'starfucker incident' - and the ensuing tit-for-tat *ratatat* ranting – had some justification in fact. I was in New York for the first time, alone and overwhelmed by the first frightening gush of success. The hoary, whorey rock 'n' roll crackpipe dream had apparently come true and my recurring nightmare was that I'd wake up. Lonely and low after a spectacularly unsuccessful recording session at the Power Station – probably the world's most famous studio – I'd got talking to this pertly petite Japanese music reporter who perched unbearably prettily on the edge of a vast sofa that double-dwarfed her (or *elved* her) and made her doubly doll-like. I wasn't, (couldn't; never could) chatting her up. My new star status (well, incipient star status, since I'd only just signed the major deal and been trumpeted in the press) lent me a gravitas that I hoped I'd never have to give back; one that attracted girls of this calibre without the slightest effort on my part. I was suddenly in an elite club; one whose members were in great demand, as I discovered later in the hot tub atop her top-flight apartment block. Although as the presenter of Tokyo's most popular teen pop TV programme and music columnist for a couple of Japan's major rock mags, she was a lot more famous than

93

I, she evidently had a thing for cock rock and rocker cock. I didn't suss this until way too late – when we'd retired to her flat to dry off and dress and she presented me with her visitors' book and an expensive-looking fountain pen. If it had been a Biro I wouldn't have thought twice. But that *Mont Blanc* suggested that great import was attached to the requested signature. My inference was confirmed by the list of rock aristocracy names that preceded mine in the well-thumbed, leather-bound and metal-trimmed volume and their lewd lines scrawled in the 'comments' column: Billy Idol, Axl Rose, Slash, all of Motley Crue (three times each), a couple of famous females not known as far as I knew for their lesbian tendencies and a number of males not known for their heterosexuality, whose names I mustn't list for fear of reverse-outing (inning?) them. I was the only name I didn't recognise! It was kind of flattering. No, not 'kind of'. Who am I kidding! I was chuffed she wanted to fuck me. But I was double chuffed to find she wanted my body not just because I was some body but because she thought I was *somebody!* It was only when I lay alone in bed that night and scrolled down that list that the dream turned to a nightmare. At least one of those names was dead – and another two were dying. And I hadn't worn a Trojan, as they so aptly call rubbers in the States.

14

My One-Whore Town

Daisy pays for a room in the one hotel of our one-horse town, where eyebrows are raised as I avoid the gaze underneath them and shuffle shiftily behind her. I'm out of my depth, intimidated by those laughing eyes that have seen so much – too much. I'm not up to this. I'm scared. But I shouldn't be. You know the cliché of the guy who goes to a prostitute and 'just wants to talk', who uses her as a sort of sexually charged therapist? Well Daisy, accustomed to being paid for her time, is simply paying for mine. She really does just want to talk. And we talk and talk and talk. She showers and doesn't bother to dress – just lolls like a contented black and white cat on the bed in a bathrobe and towel turban, scrubbed clean of make-up and, amazingly, kind of fresh-faced. *Fresh as a Daisy,* I think.

The 'eyelid incident', as she calls it, wasn't the start of her six-year ordeal at the hands of her dad's perverted piety. It had begun some months before when he first made her pose in school uniform for him and then began to parade her for men he brought home from 'prayer meetings'. But that night signalled a new, more painful, more penetrative phase that went on and on and on until, at fifteen, she realised that it wasn't right. Then, a while later, she worked out that it was wrong. And that the preaching each night before he came, and the prayers when he'd come, were a warped and sticky web of tortuous self-justification, constructed over years of self-serving bible study in which what Raines Senior didn't like was a sin and what he did was a virtue. And she'd swallowed the lot – time and time again. She was bad. She was Eve. She

was Evil. She was dirty. She was filthy to the core and she was a whore
– as all women apparently were. So she had to be purged and she went
through purgatory until finally she spat it all back in her father's face.
Literally.

And, with his own sticky goo still dripping off his graveyard face,
he threw her out onto the street.

'And he had the fucking nerve to call me a slut as he slammed the
door shut behind me!' Daisy says quietly, staring at an invisible place on
the ceiling.

'I walked ten miles, crying my eyes out, to the station and bunked
the train. Ended up in King's fucking Cross at about ten in the evening.
No money. No coat, nothing.'

'Bloody hell,' I murmur, helpfully.

Silence. She lights a cigarette, slips it between my lips and lights
another for herself. Both stretched out, hands clasped behind heads,
maintaining the one–inch no–man's land between bodies, we smoke in
a taut, fraught silence, which is finally popped by the pointed arrow of
the town hall clock outside hitting the twelve and chiming. She flexes
at the middle and springs to her knees, playfully half–bouncing on the
mattress.

'You can fuck me if you want,' she says, out of nowhere, as if offering
me a pint, her robe falling open – I couldn't tell whether by accident
or by well–rehearsed ruse. But it isn't the milk–white balloon breasts
or the nipples that suggest inflation valves that have me gobsmacked,
dumbfounded and dumbstruck so much as the tattoo that flexes across
her drumskin belly: I'M MEAT. EAT ME.

Lying on my back, hands behind my head, I read the four words like
they are a page of A4, letting their significance sink in. Then I look up
to see her eyes. There isn't a hint of a twinkle.

'Fucking hell,' I mumble.

She raises an eyebrow as if to say *do go on.*

'You gave me Hepatitis!'

A purr grows to a growling chuckle in the back of her throat like she's gargling something thick and sticky.

'So it *was* you with Bart in the King's Road! Thought so!'

'Yes,' I *oh shucks,* reddening as I remember how I prostrated myself for her. 'But Bart never said...'

'He didn't recognise me. Hadn't seen me for about five years, remember – and I had changed a bit, even if he hadn't.'

'Yes you had,' I agree hotly.

'Anyway, Bart never really forgave me for the eye thing – so I couldn't bring myself to tell him he was trying to grope his little sister... I don't know what he might have done. Don't know what I might've done... And if I ever saw my dad again I'd have to stab him.'

'Can't say I blame you! In fact I'd do it for you.'

'Thanks babe,' she smiles, suddenly softening as if her fine-cut bone structure's just melted a little round the edges.

'Sorry about the Hep. But you did ask for it you dirty sod! Mind you, I could've given you something much more exotic at the time... But less said about that the...'

'Yes. Right,' I agree quickly, to pre-empt whatever's coming next. Silence again.

'I'm clean now – if that's what you're worried about,' she begins, casually pinging a miraculously conjured condom like a schoolgirl with an elastic band.

'I'd rather just talk,' I say.

She feigns a corny version of dismay, which fools me.

'It's not that I wouldn't... I mean, I don't want to be just one of your...'

She rolls on top of me and plants a lingering kiss on my clamped lips.

'You're a darling,' she grins, rolling off and tying her bathrobe. 'You really did look after my brother didn't you.'

It's a statement, not a question.

'I mean, I thought it was just him always needing someone to look up to,' she goes on, 'All those fights he told me about, I thought they were bullshit, but I can see now...'

'Well he got bullied...'

'Yeah but why you – why the Guardian Angel?'

I shrug.

'Cos I could?'

'He's such a git. He didn't deserve it.'

'No he didn't - deserve what they did to him, I mean.'

'No, course not. I mean he didn't deserve a friend like you,' her answer comes too quickly and she turns away, too much given away.

'You didn't deserve what your dad did to you – but anyway, I wasn't that great for Bart,' I say, knowing the truth would be mistaken for modesty and hating myself for saying it anyway.

'Bet you were,' Daisy schoolgirls cutely, digging me in the ribs and cackling, then suddenly dropping the brave face and taking my hand. Evidently he hasn't ever told her about Goalgotha.

'I need a friend like you too,' she states simply with an earnestness that, in her, I find unnerving.

Typically, the 'friendship' she has in mind is to be paid for – but this time she's the buyer. I'm not sure she knows there's any other kind.

'You're working for a couple of quid an hour in a shit job.'

I nod.

'And you need money to finance your band – your demos or whatever.'

I nod again.

'OK. I need a driver. Eighty quid a night. Three nights a week... All you have to do is take me to the client, wait outside for an hour or two and take me to the next one...'

Tempting. But then she's a professional temptress. £240 a week is more than twice what I'm earning. And for three nights instead of five days.

'But I haven't got a car,' I mumble.

'I'll buy you one,' she says, again like she's offering to buy me a pint.

'Come on – it'll be fun. And you need the money. And you can look after me like you looked after Bart,' she cajoles coquettishly.

'Thanks, Daisy. Really. But I'd be no use as a minder – and to be honest I don't like the idea of waiting while some bloke fucks you for money.'

It takes quite a while for the squall of squawking to die down to a sexily gruff rattle in the back of her long swan's throat.

'You're jealous!'

'No I'm not!' I protest unconvincingly.

'You are!'

'Yeah I am,' I admit so bashfully I might as well round it off with a 'Gee shucks'.

'So you'll do it?'

'Daisy, I can't. Sorry. No way.'

'And you really don't fancy a freebie?'

'Certainly not when you put it like that. I mean, I can see you know what you're doing now; that you're in charge now... But when you were fifteen?'

'Do you know how many people ask me that? Even while they're screwing me?'

I shrug.

'I never tell them. But I'll tell you.'

I sit up on the bed, crossing my legs beneath me, my arms locked round a cushion in front in a manner Freud could have written a book about.

'Sitting comfortably?' she Mary Poppinses, reaching across the cushioned gulf between us and placing her hands over mine – sealing an unspoken pact. 'Then I'll begin.'

★　　★　　★

Daisy had been one of those bright kids who drive teachers up the wall by using their wit to take the piss and to turn in essays that glean maximum marks from minimal knowledge; who piss them off by dashing off a three-hour exam in half the allotted time, pissing off and *passing*. She told me about Biddle, the callow 'new man' with a moral mission at odds with his crush on his most talented and wayward pupil; how she'd tortured and tempted him; how she'd now like to see him again, give him a hug and apologise.

'Why?' I asked, genuinely curious. Although her teacher hadn't touched her, his interest obviously hadn't been entirely wholesome.

'When you've met the kind of blokes I've met you forgive the rest more easily,' she explained. 'Anyway, he never gave in. He was a decent bloke... I should've left him alone.'

'But when you were fifteen? On your own in the middle of the night at King's Cross of all places and grown men who could've helped just took advantage...' I trotted out on my high horse.

'It wasn't all that bad,' she said, unconvincingly, then went on, ignoring my incredulity. 'Anyway, it wasn't a man... I was just walking and crying and this woman stopped me and asked what was wrong. I told her and she said she could give me a room and food and some money and a job if I wanted it.'

She caught my knowing look and dismissed it with a dry laugh.

'No it wasn't a brothel. It was a hostess bar.'

'Same thing in the end,' I stated as fact.

'Actually no,' Daisy's tone sharpened, then softened. 'Rowena really did look after me.'

'But?' I held out, waiting for the inevitable horror story.

'But nothing. I was a hostess in Mayfair for three years. Every night I danced with businessmen with loads of money, Arabs mostly, and got them to buy me fizzy grape juice at a hundred quid a pop...'

'Pop being the operative word!' I quipped, failing to lighten the tone.

'And usually I'd have to go to their hotel suite. Always a suite.

Always at the Hilton or Dorchester – nowhere imaginative...'

'I rest my case.'

She stood up and lit a cigarette.

'Actually, no you don't. I always got paid. But I never fucked any of them. Not one - for three whole years.'

Sitting down, she eyed me coolly as she exhaled straight at my face like a, well, like a high-class hooker really.

'You're kidding.'

'Nope. Not one, Rowena trained me. Told me I could make a fortune and never get fucked... And I did.'

Basically, there was no scam or scheme – just a woman of experience explaining to a young girl how to manipulate men. Most of the 'clients' were Arabs making the most of their freedom to drink alcohol and screw around while they were away from Islam's holy lands. The key thing was only to accept a 'date' from an Arab. Then, once in their hotel, to insist upon being plied with alcohol to 'get them both in the mood'. Daisy and her cohorts were inured to the effects of booze – in fact they practised – and could drink all night without losing the plot. In case of difficulty, Rowena furnished them with plenty of cocaine to sharpen them up when necessary and some downers to slip into the clients' drinks as an insurance, which was underwritten by a hefty henchman outside just in case.

The client, on the other hand, was invariably alone in London, a lightweight in the boozing stakes, and would collapse in a stupor shortly after the vision of Daisy in nothing but stockings and suspenders started kaleidoscoping in front of his eyes. As he slipped into unconsciousness his last memory, if he had one at all, would be of Daisy enthusiastically unbuckling his belt and whispering sweet nothings (actually, their command of English being rudimentary, she generally whispered something along the lines of: 'You think you're going screw me but you're going to crash out any minute now and then, my darling, I'm going to screw you!'). So, when the screwed but not fucked would-be fucker woke up in the morning with a banging, blinding headache, his head heavy and his wallet a couple of hundred pounds lighter, he'd assume he'd got laid. Simple. But effective.

'Fucking risky though!' I breathed, impressed.

Daisy shrugged.

'OK,' I admitted, 'so I was wrong – well a bit wrong. But what about after that?'

'Oh yeah, of course it had to happen in the end. But I was over eighteen by then. And I could choose who got the privilege!'

'Ooh, *privilege,* she says,' I camped.

She stuck out her tongue.

'Yeah privilege!'

'But even so, it must've been hard to take? Mustn't it?' I ventured.

'You're so fucking provincial aren't you!' she sneered, but not unkindly, I felt.

'Suppose,' I allowed.

'I had my moments, I must admit – but you're doing that victim thing...'

'Well aren't you? A victim?'

'Only of my dad. Not after that. Not really. I don't know how to explain if you've never...' she frowned and slumped a little, pensive for a few seconds, then stiffened, galvanised by a thought.

'Here it is. Because you've never had anyone touch you, fuck you or made you do anything you don't want to, sexually I mean, you can't imagine anything worse. I've had much worse than when I've agreed to do something I don't much like for the money. At least I have a choice – and it was always for a LOT of money. I do have some self-respect you know.'

I nodded. Made sense. I supposed.

'But...'

She shut me up with a what–the–hell–do–you–know look.

'Let me finish. In the end it's just a job. It's separate from love – it isn't even really sex for me. I save that. Been saving that for ages for someone of my own... What I do is think like a doctor or a midwife or a nurse... Or a scientist...'

Her eyes rolled up, looking for words, as if there were an autocue inside her eyelids.

'Or a plumber even!' she announced triumphantly.

I smiled, cringing inwardly. That bloody word again. She went on.

'Seriously Rich. Sex, biology, anatomy... It's all as easy as flushing a toilet after a while. It's all just plumbing: pumps and sumps and valves and vulvas, screws and sockets, pipes pipettes, suction and ducts... Just mechanics with soft moving parts. Well,' she chuckled throatily, 'some of them have to be hard! It's like....'

I watched avidly while she took a long French film drag on her fag.

'...like clockwork with a silent "L"!' she concluded triumphantly, bouncing up and down with real glee, laughing and repeating the phrase to herself, forgetting herself, being herself, being a girl.

'Clockwork with a silent "L"!'

The giggles rippled through her, jiggling her breasts like Barbara Windsor's in a Carry On film – so unerotic, so much at odds with her usual feline stealth, that I giggled with her and the invisible buffer-zone between us vanished in paroxysms of the kind of laughter I'd only ever shared after smoking some serious grass. Which meant once. We rolled around like kids in a playground, trampolined on the plump mattress and fought with pillows and I was kind of proud and also relieved that I was in her confidence; that I was trusted; that I was a real modern man who didn't need to bolster my ego with a sexual conquest; who wasn't afraid to say no.'

And then she stopped laughing. Stopped moving. She'd straddled me - and the towelling dressing gown that was nearly as white as her skin was gone.

I'M MEAT. EAT ME

The words quivered just a foot from my eyes as she shifted her centre of gravity, finding the growing ridge in my jeans and nestling its strut into her groove. For the second time that night I slowly raised my eyes to meet hers — and was surprised to find them so serious. I think a tear was brimming there, which she wiped away, simultaneously wiping a warm smile onto her face like paint. She'd scrubbed off the make-up hours before. But still, for an instant she looked freshly-scrubbed, rosy-cheeked, almost cherubic. *Fresh as a Daisy* I thought again and inwardly groaned. Suddenly her cleansed features were dirty — no *filthy*. Her pout stretched to a leer as she lowered her face to mine, shrouding me in crow-black, coiling curls.

'Good analogy,' I puffed with difficulty, eyes clamped blissfully shut and muffled by a tempting tress. 'Think I understand now.'

'Good,' she half-voiced, smothering the word with a lingering kiss so expertly lascivious it scared the crap out of me and made me shrink. Her breasts, which had cleaved gently to my bursting chest, now cleaved gently and almost reluctantly away, the gentle Velcro of our interlocked goosebumps tearing apart as she straightened like a layer of me went with them. I gazed through half-closed eyes with lazy loved-up lust. She was just a beautiful girl. Nothing more or less. And she loved me — and I loved her. This was just us — no one else. And all the sordid stuff in her past was just that — in her past. History. All that mattered was a future together, just now beginning... *Daisy, Daisy give me your answer do, I'm so crazy over your eyes of blue...* Well, green, I corrected myself. *Daisy, Daisy, I don't care where you've been, I'm so crazy over your eyes of green. Our love is where we're going, I don't mind where you've been, we'll get married and...*

'Oi,' she prodded me in the chest, rousing me from my rose tinted reverie involving rose covered cottages with rosy-cheeked kids and...

'Not dozing off are you?'

'Nope,' I smirked. 'Just dreaming.'

'Good!' she schoolmarmed with a kind of cosy authority that I liked a lot.

'So, you gonna be my driver and friend and protector?' she continued in a confrontational tone that I didn't like very much at all.

'No Daisy, I can't... I really...' I said as evenly as I could, trying to hide my dismay at her reversion to stereotype.

'OK,' she sighed, almost despairingly, like a teacher whose pupil's just not getting it.

'I just...' I began hopelessly and halted as she lunged at my hands, took them in hers and clamped them against her tits with a loud and, rather lovely I have to say, slappety slap. (I think it's important to note that at this point they're no longer breasts. They're tits. A significant change.). Her hands dropped and then rested at kidney level, palms and elbows outward in a whole paragraph of body language that men can't do unless they're gay − and it says: *WELL??????* Unaided, my hands stayed clamped against her milky jugs, tits, knockers, udders... Nope, it was no good. I couldn't. They were breasts, a bosom, beauty... I wanted to pluck, not fuck, a different Daisy.

'Oh for God's sake, how d'you want me? Up the fuck duct or the muck duct?'

'You what?' I spluttered. Then, 'Oh... right... ducts and pipes and that...'

'Gentlemen,' Daisy announced in a disturbingly stentorian voice as she took charge of the situation, 'Smith is going to be a plumber!'

15

Daisy Chains

Turned out her professional name was Daisy Chains. Catchy and clever, I thought, juxtaposing the *faux* naivety, delicate floweriness of her first name with the *fuck you* (or *fuck me*) SM suggestion of the second. Sitting in the Jag she'd bought (cash in wads from that great big handbag) listening to The Clash, I morosely counted the night's takings. Two visits to two stratospherically expensive hotels and already she'd made four hundred quid in fresh-minted fifties. *Unbelievable,* I muttered to myself. But then with a token hat-doffing a top-hatted Dorchester doorman stepped back as a fur-coated Daisy swept like royalty through the door he held open. The phrase 'fur coat and no knickers' came to mind. It was believable all right. She looked incredible. As she folded herself with feline expertise into the back seat and busied herself with preparations for the next call, I pushed away the rear view mirror to avoid a sight that would be at once erotic and upsetting. That mirror had taken its name too literally of late. In it I'd glimpsed several times the twin moons of Daisy's china-white marbly bum and almost swooned. But the moment was always spoilt by her decidedly un-erotic gynaecological ablutions routine, which involved certain lotions, moist wipes, some sort of pump and an immaculately laundered supply of dainty little towels. Once cleansed, she'd rummage in a suitcase and pull out a fresh outfit, a fresh wrap and a fresh hit – cocaine while working. The brown was for relaxing. And here's the thing. Daisy had a bit of a niche marketing thing going on. Or a nook, or a nookie marketing thing. She was a schoolgirl. The fur coat, diamonds and *Prada* accessories served only to get her through the hotel lobbies and past the scrutiny of watchful concierges. Underneath she would be wearing an erotically enhanced version of the uniform she'd been made to parade for her father. In a ponytail, pleated miniskirt, laddered stockings and slack black bra she was rewinding and re-running the tape loop of her childhood I never saw. And didn't want to. My mind's eye was as unblinking as her brother's as it focused on fat cat millionaires chaining Daisy to bedposts or radiators or themselves, their coke-focused pupils sucking her in, porno-prone and girly giggling. At least, I imagined, now there was no pain – only financial gain – in her selling a sequel to the innocence she'd had plucked from her with an incestuous fuck. But knowing this sick parody's inspiration made me sicker still.

It wasn't lust. It was love. The trouble was that she was utterly loveable. But she couldn't be loved. So one night, while some fat cat chained Daisy, fiddled with her and fucked her while pretending she was a child, I took what I was owed for the night's work, left the keys in the ignition of the pimpmobile and started walking to Kings Cross – Hooker Central - where she first started whoring and where I finally left her behind. I left a note on the dashboard:

Daisy
I'm sorry. I can't do this because I think I love you. But I'm still your friend. Even poorer without you, Rich.

As I slumped against the railings outside the station, a junkie hooker grabbed my arm with a bird-claw hand.
'Twenty quid for a fuck!'
'You'll have to pay me a lot more than that love,' I quipped.
A stiletto in the balls is a very effective revenge – and one that chastens you literally and figuratively. That could have been Daisy.

★   ★   ★

For four or five years she went off the radar completely. I'd have gone back to her like a shot had she asked. But whether out of respect for my feelings or simply because she didn't care, there were no phone calls, no letters, nothing.

So I vented my feelings in several songs that ended up on the first Airstrip One album, including *Bring It On* – which, to my incredulous delight was odds-on favourite for the 1991 Christmas number one. To celebrate, the record company had treated us to the kind of end of tour party every aspiring rocker dreams of. They booked out the entire top two floors of the Kensington Royal Garden Hotel, the penthouse for the party and countless suites for the band and our 'guests'. It's amazing how quickly you become blasé about the trappings of stardom. A mere six months since we'd finally signed a major deal and it all bored me – the party, the specially-imported hip-list names creamed off the top of all London's coolest private clubs, the clamouring, glamourless groupies and the gormless, charmless roadies. So having sloped off to my room to hit the mini bar hard and wallow in some precious solitude and darkness, I wasn't happy to hear the swipe and click of a passkey in the door.

'Fuck off, whoever it is,' I roared without bothering to look up.

'Hello Rich,' came a familiar voice, with a decidedly unfamiliar and tremulous timidity, from a slight figure silhouetted by the corridor's lights.

'Bloody hell. Daisy?' I spluttered. 'How the fuck did you get in here? How did you know where to find me come to that?'

'I'm a whore darling – I'm in and out of this place every other night!' she said with a sniff, then stepped into the room as I jumped up from the bed.

'Oh my God,' I whispered when she hit the light.

Bruised, bloodied and beaten. I'd never seen her so broken and frail. That pearly white skin tattooed with the marks of rough manhandling. Blue and purple imprints of big fingers clamping her upper arms. Panda eyes, for once made without make-up. Lips pouting with scabbed-up blood instead of the sulky pulchritude I remembered.

'Come here,' I said, holding out my arms.

She sank sobbing onto the bed and eventually we very gently and tenderly made love and then I held her all night, wishing I'd never left her so that I could have protected her. I didn't ask who or what or how or why. No point because she wouldn't tell. She'd always maintained that invulnerable front – so that even when I wanted to protect her from the scumbags she screwed for money, I felt I was superfluous - useless. If anything, I was the one who needed defending. She'd always been impregnable then.

Not now though.

Not now.

Now I was *somebody,* I had the power, the money and the wherewithal to protect her. And as she slept and I watched her eyelids flicker at the movies her mind was projecting on their inside, I resolved to sort her out, get her a job with the Airstrip One machine somewhere. Save her...

But when I woke in the morning, she'd gone.

16

The Other Daisy Chain

Crouched in the dark behind Raines's imperious bureau desk in the Daisy Chain's oak-panelled 'state room', Burroughs burrowed, delving in the dirt that held the seedy secrets from which Raines's filthy riches grew. For months now he'd been sneaking in here every time Raines left the ship, frantically failing to hack into the vast database that was the source of his employer's unfathomable power over A list celebs, politicians, business tycoons and even royalty the world over. Finally, he'd come across the password – embarrassingly literally in fact – while wanking over a porn mag depicting several teenage boys enjoying the variety of group sex known as a daisychain. Now, almost on a whim, he tapped in the word and, *eureka,* the humdrum laptop hummed and thrummed as its wireless connection hooked up with a mega-server somewhere in the world and a screen projection flickered into life, filling the room with bluish light.

'Shit,' he muttered, stabbing blindly at the wall for the button that closed the blinds.

The 'daisychain' that password referred to was Raines's own personal worldwide web – for which the spider's web analogy was a lot more apposite than for the easily accessible subset of the internet that the term usually refers to. It was a carefully constructed, utterly invisible network of unblinking eyes through which streamed a good googol of gigabytes of exploitable data – mostly in the form of voyeuristic video relentlessly garnered by CCTV networks hooked into Raines's global 'security monitoring' service. What his high net worth customer base didn't know was that the installation team went a long way beyond the call of duty by installing additional cameras in intimate places that other cameras couldn't reach. Like bedroom, bathrooms, boardrooms, toilets and many of the very best rooms in many of the world's priciest hotels. Anywhere and everywhere, in fact, that the rich, famous and powerful could be caught with their pants down, literally and figuratively. The digitally enhanced, lasciviously edited recordings would then appear on a password-protected website accessible only to Raines and his fat cat victim – for a while. With characteristic grammar school humour, the format of this elaborate scam was based on the Monty Python Blackmail sketch beloved of the boys in our year at school and second only to the Parrot Sketch for playground parroting. The victim would receive an innocuous-looking email purporting in its subject line to come from someone they knew – a business associate, a loved one, an agent, a publisher – anyone whose name would ensure that the email was opened. Then with one click whole lives could fall apart as a suggestive ten-second movie appeared, which they'd instantly recognise as showing the moments leading up to an act of indecency, infidelity, dishonesty or that was in some other way shameful. And then, in a heartbeat, the image would be gone, leaving its viewer panicked enough to click on the weblink, enter the personal code prompted by the email and sag despairingly as the film showed their shame in glorious Technicolour – often from a number of cute camera angles, pans and zooms accompanied by an upbeat soundtrack dripping with irony and Rawling's gleeful *schadenfreude*. The jocular faces of a youthful Michael Palin and a positively juvenile Eric Idle would leer manically from the screen with an overdubbed running commentary on the proceedings, generally in the style of a sports commentator...*'he mounts the mare and now they're really off and running and if he wants to make this spectacular jump he's really going to have to whip that rump!).* Or in the case of, say, a businessman handing over a backhander or bribe, the voice-over's tone would take on the hushed reverence of David Attenborough *(...and as the pigeon carefully feathers his nest and his mate delivers a sizeable nest egg, notice how he preens while the other's feathers ruffle uncomfortably...).*

The confluence to which all these polluted streams flowed was, appropriately enough, the Mediterranean Sea – or more particularly the luxury yacht known as The Daisy Chain, whose prickly, constantly revolving and evolving array of laser scopes and satellite dishes trawled the net to trap the biggest fish and let the tiddlers off the hook. And, lounging in his plush leather executive chair at his plush marble-top bureau, Raines would watch, chortling quietly to himself, as his stricken prey panicked, sweated and hyperventilated. As the movie drew to a close, the 'credits' would roll, listing the hapless victims peccadilloes and misdemeanours in depressing detail. But that wasn't the worst of it. Just as the initial shock settled into anger, disbelief and denial, the whizzbang graphics would alert them to the countdown clock in the corner of the screen, which marked each passing minute with a comedy hooter's *waaaap waaaah* straight out of Tom & Jerry. Intermittently a lurid porno-purple neon headline would be emblazoned across the screen:

THE LATER YOU PAY THE MORE IT COSTS
Quickly followed by:
Terms and conditions apply – this contract is on our terms, which are unconditional and non-negotiable. The price of your ransom may go up and certainly will not go down. Should you fail to pay the amount due by the specified date, however, you will go down in flames the moment we remove the firewall from your temporarily secure website. This process is entirely automated and cannot be stopped once the timer reaches the final sixty minutes and enters your hour of reckoning. When the digits hit zero you will hear an air raid warning. You should at this time take cover and dress in protective clothing to protect you from messy aftermath of the fertiliser's collision with the air conditioning device. Please look at your computer screen. Along the bottom you will find a remarkably lifelike animated graphic of a turd, representing your good self, being extruded from the left and curling slowly but determinedly towards the equally lifelike graphic of a fan. At the zero hour, if the requisite

funds have not been remitted as instructed, the shit hits the fan. Your career/ marriage/reputation/professional status/celebrity (delete as applicable) is over unless you choose to preserve it. The figures stated have been carefully calculated to represent a mere 20% of your net worth. A very reasonable price to pay, and one that we know you can afford.

And then came the FAQ section – chummily phrased like some building society customer leaflet:

If I don't pay how does it work?

It's very simple. Your private web area displaying your incriminating material is programmed to go public. At that time an email is generated and mass-mailed to the global media and/or to your business associates/fans/friends and relatives. This shows a short clip of your little home movie and invites them to see the unexpurgated film at the now-public site with just a click of their mouse.

How many other prominent figures have been targeted in this way?

Hundreds. You are not alone. We only reveal the identities of those who failed to comply. You and the rest of the world will never know about those who paid. Take comfort from our assurance that some of the most powerful, famous and wealthy figures in the world have become our clients – and have come to appreciate our integrity.

How do I know you won't keep coming back for more money?

You don't. However, we assure you that it is our policy to protect those who co-operate in this scheme. You may, if you choose to co-operate, take up our invitation to discuss the arrangement with some of our other clients who have agreed to allow limited disclosure by way of a testimonial in return for discount on their payment plan.

Payment Plan?

Yes. We are a reasonable organisation and appreciate that even the wealthiest individuals might have difficulty accessing liquid funds without arousing unwelcome interest. Therefore, we offer a range of amortised payment plans combined with life insurance, payment protection cover and a host of other benefits. The rates of interest are somewhat higher than standard bank rates but we make every effort to keep them in line with those of reputable lending institutions.

I'll call the police

Fine. We monitor all your outgoing and incoming telephone, fax, internet and email communications. We also monitor those of every police service in the Western world as well as those of much of the Middle East. In our experience, new clients are inclined to doubt our global reach and data handling capacity – which is why we have developed a simple test that you can carry out with a minimum of fuss and which will leave you in no doubt about our capabilities. Simply follow these instructions:

Leave your house/office and drive to a location of your choosing. Find an internet café and go to Hotmail, Yahoo or Google or a similar web-based email provider. Open a free web account under a fake name and send an email to anyone. It can say anything at all.

Next buy a Pay-As-You-Go mobile phone and pay cash, thereby remaining totally anonymous. Call the police and report a minor incident. We suggest a prowler or a minor act of vandalism, which would not be serious enough for them to want to rush out to interview you.

Then go home/to your office and check your email. In your inbox you will find a) a transcript of your telephone conversation with the police and b) the precise contents of the email you sent.

What if I'm not convinced?

You will be. Big Brother is watching you.

Not that Burroughs gave a flying one about the rest of the web's captives – he just wanted the fuel to achieve escape velocity. First he had to find the dirt on himself with which Raines had sucked him in and he simply had to wipe it clean. And second, more ambitiously, he aimed to rake up enough dirt on Raines to ruin him. Failing that, he thought he might go freelance: start up a few blackmail schemes of his own.

★   ★   ★

I punched out the greasy git's strange-looking satellite phone number like I was punching his smug mug.

'What the fuck's this about Bart?'

'Hello old chap, how lovely to hear from you,' came his unruffled reply, slick with unction.

'Don't "old chap" me you sneaky fucker,' I growled. 'What exactly are you playing at?'

'I don't play at anything. You should know that. I do what I do. I watch. I observe and I record what I see. '

'And you've been watching Georgie. *My* Georgie!'

'Naturellement!' he purred.

'Filming her!'

'Yes...'

'Why?'

'Why does the Pope shit in the woods?'

'You're a voyeur,' I accused, kind of unnecessarily.

'Yep. And she's an exhibitionist.'

'Bollocks!'

'More bosoms generally. Although I do have your bollocks on the old hard disk,' he tittered like some Bond villain.

'No you don't!' I barked.

'Oh yes I do,' he singsonged with a *Beano* chortle.

'Cheer up,' he cajoled in a tone designed to make me feel churlish, which somehow worked. 'Let's have a pint and I'll explain!'

'I'm not really in the mood for a chat about the good old days,' I grated, cringing at the thought of my low-slung *cojones* appearing on one of Bart's not-so-private movies.

'They weren't good – and I don't want to talk about them. Come on. A few drinks, and I'll tell all...'

'Where?' I heard myself emit, clearly nowhere near as guarded as I thought I was being.

115

'There's a great little punk rock joint in a cellar in the backstreets, way away from all the poncey places. I think you'll like it. They play all sorts of old obscure stuff. They even play *you!*'

'Very funny.'

'Well *I* thought so!'

'Well fucked if I'm meeting you there.'

★   ★   ★

The French are crap at rock 'n' roll. Always thought so. Always been right. We've got Jagger, Lennon, Bowie, Rotten, Strummer. And they've got Johnny Halliday. Which sums it up – even he had to have a cod-English name. Otherwise he'd have been Sacha Distel with a quiff. But then again... The only half decent French punk number was *Ca Plane Pour Moi* by Plastic Bertrand. And he was Belgian. And it was a rip-off of the New York Dolls' *Jet Boy Jet Girl*.

This bar was the pits. Which was handy because that was its name. The Pits was full of greasy fuckwits whose idea of punk was a floppy Mohawk or a sprawl of scrawly DIY tattoos. One thing about the place lent it an air of authenticity – and that was the shitty, pissy, tampon-y toilets whose reek mingled nauseatingly with that of pungent French cheeses and luxuriantly swampy armpits to evoke the sweatpits of mid-seventies London at the screaming, bloody, pissing, shitting and stinking birth of the spoilt brat that was punk.

'Hello Bart,' I mumbled unenthusiastically as he sailed over, flanked by a flotilla of cruisers.

He was pissed.

'Ahoy there!' he swashbuckled unconvincingly, grappling from one handhold to the next like he was crossing the heaving deck of a storm-lashed, hatch-battened brig. The deck was a dance floor, steel plated, pockmarked and riveted and awash and ice-rink slippery with the sea of lager tossed by the surging tide of bodies that seethed and spat in the

116

mosh pit. An anodyne 'punk' band swaggered the stage with guitars slung slightly too high and volume too low for authenticity. So I leant back against the box encasing the mixing desk with arms folded to say: *impress me.*

Captain Raines lurched and reeled towards me with a salute as he threw his weight against a wall that was two feet further away than he thought and collapsed in a giggling heap. I bent to hold out a hand, which he swiped at, missed, caught with butterfingers and slipped back to the beer-sticky floor. I dropped to my knees to scoop him up – then suddenly straightened. The band was playing one of my songs. One of *my* songs! Shaking my right leg to disengage Bart's clutches like he was a dog snapping at my feet, I strode, then struggled, through the sweaty mob and placed myself at the centre, at the front, at the lip of the stage, one arm casually laid on the top of the lead singer's monitor. Deep breathing. In. Out. In. Out. Oxygen stashed for the big opening line. Not to run out of breath. Do it like the record. But better. When they realise it's me. When they realise it's me. When they realise... The vocalist looked down at me. I winked and waited for the announcement of my name but he turned away and launched into my (MY!!!) 'ad lib' spoken piece of *ad schlock* poetry that meanders through the poignant middle eight.

'He doesn't know who you are!' someone shouted in my ear.

Thanks Bart. I'd worked that out. *This time next year he fucking well will,* I thought savagely. Raines's undisguised glee at my mild humiliation was sickening. He'd seen my eagerness to take the stage as if it was my right; the desperate craving for limelight of my etiolated career; my every sinew straining towards the microphone like a dog on a choke chain.

Drunk, wired and humiliated, I felt the tears rush up to complete my shame and shook my head so they mingled in disguise with gobs of thick cocaine sweat like Castrol GTX. Then, BANG, the double door fire exits against which I'd been leaning imploded and in rushed about twenty of the local Gendarmerie – and they really gave me something to cry about: tear gas and batons to be exact. I was choked — and not just by the smarting in the back of my throat. Doesn't matter how loaded you get, ditching a couple of hundred quid's worth of finest Peruvian Flake on a beer-puddled floor for the cops to pick up and sell on at their leisure is very, very depressing. I suppose I was lucky to have been so close to their point of entry. The force of the bursting doors sent me tumbling across the floor and out of their line of attack; for a moment it seemed as though the couple of hundred punters were retreating as one just to make space for my involuntary acrobatics. Of course that was before my final flip, roll and undignified halt, arse upwards in a beer puddle, which left me facing a rank of marauding, riot-helmeted and baton-wielding cops. With a presence of mind learned from my broke and regularly busted pre-fame days I slipped my wrap from my back jeans pockets as I exaggeratedly struggled to stand and dropped it into a puddle, then submerged it with a flattened hand as I pushed myself to my knees. One *Agent* stepped menacingly towards me and I rehearsed my grown-up, get-out-of-it greeting: 'Bonsoir Monsieur, je m'appelle...' But I didn't need it. He flipped up his visor to reveal the face of a twelve-year-old. Well, no more than twenty anyway.

'Monsieur, vous êtes le rock star Winston Smith, n'est ce pas?'

Which was a refreshing change after my earlier failure to be recognised.

'Oui. C'est moi,' I replied, struggling not to sound smug.

'Je dois vous demandez, est ce que vous avez....'

'Les drogues?' I interrupted, rather urbanely I thought.

'Oui,' the copper replied with a sheepishness I enjoyed quite a lot.

'Parlez vous Anglais?'

'Oui — un peu. You would like to speak English, yes?'

I grinned — my turn to act sheepish.

'Yes please my French is rather rusty.'

'Rusty?' he enquired.

'Um... Vieux... No... Je veux dire que j'ai oublié beacoup.'

'Ah. OK Monsieur Smith. I think you can go.'

'Merci beaucoup.'

'But if you would please sign this,' he ventured shyly.

That old joke where the pseudo-famous sign an autograph only to find the piece of paper is some official document. I laughed.

'Yeah right. I'm not signing any...'

But it was just a piece of paper. He merely, really, wanted my autograph! Result!

Just as I signed with a little-used flourish recalled from muscle-memory, Raines appeared at my side, white linen creased and smeared and redolent of subtle corruption.

'Is there a problem officer?' he greased, already rifling well-lined pockets for bribes.

'Non, Monsieur,' my new-found fan replied, his face darkening with new suspicion.

'Shut up, Bart. Let's get out of here,' I grumbled. The young policeman stepped aside like a soldier snapping to attention and, with a salute, waved us toward the almost unhinged fire doors. I caught his hand, mid-salute, grasped it with both of mine and shook it warmly – and the affection was real.

'Thank you,' I rasped in his ear.

He smiled. And as my friend's colleagues barked and prodded at the corralled hoi polloi, marshalling them into lines for body searches, Raines and I stepped out into a cordoned-off street. Crossing the police line, we were accosted by another Gendarme, but he relented when a now-familiar voice called out from behind us instructing him to let us pass.

★　　★　　★

Before that, I'd been all for packing our bags and grabbing a cab to the airport – leave the sick scheming git and his jet set friends behind. But then I didn't actually have all that publishing money in the bank yet.

The transfer awaited the fulfilment of certain contractual conditions, which the lawyers were still ironing out. In the meantime I wasn't exactly skint – on the contrary I had anything and everything I could want. It was just that it was all paid for remotely; all on a tab; including the generous *per diems* for the duration of the trip that were delivered to the suite each morning with our breakfast. Not only did I not have the cash or credit for two flights – I'd also be blowing out this life-saver of a deal and losing all this new-found opulence. So I rejected my adrenaline's suggestion of flight and went with the other option it proposed: *fight.*

'I'll wait till the fucker's minders are out of the way and give him a good kicking!' I Ray Winstoned unconvincingly.

'But that's exactly what he wants,' Georgie pointed out. 'Touching me up, having you beaten up, spying on us – he's trying to get under your skin.'

'And into your pants!'

'Same thing isn't it?' she smiled, tousling my hair. I leant heavily on the balcony rail, squinting out to sea where the sinking red sun was setting ablaze the twiggy rigging of the yachts in the harbour. Shimmying up behind me, she laid her head on my shoulder, clasping slender brown hands round my waist.

'Which is his boat?' she breathed.

'Dunno. They all look the same to me – probably the biggest.'

We fell silent, watching a tiny white arrow detach itself from the wing of the largest ship, anchored regally aloof, some distance from the others – a swan set apart from all the ducks and geese. The arrow darted with expensive *élan* in and out of the motley flotilla and accelerated.

'So what do I do?' I nodded in the direction of several billion pounds worth of floating boats – or more accurately floating *boast,* since few of them ever actually set sail for anywhere other than the next show-off harbour.

'Let's play him at his own game – let him think he's forgiven, hang out with him...'

'No way!'

'Yes, way! You can find out what he's up to and...'

'And what? Anyway, I know what he's doing. He's getting revenge.'

'But I thought you were his saviour and protector...'

I shook my head.

'Up to a point, yes... But when it really counted I let him down.'

So I told Georgie about 'Goalgotha', confessing for the first time to the cowardice that had cowered in the back of my mind for nearly thirty years.

'And you think after all this time he's torturing you because you couldn't fight off a mob of bullies?'

'Yep,' I grimaced.

'Why now? Why leave it so long?'

'Maybe he didn't know where to find me till now − I've been ex-directory since the first record came out and my agent never gives anyone my address.'

'You reckon he's been hanging out with the rich and famous purely so he'll eventually bump into you?' she laughed. 'That's ludicrous!'

'I know. But so's he.'

The smile settled into a frown.

'Well we're not letting him win. You've got to go and see him − get to the bottom of this.'

Which is why I'd ended up in The Pits. And why I'd accepted Raines's slurring invitation back to the Daisy Chain for drinks.

★   ★   ★

'Do I have to?' Burroughs schoolboyed, propping himself up on one elbow, shoving his shades up onto his forehead and squinting at Raines, who lazily opened his eyes and failed to wink with the lidless one.

'A lot of people would give good money for the privilege...'

'A lot of *straight* people, yeah.'

'Actually I know for a fact that they have. Half the cunts in Cannes would give their right arm to shag the gorgeous Georgie Jordan.'

'Since you've got your right arm down my shorts I'd have thought you'd remember I happen to be a queer!'

'Oh and out comes the Burroughs vintage whine! You're turning into a spoilt brat, you know that Bunny?'

'Don't call me that. I won't do it,' he sulked.

'Bugsy Bunny Burroughs,' Raines nursery rhymed, suddenly joining the slab of bronzed muscle beside him in his figurative playground. 'You fucking well will. Christ, it's not as if you have a hard life.'

'I won't have a hard anything – that's the point!'

'Oh but you will!' Raines smirked, withdrawing his hand from Burroughs' shorts, wiping it on his own and tugging his wallet from their back pocket.

'And don't think plying me with charlie's gonna do the trick.'

'Stop bugging me, Bunny!'

Raines held out his clenched fists knuckles upwards.

'Pick a hand.'

'Oh for Christ's sake,' Burroughs sighed, tapping the left hand.

'Da daaa!' Raines fanfared as he held out an open palm on which sat a blue elongated diamond-shaped tablet. 'You could shag Margaret Thatcher after one of these!'

Burroughs softened in spite of himself.

'Viagra. Oh my lord and master you think of everything. Actually, if I had to do one woman...'

'Keep hold of that fantasy my boy – it will serve you well in your mission! Oh, and you'll also need this,' he twinkled, handing over a vial of clear liquid. 'I think you'll find her quite compliant once you get this into her.'

'Any chance you're going to tell me what the point is? You just want to watch me screwing Smith's bird – bit sad isn't it, even for you?'

Raines ignored the jibe.

'Well, I'm quite looking forward to it, I must admit, but no. The gratification's not that instant. And anyway, the private bed show's not for me – it's for Smith.'

Burroughs looked bemused for a moment – then very amused.

'You bastard!' he smirked, working it out. 'You've resurrected his career, made him rich, got him the girl and now you're going to take it all away.'

'There's a clever boy!'

'There's a sadistic motherfucker! But what makes you think the girl's going to leave him?'

And Raines took great pleasure in explaining how he'd watched and waited for his chance – the optimum point just on the downside of his career's apex to control the descent to its nadir – then resurrect the rock star, raise him up and finally nail him. He gleefully detailed the myriad information streams that he had programmed to trawl the net and dig the dirt for mentions of Winston Smith and of Georgie Jordan; how his hordes of geeks edited, collated, prioritised and summarised it all – the cyber-equivalent of hunting through celebrity dustbins. How he'd compiled a dossier on Georgie's love life for the last ten years: a shopping list of hip, rich and powerful names, each of which had been ticked off and fucked off when they failed to realise her ambitions. Winston Smith was just the latest in the parade of gullible men, not to mention a couple of women, who'd soared too close to her radiance and fallen at her feet. As far as Raines was concerned Smith had a lot further to fall.

'So he'll be utterly at my mercy,' he concluded, rubbing his hands together in anticipation. 'I'm the ultimate Bond villain!'

'Ever seen Austin Powers?' Burroughs sniped.

'Fuck you,' Raines leered. 'On second thoughts, fuck *her!* Go on, get the Viagra down and get it up!'

'You really make me sick sometimes, Bart.'

'And I make you suck! Bleep the boy and tell him to get the fast boat out. I'm meeting Smith at eight. Give her half an hour to chill out and then get in there.'

17

GBH

The gleaming white arrow stabbed the pristine and deserted beach, riding up and rocking onto one side with engines idling and propellers stowed as Burroughs leapt over the gunwales, heaved against its bow and shoved it back into the lazily lapping waves. Nodding expertly as the stern bounced eagerly into buoyancy, he gave the boy at the helm the go-ahead to power up and the craft dipped deep into the trough between waves, swivelled as the giant twin engines reasserted themselves, and slashed its way back through the surf to its mothership. Fancying himself as a bit of a Bond, the over-groomed and black-clad Burroughs strolled languidly up the man-made and manicured beach and stepped into the limelight of La Croisette.

★   ★   ★

Somehow, miraculously, Raines must have sobered up on the short stroll to the jetty where his tender youth bobbed about, the supersized dinghy's engine idling in an ostentatious waste of petrol. Because, once aboard the yacht proper, he ceased to sway - maybe the ship's gentle rocking was simply countering his own reeling to keep him on an even keel. We lounged on the aft deck and Raines was as bubbly as the Champagne that he kept on pouring - and glass by glass my guard dissolved and a clinical sort of suspicion gave way to a much more genuine curiosity and my covert interrogation turned to a conversation.

'So what is it exactly that you do? Something to do with security cameras is it?'

'I watch.'

'No change there! Still spying on the neighbours in their undies are we?' I joked, referring to one of many ignominious episodes in his turbulent teens.

'Absolutely!'

'Come on – what is it you do really?' I pressed.

'I keep the rich, famous and powerful on the straight and narrow – and I charge them astronomical sums of money for the privilege!'

'Yeah right,' I snapped back. 'Like who?'

'Name a famous person – and they're almost certainly among my, er, clients.' Noting my incredulity, he went on. 'It's very simple really. Over the years I've built up a massive surveillance and monitoring network, which the truly monied pay for as a security service. I'd been doing very nicely indeed for ten years or so, when one of my employees fell foul of the CIA – they monitor all the email and phone traffic in the UK you know...'

'I thought it was an urban myth,' I breathed, now intrigued despite myself.

'Don't you believe it! They put it about that it's apocryphal because it defuses opposition. Anyway, they'd sussed that we were hacking into various email accounts – and felt that that was their job. We were warned off and got away with a slap on the wrist in the interests of national security – though which nation's I'm not sure. Then a client neglected to tell his wife that he'd installed our CCTV system and we had weeks of fun watching her shag everyone in a five-mile radius until she sussed it. And that gave me an idea.'

He took off his dark glasses and fixed me with his unwavering eye.

'Knowledge is power!' he hissed at me with unnerving zeal.

'Pope took a different view,' I objected.

'A little knowledge is a dangerous thing? Yeah, yeah but I've got lots and lots!'

It took me a while to absorb this – along with a quick toot and a gulp of Champagne. Then I lit a fag while I rummaged around for words.

'So... Instead of spying on girls in the bathroom you spy on everyone, everywhere.'

He nodded proudly.

'Instead of collecting rocks and fossils and dead animals and Second World War shrapnel you now collect information?'

'That's about the size of it.'

'You're a fucking blackmailer!' I spat.

'I prefer the term extortionist dear boy. Sounds so much more professional,' he smiled.

I couldn't help chuckling.

'You always were an evil bastard. But I suppose a lot of these dodgy celebs deserve all they get. What do you do, show them a tape of themselves doing the dirty deed and charge 'em a few grand for the master?'

'Nothing so trivial – though I'll admit it started out pretty much like that. No, these days I deal with the most powerful men and women in the world. And they pay me in a currency worth much more than money...'

'You're losing me now,' I mumbled, baffled.

'Power, dear boy,' he beamed oleaginously.

Clocking my puzzled frown, he expanded on this.

'To use an example you'll understand from your own business – let's say a rock star gets busted with a vast amount of Class A drugs. Technically he could go to prison – and even if he got off with a fine, the criminal record would prevent him touring in certain territories, which would be extremely costly for his record company.'

I nodded sagely. This was fairly close to home.

'So what do you think it would be worth to said record company for the whole thing to go away with no questions asked?'

'A fortune. But you're not suggesting you have the whole of the fucking British filth in your back pocket.'

'Heavens no – most countries in the world really.'

'Bollocks! You can't bribe entire police services. No one can.'

'No. But you can get powerful people to do anything you want if you have their deepest darkest secrets, transgressions and perversions on file.'

I stood and leaned over the deck rail, watching a distant Gendarmerie patrol slowly cruising La Croisette, protecting the super rich from the super poor and ignoring the in-betweens.

'Call me old fashioned, but there is still the law. You saying there's one law for the rich...' I protested.

'Yes that's exactly what I'm saying.'

'Rubbish. Not really. Not formally.'

'Explain to me then, why the police have never done a drugs bust on the Brit Awards, the MTV Awards, the Oscars, MIDEM or the Cannes Film Festival? Because they don't know each one of them's a massive coke-fest?'

I shrugged. He joined me at the rail and waved over at the twinkle, chintz and glints of light peek-a-booing through the breeze-blown trees lining the famous esplanade. A missile powerboat carved a wide arc of wake, zoomed in and slid between the open white thighs of a giant catamaran. Motor dinghies, even at this late hour, beetled and bobbed to and fro and warm wafts of wind carried across the tinkle of cut glass laughter and plastic pop music from a hundred yacht parties, their exclusivity guaranteed by half a mile of sea.

'In every other hotel room, every bar and every club and every showbiz party there's enough coke to win a Colombian export award. What do you think that speedboat's doing? He's bringing in tomorrow night's stash. So why does nobody - I mean nobody - get busted.'

'Cos the pigs are stupid?' I ventured.

'No one's that thick.'

'So maybe they just don't care.'

'If that's the case, why do they go charging into lowlife joints like The Pits with batons drawn just to seize a couple of wraps of coke and a few E's? Just for the fun of beating up proles? OK, bad example, but you know what I mean.'

'Go on. Tell me. You're going to anyway.'

'Yes I am. It is partly, I admit, down to pragmatism. The rich can afford their vices. They're not going to mug anyone or rob any post offices to pay for their charlie habit – so why waste resources pursuing them...'

'Actually you have a point there,' I interrupted. 'It's not the drugs that kill – it's desperation.'

'Exactly. So pragmatism wins...'

'And the fuckers protect the rich and persecute the poor. Fuck pragmatism if that's what it is.'

'That's not my concern.'

'Evidently,' I sniped.

'Thank you, Mr Geldof. You're not exactly one of the underclass yourself.'

'Doesn't mean any of us has a right to stand by and... I mean all that's...'

'"All that's required for evil to triumph..."? All it takes for good men to succeed is the evil man does bugger all too! You can shove Edmund Burke right up your arse!'

'And up yours too – except you'd enjoy it. Anyway, how does all this justify your nefarious activities?'

'I never said it justified anything. It's just why it works. I also said that this rich man's law, for want of a better phrase, is only part of the reason. I've taken the status quo on board – literally really – and made explicit what was implicit.'

'Haven't a clue what you're trying to say.'

Raines stooped and loped along the deck, deliberately dragging a foot behind him.

'Smith,' he boomed imperiously, 'is going to be a plumber!'

'Very funny. I've seen better impressions of the old git.'

'Generally the people in power have got where they are by becoming diplomats. Reeds — not oaks. They know which way the wind blows and faced with a hint of disastrous scandal and public shame they bend over backwards...'

'To let you fuck them,' I interrupted, wincing with distaste at the image I'd just conjured.

'Or not. You see the "requests" we make of them are not blatant or usually even radical. They're just minor adjustments of the way they'd normally handle things...'

'Because the status quo's already bent.'

'You're catching up. Not so much bent as skewed in our favour.'

'Yeah but there must be some integrity, some honour left, surely! Even I can't believe there's no such thing as justice.'

'Of course. And those people are to be admired — and then retired.'

He smiled at my open-mouthed amazement. I'm not sure whether it was at the enormity of what he was suggesting or the enormousness of his arrogance.

'Yes I am saying what you think I'm saying.'

'You have them killed?' I blurted in shrill-voiced horror.

Raines burst into gales of laughter, choking on his bubbly, which spumed from both snorting, chortling nostrils.

'Christ no! I just mean if they're squeaky clean we either set them up and stitch them up or simply have them replaced!'

'Oh well that's all right then. Thought for a moment you had no scruples!' I replied coldly.

When his coughing and spluttering had died down, we both settled back into our chairs and surveyed the shoreline in silence.

'How high?' I asked, unable to resist my curiosity.

'That's what they say when I say jump,' he ad glibbed.

I tutted.

'How high up in authority, in government, whatever?'

'All the way old son. Right to the top.'

'You're saying you control governments?'

'No – that would be arrogant. I just change them when the need arises.'

I raised a querulous eyebrow.

'You're a plumber – so you know all about leaks…'

I scowled – to no effect.

'Well I've instigated some of the biggest cabinet leaks in history,' he went on. 'I even set up an armed takeover of an African dictatorship - which was a bit of a coup!' he giggled at his quip – and even I couldn't help grinning.

'You don't mean Equatorial Guinea?'

'The same. 2004.'

I laughed.

'But it fucking failed! It was pathetic. Mark bloody Thatcher nearly ended up in jail. And of course the nasty little fucker got away with it thanks to Mummy.'

'That was the object of the exercise. Jail, I mean, not getting away with it. I had no interest in oil money from dodgy despots. A client of mine needed Thatcher out of the way for a while and I obliged. Still got that Maggie-shaped chip on your shoulder, I see!'

'How the hell do you put together a thing like that and get away with it?'

'I was introduced to Severo Moto, the opposition leader, at a yacht party in Spain – he was exiled there you see – and became aware of suggestions that it was time President 'I am God' Obiang was deposed.' A fifteen mill carrot got Scratcher's tongue hanging out – and a lot of the other arrangements were made by twisting a few guilty consciences.'

'And all this started with a telescope,' I marvelled.

'I suppose so. It's all long distance information, amplified and magnified and then concentrated on a target like a laser.'

'It just a power trip isn't it. You get off on their helplessness.'

'Yes! Great isn't it,' he replied gleefully. 'That's why I still have my telescopes. They're not as effective as fibre-optic camera systems and web-based surveillance but they're a lot more fun. The geek shall inherit the Earth!'

He lurched out of his low-slung chair and reached for a streamlined eight-foot white cylinder I'd taken for a lifeboat capsule. With a chunky clunk, satisfying like a Rolls Royce door shutting, the capsule swivelled with counterweighted ease and the casing clicked open like a giant egg to reveal the single glowering eye of a telescope lens.

'Check this out!' Raines enthused, suddenly boyish.

At the flick of a switch the instrument was aglow with soft green lights and a console unfolded from within and whirred into place. Intrigued, I shuffled my chair up behind him as an outline map of the local coastline flashed up over a fine grid. As Raines clicked his mouse over a set of co-ordinates the telescope hummed into action, slowly wheeling, ranging upward and extending to twice its compressed length. He placed his lidless eye against the eyepiece and emitted a low wolf whistle.

'Your turn.'

I stepped up, put my eye against the rubber flange and barrelled several miles in an instant, across the black waters, over the myriad fairy lights lining La Croisette, to a hotel room. My fucking hotel room at the Gray D'Albion! Where a naked Georgie was padding around in time with the unheard music (almost certainly Massive Attack's *Blue Lines*) with the heartbreaking innocence of the unknowingly watched.

Of course I had to hit him.

★   ★   ★

Georgie scrolled through a hundred and thirty pages of script on her laptop, pensively rolling a joint in preparation for an uninterrupted evening devoted to her *meisterwerk*. She scribbled a couple of notes on a hotel pad and strolled round the suite, placing and lighting candles and incense, turning off electric lights as she went. Mood was everything. And, thus readied, she ran the bath and consecrated it with another array of candles and a selection of expensively inessential oils before sinking into her meditative womb.

With Champers on ice, a spliff in the ashtray, Massive Attack brooding on the sound system and a couple of lines on a mirror begging to be inhaled before condensation made them mud, she meant to sink into utter relaxation and almost simultaneously fire herself up for a stint of blazing, incandescent creativity. *This is the life,* she thought, as she sank under the oily surface, her locks bobbing obstinately on the bath's viscous meniscus, droplets running off them as if afraid. The troublesome scene she had decided to tackle coalesced in her mind and the solution came clear. Now she'd write and get it right. Any minute now she'd burst out of this primal goo reborn as a writer... Or maybe even a movie star. Or a director.

Submerged, with eyes clamped shut, she started the countdown to action. Ten, nine, eight, seven, six, five, four, three, two, one... Nothing. The launch was aborted. Her happy head hit an invisible ceiling – as if somehow the simmering human casserole had iced over. The bouillabaisse bubbled as her mouth gaped fish-like in a futile and self-defeating gasp for air that filled her lungs with bubbles. Her black and buoyant coiling locks writhed on the water's surface as one of Burroughs' giant flattened, flatfish hands pushed Georgie's head deeper and held it there and the other calmly reached out and clamped her ankles together. Waves tipped by scented spume crashed over the sides of the huge tub as her body bucked and thrashed, like a fish out of water. Or a human out of air.

★ ★ ★

'Wiggle like that when he's doing you, do you?' Burroughs sneered as he hoisted her by the hair from the water, like a fresh-landed fish. Fists flailing, breath failing, she laid into his face, albeit fairly ineffectually, before slumping to the slopping floor. The big man, evidently feeling even bigger, glanced around automatically like he was expecting someone to weigh his trophy, wrap it up and take it home for gutting and eating. Bullying's nowhere near as much fun without an audience. He knew he had at least one avid watcher though – he just had to work out exactly which part of the suite was to be the stage.

Georgie was gutted all right. In fact she was downright livid. And, despite his earlier protestations, Burroughs couldn't help thinking she was good enough to eat – and that maybe the Viagra hadn't been quite as essential as he'd thought. But he'd got the stuff in his blood – and it felt like it had all rushed to one place, reducing the rest of his considerable bulk to a floppy appendage attached to a dick.

'Fuck you,' she blurted in a blended spray of literal and figurative bile and expensive bath oils.

'Oooh that'd be nice,' he queened insincerely, wiping the slime off his face like it was moisturiser. 'Maybe I will then – fuck you, that is.'

'You couldn't fuck me if you tried you limp-dicked fuckwit,' Georgie summoned an apposite phrase from a well-used repertoire of abuse usually reserved for the over-inflated and therefore easily pricked ego of a certain rock singer.

'You'd think, wouldn't you!' Burroughs grunted as he grabbed her by the hair with one hand and hauled her to her feet, his free arm scooping her up with a degree of ease that suggested resistance was futile – for now at least.

'Bet you've never been swept off your feet by a poof before,' he snarled as he threw her casually onto the bed, where she landed, bouncing pornographically, legs uncontrollably and gynaecologically splayed in the least dignified way conceivable.

'Rich'll be back any minute.'

'I don't think so darling,' he chuckled. 'I think you'll find he's anchored offshore... Wankered as well...'

'This is GBH!' she shrieked.

Burroughs pulled a little glass bottle from his inside pocket.

'Think you'll find it's ABH actually. *This* is GBH!' he smirked as he pounced, grabbed her again by the hair and pinched her nose shut with the other hand.

Both Georgie's hands strained to hold back the open bottle from her mouth as if it were a knife. But Burroughs pressed them down like a flattening car jack and the clear, tasteless liquid trickled between her plump lips as they parted for air.

'I think you'll find it's called GHB you fucking....'

But her eyes rolled back in her head and she slumped to the floor, soapy water pooling around her splayed locks. Burroughs gave her flaccid torso a desultory kick. Nothing. Maybe somewhere deep in those cloudy brown eyes there was a flicker of defiance – but nothing her mashed brain could act on.

★   ★   ★

The micro thunderclap as my less-than-lightning-fast fist struck his pudgy face let loose a pitter-pattering rain of blood onto the deck, polka dotting his white linens in a pattern I found rather satisfying. Less satisfying was his response – after hitting the deck like the sack of shit he was, he sat up, chortling good-humouredly through gobs of blood and snot and pinching the bridge of his nose.

'S'pose I asked for that!' he chuckled. If that was meant to soothe my rage it didn't work.

'Quite an instrument though isn't it!' he bragged, one eye blinking stroboscopically. 'I thought you'd be impressed!'

That did it. I swept the bottle of *Cristal,* glasses, ice bucket and all, off the table in a tinkling cascade as I hurled it at the telescope. As the giant glass lens-like table-top glanced off the console, the casing sheared off and the electrical innards died slowly with a final Champagne fizz and crackle. Instantly, Raines was on his feet. I sidestepped neatly what I thought was a lunge. But I wasn't its object. Snatching a wireless headset of the sort worn by Neanderthal disco doormen everywhere on Earth and probably throughout the galaxy, he spoke with irritating composure.

'Engineering? There's seems to be a fault with number one 'scope. Please have it sorted by tomorrow, there's a good boy.'

'Very good, Sir,' came the clipped naval response. 'Is it a Champagne infiltration scenario like last time sir?'

'Don't take the piss boy – just get it done,' Raines replied without emotion. 'And send Charlie up here pronto with more bubbly. Mr Smith seems to have spilled his.'

He smiled. I glowered.

'Who's Charlie?' I grated.

He nodded his head at the young boy, who'd appeared by his side like a genie with another bottle of the unbearably pricey *Cristal* on ice.

'Not his real name, obviously. I named him thus because I used to do him on the toilet seat in the Gray D'Albion's bogs!' he simpered.

I glared. Raines's lidded eye fluttered like a moth while the other returned my glare with its expressionless and endless gaze. Charlie handed him a tiny bottle, from which Raines dripped eye drops into the corner of the drying eye – a windscreen without washers and wipers.

'Ironic isn't it,' he said, waving a hand at the expanse of the Mediterranean behind us. 'All this salt water and I have to send Charlie ashore for a drop of saline to squirt in my eye – my precious bottled tears. Doesn't matter how much you've got, you never have enough of the right stuff! That's why crying's the one luxury I can't afford.'

I shrugged. He righted the chair I'd sent flying in my rage. He patted it, like he was inviting a dog to sit down.

'How about a peace offering?'

My blank gaze obviously wasn't as inscrutable as I'd imagined – a question had written itself across my forehead.

'Come on – some marching powder for the road?' That bloody chuckle again. Something rock 'n' roll had written into my DNA over the years made my whole body signal acquiescence and, resigned, I slumped into the offered chair.

'Bring it on then,' I sighed, coke whore that I was.

'There's a good chap. I think you'll enjoy it – pure as the driven snow that is, if you'll excuse the pun. I get it straight off the boat – and straight onto this one as it happens.'

The doubly aptly named Charlie-boy reappeared with one of those vials with a screw-top complete with tiny folding spoon. That wasn't unusual in the circles I moved in – except that this one was obviously made of silver. It was also the size of a bottle of lager – and the spoon was in proportion. Not so much a phial as a fucking flask. Flash bastard. Of course I sniffed a spoonful, which must have been a good half a gram. Then another. And another. Even the cabin boy, rent boy or whatever his job title was had his fair share. It took me a while to realise that Raines abstained – not that I cared. I'd take as much as he was willing to give and deny him the satisfaction of my gratitude. Soon I had to request something stronger than Champagne to offset the tooth-grinding, headachy coke sweats – and was instantly obliged with a bottle of Jack Daniel's.

'That's what you rock stars drink, I believe,' Raines simpered.

'Not neshessarily,' I retorted through rubber teeth and sucked back a hefty hit.

★   ★   ★

Where the silver studded black sky met the iron, copper and chromium sea, strands of iridescent pink intervened, the colour of the bloodied whites lining the pencil point black dots of my eyes. Seagulls swooped and cackled with mocking laughter as the Daisy Chain rocked in the wash of wakening sea traffic. Imperceptibly, and almost instantly to a mind on the cocaine clock, midnight had turned to six in the morning.

'Oh fuck,' I groaned, wiping my hands on my jeans to rid them of the sooty grime that I'd always thought was the white powder's excreted form – pure white powdered corruption, turned black by grubby coke-stoked thoughts; sleazy sensations oozing out of your pores.

'What?' Raines enquired.

'Georgie. She'll be worried.'

'Oh I don't think so,' he smiled disconcertingly. He picked up a headset from the table full of empties.

'Burroughs? Is number one scope operational?'

He nodded. 'Set it up and turn it on then.'

A hatch clattered open a couple of feet from my chair.

'Fuck!' I shouted, more than startled as the jitters got the better of me.

'Morning, Mr Smith,' the big henchman said evenly, and as far as my coke-rattled nerves could tell, insincerely.

'All right,' I nodded grudgingly, hoping to reassert my rock star status and its contrast with his as a lowly servant.

I looked at my watch, which had managed to compress another unwanted and depressingly objective hour into my last few subjective minutes.

The telescope did its phallic telescoping thing again as Burroughs stroked it into full erection and Raines looked on appreciatively and stuck the Cyclops eye onto the eyepiece. As if he couldn't be torn away, he scrabbled around blindly for the mouse, found it and shuffled it around the newly replaced green-lit screen like an expert roulette croupier.

'Eureka!' he giggled, beckoning me without removing his eye from the vaguely SM pornographic-looking flange that half-covered his face like a Phantom of the Opera mask.

I clambered out of my seat, with some difficulty. And while I was trying to stamp painful life back into bloodless, coke-constricted, needling pins, Burroughs took my place at the private 'What the Butler

Saw'.

The pins and needles from my legs ran right up my spine, fleeing the sadistic laugh I'd last heard on the school sports field almost thirty years before. It didn't seem to bother Raines though. Clearly he'd managed to de-activate or emasculate his old Nemesis somehow – but now I saw that, like a decommissioned firearm, it only took a little work to make him as lethal as he ever was.

'Have a look at this then Smith... I'm sorry. *Mr* Smith,' Burroughs urged. The emphasis on the 'mister' dripped with sarcasm. Suddenly the servility had gone out the porthole - he was making no attempt to hide his contempt.

Oh shit, I thought as I moved warily towards the great white cylinder.

'Oh shit,' I screamed when my eye adjusted and focused in on the balcony of what was clearly my suite at the Gray D'Albion.

'We've been watching a bit more of your girlie!' Raines sing-songed mockingly.

'So what. Wouldn't expect better of you – you fucking pervert,' I growled defiantly.

'Burroughs old chap, put on the recording would you!' Raines ordered blithely.

'Oh shit oh shit oh shit oh shit what have you done you fucking bastard!' I screamed as the live image fizzed into a silent video close-up of my gorgeous Georgie's face, which was wreathed in the lazy loose smile I knew all too well. It was her, 'yeah come on baby let's do it smile.' It was the one she used to smile when we first met; when we first slept together with teenage abandon and before familiarity bled away temptation and the carnal became banal.

'Turn up the bug, Bunny!' Raines chuckled and suddenly the air turned blue with porno gasps and grunts and the sickening rhythmic slap and squelch of flesh on flesh.

'Oh Jesus no!' I whimpered as the camera panned out and up along her lovely legs to where her dainty feet hooked over a pair of naked ox shoulders and a tree trunk neck – then to a big oblong face in a rictus of effort as he dispassionately rogered the former love of my life.

Burroughs and Georgie.

I couldn't believe it. I grabbed the table with rubber hands to lever myself up on rubber legs, swivelled to get Burroughs in my sights…

'Gotcha!' tittered Raines as Burroughs appeared behind me, seized my arms and deftly tied them with a plastic cable tie. I didn't even try to struggle. Too busy puking, dribbling and weeping. Hog tied and whimpering on the deck, I bucked and writhed pointlessly as Burroughs' big rectangular head loomed over me, as his fat sausage fingers pinched my nose and he shoved a rubber teat on the end of a little medicinal-looking bottle between my teeth as I gasped for air. I bit on it and cool liquid burst into my mouth like I'd popped a zit. I gagged. Tried to spit. Heard the familiar rip of gaffer tape torn off a reel – and then Burroughs' hands smoothed the silver sticky gag over my mouth. As my eyes bulged and the blood drummed in my ears like I'd had a hit of poppers, those hands clamped either side of my head and forced my face into the telescope's rubber flange like an anaesthetic mask. I shut my eyes and wrested my face away. The rip of gaffer tape again. Then fingers stabbing at my eyes, pulling back both lids till I thought they'd tear off and anchoring them to my eyebrows with the tape.

'Don't want you to miss anything Rich!' Raines simpered. Then, to Burroughs, 'Fast forward it to the end – he'll be out in a minute.'

Head held tight into the stifling rubber flange, eyes unable to shut off the flow, I took in the rest of the triple-speed Buster Keaton shagfest before the frames slowed, flickered and settled on the naked carcass of my gorgeous Georgie, tied and crucified on the giant H formed on our terrace sundeck by the two pillars and crosspiece that supported the Clematis-draped trellis. Shiny and streamlined in the morning sunlight, her golden limbs hung limp like a mermaid or the fresh-caught fish dangling from booms in the harbour below. Goalgotha in the Gray D'Albion. A final retch left the viewfinder awash with vomit before I sank out of my conscious nightmare into an unconscious one in which Raines' and Burroughs' laughter featured heavily.

18

Big Brother

Daisy was keenly aware of the irony of it: her estranged, and very strange, brother was still attached to his beloved telescopes decades after he'd been so savagely detached from his very first and left his blink behind in the wink of an eye. And now she'd found herself almost as stuck on the top-of-the-range pair of binoculars she'd acquired a few months back.

Not that she'd been in touch with the bastard. Just taking a leaf out of big brother's book and watching at a safe distance.

She hadn't meant to track Bart down – in fact she never wanted to see any of her family ever again. But somehow the sort of work she did, and the people she met through it, brought her inexorably back into his orbit and its world of watchers and the watched.

Forty-five going on sixty, young-fogey neat and too tidy by half, Roland Chalfont was the extremely successful proprietor of a discreet shop in Bloomsbury that sold high tech espionage equipment, ostensibly for the purposes of keeping tabs on errant spouses and pre-empting industrial espionage. If truth were told and if he were indiscreet, which he never, ever, was, he'd just emblazon *VOYEURS R US* in neon lettering across the blank shop window. Another irony: Chalfont, the provider of accoutrements and paraphernalia for those who loved to watch, got his own kicks at the other end of that particular peccadillo's continuum. Although he'd first encountered a domineering version of Daisy at the wrong end of a whip, the inside of an iron cage and two sets of shackles, he was, first and foremost, an exhibitionist – and one with the wherewithal to turn his pastime into an art and an exact science. That entailed loading up Daisy's designer bag with state-of-the-art surveillance technology. Her brief, in brief, was to test this array of voyeuristic weaponry on its provider. He was never to know when or where he was being watched. All he needed to know was that sometimes, somewhere, somehow, his every move was watched and enjoyed – the latter part of the deal drawing on all Daisy's considerable experience and talent for acting aroused. Beyond that, it was just a question of noting the precise details of what he was wearing and when and where and emailing him this information as proof in the lewdest, rudest detail conceivable.

After all those years of prostitution and the various degrees of muckiness that entailed, this was a walk in the park for Daisy – literally as it turned out. Her first 'mission' led her on a trail through North London that she found she was enjoying in spite of herself. It started with lunch at the Engineer gastropub, where she trained a covert video camera on her target as he enjoyed a lingeringly leisurely three-course lunch and she picked at a platter of tapas. From there both watcher and watched walked off their lunch through Chalk Farm, up Haverstock Hill to Hampstead Heath, where a pair of military calibre binoculars came into play as Daisy's subject wheezed off uphill and into some dense bushes accompanied by some moustachioed bloke in Freddie Mercury fancy dress who'd been leaning against a tree in a pose that meant to be coolly casual but was belied by his pumped muscles.

'Fuck, fuck, fuck,' Daisy rasped, scrabbling in her handbag of trickery for the manual. The dense foliage rustled as she tentatively delved – too loud not to be noticed by ears keenly tuned for the sound of approaching coppers, marauding kids or queer bashers.

'Fuck me, fuck me, fuck me,' groaned a trembling voice from the shrubbery.

'Fuck me!' Daisy exclaimed as she found the button that made the binoculars' infra-red imaging function kick in, in all too graphic detail. The ghostly green image left a trail like ectoplasm as two heat sources merged, then separated, merged then separated. And then Daisy separated herself from the viewfinder, more out of boredom than distaste, blinking the dancing green blobs out of her eyes.

'That's one way of exacerbating your Chalfonts,' she muttered, flicking the device onto 'record' and hooking it up to the USB drive clipped to a Batman-style array of pointless gadgets and gizmos strapped round her waist, which she referred to privately as her 'futility belt'. The grunts in the undergrowth turned to squeals. *Like a stuck pig,* Daisy thought. *No. Not like* — it *is* a stuck pig, she continued musing with a grin. Her arm tiring of holding up the tangle of apparatus, she draped the USB leads over a branch, leaving the electronic eyes to carry on leering silently while she sat down for a smoke and a smirk. Having weaned herself off the smack and crack and coke some time back, she laid out on a magazine cover the paraphernalia of the class C user: Rizlas, baccy and the last sprinklings and buds from her baggy of oxymoronically strong weed just as a jellyfish out of water came flying out of the greenery and landed with a splat on her own little clutch of green. She eyed the washing-up-gloves-calibre rubber and its dribblingly viscous contents with unsurprised revulsion and abandoned the whole tainted lot, grass and all, on the balding ground.

Stalking off, understandably peeved, she halted suddenly and turned back to retrieve several thousand pounds' worth of technology from the bush where she'd hung it just in time to bump into Freddie Mercury as he clambered out of the greenery like he was climbing out of a cockpit — which he actually was, she giggled to herself — and struggling to re-buckle a dungeonful of leather straps and buckles.

'What the hell do you think you're doing?' he squealed, the hand-on-hipped stance and high pitch at odds with the ultra-macho get-up.

'Bird watching?' Daisy ventured, unconvincingly.

'Well you don't look much like an ornithologist to me!' he squawked.

'And you don't look a lot like a botanist — I assume that's what you were doing in there... Studying the local flora?' She nodded in the direction of the bushes, where Chalfont's now rather less-than-debonair figure was stumbling about in a tangle of brambles.

'Good afternoon Daisy,' he said as if they'd met outside the church at Evensong. 'This is...' He stopped, realising that exchanging names was the one intimacy he hadn't shared with his new acquaintance.

'Hello Roland,' Daisy simpered, holding out a limply ladylike hand to her employer's new beau.

'Is this what I think it is?' Freddie (for that's how Daisy had already christened him). 'Is this some kind of set-up?'

'It's not what you think...' Chalfont began.

But Mercury was off, winging his way to his next assignation, wherever that might be, his skin-tight leathers squeaking like new shoes – or farts.

'You wanna cut down on the baked beans mate!' Daisy called out after him.

'Thanks very much!' Chalfont muttered, hurriedly brushing his neat grey suit down and fastening buttons.

'Sorry love – but I can't be expected to have all these bloody contraptions sussed from the start can I!'

'Well I suppose not,' Chalfont allowed, his demeanour softening. Accustomed to keeping his dealings with most people at the end of a telescope or a data cable, he really wasn't very good at confrontation. Not like Daisy.

'I suppose I could teach you,' he ventured.

'You'll bloody well have to if you don't want a repetition of today's fiasco!'

He helped her pack away the multifarious attachments and cables in their fetishistic leather cases and as dusk gathered and brought out the evening cruising shift the unlikely couple strolled back to Hampstead's genteel bustle and then the cocooning anonymity of a black cab back to Bloomsbury.

'Are you really happy with what you do?' Chalfont ventured timidly.

'Oh Sugar Daddy!! Are you going to take me away from all this,' Daisy mock-gushed bitterly.

'Don't be like that. Of course not,' Chalfont's lips puckered up like a sphincter. 'I simply mean that perhaps you could work for me full time. You know – a job, if you're at all familiar with the concept.'

Shoving herself back into the opposite corner of the cab's bench seat, Daisy turned to face him, scrutinising his face expertly for evidence of insincerity. She found none. Old Roly might be a bit of a perv, but he was at least an honest one. Now that she was a 'Madam', she was rarely required to have sex with anyone – at least not for money. And on the odd occasion when some self-important punter insisted on doing the business with the top dog (and they'd actually put it like that, the bastards!), he'd have to pay top dollar. These days that was at least five hundred quid. But because she no longer needed the money, the deed felt doubly dirty. So the idea of installing one of her best girls as a sort of Junior Madam while she raked off a modest twenty percent and at the same time 'went legit', was rather appealing. In a year or so maybe she could even knock the knocking shop on the head altogether.

'Go on,' she said. 'I'm all ears.'

'Well,' he began, 'As you know, a good deal of my merchandise is of, er, questionable legal status.'

'It's dodgy as fuck you mean!'

'That's my point actually. A lot of surveillance equipment is perfectly legal as long as it's sold for legitimate purposes.'

'Like those speed camera detectors that say they're designed so you can practise moderating your speed and become a safer driver?'

'Exactly – and we all know that what they're selling is a way of flouting the speed limits with impunity.'

'So?'

'You know that quote by Charles Revlon?'

Daisy shook her head.

'Something like, "I know that half the money I spend on advertising is wasted. The trouble is that I don't know which half." Now, in my case

I do know which half – but I don't know how to stop wasting it.'

'I haven't the faintest idea what you're talking about,' Daisy replied, her interest piqued nevertheless.

'Right. Take those infra-red surveillance binoculars.'

Daisy nodded.

'I order them in from some survivalist nuts in the US where there's a vast market for all sorts of defence-related crap in all the redneck states.'

'But not here, right?'

'No – not here. And if there were, I wouldn't want to deal with those kind of people – Nazis and the like...'

'Don't mind hanging out with a lot of old sickos though do you...'

'Those "sickos", as you so delicately put it, are my bread and butter. What's more, all they're doing is indulging some completely harmless fetishes in the privacy of their own...'

'Public park? Heath? Lavatory?' she teased.

'Homes, actually' he sighed. 'Come on Daisy, you of all people should know that.'

'OK, OK, point taken.'

'I have to maintain a veneer of respectability for the business – for the clients' sake as much as for my own.'

'Yeah I always wondered what your wife and kids thought of it...'

'If you'll allow me to finish!'

'Sorry. But I mean, if I had kids I...'

Daisy was silenced by Chalfont's wearily patient pause.

'So I advertise in ornithological, ecological, naturalist magazines and the like.'

'Ah I get it! "Ideal for observing nesting and mating behaviour in the natural habitat" - that kind of thing!'

'Exactly – but *sans* innuendo.'

'And do you sell any?'

'Absolutely bugger all – but you see it gives my customers a reason, well an excuse I suppose, for buying them. The cost of the extra advertising is to some extent reflected in my rather steep prices – and my marketing materials explain that the premium is the price of absolute discretion.'

'So what's the problem?'

'Well there isn't a major problem. It's just that since a good eighty percent of my trade is repeat business, the cost of that camouflage advertising is getting harder to justify – at least to my accountant. What I need is a streetwise front person with some charm, who understands my customers' er, special, needs... Who can develop the business while reducing costs and preserving the utmost secrecy...'

Chalfont studied Daisy's face for a reaction, afraid she'd take umbrage at being thus stereotyped. And sure enough, her face darkened to a frown as she clicked a black-varnished talon against her teeth. Then she brightened, her pout splitting into a goofy grin.

'Yeah, baby, Yeah!' she Austin Powered.

Chalfont's relief was palpable. Dabbing his brow with a silk handkerchief, he leaned forward and grasped Daisy's hand with both of his.

'You'll do it then?'

'Well hold your horses, Roly Poly. What's in it for me?'

Back at Chalfonts of St Giles (yes that really was the name of his establishment – an attempt to give the impression of a long established firm with stolid, gentlemanly credentials), Roland spent an inordinately long time bleeping bleepers, tapping in codes and unlocking locks before ushering Daisy into his inner sanctum.

'Bit over the top isn't it. Fort Knox or what!' Daisy observed.

'It's not to protect the stock – it's for the clients' peace of mind. I've got the names and personal peccadilloes of an awful lot of rich, famous and powerful people on file in here. If someone gained access to it... Well it doesn't bear thinking about...'

Daisy nodded gravely. She fully understood.

'All mine are in here – and no one but me ever sees it,' she breathed, tapping a bulging elastic band–bound black book.'

'Well you obviously don't take security as seriously as I do,' Chalfont replied, eyeing her book of blokes with distaste.

'Wanna bet,' she shot back, and Chalfont gulped hard as a switchblade appeared perilously close to his jugular.

'Yes – well I suppose your system's quite effective too,' he stammered as Daisy snapped the knife shut and tucked it back under the elastic band.

'A flickknife – very impressive,' he gasped.

'I prefer to call it a stiletto – so much more ladylike I feel!' Daisy purred.

'And that concludes the "street wise" section of the interview,' he quipped, regaining his composure.

'Oh, this is an interview is it?'

'No – course not. Just joshing,' he replied hurriedly.

'But I pass, do I?'

'Oh my dear, you passed the moment we met!'

'Bless you darling,' Daisy planted a kiss on two fingertips and dabbed them at Chalfont's paper-thin lips. 'But you still haven't told me exactly what's in it for me.'

'Well, I thought we'd call you the Marketing Director – and your remuneration would be commensurate with that position...'

'How fucking much Roland?' Daisy assumed her much-revered and highly effective dominatrix persona.

You could almost watch the bubbles of sweat burgeoning like hot springs on Chalfont's forehead.

'Fifty thousand,' he blurted quickly.

'A year?'

He nodded – and gulped.

'I make that in six months.'

'Yes but you could still...'

'Turn tricks as a sideline? Nah – if I stop, I stop for good. Make it a hundred and we're in business.'

'If you'd let me finish, you'd have heard the other part of my offer,'

Chalfont rallied. 'And which, I'm confident, puts your total on-target earnings well above the figure you just mentioned.'

'Do go on,' Daisy simpered, head cocked and hawk-eyed.

'I'm thinking of taking a back seat and handing over a significant part of the company's day to day running to you — and in return I had in mind an equity share of ten percent initially, rising to a maximum of thirty percent in about a year assuming you meet certain targets...'

'And the company's worth what? Fifty grand tops?'

Chalfont smiled as he tapped a laptop keyboard and a spreadsheet appeared on the screen.

'That's last year's balance sheet,' he said, his pride radiating through his usual veneer of modesty. 'And here,' he tapped the screen, 'is the net profit for the financial year ending April 2005. I'm projecting a modest increment to that in next year's figures – even without your contribution, which I fully expect to increase that by at least fifty percent if you're as good as I think you're going to be.'

Daisy scanned down the columns with the expert eye of one with years of experience auditing double entry books with double sets of accounts – one for her and one for the Inland Revenue and police. A razor sharp fingernail tapped the screen and clickety-clicked down the trail of digits, arriving once more at the total, which contained considerably more digits and commas than any seen in her own spreadsheets.

'Fuck me!' she breathed.

'Well I wasn't actually expecting that particular privilege but if you insist...' Chalfont smiled.

'For that money you can fuck me sideways with a two-man canoe babe!'

'Well, thanks for the offer Daisy but I think I'll be happy with the services described in the job spec.'

She jumped to her feet, towering over the diminutive and seated Chalfont in her five-inch heels.

'As you know darling, I don't do kissing - but for you...'

She seized him, drew him up to his feet and planted the smacker to

end all smackers on his John Major lips: MMMMMMMMMWAAAH!!!
And then released him with a gusto that sent him spinning on the
studio-style chair.

'I'll take that as a yes then?' a dizzy Chalfont gasped, struggling to
recover his balance.

'Yes, yes, yes. Quarter of a million in my first year! Oh God yes!'

Chalfont shut down *Excel* on the laptop and busied himself with the
combination lock on an imperious steel door not much less hefty than
the kind that barricade bank vaults. Daisy beamed, radiant.

'Let's have a drink. Celebrate!'

'All in good time Miss Marketing Director. First I need to give you
an insight on the intricacies and delicacies of this operation.'

'Can't we do it later?'

'I really would prefer that you understood the position fully before
we finalise anything,' Chalfont grinned apologetically. 'I know you'll
think I'm a bit anal but...'

'Think? I *know* you're anal mate,' Daisy shot back with an I-don't-
mean-it grin.

'Touché,' Chalfont countered, slightly sheepishly.

'Come on then, gimme the lowdown you old bugger!' she yapped,
jumping at the vaulted door like a waggish dog.

'Exactly which particular meaning of bugger are you alluding to,
might I ask?'

'All of 'em mate!' she cackled as Chalfont spun the hefty wheel and
metal tumblers clunked into place.

It was more of a hatch than a door really. As they stepped over
a foot-high threshold into a clanging metal-lined room, it was like
stepping aboard a submarine, lacking only a decompression chamber. A
lone, dim bare bulb half-heartedly showed them a stairwell into whose
gloom an iron fire-escape-style staircase spiralled. Daisy's tentative first
step almost ended in arse over tit disaster but Chalfont lent a steadying
hand, which guided hers to a sticky rope that hung limply against the
spongily damp brickwork, dismally failing in its role as a handrail. In a

well-practised manoeuvre, Daisy shed her 'fuck me' shoes and clutched them together, spike heels outermost. Chalfont towered over her from a couple of risers above. No he didn't – he was on the same step as the de-heeled Daisy. Life looked a lot more depressing without height. With every downward turn round the stairwell's hub, a light above them faded to black and a new one swelled into life below, each one failing to illuminate more than a few feet ahead. Daisy wasn't easily spooked though. It took a good twenty stockinged steps before, glancing over her shoulder at his eerily up-lit features, she could swear he was about to say 'Boo' to her goosebumps.

'Where we going – into the fucking sewers?'

'Metaphorically speaking, yes.'

'Or a dungeon?'

'That too,' Chalfont replied with an equanimity that sent a shiver down Daisy's spine – unless it was just the bone-deep damp, of course. Probably it was both, she privately concluded – before a new thought occurred to her.

'Oh Christ – please tell me it's not a crypt,' she whispered, instantly cursing herself for the knee-jerk impulse to lower her voice.

'Course not – don't be silly,' came Chalfont's blithe reply out of the darkness as a switching off light switched on a wall of black. Then the next leading light reluctantly lit, revealing his face in a flickering flash, much closer than expected – suddenly too close for comfort; suddenly somehow sinister.

'Although, you could say this is where the bodies are buried,' he chuckled cryptically as Daisy's hand frantically felt around in her bag for the flick-knife tucked into her big black book.

19

Gift Whores

Gift Horses, which I'd now renamed *Gift Whores* in anticipation of the inevitable sell-out to come, wasn't going well. In fact it was pony (That's 'Pony and Trap = Crap' if you're not conversant with cockney). The working title (which I was keen to use for the finished thing) had come to mind when Jimmy Gold had first announced this mysterious and very welcome new deal. I knew it was something of a rock cliché, using a snatch of a proverb as a title – but with its echoes of the Stones' *Wild Horses* and Neil Young's (or even the bleedin' Osmonds') *Crazy Horse(s)* and Patti Smith's *Horses,* it seemed like destiny somehow when Georgie had uttered the fateful words, 'don't look a gift horse in the mouth'. But of course that was when I thought she had my best interests at heart. Before she screwed some bullying henchman and left me without even telling me for that deceitful, conniving, stupidly loaded bastard who once was my friend. So, in my songwriter mind, there was a hint of the 'get back on the horse' thing. And that, I suppose, was what I was trying to do.

The trouble was that I'd saddled myself with a title before I'd written a song, let alone an album. The title was supposed to be a theme – but not, you understand, a concept. No old punker worth his spit and salt would make one of those prog-rock monstrosities... So I was caught between a rock and a... Oh for fuck's sake, there I go again: trotting out rusty old saws as poor substitutes for the cutting edge. Jimmy had lectured me about taking care of the budget.

'It's a generous deal, Rich. But that doesn't mean you can blow it on...'

'Blow?' I'd interjected with a sheepish grin.

'If that means coke – yes!'

He clicked his tongue at my crestfallen schoolboy look.

'I mean it. It sounds like a lot of money but the actual recording budget's only thirty grand.'

'That would've been the drug budget back in the day,' I whined.

'Yes – and back in the day you took two fucking years to make an album. This needs to be written, recorded, mastered, done and dusted in three months tops.'

'Well *Shit and Corruption* only took two weeks.'

'Actually, love, you spent two weeks pissing about in the studio and we spent another three months polishing your turds.'

'Come on Jim, it wasn't that bad!'

He grinned.

'It was fucking brilliant – but you can't get away with that sort of anarchy now. You just can't. It's tough out there!'

'Don't worry – I've got the songs,' I lied. 'All I need now is somewhere to do the pre-production.'

'Well you only need about nine good ones – they want a new recording of *Bring It On.*'

'No way.'

Jimmy smile.

'I told them you'd say that.'

'And you were right.'

'I know. But unfortunately it's a deal breaker.'

'You're kidding me, surely,' I whined. 'It's bad enough having to trot it out every fucking Christmas but...'

'You've never objected to the royalties though – it's only that song that's kept you afloat for the last two years. You do know that don't you?'

'Yeah,' I shrugged like a recalcitrant school kid. 'But I was looking forward to leaving it behind. I want to do something fresh and new...

Reinvent myself, a bit like Bowie or someone.'

He shook his head sombrely. If he was tempted to point out the yawning creative chasm between Bowie's talent and mine, he resisted it.

'Well you can – but you have to reinvent *Bring It On* while you're at it. Think of it as a creative challenge!' he ventured half-heartedly.

'But why?'

'Isn't it obvious?'

I shrugged sulkily.

'It's insurance. They simply want to cover their arses by re-releasing a new version of your biggest hit and giving those residual sales and airplay a big shot in the arm. They want to exploit the song's use in the pseudo-religious market – and get various name DJs to remix it. Come on Rich, you know the score!'

'Well I suppose it can't hurt,' I muttered.

'That's my boy,' Jimmy agented. 'You can pretty much do it in your sleep!'

'It'll put me to sleep you mean.'

'Look Richie, don't knock your biggest song. The reason they want it is that it's so big.'

'Any chance you could stop calling me Richie?' I shrugged again, re-discovering my spoilt rock brat persona with an ease only slightly less breathtaking than the way he shrugged it off.

'People love it. It's uplifting. It brings people together – and wouldn't you rather all these religious fuckwits sang along to *your* big anthem than one of Cliff fucking Richard's?' Jimmy insisted.

'I suppose when you put it like that...' I said, brightening a little.

Jimmy knew when he was winning.

'You were so happy when it went to number one; when you heard it blasting out of every other car on the road – you said you could stop now. You'd got a bit of yourself into the heads of millions upon millions of people....'

'I know – that time when I quoted Lennon. "Bigger than Jesus" –

fucking hell, what a wanker!'

'You or Lennon?'

'Both.'

I reddened slightly at the memory. Too much charlie and too much ego. God, what was I like! Hordes of fundamentalists had picketed the record company offices, my gigs, the Beeb, and even my house with ill-spelt placards and poorly rhymed rants decrying my blasphemy. The Christians were quite annoyed too. Could've been worse, I suppose. At least I'd only alluded to the Beatles and Jesus Christ. I winced at the consequences had I thus maligned Mohammed, or even worse Elvis. Could have been more dangerous than when I hacked into the national crime computer and added myself to the list of registered sex offenders. That really put the cat amongst the pigeons.

'Why on Earth would anyone voluntarily and, I might add, illegally place themselves on the list of sex offenders?' Paxman had challenged on prime time telly.

Shitfaced and giggling, I'd mumbled the basis of my original plan, dreamed up at the tail end of a five-day binge.

'Because it's the one sure way to make people keep their screaming, shitting little brats away from me!'

'If you're thinking about that sexual offenders nightmare – don't even go there!' Jimmy warned, clocking my schoolboy smile at the memory.

I held my hands up.

'OK then. All you need to do is fuck around with it a bit. Try it as a solo acoustic number – or maybe we'll sort out some horny bit of stuff to duet it with you. Or how about an orchestral version? We've got the budget.'

Budget! I took the bait, in spite of myself.

'So,' I wheedled, 'if I did an orchestral *Bring It On,* maybe I could use the orchestra on some other songs in the same session – and just bill it for the one track.'

Jimmy smiled.

'Now you're talking my language!'

★   ★   ★

The beauty of modern recording technology – you probably know the kind of thing (or more probably you don't), recording direct to your Apple Mac, using Pro Tools and Logic Gold and stuff like that – is that you can do it pretty much anywhere. As long as you don't want to record drums live. So I found myself happily ensconced, all alone except for a big pile of flight-cased technology, at Babington House – Soho House's country retreat. *Not bad at all,* I thought smug as a bug in a rug – or to be exact in the deep, deep, green long and wide infinity pool in the famous 'Cowshed'. Not only was this the life. This was the life I'd been used to five years earlier – and with which I intended to become thoroughly re-acquainted. Reassuringly, the staff remembered me. Or at least took the trouble to pretend to. Of all the swanky hotels around the world that I'd graced with my rock star presence, this was my favourite; the only one whose 'S' wasn't silent. To be more accurate, it had everything the others had but it was absolutely NOT swanky or wanky. It was cool in a warm and friendly way. It was hip but not in a trendy way. It was stylish yet not, in a Marmite and Corn Flakes and Heinz Ketchup on the breakfast table way. And in the maid not a) stealing or b) reporting, the modest mess of coke you'd left on top of the state-of -the-art brushed aluminium telly but instead scraping it into a neat and tidy and choppable pile. In every way, I just fucking loved it.

20

The Batcave

At the foot of the stairwell, a door swished efficiently to the left and in a blinding flash Daisy was dazzled by myriad floor and ceiling lights – those fierce halogen jobs that are *de rigueur* in restaurants and bars everywhere. Having walked ahead into the sterile white room, Chalfont had turned to find his protégé looking distinctly un-*protégé*, stiletto knife in one raised hand, stiletto shoes in the other.

'Oh God, I've frightened you!' Chalfont's dismay was genuine. 'I'm so sorry... I was just kidding.'

Daisy's blush bloomed through mother-of-pearl skin from cheeks to chest as she hastily clipped the knife shut and dropped it back into her bag. Even for Chalfont, whose proclivities tended to the other gender, her fleeting vulnerability was curiously arousing – though he wasn't sure whether the emotion she'd stirred was carnal or just some wakening paternal instinct. Stepping towards her, he made to put a reassuring arm round her shoulder but now re-high-heeled, she was way too tall for that to work, even when she shrank from his hand.

'I wasn't scared – you just spooked me OK!' she sulked, tossing her hair and dismissing her pink flush like she was shaking an *Etch-a-Sketch* to start a new picture. 'I mean what the fuck was that all about? "Where the bodies are buried!"' A laugh infiltrated her mock-strop, then infected Chalfont with a wide grin.

'I just meant that this is where I keep all the information on every customer I've ever dealt with. The information in this room is enough to ruin careers, end marriages, wreck lives...'

'Oh – silly of me not to realise!'

'Let's start again, shall we,' Chalfont smiled, pulling out a chair for her and bringing a PC screen to life with the tap of a mouse.

'I'll just run through the basics with you and then perhaps you'd like to spend some time rummaging around the database to get a feel for the way it works,' he murmured, pointing, tapping and clicking at speed through an obstacle course of passwords, codes and security checks. But Daisy was no longer at his side.

'What's all this then?' she called from the far end of one of three narrow aisles of library style floor-to-ceiling shelving.

'What? Oh – archives. All the stuff that pre-dates computerisation. I've never got round to digitising it all.'

Wide-eyed, Daisy surveyed the rows upon rows of box files.

'You mean every one of these boxes represents a different customer?'

'Yes – all alphabetised within their country's section.'

'You sell internationally?'

'Oh yes – I think you'll find clients in most countries in the world – well, the developed world anyway.

She strolled along the ranks of files trailing a finger along the ranks of files. Alaska, Andaman Islands, Angola, Australia, Austria…

'Alaska! You *are* kidding aren't you!'

Chalfont stood and joined her, pulling out a box from the Alaska section at random.

Moistening a finger on his tongue like a post office clerk, he flicked through the wad of invoices, statements and correspondence before pulling out a particularly thick wad of dog-eared documents.

'Mr Robert Kowalski – oil company engineer. Spends half his year travelling round the most God-forsaken parts of the planet and… Let me see, yes, manages to pass off his private, er, investments, as accessories and upgrades for his legitimate engineering survey equipment.'

'And you have his real name?'

'Oh yes – that's part of the deal. For billing purposes. Generally they pay a fixed monthly fee by standing order, disguised as something innocuous of course. Then they can order goods at any time as long as they don't exceed an agreed credit limit.'

Daisy reached up and pulled out another box in a puff of dust, nose wrinkling to stifle a sneeze.

'But these invoices are all in different names.'

'All part of the service you see. I ask the clients to brief me on the nature of goods or service they're ostensibly being billed for — and sometimes they also suggest the name of the fictitious company.'

'So what's Chalfonts of St Giles?'

'Just a name. A private joke really — because it's a pain in the bottom. Rhyming slang for piles? I actually own several thousand limited companies — each of which handles the invoicing for a handful of customers.'

'Bloody hell! Roland, this is incredible!' Daisy exclaimed.

'I'm glad you're impressed!'

'You really are a dark horse aren't you!'

'I like to think so.'

'Seems a bit over the top though — all this secrecy. I mean, you're not doing anything really illegal are you?'

'Depends which country you're talking about — and anyway, legality's a bit of a red herring. So's morality come to that. It's about the level of public humiliation involved were any of these people's secret lives to be exposed — but of course, you know as much as I do about that sort of thing. It's all about shame — or protecting people from it.'

Daisy nodded. Sometimes being a hooker, and especially being a madam, was akin to being a priest. Once you knew someone's deepest, darkest sexual fantasies, they often felt some compulsion to open up and confess the rest of their lives to you, often in sordid and boring detail. It came with the territory.

'But it's just technology — there's always another reason for owning this sort of equipment isn't there. Otherwise, why the ads in birdwatchers' mags?'

Now it was Chalfont's turn to redden.

'Ah, well I'm afraid I haven't told you the whole story. Couldn't, you see, till I'd made sure you were genuine.'

Daisy's dominatrix eyebrow arched and she struck a self-mocking Cruella de Vil pose.

'And what other disgusting practices exactly have you been keeping from me young man?'

'Well what I've told you is all completely accurate – but there's more to it than that.'

'Do go on,' Daisy simpered, sitting down and lighting a cigarette to see if he'd dare to object. He didn't.

'It started out as I told you – supplying surveillance and espionage devices. After a couple of years it became clear that most of my customers weren't using the stuff for the purpose advertised on the box.'

'How could you know?'

Chalfont pinched the bridge of his nose, avoiding her gaze.

'I saw myself in their eyes.'

'Explain.' Daisy insisted.

'I saw my shame. They'd come in all flustered and avoid looking me in the eye – asking questions that didn't ring true; didn't tally with what they said they wanted stuff for....'

'Like schoolboys buying porno mags.'

He nodded.

'Like me trying to buy condoms at the chemist when I was a lad,' he chuckled. 'You know, the old cliché, walking out with a tube of toothpaste, throat sweets, plasters – anything but the flipping contraceptives!'

'Why don't you just say "fuck"?' Daisy interjected.

'I'm sorry?'

'Say "fuck" when you mean "fuck". Why say "flip" – we all know which word you mean.'

'I find swearing vulgar.'

'You don't like the words but you do like the action. You're weird.'

'As you say, I'm a bit anal,' Chalfont confessed.

'Better than being an arsehole!' Daisy said with glee. 'Come on then Roly, gimme the down and dirty nitty gritty baby!'

'So I started quietly approaching one or two of the regulars, implying that there was more I could offer – you know, personal services...'

'You're a secret madam!' Daisy bounced delightedly and spun in her seat. Chalfont smiled sheepishly.

'I suppose you could say that - although cross-dressing was never my thing. Seriously though, I simply suggested that I could put people discreetly in touch with the services they required – but at arm's length, thereby removing their fear of being caught with their pants down as it were.'

'Drugs?'

'Sometimes, yes.'

'Girls?'

He nodded.

'Boys?'

He nodded again.

'But only of legal age. I've always been very rigorous about that. I know it sounds ridiculous but I have a strict code of conduct to which all my suppliers and customers must adhere – if they don't I withhold payment and cease trading with them straight away.'

'You should have been a vicar!'

'I very nearly was – a long, long time ago!'

'Hence your interest in vicarious pleasures! Daisy cackled.

'OK. Let me say first of all that I don't have anything to do with practices that I consider immoral.'

'In other words you deal with things other people would find immoral.'

'There's almost nothing that someone, somewhere won't object to. Take the Taliban...'

'No, thank you. Point taken though.'

'Seriously, when my mother was a child her parents forbade her to bounce a ball on a Sunday. To enjoy yourself on the Sabbath was tantamount to mocking God. If someone had suggested opening a shop, having a disco or spending a Sunday getting lost in Ikea they'd have been run out of town as heretics.'

'One man's fundamentalism's another man's fun!'

'Something like that.'

'Another man's mentalism!'

Daisy stood and meandered pensively along the aisles, then turned back to him like a rock 'n' roll Jessica Rabbit.

'So what you're saying is that you're like a porno version of those internet concierge services that book restaurants and club guest lists for lazy rich bastards.'

'I suppose that's about the size of it.'

She leaned over him, her bosom, cupped like overdeveloped pearls in a ridged oystershell bra, too close for comfort, and fixed him with her feline green gaze, noting that he was one of the few men who could meet her eyes without his own being drawn magnetically down to her cleavage.

'So our businesses are more alike than you first had me believe!'

He nodded, sheepish.

'When do I start?'

'How about Monday?

Daisy nodded.

'But there is just the matter of the company's image. As you know, I've gone to a great deal of trouble to keep it discreet and businesslike – so I er...'

'...don't want me looking like a hooker – I'm way ahead of you!'

He smiled.

'Is that OK then?'

'Course it is – I can go from Goth rock chick to office goddess if I feel like it.' She brandished a gold credit card like a blade. 'Come on! Only three shopping days before Monday!

'What for?' Chalfont blinked.

'A little black twinset and a more substantial pearl necklace than the ones I'm used to! South Molton Street here I come!'

21

Let Us Prey. Sunday 24ᵗʰ April 2005.

'Beauty is a duty' the flock sheepishly intones like a mantra, its murmur resounding round a room more usually alive with the polite pitter-patter of cricket applause or the clatter of rugger studs on wooden floors. In time with their incantations, in the dank, cold mirrorless changing room where reflection's discouraged, a more fundamental changing than usual takes place.

'Beauty is a DUUUUUUTY!' he yodels with a final voluptuous thrust (the last of ten), tearing his slack, slavering maw from the girl's antelope neck, wiping away the twanging string of drool that slides onto her forehead like baptism, leaving the slimy calcified shower head to take over a slow, patient drip, drip, drip water torture that promises to cleanse her but won't deliver. With a ceremonial flourish, he whisks a white terry gown from the coat hook that hovers nearest the border between the communal showers' toilet tiles and the dingy pastel green wall cladding of the changing area. She looks up, rabbit-scared, as he folds the soft towelling around a grey torso like a sagging suet pudding. But he doesn't complete the job. The dressing gown's tie hangs loose – as would his prick if it had the length to hang. Instead it cowers like a slug against two shrivelled and dangling purple prunes nested in a blossom of grey fuzz growing on two rickety grey, scaly-barked trunks. Impossible to believe this is the thing that penetrated her; that this is what men are. What boys are.

'Good girl,' he mutters, avoiding her eyes. 'Tonight you have done your duty.'

He throws her a cheap and nasty nylon gown. It's scarlet. To replace the white one her dad had draped her in when he brought her here. And which is now sporting a subtle polka dot motif in red around the lower front.

'Now cover your shame,' he spits.

Lily Bunton doesn't need telling twice. She catches the red rag and clutches it to herself. Drawing her legs together and up and locking them tight in her arms, she rolls up like a hedgehog without the prickles but with the spine. She rocks from side to side to offset the spasms of nausea and unbidden shame and pain and revulsion and horror and confusion.

★   ★   ★

'Sex is something you do with someone you love,' Mum had always said.

'Sex is wrong. It is a sin unless within marriage for the purpose of having a child,' Dad had always said.

Mum's screaming through the flat's cardboard walls suggests that Mum and Dad are trying constantly to have another child. Clearly Lily isn't good enough. Otherwise why would Mum go through such pain so often? Lily can't bear the screams. Most nights she huddles under the covers and re-reads her secret text messages from Joe, accompanied by MP3s of their favourite songs in her earpieces. Especially *Bring It On*. Which is their song. Although her boy tries to laugh and say it's by such a cheesy old band and it's way too close to home, it really is *their song*.

★   ★   ★

Unlike the lithe-limbed, hairless and handsome boy-band boys who swan through her swooning dreams, there's no heroic princeliness in Erich Raines's stance; nor is there any of the turbulent and self-balancing mix of lust and love and shyness and fear that she can divine in even the most laddish of her classmates. She's slept with her boy. Well, not slept exactly. But been to bed. When she was off school 'revising' and so was he and Mum was at work. And it was nice. Then not nice. Then it hurt a bit. And he was appalled. And she gritted her teeth and said 'don't worry, it's supposed to'. Because they say it's always like that the first time. Of course Mum and Dad think she's still a virgin. Well Dad anyway. She thinks Mum knows. It's in her smiles. And the way she says 'be careful love'. And it was with Joe. That is his name. Beautiful David Beckham-y Joe. The one they all loved and so did she. Good at football and not rugby. And clever too. Good at English. A painter and a guitar player. It was OK. And it was like it said in the magazines and everything. And he was nice. He was trying so hard to make it good. And afterwards he said sorry. And she said it's OK. And they were both kind of shy. Which was weird because it was the first time either of them had really been naked with anyone else. And the first time they'd... *done it.* Funny to be shy after that. After doing that thing and being like one person with him inside her. Then being shy. Joe was funny. He wouldn't get out of the bed because she'd see him without any clothes on.

'But I've just seen every little bit of you!' she giggled. And he smiled sheepishly and went, 'Yeah but it's gone all small now.' Like that mattered. And he said he loved her. Not before. Not trying to make her do it. And not even when they were doing it. Everyone said about that. They always say stuff like that when they're getting it. But Joe didn't. He sent her a text the next day. And it was lovely.

I HOPE WAS OK. LILY, I LUV U. U R GR8. XXX

Lying in the same bed alone that night, aware of the faint trace of his scent in the sheets and wishing his warmth was there with it, Lily Bunton is full of love. Full, still, of Joe. And hoping he's thinking about her too. So she fumbles in the dark under the bed for the mobile Dad doesn't know she has. Under the covers she smiles back at Crazy

Frog, hearing his cute little voice in her head and smiling like at a baby although she's muted the sound.

WISH U WERE HERE. XXX, she texts. And waits, projecting her private movie of herself and Joe on the ceiling, drawing out the tenderness and replaying his vulnerability, freeze-framing moments, her longing making them linger longer. The muted phone tingles against her skin. It must be him.

SO DO I. J+L 4EVER 2GETHER. XXX.

And then Dad's voice rattles the floorboards. Shouting at Mum. Shouting about God and whores and immorality. And Lily Bunton is full of fear. *I'm pregnant. I'm diseased. I have AIDS. I'm evil.*

'Lily!'

The stentorian Old Testament voice and the clumsy beer-stunted steps on the stairs preceded the opening of the door with countable predictability.

The door opens.

Lily's legs close. And her eyes open.

'Our preacher has asked for you.'

She peeps out from under the duvet's armour.

'Hi Dad.'

'What are you doing under there?'

'Nothing?'

'No one is ever doing nothing.'

Bunton hits the light and strips the covers back to lay his daughter bare, forbidden phone and secret love exposed along with everything else. Lily curls, unblossoms into a bulb; time reversed. Sunlight's flower cowers in dadlight.

'What do you mean, Dad?'

He surveys the almost familiar centrefold or webpage he's just opened, loves it and hates loving it and blames his shame on her.

'Beauty is a duty. You'll soon see.'

He snatches the phone from where she's guiltily left it beside her.

'Please Dad, I need it.'

The phone throbs in his hand and he drops it like it's red hot.

'Dad, please,' she pleads. It has to be Joe. Can't be anyone else. And Dad can't see this.

He stoops and picks up the handset gingerly as if it's a turd. Crazy Frog must be leering at him with his stunted genitalia on view because the backlight flickers round the room. Even now Lily can hear his childlike giggle – but for the first time it doesn't raise a smile.

'Who's Joe?' Dad growls, now clicking through her phone's memory with a finger and thumb dexterity she's never seen before.

'My boyfriend.'

'You're fourteen. You can't have a boyfriend.'

'I have!' she bleats defiantly.

'No you haven't.'

'I *have* – and I love him and he loves me!' she shouts back.

'Not any more you haven't,' he states with grim certitude. 'Joe – that his name is it?'

Lily can't reply.

'He doesn't love you. He doesn't know the meaning of the word. I know his sort. I'll find him and that'll be the end of that.'

He closes the door. She closes her eyes to look for Joe – but Dad's just fucked up the ending to the fairytale. And Joe, in her mind, is indistinguishable from Dad and, only slightly worse, from Erich Raines.

★   ★   ★

The service had been more than satisfactory. The campaign of fifty thousand leaflets inserted into the local free rag and deposited on the counter tops of youth clubs, rock venues, nightclubs and snooker halls had targeted the young and the dumb; the voiceless unless they shout, shag and stab; not necessarily the jobless – but the careerless, careless, loveless, friendless and fearful. The radio campaign used a famous rock song, one that would ring bells for Erich Raines' church. The irony of the fact that this was the ballad that had taken the pansy's school friend and corruptor to the top of the charts some fifteen years earlier and made him rich and world famous was not lost on Raines senior. On the contrary, he rejoiced in using this voice of corruption and sin to reel the sinners in.

Bring it on, bring it in
In this we sing, of ageless sin
Bring it on, bring it in
This is where our lives begin...
Let's play, let's pray
To the lord above
To bring it on, to bring on life
Yeah bring it in, yeah bring me love

went the chorus of *Bring It On* in a massive Spectoresque wall of sound that had haunted every Christmas since with its irreligious schmaltz. The so-called singer, so-called writer, not only had the temerity to write this doggerel about love as if he were addressing our Lord Jesus Christ, rather than some slut that he wanted to screw – he also compounded the blasphemy sixfold by augmenting his atonal whining with the seraphic voices of a gospel choir. And this was the moronic, godless noise of the school friend his pansy had so adored. And worse still, whom Daisy had worshipped. This Judas friend who had led the pansy and Daisy astray.

But never mind. The sacrilegious fuck had unwittingly served his purpose and the 'church' had been almost full for the first time in its thirty-year history. Full of empty heads; pretty, vacant and ready to be filled.

Erich Raines had been a lay preacher – lay being the operative word – for more than thirty years now; having slowly transformed his clutch of woolly-sweatered real ale pub disciples into something like a congregation and covered himself in spurious pseudo-religious trappings, he'd managed to attract a loyal and compliant following whose credulity appeared endless. Not that he saw his tambourine-wielding proselytising as anything but genuine. Like the millions of Africans who believed that sex with virgins would cleanse them of HIV and continued to spread the disease with the Pope's two-faced blessing, he'd convinced himself and those around him that intercourse with the unsullied young was an act of purification. Their purity made them receptacles, sin eaters, for his and his cohorts' sins — the theory being that untainted as they were, their white and absorbent souls could afford to mop up a few minor blots. Maybe he was right; the monthly servicings certainly left him temporarily purged of the wicked urge to fornicate — and it invariably left the repository of that sour seed feeling soiled and suddenly old as if he'd tainted their youth with the disease of his age. Outside of his 'church' he eschewed carnality with pious zeal on the stony grounds that his wife Rosa's admittedly limited attractions were already corrupt and therefore incapable of providing the cleansing that his soul required. After all, she'd served her purpose by producing two offspring; an empty vassal now, she was mutton now - there only to serve him in her stoic style and stand by as he furthered his apostolate mission to breed new lambs for the slaughter.

She had, on occasion, had the nerve to suggest that all was not right with Erich's *project,* as he called it. But while he shunned carnal contact with her like a bad smell, he didn't turn his nose up at contact, and punishment, of the corporal kind — and a couple of well-aimed punches unfailingly silenced her objections.

This evening's service had been a prime example. Brother Bunton had conscientiously complied with his obligations and prepared his lovely daughter Lily for the ritual deflowering that had become the centrepiece of the monthly meetings. Bunton's wife Mary had made the fuss typical of women, missing entirely the point that this was a painful business for the father who put the female fruit of his loins forward and for the preacher who was duty bound to sully her innocence as part of the cleansing. As the girl was brought forward, pneumatically cherubic in her white vestal gown, first Mary, then Rosa had ruined the necessary air of reverence by clucking about the girl's innocence. Even now, with the deed well and truly done, Erich's lip curled in contempt. As if the little whore wasn't looking forward to what was about to happen; as if they all didn't live for the way they made men feel; they way they infect the good and true man with dirty wants and needs. How could they object when that filth was injected back into them?

'Rosa. Mary. Be quiet,' he had intoned with priestly dignity as he made the sign of the cross. 'You know what must come to pass.'

'Erich. Please. Not Mary's girl. This is...'

Her words dried up and shrivelled in his hellfire glare.

'Mary. Rosa. Lily is fourteen. She isn't a girl. She's a woman and a daughter of Eve. Remember. Beauty is a duty.'

'Beauty is a duty,' they'd echoed dully, the spark of rebellion extinguished by his Communion whine.

'Beauty is a duty,' the congregation had murmured in unison as Erich led the girl into the 'vestry', although the resonance such occasions demand was lacking. And the vestry was actually a testosterone-soaked changing room that reeked of rugger and buggery. Because the 'church' was the cricket/rugby pavilion of the local anachronistically single sex comprehensive-used-to-be-a-grammar-school-with-pretensions-to-quasi-public-school-status.

22

The Tunnel

The footpath was the conduit from the arse of the town to the poky promenade where the shit got diluted in the ominously brown and frothy milkshake sea. From the bypass that fenced in the ostentatiously detached houses with names (not numbers) and stonewalled the countless unnameable boxes outside its curved concrete curtain, the trail curled down like a long turd into the slurry stream right behind the aloof archipelago of separate and unspeaking homes whose windows were blinded to the squalor of the all-too-close other side of town. There was a hole in the chicken wire fence by the little bridge that crossed this desultory moat. If you slipped through, slid down the bank, paddled underneath and parted the undergrowth you could find the flood tunnel that ran several yards under the road and spouted into a scrubby patch of salt marsh corralled by the coast road to create a fly tippers' (and flies') stench trench. In summer the tunnel was reliably dry – only exceptional rainfall from one end or tides from the other created water enough to seep through after Joe and a couple of friends had dammed and walled off both entrances with corrugated iron sheets camouflaged with foliage. It had been their secret place since primary school; where they hid from angry parents or policemen after misadventures involving sticks chucked at horse chestnut trees that went astray and into the windows of passing lorries or stripped down motorbikes that shouldn't have been on a public road.

The only adult that ever found it was Danny the Drunk, the town's imaginatively named amiable vagrant – and since Joe (AKA Stig – as in dump), Neil Parry (AKA Nelly), Darren Spitz (AKA Dogshit) and Aaron 'Sweater' Bettridge were rarely allowed out after nine in the evening, they were happy to share it on a shift system. Especially because Danny paid 'rent' in the form of the odd pack of fags (assorted brands, cadged from passers by) and the occasional half-drunk bottle of sherry or cider or can of Special Brew.

When Danny died as he'd lived – alone and on the street – they'd grieved as if for a grandparent. After the funeral, they had the press photo encapsulated and nailed it to the tunnel's wall above a makeshift shelf bearing birthday cake candles. Dogshit toured the town's alleys and squats and popular park benches, inviting Danny's fellow pissheads to a private wake.

Big mistake. They came. They saw. They were bonkers. And they never left. Lacking the kindly twinkle and warmth that made Danny a local treasure, the others marked the tunnel as their territory with their piss and all-pervading stink. Something had to be done – and Nelly came up with the answer. His dad was a builder – and Nelly was already learning the trade. So one morning, after watching the interlopers cough, splutter and chunder their way out of the tunnel to wait for the Happy Shopper to start selling Special Brew, the four of them put Nelly's plan into action. Sweater and Dogshit came careering down the footpath behind overloaded wheelbarrows – one full of bricks, the other of sand and cement mix nicked from one of Nelly's dad's sites. Joe, bucket and shovel at the ready, scooped up water from the stream and started to mix the concrete while Nelly clinked and scraped like a real pro with his brickie's trowel. By mid-afternoon the tunnel was secured by double brick walls, half a door they'd found in a skip and four hefty padlocks.

'No one's gonna get in now!' Nelly pronounced with satisfaction, hands on hips as he admired their handiwork.

The others murmured agreement.

'Only thing is,' Joe piped up. 'What if the stream floods?'

'Who cares?' Dogshit shrugged.

'I mean, if the water can't go through the tunnel, someone's going to come and see why aren't they?'

'But it *can* go through!' Nelly grinned. He'd been waiting for this. 'Check this out!'

He waded under the bridge, crouched and pulled a cinder breeze block out of the water, around which was tied a nylon rope. Untying it, he reeled it in, folding it over his left hand and elbow and the other three gazed in amazement as a huge bright yellow corrugated raft, a good ten yards long like a giant rigid and elongated lilo, hove into view. Then another. And another.

'Plastic soil pipes!' Nelly explained. 'That big house the other side of the cemetery – they're having new drains and stuff. I capped them at either end, roped them together and floated them.'

'Suppose you think you're clever,' Sweater whispered, clearly impressed. 'But...'

The others nodded.

'God you lot are thick!' Nelly exclaimed, enjoying the moment. 'The tunnel runs slightly downhill, right! I've checked with a spirit level.'

They nodded.

'We run a few drainpipes through and put boards on top to make a floor. If there's a flood, the water just runs under us and out the other side as long as it's not a real Noah's Ark job. Piece of piss!'

He kicked two bricks at the foot of the new wall and amazingly they fell away. He'd left them uncemented. Then he fed three of the pipes into the gap.

'You clever bastard,' Dogshit said admiringly as they all set about connecting up lengths of pipe and building a three-tube drainage system like a miniature Channel Tunnel.

To complete the coup, Sweater had purloined some plywood hoardings, a couple of paraffin lamps and a few amber flashing lights from a roadworks site. The lamps served as heaters now that there were no draughts and the boards rested on the pipes to make a floor. With his usual ingenuity, Nelly opened up the roadlights and, with copper wire and crocodile clips, bypassed the bimetallic strip that made them flash. Bathed in orange light, they toasted their success with warm cider, smoked ragged roll-ups and pored over porno mags gleaned from roadside tips and unlocked lorries outside the transport café.

When Joe ran away from the children's home they'd put him in after running out of foster parents this was where he hid and lived for nearly a week on cold school dinner scraps smuggled to him in Tupperware lunchboxes by his mates. It had been in the local paper: *LOCAL BOY MISSING – Tragedy of prostitute's runaway boy.* The police had been out combing the countryside; his school's headmaster had rounded up a posse to search the derelict warehouses and train sheds that still lined the ragged scar of the long-gone railway. But they never found him. He just turned up at breakfast one morning, dishevelled but unharmed. Despite their gentle coaxing, then the exasperated interrogation, he never explained; never said where he'd been or why he'd gone.

Attention seeking, the local paper's cod psychology columnist called it. Actually it was quite the opposite. All he wanted was to be alone for a while, away from the dormitory, away from that creepy preacher's hellfire and brimstone drone every Sunday, away from the endless drumming in of Old Testament prejudices. Just away. If, underneath all that, it was attention he was after, he certainly got it. Notoriety in the local press meant fame among his peers, a new if grudging respect from the older lads about town and the adoration of the girls. For the first time in his life, the misfit fitted. And then they sent him away. It was supposed to be a good thing – a fabulous opportunity, the Headmaster had told him...

Of course, having tailored himself to fit Hartham-on-Sea, he was extremely uncomfortable at cut-glass Dartington – or at least he had been for the first few months. Now, this so-called 'benefactor' of his was lording it over him once more and ruining his life. Now he'd made friends. Now he fitted in again he'd been uprooted and replanted in the decidedly stoney ground of his home town and his old school – where he hadn't exactly been welcomed with open arms. His only friends, all a year older, had left for apprenticeships and pubs and grown-up life. Three months on, he still had no one he felt he could call a friend. Except for Lily. If it hadn't been for her, he'd have run off again the day he arrived.

23

Lily's Pavilion

Lily waited and waited while the congregation clump, clump, clumped out of the pavilion. She was till holding the scarlet robe against her; she hadn't put it on. She'd kind of worked out somewhere in the back of her mind that it was supposed to make her bad; meant to shame her and not them. Maybe Mum will come. Even Dad... But neither showed their face in this dark, dirty room. A final bang of the front double doors, and the turning off of lights, proved they'd relinquished her to whatever Raines deemed was her fate. A rattle and click of the bolts and the clunk of the Chubb lock confirmed she'd been abandoned; she'd served her purpose. She was alone.

So she sat in the touchable, visible gloom and shivered and quivered and cried. For how long she couldn't tell. But somehow, suddenly, the unbreachable continuum of darkness was breached by a ghostly flickering. As much as she yearned for light, Lily's eyelids fluttered in panic. And then, in spite of it all, she smiled. Accompanying that spectral guttering glow was a friendly giggling voice.

'Crazy Frog!!' Lily whispered, suddenly heartened as if rescued by a trusted friend.

And she had been.

The Crazy Frog called her; she could kiss him – and maybe the frog really was going to be her prince. There was a mobile phone in the building.

Clutching the red robe against her nakedness, she jumped to her feet and ran out of the showers into the main room. The frog was still burbling happily away on his imaginary motorcycle in the far corner – and the light from a phone was pulsing like something out of ET. Realising the robe was pointless, she dropped it and ran towards the light and sound.

It was her rucksack. The phone was tucked into the top pocket. It went dead. And the room went black. Hugging her nakedness to herself, against the cold and against who might be watching, she snatched the mobile from its little pouch.

MESSAGE RECEIVED

She hit *MESSAGES*.

PLEASE DON'T TELL DAD. THOUGHT U WLD NEED THIS. LOVE YOU. MUM

Her first thought was Joe. Not Mum. Not Mum, who'd let this happen. Even if she now wanted to help. She'd let this happen. 'Be careful love,' she always said. And Lily never knew till now that she wasn't just talking about the boys at school.

Of course Dad had wiped all her precious, treasured texts. And Mum had let him. And he'd wiped all the numbers in the memory. And Mum had let him. But he couldn't wipe her memory. Joe's number was hard-wired there forever.

Lily peered out of the window past the cricket nets over the blank expanse of the sports field, the giant aitches of the Rugby goals, luminous in the moonlight, framing the churchey school clocktower, which was backlit by the orange glow of the town. She unclipped the catch and tugged at the sash. Nothing. Painted up tight by decades of glossing over the rot. Tears rushed back and she slumped on ragged wooden boards under the window, the damp cold numbing her bare bum against the splinters. It must be late. There was no traffic hum; there were no sirens to break the hush – only her sobs and sniffs.

'Please be awake,' she whispered as the screen lit up and Crazy Frog blinked benignly at her, telling her it was just after midnight.

JOE. PLS HELP ME. URGENT. CALL ME QUICK. X, she tapped, cursing as her trembling fingers fluffed the buttons.

She clamped her eyes shut.

'Please, please please,' she pleaded to no one in particular.

★   ★   ★

Since Lily had been hauled off to one of her parents' bible bashes, Joe had spent the evening at a loose end. Drunk on three pints of lager and wearying quickly of a bad band's even worse posturing in the Black Horse, he'd sloped off for a quiet meditative spliff in the tunnel – which wasn't as simple a plan as it once had been now that the local authorities had barricaded the entrances with a steel fence (Evidently they hadn't realised that the rough brickwork across the tunnel's openings was not an officially sanctioned job). After wrestling a ladder over the back fence of a nearby garden and using it to scale the battlements, and with the band still ringing in his ears, somehow amplified by the tunnel's sepulchral silence, Joe skinned up and smoked in the darkness. Eyes closed and pleasantly wasted, he hummed the band's final, fated, tune of the set – The Who's *Pictures of Lily* funnily enough – and smiled contentedly as he projected some of his own pictures of Lily onto the screen inside his eyelids. Pure, demure and pretty Lily, who'd given herself to him so completely. *Bloody hell I don't half love you,* he thought – then, realising he'd said it aloud, burst into a pleasurable fit of giggles, which was cut short by Crazy Frog's helium chuckle as Joe's phone lit up with a text.

Lily's message dismissed the effects of the grass and the lager like a cold shower and he feverishly punched in a reply.

★   ★   ★

Lily waited and allowed hope to fire her imagination. Joe would come to her rescue. He'd wrap her in something warm and take her home with him and they'd be alone and he'd bathe her gently before taking her to bed... Joe: her knight in shining armour; her light at the end of this tunnel. But that train of thought just brought back the horror of her sacrifice – and the pain and the humiliation. Joe wouldn't want her now – not once he knew what had happened. She was spoilt. How could he enter where that vile pervert had left his tainted muck?

She jumped to her feet. He mustn't see her in this state: red-eyed, filthy, snotty and bedraggled. And naked. Worse, she didn't even have any make up on – Raines insisted that any adornment was work of the devil. She laughed out loud at the breathtaking hypocrisy.

'I need a mirror,' she muttered and padded over to the ladies' toilets where she could just about make out her image in the scaly and flaking glass above an ancient crusty basin. Dampening a wad of coarse paper towels in icy water, she wiped the tears from her face and then applied it tentatively to where she really felt soiled. Shivers turning to shudders, she pulled the red robe over her head. It was too short, leaving the lower curves of her bottom on show. It was a Shirley Temple frock, meant to mock her. Opening her phone to use its light, she examined her face, slipping into that routine primping and preening ritual that women do in traffic jams and supermarket queues and in chatty groups in lavatories. A comforting thing. And something Raines hated. Running through the checklist: eyes – puffy and red. Cheeks – one with a light graze like a carpet burn. Lips – poutier than usual. Bruised by Raines's maw and pricked by his porcine stubble.

As she held out a long lock of her rich dark hair against the phone's glow and carefully combed out something glutinous and gluey, the Crazy Frog gleefully cranked up his imaginary motorbike and Lily laughed with him as she hit the green.

'Joe?'

'Where are you what's happened what's going on are you all right?' he babbled breathlessly.

'I... I...' she began but his concern kick-started her heart again and its palpitations turned to trembling and the quiver in her voice got sucked up into a strangled sob.

'Lily? What's happened? Lily?' Joe urged, scrabbling at the tunnel's door, flinging it open and running up the muddy banks to the footpath.

'I'm locked in the sports pavilion,' she finally managed to reply.

'Locked in? What the fuck?'

'It was horrible Joe. He did things...'

'Who did?' Who did what? Don't worry. I'm on my way.'

'I love you,' she cried. 'I can't explain... Not yet...'

'I love you too,' he puffed, sprinting now. 'Don't worry. I'll be there in a minute. Don't worry.'

★   ★   ★

Alan and Mary Bunton never argued. Instead, she wept and he walked the dog.

Tonight she was crying about the service; about having left their beautiful, dutiful daughter at Brother Raines' mercy – or rather the lack thereof.

'Oh ye of little faith. Remember: beauty is a duty,' Alan incanted at her with dead eyes as she railed at God down the U-bend and hurled her dinner at the traitorous deity. 'And don't take our Lord's name in vain.'

Mary tried to reply but was gagged by the next eruption of bile from the pit of her gutless stomach. Bunton turned his head from the sight, his nose from the smell, as his own Pavlovian bile rose to his throat.

'Better walk the dog,' he grunted. 'Daisy!! Here girl!! Walkies!!'

The fluffy grey bundle of puppy love bounded yapping and joyful from its basket, lead in mouth and bouncing like she was on springs. A gift from Brother Raines, the daft little mongrel bitch had already been 'Christened' – and the remainder of the litter, Pansy, Lily and Daff, had been handed out among the flock.

'Thought I'd let you have Daisy,' Raines had joked, placing the mewling little pup in Bunton's arms. 'She'd only run away from me. You can't have two Lilys in the house can you! And anyway, Lily's mine now!'

Closing the front door of the terraced Georgian 'cottage' that cowered under the thundering flyover, Bunton stepped into the pool of orange sodium streetlight just as it changed shifts with the sunken sun. Lily darted into the faecal-stinking cleft between the end of the terrace and the Clutch, Brake and Tyre Centre at the arse end of town and cursorily pissed.

'Come on,' Bunton growled, yanking her away mid-flow and striking out onto the hedge and dogshit-trimmed footpath that ramped sharply up over the industrial estate, across the bypass and then meandered meekly down into the twinkling trees and shrubbery of *avenue* and *cul de sac* land, where the *faux* Dickensian street lights glinted like jewels through immaculately manicured trees. Here and there, now and then, another respectable dog walker nodded and *good eveninged,* but for the most part the neat streets were hushed, the gentle lamplight interrupted only by patches of unthreatening darkness and the homely blue flicker of televisions like fires in hearths. Here the detached houses were smart – but too tarted up for Bunton's taste. A couple of hundred yards further, he crossed the dinky little bridge over a pissy little condom-strewn stream where often young fornicating couples were to be observed for a while and then disturbed and sent scurrying back to their mummies' and daddies' ideal homes. Not tonight though. A couple of smoking, hooded, baseball-capped and shell-suited kids whose gender he found impossible to discern cut short their talk and hid their fags badly as he passed.

'Going to see the wolf man are ya,' came the donkey-bray snicker of a half-broken voice. Bunton ignored it, silently cursing Raines' nasty habit of leaving the dogs alone in the house to piss and shit and howl the place down every time he went away for a few days on one of his walking expeditions or the route marches that passed for family holidays.

And when he looked furtively back, he caught sight of the adolescent rabble slipping into the bushes and tutted to himself in disgust. Daisy whined, pleading to follow them. A lupine howl from the undergrowth was for a moment chilling, before a squall of childish giggles ruined the effect. Bunton half-turned towards its source. Then, with a more urgent mission on his mind, he tugged at Daisy's lead and dragged the dog along determinedly. The footpath cut through the woods where lovers did their loving and opened out onto an older street; an arc of cottages cut off and left behind like an oxbow lake from the elegant new developments deposited by the incessant flow of modernity and affluence, whose cess and effluence was represented by those precociously sexual brats. Nevertheless, for Bunton, Mimram Crescent retained a quiet dignity and a dilapidated elegance that the upstart intruders could never match. Down at heel, certainly, these houses were not status symbols – nor did they bear the satellite dish badges of the great Godless unwashed like the sullen council estates' square-eyed and soulless boxes. No televisual flame flickered at these windows – instead real blazing fire reached from its hearth through misty leaded lights to welcome him to the Raines household.

★   ★   ★

Raines must have heard the rattle and grate of the rickety gate opening because the front door opened in perfect synch like it was tied to it on a rope. It was almost as if he'd been watching out for his arrival.

'Brother Bunton! What a nice surprise. And hello Daisy dog! Come back to see Granddad have you!' came Raines' hearty welcome. 'Come in, come in! Glass of stout?'

Bunton left Daisy to dive into a yapping rough and tumble reunion with her yelping siblings and followed him into the humidly hot living room, disguising his distaste as his host poured them both a too-warm

Guinness. Lit only by a dim standard lamp and the embers' glow, the place smelled like an Oxfam shop with a delicate top note of damp dog. As he'd expected, Raines didn't look at all like a sixty-five-year-old man who'd just ruthlessly rogered a helpless fourteen-year-old girl - but then he never did.

For a painful instant, Bunton's unruly subconscious conjured up an all too graphic image of Raines's sagging frame lowering itself onto the slight, frightened, prone and trembling form of his virgin daughter. With a visible shake of the head he dismissed it. This pain - and hers - was the price he had to pay. One must suffer to earn one's reward – on Earth as it is in Heaven. What form that would take after passing through the pearly gates he had no idea – but unlike those Muslim martyrs who manned the barricades so vocally he knew that he didn't have to die to get the benefit of a supply of supple and compliant virgins. Having sacrificed his precious little girl, it would be his turn soon to deflower another Lily, Daisy or Rose. But would it? This so called boyfriend; this Joe, whoever he was, might already have defiled Lily, robbed Raines's ritual of its essential purity. The imagined grey porridgey form of the naked Raines with its pigskin-white bristles morphed in his mind into a wiry, hard-wired and lithe male body that was, by contrast, almost hairless with only the early sproutings of pubic hair. A hot flash of anger; then a sizzle as the flames consumed the image as he projected this Joe's vile nakedness onto the fire in the grate, sending it to burn in Hell.

'Erich, about tonight...'

Raines put a reassuring hand on his shoulder as they both sank into slightly soggy armchairs and gazed at the fire.

'It's natural to feel confused brother. You've made a great sacrifice tonight and the Lord appreciates that. And so do I.'

'Well, I do feel confused... I mean there is some pain. Not that I...'

'I know, Alan, believe me I do – but you will come to terms with it and so will Lily.'

'I'm sure you're right. Is she? I mean, was she?'

'Was she all right? Yes of course. As I explained, I had to leave her there in the darkness to meditate on the sin that she has taken upon herself. It's hard, I know – but that darkness symbolises the wilderness and by the time the cleansing sun rises she will understand that she has simply taken back the evil temptation that all women since Eve have visited upon good men. And when she is reconciled to this, she will be redeemed.'

'I understand all that Erich but... Well, do you know this boy?'

He pulled out a piece of paper on which he had written all the names and numbers in Lily's mobile phone's memory before purging it. One name was circled, ringed in red and underlined. The Biro had penetrated the paper, leaving a red-edged rip like a knife wound. He handed it to Raines.

'Joe who?'

Bunton shrugged.

'I thought *you* might know. It's just that I'm worried that tonight's ceremony has been spoilt...'

'Spoilt?'

'Lily claims she has a boyfriend,' Bunton murmured.

'Boyfriend – rubbish,' Raines spat. 'She's only fourteen!'

'That's what I said, but she was adamant. Says she loves him – that he loves her.'

'At that age? They don't know what love is!'

'That's what I told her but...'

'You're saying Lily might have been... *Sullied?*' Raines's face clouded.

'Well I don't know...'

The clouds gave up their thunder.

'You don't know!' Raines roared, jumping from his chair and facing the fire like it was an altar. 'You don't know! You're her father for God's sake – it's your job to preserve her innocence at all costs; to protect her from dirty little boys!'

Bunton shrank into his armchair.

'But I didn't know – I *don't* know, I just...'

Raines turned back from the fire, red and fuming like his face had caught alight.

'Well you should bloody know! Your little whore could be diseased – *I* could be diseased!"

'That's why I felt I had to come and tell you,' Bunton whimpered. 'I'm sorry – but, it's quite possible they haven't, you know...'

'In this vile day and age – you must be joking. She's probably been fucked by half the school the filthy little slut!' Raines raged.

Bunton had never heard him say *fuck* before. He'd seen those clouds before – but this thunder and lightning; this fire and brimstone, he'd never witnessed outside of Raines's cricket pavilion 'church'. He cowered, waiting for the storm to pass. And it did, as quickly as it came.

'I'm sorry Brother Bunton. Sin makes me so angry I can't control myself sometimes. Please forgive me,' Raines muttered, kneeling in front of him and taking both Bunton's hands in his.

'So what do we do now?' Bunton whispered though a watery smile.

'We have to find this Joe and get the truth. The implications are quite devastating – potentially.'

'How do you mean exactly?'

'What if Lily's pregnant?'

Bunton winced at the suggestion, then turned it into a shrug.

'The child will join all your other issue as part of the flock - what is it, twenty-three of them now? - in your image and hence in the image of the maker.'

'You miss my point Alan.'

Raines's fire had died down to the chummy warmth of his initial welcome.

'If – and of course it's a big if – your lovely daughter is with child, it will be yet another blessing on our congregation, and one for which you will be richly rewarded. *But only if the child is mine!*'

The words whistled through the tiniest gap between his clamped teeth.

'Oh damn,' Bunton mouthed.

'Damn indeed. If this Joe has defiled your little flower and she bears his child, our precious little Garden of Eden will be poisoned by the fruit of one bad seed. And I'll be damned if I'll let that happen.'

Bunton sat, Raines kneeled, in silence for minutes until finally he released Bunton's hands but not his eyes. His gaze still fixed on his trapped pupils like he was pushing information in.

'I've got to find this boy and sort it? That's what you want isn't it?' Bunton ventured.

Raines nodded, handing back the piece of paper and shoving the ancient grey dial telephone towards him.

'Call him.'

'Now?'

'Now.'

Bunton dialled slowly, unaccustomed to the click, click, whirr of the ratcheted old machine.

YO. THIS IS JOE. SPEAK ON THE BEEP chirped a reedy brittle voice about to break.

'Answering machine. Probably in bed – it's after twelve.

'Yes – probably busy defiling some other young girl. Anyway, it's called voicemail. Doesn't mean the phone's off. Probably talking to some slut,' Raines announced, asserting his superior knowledge of the vices of the young.

'What if he'd answered?' Bunton ventured.

'You'd have muttered something ineffectual as usual and I'd have taken charge, I imagine,' Raines snapped.

'Yes. All right but… What would you have said?'

'Well I wasn't going to ask if he'd copulated with Lily Bunton if that's what you mean! No, I'd have said I was a friend of Lily's family and that she'd asked me to call him because she'd been taken ill – or something along those lines.'

Bunton looked baffled.

'To get him to come and meet us you fool! Then we could get the truth out of the little bastard!'

Now Bunton looked worried. Raines faced the fire, leaned on the mantelpiece and gazed into the flames. After what seemed likes ages, he looked over his shoulder at Bunton and, like Poirot announcing the murderer's identity to the gathered suspects, he said,

'Much quicker and cleaner to get it from the horse's mouth.'

Bafflement was getting to be a habit for Bunton.

'Lily!' Raines barked. 'Lily will tell us who he is and where he lives.'

★   ★   ★

Heart fluttering in anticipation, Lily crouched in the darkest part of the room. Five minutes at the most it would take Joe to run from the tunnel, through the cemetery, cut through the woods and across the sports field to save her. Suddenly she heard the scrape and clunk of a key in the lock. *He's such a good runner,* she smiled to herself, leaping to her feet and bounding to the door in a single movement.

'J...' his name died in her throat with her hope as the door swung open to reveal not her knight in shining armour but Raines, smiling at her with pitiless piety as he hit the light switch. Lily shrank back and shrivelled, huddling in the remotest corner as if withering under the fluorescent strip lights as they flickered into life, driving back the darkness and leaving nowhere for her to hide. The oily preacher stepped towards her, hands open and outstretched in a horrid Christ parody and only then did Lily notice the hesitant figure hovering in the doorway.

'Dad!' she bleated helplessly.

'Hello Lily,' Bunton breathed, looking to his mentor for guidance. 'Brother Raines needs to talk with you.'

At this, Raines smiled, his grey oleaginous pallor going green in the unforgiving light.

'I hope you weren't about to take the name of Our Lord in vain

188

young lady,' he smirked.

Lily blinked uncomprehendingly at her tormentor.

'Or was "Joe" the name on the tip of your sinful little tongue? Yes — I see from your expression that it was the latter. In fact it's about your little "boyfriend" that we've come to see you. Talk to your daughter, Alan.'

Lily's father stepped tentatively from his master's shadow.

'Now then, Love, there's nothing to be frightened of...'

A great wobbling sob turned to a scream in Lily's heaving chest as she jumped to her feet and, forgetting to hide her nakedness, let the scarlet robe flop to the floor.

'Nothing to be frightened of!! Nothing? That's what you told me before this evil fucker...' she blurted.

A coarse, spade-sized hand connected with her face and she connected once again with the slightly less coarse floorboards. Holding a hand to her thrumming cheek, she glared defiantly up into Raines's face. He didn't even try now to disguise his lecherous appraisal of her elfin vulnerability. Her father turned away, leaned heavily on the windowsill and gazed out across the sports field as if he'd seen something of great interest.

'That's what you told me,' Lily persisted coldly and quietly, 'before you offered me up as a sacrifice.'

Raines stepped forward menacingly. Bunton swivelled and put a hand on his shoulder.

'Erich, please...'

Raines relented and stepped back. Bunton squatted next to his daughter.

'You're just too young to understand Lily — that beauty is a duty,' he murmured.

'Duty!' she spat back. 'What the fuck would either of you know about that?'

Her father reeled back as if she'd punched him.

'Lily — young ladies don't use that word.'

'Yeah? And they also don't say CUNT! And that's what you both are. CUNTS. CUNTS, CUNTS, CUNTS!'

Bunton sighed, bent and picked up the red robe.

'Cover yourself, there's a good girl.'

As Lily took the despised scrap of nylon – a man-made garment for a man-made misery – Raines struck the swaggering Jimmy Swaggart pose he always assumed at the onset of his hellfire and brimstone sermons. If it was calculated to scare her, it did the trick. As he bent towards her, and turned his head to her father for approval, she could see where his uneven DIY short back and sides left greasy grey bristles clumped like spots of mould around the clutch of warts and moles that nestled behind one ear. She shuddered half in fear, half in revulsion. *This THING has been inside me.*

'Now then young lady,' he said more unctuously than she'd have thought possible. 'You should consider yourself lucky...'

Lily laughed without humour.

'Yes you can laugh. But that's the Devil laughing. You were left here to meditate in complete isolation – a little time in the wilderness to consider your sins and repent.'

She spat. Literally this time. Raines didn't react – not at first. He let the foamy rheum-free saliva trickle down his grey pockmarked cheek. Then he slapped her. Hard. The blow knocked her to the floor, her mobile phone flying from her hand and clattering across the boards. Bunton, in spite of himself, jumped up.

'Now, Erich, please. You can't...' he began.

'Shut it Alan,' Raines grated under lustfully heaving breath, then to Bunton, 'Thought you said you'd confiscated her phone!'

'I did,' replied a baffled Bunton.

'Well what the hell is this then?' demanded Raines, picking up the phone, now in bits.

'How did you get your phone back Lily?' Bunton probed, hoping to spare her Raines's infinitely more aggressive interrogatory style. But Lily just glared defiantly at them both.

Cheek stinging, head humming fit to burst, she splayed her arms and levered herself back to sitting position. Levelling her dark eyes on Raines's pink-edged and rheumy sockets, she held his gaze, swivelling her glare as she slowly, deliberately, turned away the smarting cheek, now flushed red like a ripe peach, and presented him with the other.

Raines missed the point. As he'd always missed the point. And missed the chance of another assault.

'You have a lot to learn,' he preached to Lily's well-turned cheek. 'When I said you were lucky, I simply meant that your father and I are here to give you a chance to cut short your time in the wilderness.'

Lily stared blankly at the floor. Anything to avoid looking at this monster.

'By rights, you should have been sequestrated for forty hours — each representing a day and night in our Lord's time. But...' he reached out and took Lily by the chin, her resistance failing against his hand's clammy but vice-like grip, 'your father and I would like you to tell us about this so-called boyfriend of yours; this boy you've told your dad you're so in love with.'

Hearing this, Alan Bunton appeared at Raines's side.

'Just answer a few questions about this lad, love, and it'll all be over, there's a good girl,' he daddied gently.

Lily looked down at the red rag she was clutching between her nakedness and all this bull and dropped it. The two men's mouths gaped; one lecherous and the other confused.

'JOE!!' she screamed.

'We know his name,' Raines started. But then he followed her gaze. In the doorway was a horror-struck kid in black leather jacket and ripped up jeans.

'JOE!' Lily shouted again, 'RUN!!!'

Frozen for a flash in the door frame, Joe mouthed 'Lily, what...?'

Then the two men turned as one on the boy — but he held Lily's eyes in his. She nodded. *You've got to run,* she was clearly saying. *So you can save me.*

So Joe ran. And he was a lot better at running than his would-be captors, who gave up the chase and turned back before they reached the first goalposts. Gasping for air like fish out of water they stumbled back into the pavilion just in time to stop Lily getting out of the door.

'No you don't!' Raines huffed as he caught her unnecessarily around the crotch area.

'Erich, please...' Bunton protested, not wanting actually to witness what he'd already acquiesced to.

Raines withdrew his raptor hand way too slowly from between Lily's legs; so slowly she felt she was being raped again. Then he sniffed its leading edge with a voluptuousness that made Bunton gag.

'Where's he gone you little slut?' Raines barked at the trembling waif. Lily clamped her eyes shut, squeezing out tears through quivering lashes as she shook her head determinedly.

'You might as well tell us. You're going to in the end,' Raines persisted.

'Erich, please,' Bunton pleaded once more. It was one thing sacrificing his daughter to an unseen ritual hidden behind the closed doors of Raines's inner sanctum – quite another to be faced with what he'd done. 'A word?'

Raines nodded and the two men stepped outside the door, Raines holding it firmly shut with a hand behind his back as they conferred.

'Look Erich, why don't we lock her in there and pretend to walk away. Either the lad will come back for her – he must be hiding out there somewhere – or she'll phone him and we'll hear. Or we can let them text one another and come back and read what they've had to say!'

'Good thinking brother,' Raines enthused, once more assuming his kindly lay preacher persona. 'But I can do better!' he went on distractedly as he fumbled with two mobile phones, his fat unwieldy fingers prodding and tugging at the delicate SIM housings.

They stepped inside. Bunton took off his anorak.

'I'm sorry my love but if you're not going to tell Brother Raines what he needs to know, you'll just have to sit out your forty hours in here.'

As Raines scuffed around in the shadows, Lily turned her back on her father, hugging herself and shivering.

'Take this.' Bunton edged towards her and, maintaining as much distance as his arms' length would allow, draped the coat over her delicate shoulders. 'That'll keep you nice and warm.'

She shrugged.

'Don't worry. I know it's a bit scary and cold but we'll be back for you before you know it...'

'Come *on,*' Raines urged impatiently, holding the door ajar.

★   ★   ★

In the scrubby bushes by the most distant of the goalposts, Joe watched the two men leave the pavilion and crawled deeper into the undergrowth as they strolled with stunning nonchalance across the grass towards him.

In the ringing, deafening silence, Lily watched the two figures turn to silhouettes and fade into the light mist that haunted the cricket table. Then she remembered. *The phone!* After scrabbling blindly around the floor for several minutes she found it, its back cover and battery. But no SIM card. Finally her fingers brushed against the plastic sliver, wedged like a splinter into a crack between floorboards by the door, and fumbled it into place. The moment she snapped it into its slot and the back onto the handset, the room lit up again and Crazy Frog announced a message.

WAIT THERE. CALL SOON. JOE.

So she waited.

★   ★   ★

Joe's phone was on silent. It vibrated excitedly to announce Lily's text – couldn't have been anyone else at three in the morning. He froze. He held his breath, convinced his heartbeat was audible ten yards away. But no, Raines and Bunton walked on, still at a horribly leisurely pace until finally they disappeared through the gap in the hedge that led to the footpath.

He hit the message button.

WHERE ARE YOU? ARE YOU OK? THEY HAVE GONE. WHERE CAN I MEET YOU? LOVE LILY.

YES. OK. AT TUNNEL.

I FORGET HOW TO GET TO TUNNEL.

Joe chuckled. Girls – so crap at navigation. And she'd only been there a couple of days ago. Suddenly elated with the marijuana high that had been so suppressed by fear, he got up and began darting in and out of the bushes in a course parallel to the footpath to be sure he didn't cross the path of Raines and Bunton.

PATH TO CMTRY. THRU HOLE. TRN RGT UNDR LTTLE BRDGE. NK 3 TMS. XXX, he tapped in as he trotted along.

SEE YOU THERE. LOVE YOU. XXX, came the reply almost instantly.

With a quick glance around, Joe emerged from the thick copse next to the stream and slid down the muddy bank, ducking under the miniature bridge, padlock keys at the ready. Once inside the tunnel, he lit a couple of candles and sat on the cold, damp boards to wait for her.

Any minute now, he thought, suffused with relief and the anticipation of her Lilyness being safe and warm and near his skin again. His phoned vibrated in his pocket yet again.

W8NG. WHRE U? X

He stared at the words. *What's she on about?* Had she misunderstood? Had he? It buzzed again, rattling on the hollow hardboard.

J? SCRD! PLS CME BK.XX

And then he got it. This wasn't from Lily's phone. It was a number he didn't recognise – and that his phone didn't recognise. *Evil motherfuckers,* he breathed and jabbed a middle finger defiantly upwards at the world above the tunnel as he sat back to wait for his trembling, delicate Lily to arrive.

FUCK YOU, he typed and hit the green button like it was the face of the devious old bastard who was trying to get one over on him. Three tentative taps on the door turned his sneer to a tender smile as he shimmied over to slide across the inner bolts. The door rattled.

'Lily!! Thank God! Hang on darling. Just a sec,' he whispered at the door as he struggled with the four hefty and rusty bolts and his phone lit up with another message. 'You won't believe what your....'

★   ★   ★

Lily's almost knee-jerk smile in response to Crazy Frog's goofy grin twisted and quivered into an uncomprehending grimace as her knight's shining armour tarnished. *Fuck you? Fuck you? How can you say that? How can you? Now — when I really need you. You're just like them. I hate you I hate you... I...*

I H8 U, she turned thoughts into text with synaptic immediacy, tears dropping on the keypad as she hit the button that sent her hate back to the hateful little shit. A strange sort of calm came over her as the last drop of hope drained away. Betrayed by Dad, then Mum, and now Joe. She had no one. No hope. Nothing.

★   ★   ★

'Hello — young Joe, I presume,' came a voice that was about as unLilylike as it was possible for a voice to be. Its warm, yet at the same time stentorian, tones were chillingly familiar, the warmth derived from hellfire presumably.

'Oh shit,' Joe muttered, picking up his phone and hitting the message button.

I H8 U.

Not Lily's number. But they were Lily's words all right. Suddenly it was clear. She never spelled whole words in texts. Nor did he.

Oh shit oh shit oh shit oh shit.

'You fucking cunts!' he blurted at the interlopers, backing away on his knees as the two burly forms shouldered in through the tiny door like greying grizzly bears.

'If you're going to use that kind of language I'm pleased to find you on your knees. Because that's just as it should be,' Raines treacled.

'What have you done to Lily?' Joe screeched, instantly pissed off that his roar had shrunk to a shriek in his throat.

'We might ask you the same question,' Raines replied with the kind of unction you could drown in. 'Have you met Lily's father?'

'Hello Joe,' came Bunton's voice, threatening yet not without a quiver.

'What have you done?' Joe repeated, summoning courage from somewhere deep inside him as Bunton's face loomed closer, the candlelight caricaturing the subtle Lilyness in his face — beautiful on her; ugly on him - that confirmed he really was her dad. Folds of flab camouflaged but didn't quite hide Lily's pointy chin and cheekbones — elfin on her; weak on him. The two bears kept coming. Joe shrank back against the wall; against the tattily ancient candlelit shrine to Danny the Drunk.

'How appropriate,' Raines commented, 'a shrine by candlelight dedicated to the kind of scum that *we're* dedicated to eradicating!'

A spade–like, grey–haired and veined hand reached past Joe's ear and plucked Danny's faded and wrinkled photo from its nook, waved it before Joe's eyes and committed it to the candle's flame. Joe lunged, dropping his phone in the attempt to save Danny's memory — and failed. Raines's other hand seized his wrist and held it locked without evident effort, forcing Joe to watch the photo crackle, burn and shrivel. As the flakes floated away from the flame like moths in reverse and fluttered down like black confetti, Raines picked up Joe's phone and sneered.

'Oh dear, oh dear. Little Lily hates you! Wonder how that happened!'

'You switched the SIM cards. You bast...'

Raines's spade hand was a sledgehammer by the time it connected with Joe's nose. The tiny explosion of blood looked black in the dim light. But all Joe saw was red as his eyelids flickered down and everything faded to a much blacker black, then swam dizzily back.

'Take it easy Erich, for Christ's sake,' Bunton ventured. 'You've knocked him out.'

'No he hasn't,' groaned a dazed but unconfused and defiant Joe.

Raines turned and bared his Stonehenge teeth in a prehistoric smile.

'See, Alan. Made of strong stuff this boy. Aren't you young Joe!'

A scowl was the best Joe could do, for the moment anyway.

Bunton started to say something – but his leader silenced him with a raised eyebrow; the same one that made his congregations quiver in awe. It still worked on Bunton, away from the 'church', down in the dark and damp of the tunnel.

'Very impressive job you've done here my boy. Solid locks at either end. Professional brickwork – and all so cleverly camouflaged. Not sure even I could have done better!'

'Thanks very much,' Joe grated, failing to convey even a fraction of the bitterness he felt.

'Almost worthy of what you've taken. Almost.'

Joe's baleful glare asked the question. Which Raines answered.

'You've taken what you should not have: the innocence of Lily Bunton.'

'I haven't taken anything.'

Bunton's livid face thrust itself over Raines' shoulder.

'Yes you have you little fucker. You've been with my daughter!'

Joe stared blankly.

'What have you done to her?'

'What have *we* done? You little...'

Raines held Bunton back as he tried, ineffectually, to punch the boy.

'You see, Lily's dad is upset because you've interfered with his lovely little girl. If I weren't here to hold him back, the Lord knows what he might do.'

'Pretty much anything from what I've heard,' Joe replied with steel he didn't feel.

Again Raines stopped Bunton from hitting him with an easy raise of an authoritative hand.

'He's a father. His instinct and his right and his God-given duty is to protect his daughter's innocence. Do you not see that?'

'I'm beginning to see something – but it ain't that,' Joe laughed bitterly.

'And by that you mean?'

'I think I see why Lily's always been so... frightened. And I can't say I blame her.'

'We don't want to hurt you....'

'But you just thought you would for a laugh?' Joe spat.

'I'm being patient with you because you're only a boy but the fact of the matter is it seems you have violated my brother's child. Will you admit to that?'

'*I've* violated her!'

'Yes. You.'

'Pot fucking kettle.'

'Yes or no?'

'No. I wouldn't violate anyone.'

24

Despair Has its Uses

Despair has its uses, Lily found. While sustained by the hope that Joe would come rushing to her rescue, the obvious hadn't crossed her mind. Sensible, sensitive middle class teenage girls don't generally smash things. So locked locks and painted shut windows told Lily she was a prisoner – and that her only hope was of rescue. She still hadn't put on that red rag. And her father's anorak, though warm, just made her shiver by wrapping her in a cloud of his stale sweat, deodorant-free signature scent. So she'd thrown it across the room – as far from her as it could be.

Now she knew she was utterly alone. Naked, violated, cold and alone. Betrayed by her father, then her mother and then, unbearably, by the boy of her dreams who'd turned into a nightmare. Just like everyone else she ever thought she could love and trust. She could just curl up and die. So cold now, she felt she would. In the end. So why not hurry things along?

When you're slightly short of five foot, a changing room coat hanger designed for burly rugby players is high enough to be hanged from. She looked up at it. Then down at her hands, still wringing the despised scarlet scrap of nylon. It looked like a blood-red rope - not that its redness penetrated the gloom. She just knew it was red. And when her dad and his hero found her slack dead carcass, they'd know exactly why she'd died. They'd know it was because of them. That they'd killed her. Tying the ends together with Girl Guide prowess and determination, she slung the loop over the hook. Funny – she'd stopped crying now.

Decided on death, she had no use for despair. That was for people who still clung to the hope of hope. Coldly, shivering from the cold in fact, she sized up the end of her short life. *I hope I can haunt them. Hope I can be a ghost. Even if there's no such thing as afterlife; if there's nothing, I'll haunt them. Even if I don't know it. I'll haunt them. They'll wake up in the night sweating and screaming and everyone will know that they killed Lily Bunton.* Now she even allowed herself a smile. The mangled dress wasn't long enough to tie a proper noose – but if she stood on the bench with it round her neck and jumped...

*   *   *

'Hi Jimmy baby,' I chirped, sat happily at the Babington bar, 'Wassup?'

'What are you doing to me,' he groaned down the phone.

'What d'you mean?' I enquired, knowing exactly what his problem was.

'You know exactly what my problem is! All these bleeps and buzzes – what's that all about? Sounds like an acid house mix circa '87!'

'They're mobile phone tones Jimmy.'

'Yeah well I worked that out – but why for fuck's sake?'

'They're text bleeps. The sound of the language being whittled down bleep by bleep. That's why I'm calling it the 'Newspeak' mix – if you haven't got the words to say it, you haven't a way to think it. Not "doublethink" – *unthink!*' I enthused.

'You sure you're not taking this Orwell thing a bit far?' he griped.

'No. I mean yes. Anyway, I've made a slight change to the album title that you might want to run past our benefactors.'

'Oh Christ – what?'

'Just a simple shift from the plural to the singular: *Gift Horse* instead of *Gift Horses* is all,' I said breezily.

'Oh all right then,' Jimmy replied, sounding relieved. 'Thought

200

we were about to go through the same shitstorm as we had when you insisted on *Shit and Corruption…*'

'They called it Hit and Corruption in the States,' I pointed out.

'You hardly need remind me,' he groaned. 'OK. *Gift Horse* it is.'

I'd tell him about the precise spelling later – when it was too late to change it: *Gift Whores.*

★   ★   ★

'So you're not going to tell us your surname?' Raines Gestapoed.

Joe shook his head, its centripetal effect tipping a telltale tear out of the corner of a squeezed-shut eye.

'Or where you live, I presume,' Bunton chipped in.

Again, the boy shook his head, eyes shut tight as if contact with theirs would let them steal his soul.

'You cocky little…' Bunton started, only to have his threat waived by Raines's airy wave of a hand.

'Doesn't matter young man. I'm sure you're easily findable. All you're achieving by refusing to co-operate is that you're putting my Brother Alan here to a little trouble.'

Bunton looked baffled, just for a change.

'Come on Brother Bunton. We know his name, his approximate age, the town he lives in and where he goes to school. That should be enough to find him on the internet shouldn't it?'

'Well I suppose…' Bunton began, taken aback by the revelation that Raines was even aware of such things.

'Well let's do it. I assume you have the internet at your house?'

Bunton nodded.

'Off you go then. See what you can find and come straight back, there's a good chap.'

'Who do you think I am? Elvis fucking Presley? You're not gonna find anything about me on the web – I'm nobody,' Joe piped up.

'You sure about that son?' Raines smirked.

'I'm not your son.'

'No – but you're someone's. And we're going to find out whose. And I bet he's not married to your mother!'

'Very fun…'

A slap cut Joe short and smacked his head against the brickwork.

'Shut your mouth you little bastard,' Raines hissed, following the slap with a shove that sent Joe sprawling on his back and rifling his pockets a little too lingeringly.

'Aha – here we are!' he crowed, waving Joe's wallet in the air and ostentatiously taking out each card, photo and slip of scribbled paper one by one. 'Now we have your full name and address – and which video rental shop you frequent and... Ah yes, a library card, which means we can find out what books you read and, look Brother Bunton, how sweet! A photo of your little girl!'

Bunton took the cards and scraps of paper, slipped the picture of Lily into his back pocket, ducked out of the hatch and disappeared.

★   ★   ★

The trouble with tacky man-made fibres is that they tend to stretch. So when Lily jumped off that bench like she was diving off the highest board at the local pool, eyes shut and stick rigid, all she got was a crick in the neck. The shortest bungee jump in history.

Understandably pissed off to find herself alive, Lily lashed out – for the first time in her fourteen years. And her delicate fist smashed straight through one of the windows. No pane, no gain. No pain, actually, because she was so numbed by the cold and the assumption of death. There was blood though. And that's what reminded her she was alive and should be and would be. Lily turned into Lara Croft and kicked and kicked and kicked at the glass panels in the door. All of them. Not just the one that would give her access to the outside door handle. All of them.

And, stepping through a moonlit shimmer of glass shards, oblivious like a firewalker to the cuts and blood and pain, she reached through, released the catch and walked naked across the flat expanse of grass.

★   ★   ★

'Mary?' Bunton called under his breath as he eased open the front door. *Asleep. Thank God for that,* he thought, relieved to have been spared an interrogation, more histrionics and, no doubt, weeping. The PC flickered into life at the touch of the mouse – left on by Lily as usual despite his incessant lectures about wasting electricity – and, referring to the details on the library card, he tapped in Joe's name. Then, anticipating a long session of fruitless Googling, he tiptoed into the kitchen and made a coffee, on which he almost choked when he saw the hundreds of results the search engine had dredged up, mostly links to local and national newspapers', magazines', television and radio programmes' websites.

ORPHAN ON THE RUN
FEARS FOR MISSING BOY
FOSTER MUM WEEPS FOR RUNAWAY BOY
MUM IN TRAGIC TV APPEAL

He clicked a couple of links at random – and there was no doubt they were referring to the same Joe. Dating back to three years before, the grainy newspaper photos showed a boy – not the sulky adolescent they'd made captive. Instead of the unruly black curls, he sported a neat crew cut - but there were the same dark, defiant eyes that seemed to see more than a young boy ought to. The initial reports of his disappearance showed a too-tidy boy posed stiffly against a screen – obviously an official school portrait. Later pieces went with a dark monochrome mug shot – one taken in a police station after the boy's arrest for some petty offence. And that was the image that had stuck, hinting as it did at some darker truth lurking under the human-interest story. The puffy dark crescents underlining the still darker eyes suggested tears and bruises. Like that endlessly reprinted and now iconic shot of Myra Hindley, that photo condemned its subject more completely and effectively than any evidence or judgement; it suggested that somehow, sometime, the orphan boy had deserved whatever fate had brought him.

Bunton clicked a few pages on. The headlines' tone grew harsher with every batch of ten or so results. Crocodile tears had turned to teeth, bared in anger when the authorities, the police and the papers discovered that far from having been abducted by some predatory paedophile, he'd simply done a runner.

STRANGE WAIF DUPES POLICE
COPS CAUGHT NAPPING BY 'KIDNAPPED' KID
BAD PENNY TURNS UP AT LAST

The little bastard had made fools of them all. And he'd had the cheek to simply turn up out of the blue as if nothing had happened. No explanations. No excuses. Not even any tears of remorse. Just those dark defiant eyes with their unflinching, unapologetic stare.

'Evil little sod,' Bunton muttered to himself, grimace turning to a grin as he copied and pasted page after page of text into a Word document and clicked on the printer icon. Brother Raines was going to be very pleased indeed. So surely he wouldn't object to a father checking on his daughter – whom, he was sure, would now have had time to reflect on her duty and accept her fate with the equanimity he'd instilled in her mother. It couldn't hurt to set her free now, could it? he reasoned.

Gathering up the sheaf of paper from the printer tray and shoving it into a carrier bag, he swiped another anorak from its hook by the door, ignoring the dog's pleas and marched purposefully back to the footpath and then through the copse to the sports field. The ancient planks creaked as he set foot on the pavilion's terrace – but the creaks became crunches underfoot. Bunton yelped as a shard of glass penetrated his Hush Puppy and the ball of his right foot. Hopping to a bench he slumped down and scrabbled his laces undone, wincing as he pulled off the shoe and blood bloomed on one white sock. The French window doors hung open, black staring squares where their panes had been.

'Shit,' Bunton muttered, scanning the field.

'Shit!' he repeated a lot more fervently when he spotted a slight figure darting from the cover of the scrub to disappear behind a slender tree like a dryad – or a ghost. He paused. Silently, the sylph slid and flitted through the air to the next pool of shadow, then the next and the next. From this distance, Lily's timorousness came across flighty. Flirty. Dirty.

'Slut!' he muttered, realising she was naked.

Stepping gingerly over the broken glass, he advanced cautiously into the pavilion and picked up his anorak from the floor where Lily had shed it like dead skin. Clicking on his key ring torch, he swept the room with light, the beam halting on a slash of red that hung like a carcass on a hook. Evidently she'd cast off the clothing they'd brought for her modesty and brazenly sauntered off cross-country in search of her dirty little paramour. So much for Brother Raines's forty hours in the wilderness. So much for her meditation in solitude; so much for her acceptance of her duty and her fate; so much for chastity.

The dryad darted down the arboreal tube that more usually siphoned schoolboys out onto the footpath and the pissy little stream. Now she was out of sight, Bunton trotted after her. He didn't trouble to run exactly. After all, he knew where she was going – and her zigzagging from tree to tree, cover to cover, necessitated by her nudity, meant he'd have no problem catching up. Sure enough, by the time he reached the far corner of the field and peered down into the wooded darkness, she was still hesitating. Crouching, arms folded over her hints of breasts, she scurried rabbit-like into a tiny clearing and tore off a couple of ferns. Covering herself with the frilled fronds, she tiptoed tentatively forth in an elfin or Eve-like parody of the dance of the seven veils. Bunton's lips curled in disgust as he eased forward to get a better look at this travesty.

A twig cracked under his not-so-Hushed Puppy. Lily froze mid-step and turned to face him, for a moment letting the ferns drop to reveal to him a Lily more fully blossomed after her deflowering than he had imagined. And the frisson he felt was her fault.

'Cover yourself girl!' he boomed with what he imagined was Raines-esque authority.

'Dad?' she ventured, quailingly.

Bunton broke cover and yomped down the steep slope, narrowly avoiding cannoning into her, and halted his momentum by harnessing the orbit of a tree trunk.

'You're coming with me,' he wheezed, seizing her arm and frogmarching her off towards the tunnel.

★   ★   ★

'Now then young man,' Raines headmastered. 'As I'm sure you can understand, you present me with a bit of a problem.'

Joe nodded but raised a querulous eyebrow.

'The problem is twofold in fact,' Raines continued evenly. 'Firstly, it has come to my notice that you have interfered with young Lily. You may even have impregnated her. Either way you have tainted her and rendered meaningless the sacrifice of her purity to my church.'

'Bollocks!' Joe muttered in disgust.

'They certainly had a lot to do with it,' Raines went on, now apparently impervious to the boy's defiance. 'What's more disturbing to me and my brethren is the unfortunate fact that you have witnessed the most sacred and secret ceremony of our church – and that you certainly can't be trusted not to divulge that secret.'

'Well you've got that bit right.'

'So you see I can't possibly let you go. The sanctity of our church is at stake.'

'So you're going to keep me prisoner here forever are you?'

'No. Obviously that's not possible...'

Raines left the implication hanging.

'So you'll let me go?' Joe asked finally, afraid to ask about the alternative.

'That is an option you could choose. Provided you agree to join our church and commit yourself to us fully and wholeheartedly.'

Joe tried to feign interest but the curl of his lip gave him away.

'Wholeheartedly, I said,' Raines reiterated, reaching out a hand and tugging with distaste at an unruly hank of Joe's hair. 'And that means getting rid of this mop for a start!'

'But surely that would be a sin!' the lad Johnny Rottened.

Raines guffawed.

'A sin? A sin? I hardly think so. Slovenliness is a sin and this...' he tweaked the lapel of Joe's leather biker jacket, 'pagan finery is exactly the sort of thing that the Devil wants you to wear.'

'Because he's got all the best music you mean?' Joe sniped.

'In the opinion of the godless perhaps,' Raines allowed.

'So if I have my hair cut like yours I'll be accepted into your church and you'll let me go?'

'A haircut would be a good start, yes.'

'Even though it's an abomination?'

'Wearing your hair like a savage is an abomination in the eyes of the Lord, yes.'

'But what about the Bible?'

'Don't you question me about the Bible, laddie,' Raines snapped.

'I'm sorry. I must have got it wrong. I wear my hair long because I thought Leviticus 19:27[1] expressly forbade trimming of hair. The punishment is death. I mean, if you say I must have it cut then I must but as long as I'm not going to die a horrible death...'

Raines didn't reply. So Joe pressed his advantage.

---

1. Leviticus 19:27: 'Ye shall not round the corners of your heads, neither shalt thou mar the corners of thy beard.'

'I've obviously misunderstood Leviticus 19:19[2], because I wear leather and denim to avoid fabric that mixes different kinds of thread – and you seem to be wearing a shirt made of a polyester/cotton mix, which means by rights, that the whole town should have teamed up and stoned you to death. I mean I'm stoned right now, but I don't think it's going to kill me. That's your job presumably,' Joe giggled, the lingering effects of the grass tickling him into a spate of hilarity at odds with how he really felt.

'Mind you, working on the Sabbath's apparently punishable by death,' he rambled, 'so maybe the town decided to leave the hard work to God! Well, I assume that since you rape young girls in your professional capacity as a full time religious nutter, that constitutes working on the Sabbath. Or did you make sure you fucked her before midnight just to be on the safe side?'

Joe girded himself, ready for the inevitable punch. But although Raines's giant hands clenched and unclenched like the iron jaws of two JCBs, smite him he did not.

'Precocious little bugger aren't you!' he growled.

'Absolutely not – Leviticus 18:22[3] specifically forbids...'

And lo the giant hand did smite him. And it didn't half hurt.

'Erich, you still there?'

Getting up from where he'd tumbled in the follow-through of his punch, Raines kicked Joe's splayed legs aside and crawled to the entrance. Silhouetted by a thin torch beam, flyaway hair fizzing in its light like a burning halo, a slight figure stooped to enter.

'Lily!' Joe blurted. 'You all right?'

Stupid question. As his eyes readjusted to the candlelight he could see she wasn't. How could she be? Her quivering lips parted to form his

---

2. Leviticus 19:19: 'Ye shall keep My statutes. Thou shalt not let thy cattle gender with a diverse kind; thou shalt not sow thy field with two kinds of seed; neither shall there come upon thee a garment of two kinds of stuff mingled together.'

3. Leviticus 18.22: 'Thou shalt not lie with mankind, as with womankind; it is abomination.'

name but the syllable became a sob before it got out and she flopped into his arms, only to be batted almost casually aside by Raines's hand.

'What's she doing here?' Raines demanded.

'She'd already got out, Erich – smashed the windows. I couldn't put her back in the pavilion...'

'Idiot,' Raines spat, holding out a hand for the papers his sidekick proffered in appeasement. As Joe and Lily poured wordless yearning into one another's eyes, he sat back on his heels and pored over them, each new headline eliciting grunts of interest as Bunton searched his face for approval like an adoring dog.

'Good boy!' Raines murmured with unusual warmth and tweaked Bunton's cheek.

And if Lily had looked ashen before, now she was positively green with nausea. Joe stuck two fingers down his throat - and miraculously the feigned gag got a laugh. A tiny, timid one, but a laugh nonetheless. Lily reached out a hand behind the preoccupied Rawling's back and reached Joe's. He took it and squeezed it gently, rhythmically, as if he were pumping hope back into her.

'Get your filthy hands off her,' Bunton snarled, bursting their bubble.

Joe held tight and glared.

'Oh yes – silly of me. She's the property of Mr Raines here now isn't she! How much did you get for her? Exodus 21:7[4] isn't it?'

Bunton lunged, missed by a mile and sprawled on the muddy floor. Then, recovering, he thrust his sad beagle eyes close to Joe's and opened his mouth to roar.

'You cheeky little...' it dribbled out in a whimper as he was interrupted by Raines, reading aloud from one of the sheets of paper.

'*...The whole town feels let down by this young delinquent's irresponsible behaviour. Not only has his selfish escapade brought near riots to our streets after this paper revealed the presence of a known paedophile in our midst – who*

---

4. Exodus 21:7: 'And if a man sells his daughter to be a maid-servant, she shall not go out as the men-servants do.'

was accused, as it turned out wrongly, of his abduction. He has also caused untold heartache and suffering to his family, friends, schoolteachers and the townspeople who gave up their free time to comb the countryside for him. I personally as head of this investigation, feel doubly let down, having appeared on countless television and radio appeals alongside the anguished carers from the Broadoak Children's Home. I feel that it is a great injustice that this tearaway is too young to be punished legally with the severity he deserves for the trouble and expense he has caused,' Raines quoted one Detective Inspector Masterson with relish. 'Well, well,' he went on, 'quite the little Robin Hood aren't you – or a hood of some sort!'

Joe glowered.

'Which makes you what? Sheriff of Nottingham? Friar Tuck? Try a Fuck?'

The barbs glanced off Raines's chainmail hide.

'I wonder where you disappeared to! Says here you never let on, never explained. No one ever got the truth out of you.'

Joe shrugged but held Raines's gaze.

'I have a feeling I know where you were hiding all that time.'

Joe flinched.

'Aha!' his interrogator crowed, 'I thought as much. You were holed up in here the whole time weren't you.'

'So what?'

'So, my little outlaw, no one knows about your little bolthole but the four of us here. If you were to do another vanishing act, no one in this town would be surprised. I doubt the police would even bother to list you as missing – especially now that you're sixteen. In fact, I wouldn't be surprised if they jumped to all sorts of conclusions – that you'd run off with the innocent daughter of my colleague Mr Bunton here to subject her to all manner of depravity!'

'And that's your job!' Joe hissed just as a backhander sent him reeling and his head landed in Lily's lap where it rested for a blissful instant before two pairs of hands clamped round his ankles and wrenched him away, head bumping across the coarse boards.

25

Bring It On

The new version of *Bring It On* was shit hot, though I say it myself. Back in the day – the start of the nineties - I never had the budget to use an orchestra. Even if I had, I'd have rejected the very idea as too old school, too prog rock. I did enjoy a brief flirtation with the sampling technology of the time, but a Fairlight computer cost about the same as my first house – over thirty grand – and a Synclavier wasn't a lot cheaper. Now, with more processing power on my Mac laptop than the priciest eighties Solid State Logic studio, I'd started with the bass and drum tracks from the original and tracked up a massive, epic masterpiece. Honestly.

I hadn't heard from Georgie since Cannes. Presumably the Cyclops with his big fuck-off yacht was what floated her boat. Not hard when you're as shallow as the gorgeous, Georgish Georgie. *Good luck to her,* I thought, insincerely and threw myself into my work. I hardly gave her a thought in all the four weeks I was installed in the buffered urban country life (*Soho in Somerset* the brochure said, and it was dead right). Apart from when I was drinking, obviously. Or when I'd had a bit of celebratory toot. So, about once an hour at the most. Georgie out of sight meant I was usually out of my mind if I'm honest. Especially since my loss appeared to be Raines's gain. The geek really inheriting the Earth, it seemed. That's what really rankled.

Anyway, in spite of, or maybe because of, all that, I really did work. Good work. Honestly.

Babington House has a cute little chapel in its grounds and I had a whale of a time roping in the local vicar and his choir. I got Jimmy to send my trusty sound engineer down with a shedload, or to be more accurate a vanload, of equipment and mike up all thirty of them. Ralph Pemberton, the vicar, was a joy to work with – about as far from the goofy stereotype of a country curate as you could get. Turned out he was in a band that supported Airstrip in Taunton in '84. *God Squad*, they were called. Not that I remembered. I think I did a good job of bullshitting though. Anyway, he was so chuffed to meet me – and to have a pint in the Babington bar surrounded by the coke-stoked Soho House crowd and to play snooker on the blasphemously red baize in the library – that he jumped at the chance to get his church choir on a real rock 'n' roll record. After God knows (I did ask Ralph to check with Him) how many rehearsal sessions to playback in the damp and draughty local village scout hut, he turned up for the live recording in the chapel wearing leather trousers, biker jacket and one clip-on earring. Bless him. So earnestly and devoutly in love with that whole rock myth. Slightly less so when he caught me chopping out a (not so) crafty line in the vestry – but I think I was forgiven. By the Lord's representative in Babington, if not by The Boss (by which I don't mean Bruce Springsteen).

I have to confess I found the whole experience surprisingly uplifting. The kids in the choir had never heard of me of course, but once informed (by me) about my monumental significance in Rock's Rich Tapestry, they treated with a degree of reverence that became embarrassing – but only when I was sober.

On the quiet, Doctor Who (the live sound engineer I've stuck with since day one and whose name comes from his refusal to be impressed by the rich and famous:

'Do you know who I am?'

'Nope.'

'I am INSERT NAME OF MAJOR ROCK STAR!'

'Who???')

made a covert video of the session. And the bastard set up a screening for all the hotel's guests in Babington's sumptuous little private cinema. In it, I'm throwing myself around in a half-arsed attempt at being the conductor and I'm visibly smug about the performance I'm eliciting from this motley bunch of kids and clueless amateurs. I'm also oblivious to the fact that Ralph's standing right behind me commanding the choral high ground – and that it's he, not me, from whom they're taking their cues. I look like a complete cock. I am one. I'm everything I ever despised. The washed-up rock dinosaur; the dippy dilettante who toys with classical forms because his ego says he's earned the right. Well, fuck it – we all had fun and the record sounds great and Ralph's faith has been renewed because this was a prayer answered.

In a funny way, it was like that for me too. *Liberating* is the closest word I can find for it. Although I was as usual giving in to utter self-indulgence, I stopped hating myself for it. Doctor Who blackmailed me with the video and I didn't really mind. I even gave him a pay rise. And then I bunged Ralph a hefty session fee, way beyond the call of Musicians' Union duty, which went to the local hospice. Saint Stone! Maybe Saint Winston sounds better?

Then one night, after a major all-day session at the Babington bar among a galaxy of stars and their satellites, the irresistibly Georgie-shaped black hole at the centre of this new happiness pulled me in. My mobile rang. Clocking the disapproving glare raid from all quarters (you're not allowed to have your mobile on) I scurried to the nearest exit, scrutinising the screen as I went. The number was withheld – or foreign. I nearly didn't answer. But then I did.

'Hallo?'

'Rich. It's me.'

'Georgie,' I said in a robotic monotone. 'What do you want?'

'To see you of course.' Her voice was faint. She was a long way away from me.

'Well since you're presumably swanning about on that fucking boat somewhere, you clearly can't,' I spat.

'What changed Rich? OK we had a row but…'

'But what?'

'I ended up on Bart's yacht yes. But you were supposed to be there.'

'You were s'posed to be in the hotel working on your fucking masterpiece.'

'I was – and they said…'

'You reciting your own dialogue now?'

'Stop it Rich. Listen to me.'

'Why would I?'

'Well you never did. Just tell me one thing then. Why did you just leave me? Hotel bill unpaid – no fucking money, nothing and not a word…'

'Very funny love. Has he got you so stoned you don't remember *you* left *me?* Getting bored with your sugar daddy now are you?' I snarled and cut her off.

I'd have hung up – but you just can't do that with a mobile. So after another fortifying visit to the toilets, I considerately picked up the shattered bits of my phone, dabbed ineffectually at the abrasion it had left on a venerable-looking painting on the wall and dropped by Reception on my way back to the bar.

'Couldn't sort me out a spare phone could you? Seem to have bust mine. Here's the SIM.'

The ever-attentive girl there smiled *yes of course* and went off to sort it as I weaved my way back to my barstool to hang out with my hangers-on.

Maybe it was the gear. Maybe it was the beer. And the Bloody Maries. And the rest… Suddenly, in the middle of a hearty, happy laugh, I cracked and gagged in the middle of cracking a gag and cried and cried and cried. Not the done thing when you're famous, or even formerly famous. Everyone turned away. My retinue retreated, slinking back to huddle round tables, fags in hands, tapping ashtrays like they were starting a séance to summon back the party spirit. I blew my nose on a bar towel and ran to my room. I put Massive Attack's *Blue Lines* - Georgie's favourite - on the CD player, cranked up the volume and stood sobbing on the rooftop terrace, staring out across the calm unruffled countryside and watching the dancing shadows thrown out of the downstairs bar's open sash windows. The unfathomably deep bass rumble must have drowned out the knock at the door – if there was one – because I didn't notice Ralph Pemberton slip gingerly into the room. Obviously I didn't – if I had I wouldn't have been racking up a monster-sized line on the outside table.

'I'll pretend I didn't see that,' Ralph murmured right in my ear.

'God!' I shouted. Then, 'Sorry. Jesus! Sorry! Christ! Sorry.'

'Try "Fuck"' my unlikely new friend smiled, putting a hand on my shoulder.

'Fuck!' I repeated sheepishly.

'There you go.'

We sat in silence for several week-long minutes, during which I smoked a pack of Marlboro, called downstairs for another 200 and downed a bottle of Pinot Grigio. While I thought Ralph wasn't looking, I built a little windbreak with a lighter and fag packet to make sure my precious blow didn't blow away.

'Oh for fuck's sake snort it!' the suddenly irreverent Reverend Ralph chuckled.

So I did. Which cheered me up. Then, with a schoolboy look, I checked whether this license was extendable to having another. He nodded.

'Chop one out for me while you're at it.'

'Fuck me!' I exclaimed.

'Don't push your luck mate,' Ralph teased, then, clocking my nonplussed gape, went on, 'I think the Lord will forgive my indulgence in a line of the Devil's dandruff but sodomy is explicitly forbidden by...'

'Leviticus 18:22,' I finished.[5]

---

5. Leviticus 18.22: 'Thou shalt not lie with mankind, as with womankind; it is abomination.'

Now *he* was shocked.

'How the fu...' he began.

'Language, vicar!' I interjected with mock severity. 'Far be it from me to make light of Leviticus but...'

'Hidden depths, eh!' Ralph observed.

'Nah – hidden shallows mate. I boned up on the Old Testament once when they got me on The L8 D-b8.'

'Never heard of it.'

'Well, it was a debate programme on a thing called a television and it was on late at night.'

'You astound me.'

'Yeah. They get the audience to text and email in and vote for whose argument wins.'

'So it's a mass debate.'

I nodded.

'Masturbate's about right.'

'Seriously though, what were you of all people doing on the Late Debate?'

'I was on there to argue against the proposition that the Devil has all the best music – my particular subtext being that not all rock stars are foul-mouthed drunken fuckwits and yobs, a recurring theme of mine.'

'And how did you do?'

'I got pissed, called some American evangelist a wanker, nutted him and broke his nose.'

'Good for you!'

'Thank you. It was actually. Our record went up thirty places in the charts next day! Astoundingly. Talking of astounding – you astound me. I know we've got gay clergy and all that – but are you lot allowed to...'

'No we're not... Until now my indulgence in the pleasures of the rock 'n' roll lifestyle has been entirely...'

'Vicarious?' I filled in.

'Exactly,' he grinned. 'Bought the records, went to the gigs, bought the T Shirts…'

'And now you've done the drugs!'

'Not yet I haven't,' Pemberton pointed out as his pointy nose lowered to table level and, with an expertise learnt from countless videos and gangster movies, he Hoovered up a line with a snotty crackle.

'Now I have!' he rasped, gagging slightly.

'Done like a professional!' I laughed.

'Not quite,' he managed to gurgle a nanosecond before he projectile-puked over the terrace rail. I stifled a giggle as the sickly splatter of vomit hitting the ground was followed by a chorus of indignation as an escadrille of high-flying fashionistas and other connoisseurs of the bulimic lifestyle efficiently and correctly identified the gobs of goo that oozed through their hair.

'Let's hear the record again,' Ralph's bilious voice dribbled from the bathroom through the general hubbub of hasty ablutions.

I slipped the disk in and instantly the Rev. Pemberton's protégés' sweet voices were rattling the room's walls, the gut-wobbling sub-bass groove I'd added providing a sinister counterpoint to their angelic tones. I leaned in through the open bathroom door, where Ralph was praying in the usual stance to a less usual (for him at least) altar. I took advantage of the rare opportunity to take the moral high ground.

'I hope you're going to be in a fit state for the launch tomorrow.'

He turned from the toilet bowl.

'As someone used to Communion wine at seven am, I think I can cope with a public engagement at noon in the bar of the local hotel!'

'If you say so,' I said, without bothering to disguise my scepticism or my great enjoyment of it.

'I do shay sho,' Ralph managed to say.

'Say "she sells seashells on the seashore" then,' I bullied.

'No – *you* shay jusht becush I'm a rock shtar don't mean I'm entitled to take the pish out of a pished up vicar.'

'Shan't!' I countered wittily.

'Can't!'

'You can't say that!'

'I said "can't." Not cunt. You cunt.'

'I cunt believe you said that.'

'Oh shut the fuck up and gimme more drugs.'

I chopped them out. And, God forgive me, I only made the poor sod say grace.

★   ★   ★

What is it with me? I find this unlikely friend who, despite being titillated and tempted by the trappings of stardom, is a real one and one to be valued – a 'keeper' as the Yanks say – and I can't help taking advantage of the fact that a couple of drinks and a couple of lines fuck him up so comprehensively. As if the years of drink and drugs that have inured me to their effects to the extent that it takes half Colombia's annual exports to get me high and almost always in a state of faux sobriety give me an edge on this man who's one of the good guys. The *real* good guys. No white Stetsons or derring do or rock star ranting. Just a quiet, gentle man in a white collar who strives with all his might to be good; the cavalry from the calvary.

The irony was that I liked him so much not because he was a good man, but because he was trying in his playful and utterly harmless way to be a little bit bad. But bad wasn't in him. Unless you really think taking drugs is evil *per se*. I don't. I think only those born again types really believe that. Not Christians. Not real ones. Not Jesus. Just those revoltingly self-righteous renouncers; the ones who were really nasty before they saw something that passed as an epiphany; the ones trailing their stinking afterbirth behind them. And I know this is crass. I know this is just what someone like me would be expected to do but I also know that for me and for Ralph at that time and that place it actually was the right thing to do.

'Come on mate,' I said with a certain authority. 'You need a livener.

That'll sort you out.'

Half an hour later it was as if someone had strapped him into a steel corset. Upright, excited, high as a kite, The Rev. Ralph Pemberton acted like everyone else on a shitload of coke. Except that his charlie chatter was reasoned, not rant; rational, not Kant – and that he somehow, miraculously, retained the capacity to listen. And listen and listen while I talked and talked and talked.

*   *   *

'This has definitely been one of the most interesting confessions I've ever heard.' Ralph observed as my account of the hazy Daisy day in the summer of '85 tailed off.

'Suppose so. Jealous?' I teased.

'Naturally,' he breezed. 'Comes with the territory.'

'Sorry – I suppose it must,' I sympathised, unable to imagine yet impressed by the strength of will that suggested.

'So, may I ask,' Ralph piped up, 'was it the "fuck duct" or the "muck duct" in the end?'

I couldn't be bothered to feign shock.

'The former. What do you take me for?'

'A dirty bugger?'

I grimaced. He shrugged.

'Just kidding. You can tell me the truth – I'm a priest you know! Well, a vicar, which is close enough,' he smiled.

'That *is* the truth… I mean…'

The silence was crying out for further explanation, even if Ralph was too polite to press me further.

'If it had been the latter,' I finally said, 'I wouldn't be worrying about taking the little shit out of private school,' I grimaced.

'Surely, though, if he's a little shit…'

He shut up mid–sentence, a quip too far.

'As far as I've been able to find out, he's actually not a little shit at all. A good kid really, considering...'

'His parentage?'

'Or lack of it,' I nodded grimly.

'Are you thinking of making contact, properly I mean? Once you've sorted out his schooling?'

I nodded.

'Not just at arm's length; not just with money you mean.'

'Yes that's precisely what I mean. Get in touch. Be a father,' he urged gently. 'It'll make him – and you – happier. It's just what you need.'

'He won't want to know me now – after I've left him alone all these years. Why the fuck should he?'

'What, a world-famous rock star for a dad? What is he, about sixteen?'

I nodded.

'Well, surely that's every teenager's dream!'

I shook my head.

'The dream's to *be* the star – not to have a dad who's a washed up has-been.'

'Come off it mate. This record's going to be a massive hit isn't it?'

I shrugged.

'The *Children in Need* factor you mean? I've got no time for children in need and all that shit. And, OK, much as it pisses me off, given the fact that every happy clappy bunch of born-again Christians knows the song, there's a good chance it could be a hit. But it won't be *hip*.'

'So your son couldn't possibly love you because you're not trendy any more. Is that what you're saying?'

'S'pose,' I schoolboyed. 'Thing is, I think I've left it too late.'

Ralph stood, stepped onto the roof terrace and gazed skyward as if consulting The Boss. I followed and looked up there too.

'It seems to me that cocaine is the twenty-first century equivalent of the confessional,' he mused.

'How d'you work that out? I mean it brings out the worst in most of us – with the possible exception of your good self!'

'Well that's what the confession does for Catholics. It allows people to purge the guilt; unburden thmselveselves – and watching all these media people and music business types in the bar here...'

'Shooting their mouths off and giving it large,' I interjected.

'Well, yes,' he smiled indulgently, 'but I can forgive them that.'

'You *have* to – I don't.'

'Well you're one of them!'

'Touché!'

'Seriously Stone, without that stuff you'd never have told me everything.'

'And you wouldn't have listened.'

'Maybe, maybe. Point is that we just spent about eight hours talking – and you looked like a weight's been lifted off you.'

I peered at my madman reflection in the terrace windows.

'Yeah, I look great!'

'You look like shit actually. And you've got to be on television in about half an hour.'

'I always look like shit when I'm on telly.'

'But this isn't just about music, is it,' Ralph pointed out. 'Your son might well be watching. It's a chance to make the right impression.'

'Point taken – but a bit fucking late if you don't mind me saying,' I replied, just as the phone rang. 'Yes?'

'Hey Stone,' said the unfeasibly perma-chilled guy on Reception (who actually was called Guy), 'you taking calls from a guy called Jimmy?'

'My agent. Yes. Thanks Guy,' I said, cringing as for the hundredth time I heard myself sounding like Keith Allen's pretentious music video director character in *The Yob*. *Could be worse,* I thought. *He could've been called 'Man'*. 'And by the way, in Britain we say "Hi,"' I grumbled. *Every sonofabitch in Britain's turning American. God dammit.*

'All set?' Jimmy breezed

'Natch,' I puffed back. 'No problemo. You still want his reverence on the case? Cos he's not looking so hot right now!'

I know I should have been ashamed of my glee at Ralph's indiscretion – and maybe I am a little, now. But, come on... A vicar off his tits on coke. You'd laugh too wouldn't you?

'Don't be ridiculous. You're going to be straight and sorted yeah?' Jimmy went on.

'Yes, mate. Don't worry. I am a grown up you know.'

'So's Shane McGowan. So's Pete Doherty. So's Iggy Pop...'

Before I got a chance to take the piss he pre-empted me.

'And yes you can smell burning martyr.'

'Big bonfire then!' I quipped pointlessly.

'Are you going to be serious?'

'Yes, sorry. Fire away.'

There was a distant snort of irritation at my barely repressed giggle.

'Look, against my better judgement, I've gone with our new publisher's idea that we ignore the international market for the time being...'

'I thought this was a global deal...'

'It is. But they want to build on the foundations of support you have in your home country – get a groundswell going and then roll it out across Europe first, then Japan and maybe the States, all being well.'

'Whatever,' I murmured. Already this sounded like the money men were losing their bottle. I'd been here before.

'So the money men are losing their bottle,' I accused. 'I've been here before.'

'No you haven't. I promise. This is different. *You* are different. The world's changed.'

'Whatever,' I said again and quietly cursed my Americanisation. 'So wassup?'

Oh shit, there I went again.

'The vibe is that you have roots. You're real. Not manufactured.'

'That's true.'

'And that's the beauty of it. Your partnership with the vicar's great – working with the real people, the kids and all that. But that's all tied up with Babington, which is cool as fuck but nevertheless part and parcel of the Soho elite that they're all slagging off now.'

'And?'

'You have a foot firmly planted in both camps. You may have been part of that scene – but because you've not exactly had a high profile lately you can rise above the backlash against the London cliques by talking about your roots in your home town.'

'Hurt 'em on Sea? I haven't set foot in the place for years – apart from checking out my old school for the kid. And since he doesn't know anything about it, how can I...'

'Thing is, Rich, things have changed...'

I didn't like the sound of that. Jimmy was as bullshit-free as an agent could ever be – which is not very. There was an angle here. A scam. Some horrible compromise of conscience coming up.

'I think you're going to have to compromise here mate.'

Told you so.

'I'm not sure how to tell you this.'

I sighed. The deal wasn't going ahead. The points had been massively reduced. Worst-case scenario: they wanted me to sing a medley of Westlife covers...

'Just tell me Jim.'

'The boy's gone missing again.'

Worse than my worst-case scenario then.

'Rich?'

I was snorting a line, knocking back a Jack, lighting a fag. Knee-jerk responses to any crisis. Or to anything else really.

'I'm here,' I gasped. 'Missing. Abducted? Run away? What?'

'Dunno.'

'What do you mean, "dunno"? You fucking tell me my son's disappeared and that's it?' For Christ's sake Jim. Find out!'

'Rich. He went AWOL a couple of days ago. The school reported it but didn't know how to get hold of you or his mother.

'Sorry,' I whined. Less than twenty-fours hours away from my new album's launch and already I was back in full rock 'n' roll prima donna mode.

'I thought I had at least a fucking day before you went into full-on prima donna mode,' Jimmy moaned.

He knew me too well.

'Sorry,' I repeated.

'I should think so too. Look, don't get too worried. I mean, he's run off before.'

'I know but...'

'I was just doing a bit of Googling to see if there was anything we could latch onto for the launch – something that grounded you in reality.'

'Makes sense I suppose.'

'And what I got was a load of newspaper reports about Joe.'

'I know – there are hundreds.'

'No – new ones. The difference now is that they're mostly about the school and the posh kids that go there. No one seems that bothered about Joe. Runaway boy does it again basically.'

'Oh Christ.'

A vague grunt of protest belched from the bathroom: 'Oi!' signalling the resurrection of the Reverend Ralph.

'Fuck off Ralph,' I said. Then, realising it had come out without the matey tone I'd intended, 'Sorry.'

'Bastards,' I said, switching back to Jimmy. 'What if he's been...'

'I know mate,' came Jimmy's unusually grave reply. 'Boy who cried wolf innit.'

Funny how I could be sickened, feel it right in my guts, when I heard that the son I'd never met or even acknowledged except as an anonymous 'benefactor' was at risk. Amazing how those genes I'd passed on galvanised me at such a distance in space and time. Or it could have been Ralph's vomit breath. The Vicar of Sick, Reverend of Retching,

Bishop of Barf had snuck up behind me and, having got the drift of the conversation, lurched up and carried out a baptism of bile.

'You can do something to help find the kid,' Jimmy ventured.

Suddenly I knew where all this had been leading. He wanted to turn the press launch of the record into a heartstring-tugging tear jerking 'human interest' story. Instantly I could picture the headlines:

ROCK STAR POP IN APPEAL FOR RUNAWAY BOY

MY HEARTACHE FOR LONG LOST SON – ROCK POP TELLS OF HIS GRIEF

'Oh no you don't. No way. Absolutely not,' I stated firmly.

'Think about it, Rich. It's not just a commercial thing. No one seems to care that the kid's gone missing. When they find out he's your son they'll start taking some interest. A public appeal from you would be better than a piece on Crimewatch. You could have the whole country looking for him!'

'Yeah and buying copies of *Bring It On* I suppose,' I grimaced at the phone.

'Well it can't hurt can it! You've got a son to lose, if you haven't already, and absolutely everything to gain.'

'Jimmy, far be it from me to expect you to understand such a concept but can't you get it through your head that I'd be publicly exploiting the loss of my only son. How the hell's that going to look? Not to mention how he's going to feel. He doesn't even know he's got a dad – let alone one he's sure to see as an irrelevant old rock dinosaur.'

'Presumably you were going to tell him at some point.'

'Yeah – I was going to wait till my career was back on track – leave it a few years for all the scandals to die down.'

'So now's as good a time as any.'

'No, Jimmy. Got that? No!' I barked as I slammed down the phone and stamped out of the room and downstairs for my rendezvous with the *meeja*. This time round I was definitely wearing the trousers. I'd get the schmoozing over with, round it off with a bit of boozing with the few journos who'd refrained from ripping me to shreds in their rags over the years, and then take a long, hard look at my life, the way I'd failed my only son, and see about how I could put it all right. Finally.

★   ★   ★

'Oh shit,' I mumbled as I lurched into the bar like it was the bridge of a wave-tossed ship, shielded my eyes against the electric storm of flashbulbs and took up my position at the table with its array of boom mics and cable rigging. Ever efficient, Jimmy's promotions team had evidently been hard at work all morning on the presentation. *Bring It On* boomed out of surround-sound speakers and two giant plasma screens flickered with beat-cut video images of my glorious career. It was the huge banner behind the table that bugged me:

PLEASE HELP ME FIND MY LONG-LOST BOY!

it pleaded in big red sans serif type over a grainy blow up shot of said waif looking suitably lost and vulnerable. Even in my anger I couldn't help noting its resemblance to the cover of U2's first album, *Boy*. The bastard had even slapped that cutesy *Children In Need* Teddy Bear character on it. Even I could see the strategy. Heart-warming human-interest story for the launch. Big exposure on *Children in Need's* nauseathon followed up by release in time for the record-buying public's customary Christmas taste bypass. Presumably I was about to be coerced into donating royalties to some anodyne charity that had earned Middle England's approval by withholding help from anyone a) foreign or b) over the age of fifteen or c) who wasn't telegenically cute.

'Nice job Jimmy,' I muttered.

The multitracking of the kids in the choir, which I'd thought of as heroically, stirringly epic, suddenly seemed grandiloquent and cynical and exploitative. The master of the *fait accompli* had done it again and with my back, literally, against the wall I miserably 'fessed up to the gentlemen and women of the press.

'Shitfaced again are we?' some shining wit piped up amongst the

226

motley bunch of reporters, some of whom I vaguely remembered as NME and former Melody Maker hacks and whose careers, going by their Paul Smith-calibre suits, had moved onwards and upwards.

'Sure am,' I announced unrepentantly.

26

Daisy's Induction

'Haagen flipping Dazs!' Chalfont swore as the door buzzer's fart rudely interrupted his usually sacrosanct and leisurely breakfast-time browse through the FT, making him jump and spill hot creamy *latte* in his lap. One of those city types, probably, ducking in furtively to arrange the weekend's entertainment. The CCTV screen on the counter beside him told him otherwise. Automatically his mercantile mind ran through a system of checks and appraisals: female. Conservatively but elegantly and almost certainly expensively dressed. Long dark hair neatly gathered up. Unusually, the subject cast no over-the-shoulder glances while waiting for a response. Not a furtive thrill-seeker then – nor was this one of his long-standing customers, most of whom he could recognise by the shifty demeanour of the watcher whose private practices make them uncomfortably aware that eyes are everywhere; watchers who dread the fact of being watched because the observer is in control of the image, while the observed is nothing more than data input, streams of modulating light flowing into someone's dark and muddied tunnel vision. Chalfont saw the symptoms surfacing in himself on the odd occasion he caught a glimpse of himself in a shop window as he hurried past, instinctively shying away from the implacable gaze of shop security cameras, speed cameras, tourist snapshots, TV news crews, guerrilla film shoots and police surveillance. Nosey, snooping, evil eyes everywhere. Watchers. Twitchers. Uninvited spies.

This woman, then, was the long-suffering wife of a cheating husband – almost certainly a very wealthy one. The brief, therefore, would be relatively straightforward and the only sexual frisson involved would be the inevitable, tiresomely euphemistic discussion of the errant spouse's illicit assignations. He reached for a glossy brochure on long-distance bugging devices and hit the door release button.

'Good morning. How may I help you,' he murmured robotically.

'You can make me a fucking cup of coffee for a start,' came the response in a throaty cackle. 'My head's banging like a shithouse door!'

'Daisy. Burger King!! You look...'

'FCUK Hot?' she mocked, touching her cheek with her index finger and pulling it back with a hiss like it burnt. 'Or are you just pleased to see me?' She pointed at his *latte*-sodden crotch

'You look very nice indeed. Very...'

'Un-whore like.'

'Yes. Indeed. Perfect in fact.'

He stood, flipped up the counter hatch and appraised the new image as she executed a slow, voluptuous twirl, her seasoned sensuality corrupting the black suit's straight-laced seams.

Chalfont busied himself with the cafétière.

'And look!'

She was pointing to the prim and proper tight collar on her pristine white blouse.

'Pearl necklace! First one I've ever had that wasn't given to me by a punter!'

'Well, well, Daisy Chains in twin set and pearls. You'll be taking up knitting next!'

Her animated face fell serious.

'I've been thinking about that. I shouldn't be called that any more – not here.'

Chalfont's relief that she'd brought it up first was obvious.

'No – I suppose not.'

'Course not. So I thought I'd revert to my real name.'

'Which is?'

'Daisy Raines. Doesn't have quite the same ring to it – but... What?'

she demanded, noticing the effect the name had on Chalfont.

'You're really called Daisy?' he asked after an awkwardly long pause.

Raines. Raines. I know that name, he was thinking. But for a reason he couldn't put his finger on, he fudged it.

'Yeah, why?'

'Well I just thought...'

'You thought it was my hooker name.'

'Yes,' he admitted.

'Could've been worse – they called my brother Pansy!'

'Very funny.'

'He wasn't christened that you moron! Dad used to call him that all the time: "Daisy come along, you'll be late for school – and where the hell is the pansy?"'

'That was cruel.'

'Tell me about it. His real name's Bart – Bartholomew - he got more shit for that name than he did for "Pansy".'

'You mean your father called him that all the time?'

'Oh yeah – proper sadistic bastard he was. One of your lot funny enough?'

Chalfont raised a questioning eyebrow.

'Preacher, God-botherer and bible basher of the worst sort imaginable. And a hypocrite.'

'I wasn't a preacher – I studied theology at university and dropped out. Since then I haven't bothered God and he hasn't bothered me,' he protested, much more animatedly than usual. Daisy was taken aback.

'Sorry. I didn't mean you were a hypocrite... It's just that...'

'It's all right. He doesn't sound like a very nice man, your father, if you don't mind my saying so.'

'And Keef Richards likes the odd toot! My dad is a vicious, evil kiddie fiddler who I hope will burn in the Hell he threatened me and the Pansy with every five minutes of our fucking childhood.'

She was shaking. Chalfont had never seen her like this; never seen anything but the seductive bloom she presented for the business of the birds and the bees. Her roots went deeper, more tangled and gnarled than he could have imagined. He sipped his coffee. Daisy lit a cigarette, hands trembling. The telephone broke a brittle silence – but he ignored it. When the urbane answering machine responded with the silken tones Chalfont assumed for his nervous new customers he ventured the question that had to be asked.

'He abused you? '

'Me and the Pansy both...in different ways.'

'Sexually?'

'Me? Oh yes. On a weekly basis – him and half his so-called brethren.'

'I'm so terribly sorry.'

And he meant it. Despite the inescapable fact that his rather unorthodox sexual mores were frowned upon by those who claimed the moral high ground, Chalfont really was quite rigorous in applying and adhering to his own ethical code. Although that code was constantly in flux, it could be summed up easily and almost completely accurately as: 'do no evil' – just like those Google billionaires.

Raines senior was obviously of the ilk of the suicide bombers who kill and maim in Allah's name all because they're looking forward to shagging seventy virgins in Heaven. In short, yet another bitter, twisted and sexually inadequate God botherer interpreting the Bible or the Koran or the Talmud in any way they liked as long as it provided spurious justification for their own sins. Just like the priests who kiddie fiddled with impunity, somehow inveigling the 'church' to forgive trespasses for which the godless down the pub would lynch them. Just like all the believers, agnostics and till-the-shit-hits-the-fan atheists; like Captain Hook Hamza, hands cut off for stealing the BNP's clothes - they're Pascal's wagerers, hedging their bets one way or another. *If there is a God up there, these people must be bothering Him one hell of a lot,* he thought to himself.

'The twisted cunt thinks he's a saint. You can justify anything if you do it in the name of God,' Daisy went on, staring past him at the blank wall – on which she was obviously re-running an old family movie, presumably a blue one.

'Evidently,' Chalfont murmured. 'Did he actually....'

'Rape me?'

He nodded. So did Daisy, tears welling in her eyes. She wiped them away with the impatience of the inexperienced weeper.

'Oh God. I'm sorry.'

She nodded grimly.

'Weirdest thing was, I was going to forgive him. I'd been gone years and I went back – spur of the moment thing. Just turned up on the doorstep. I thought maybe he'd changed or I had or something.'

'And had he?'

A shake of her head broke a teardrop off its clinging meniscus.

'Nice as pie at first. Then he locked the door, called me a whore – again. Least it was true that time... Then he punched the shit out of me and fucked me on the kitchen floor.'

'Oh you poor...'

'At least two hundred quid's worth and the fucker didn't pay me!' she grinned bravely, tears now running black mascara rivers down her face. She looked like the fucked and fucked up schoolgirl she was.

Roland's mouth goldfished, as if the words he couldn't find could be caught in the air in front of his face.

'Terrible thing... I mean... You must have been so awfully shocked,' he finally mumbled, with hopelessly British understatement.

'Not half – I'd have sworn he was into little boys!'

He guppied and gulped again.

'It's all right Roland. No need to find words – there aren't any.'

'But the religious – the flipping... No the *fucking* pious do these things and I... I do stuff that...'

Chalfont tore at his tie, struggling to slacken it as if that would hurt them; disassociate him from them somehow.

'That doesn't hurt anyone,' Daisy continued, instantly getting the drift. 'You're not like them Roly. I know that.'

Shivering and shucking the horrible memory off her shoulders like a clammy coat, she reached out with both hands and tackled his now un-loosenable knot with expert talons, simultaneously undoing the top two of his shirt buttons. He sighed with relief - like it was his collar that had him so hot and bothered. She cackled – the instantaneous switch from grief to hilarity almost knocking him off his seat.

'You said *fucking*!!' she accused with glee.

'Well,' he mumbled. 'There are some things...'

She kissed him on the lips in a way that was, impossibly – yet truly – chaste.

'What?' she asked as she slowly withdrew and levelled her gaze to meet his scared rabbit eyes.

'Well, you and me... We're not what you'd call saints.'

She nodded.

'But we don't hurt anyone,' he went on, 'and we don't say we're good....'

'No – I'm pretty bad. Not all that bad but...'

'NO! You're not bad. You're not vicious... You don't exploit anyone that's not grown-up enough to look after themselves and you're not one of those evil, preying, hypocritical bastards!' Roland shouted, slamming both fists down on the desk. 'Barry Manilow!!' he cursed, wincing, rocking backward and forward and nursing his hands between his thighs, 'That really hurt!'

'Bloody hell – never seen you so masterful!' Daisy mock-mocked.

'Please,' he pleaded with a quiet urgency that shut her mouth and opened her mind and which was something of a first for both of them. 'I think you're the first person I've met who I can say this to.'

'Thank you,' she murmured.

He checked her face for traces of cynicism. None. She just nodded.

'OK. If you really, truly believe there's a Heaven where you'll live in paradise for all eternity how can you be a saint? If you believe that, anything you do has the ulterior motive of a reward in the afterlife.'

'I suppose – yeah,' Daisy agreed guardedly.

'So a believer can't be altruistic. There's something in it for them, as long as they do what's supposed to be the right thing.'

'But a lot of the time what they do in the name of religion is the wrong thing as far as the rest of us are concerned.'

'Exactly. Whether they do good or bad, they're still doing it for themselves.'

'So what – why the fuck do we care about them. They don't give a shit about us!'

'That's precisely what I mean. The only way anyone can be a saint in the true sense of the word as we understand it, outside of the Burger King Catholic Church making it up as it goes along and canonising anyone that suits them, is to be an utterly convinced atheist.'

'Now you've lost me.'

'A true atheist – if there is such a person; someone who doesn't hedge their bets on the deathbed – is the only person who can be a true saint. If someone who really, totally, in their heart and soul doesn't believe they have a soul; doesn't believe there is a god, invests their time and energy in helping other people, they have no expectation of reward.'

'They're genuinely nice people,' Daisy agreed.

'No!'

She was visibly taken aback by his fervour.

'Sorry,' he mumbled, chastened by her astonishment.

'Don't be,' she murmured. 'Strident is good!'

'Oh. Thank you. Um. Oh yes. Not just nice people. Really good people.'

'You're talking about Karma really aren't you?'

'Am I? I don't know.'

'Well if by being good; doing no harm, you can be this saintly person… You're protected by protecting others. It's like Karma plating!' Daisy clapped her hands with glee.

Roland's face clouded.

'Sorry – just liked the sound of it,' she simpered.

'Maybe that's it. All I can think is that only the devout unbeliever – the faithful infidel – the contradiction in terms who devotes himself unselfishly to the benefit of others can really be described as an altruist...'

'Or a saint,' Daisy finished.

'Yes,' Chalfont agreed with an uncharacteristic flourish.

'You're saying only the irreligious can be saints then?'

'Yes I flipping am. But only the wholly, the holy infidels...'

'I really flipping like that!'

'You really *fucking* like that, you mean.' Chalfont grinned an entirely new untried grin.

'I F.C.U.King love it you dirty old saintly cunt!' Daisy beamed and gently tweaked his genital area in a way that only a hooker could make platonic – or at least make clear that the gesture's intention wasn't exactly sexual. Chalfont's equipment picked up the signal with the efficiency of his technological wares and responded as if the transmission hadn't transgressed his usual gender preference. He raised an erection. For a woman!

'You're all right, Mr Chalfont.'

'Fucking hell,' he whispered.

And raised a smile too.

'Flipping heck,' Daisy corrected. Then, clocking his confusion, 'It's all right Roly – I can do it for anyone.'

'And *against* anyone I imagine,' he breathed.

'If necessary. How do you want me?'

'I don't. I'm gay.'

'That's not what a certain part of your anatomy's telling me.'

'Well it's a knee-jerk reaction!'

'It's a clockwork reaction,' she giggled. 'With a silent L.'

'Flipping heck...'

★　　★　　★

'Hello Winston!' Georgie breathed, grabbing a brimming Champagne flute just in time to stop the gentle swell under the ship tipping it onto the laptop just as the Babington press launch and her erstwhile lover's still-famous face coalesced on its screen. *Winsome Winston,* as they used to call him, didn't look so winning now. He'd lost it. Completely.

Winsome, lose some, she thought with a wry grin. Pissed as usual, he looked physically diminished somehow. Dispelling the fleetingly satisfying thought that she'd done this to him by forcing herself to hope not, she nevertheless wondered, *What have I done to him?* as she watched his vitamin G-for-Georgie deficient and evidently vitamin C for Charlie OD'd form shake and shape up to the cameras' onslaught.

'Bart,' she half-chuckled, half-called down to the stateroom with en suite lavatory that Bart laughingly referred to as the 'Poop Deck'. 'Take a look at the state of Stone!'

Pot belly resting gently on stiff white shorts, a prattily piratical eye Adam Ant-style patch covering his unsightly eye, her sugar daddy stepped blinking from the shade below with the usual dirty chuckle — which was silenced by Georgie's halting hand.

'Oh fuck,' she whispered as the story of the missing boy unfolded and the broken Stone muttered his set piece.

27

Tunnel of Love

Joe could just about make out Lily's form in the guttering glow of the single almost exhausted candle their captors had left lit, and he couldn't help but allow its failing pool of light between them in their long tubular prison to symbolise his dwindling reserves of hope. But the hood of her parka was pulled so far forward it was like a monk's cowl; too deep a mask of darkness for this dim glimmer to penetrate. When Raines had left Lily behind, despite Bunton's characteristically feeble protests and probably because of his own more forceful but even more futile ones, he'd felt a small sense of relief – at least he wasn't to be abandoned here alone. At least they'd be together – even if they couldn't touch. She'd be there. But as soon as that little warmth touched him, he'd been chilled again by the selfishness of the reflex.

'You've done this before,' Joe had commented as Raines tied his wrists together, then his ankles, with plastic cable ties and then moved on to do the same with Lily. *At least we can cuddle up together. Anything will be bearable if we're touching,* he thought, hoping Lily could read it in his eyes. He doubted it. With the flickering candlelight and her terrified strobe-blinking, none of their usual ocular telepathy was going to get through. He squeezed his eyes shut to hold the tears in – but only succeeded in squeezing them out. A metallic rattle redolent of chain mailed and shackled ghosts in mediaeval castles opened his eyes. Raines was tugging at the padlocks securing the hatch nearest Joe.

'Pretty solid bit of workmanship - I'll give you that. You'll be safe as houses in here!' said the black slit that split the grey and monstrous uplit face, rectangular, pocked and etched with age like a weathered gravestone.

'Until we die of cold or hunger,' Joe replied, drawing on an unexpected rush of defiance.

'What kind of people do you think we are! As if I'd allow my own daughter to be...' Bunton's reedy whine piped up from his daughter's magnified shadow in the darkness by the hatch at the tunnel's far end.

'Raped by an old perv...' Joe's interruption was ruptured by a kick in the groin from Raines.

It was hard to tell whether the wave of nausea that engulfed him was down to the ball-crunching blow or Raines' oleaginous hypocrisy.

'Now then, children. No one's going to be cold and no one's going to go hungry — at least not for long. Young Lily here must finish her forty hours of penance and prayer. And think yourself lucky young lady — because Our Lord suffered forty days and forty nights. You are merely undergoing a brief, symbolic version of that ordeal.'

'Dad, please can you...' Lily whispered.

But her father turned his face away.

'Can't look her in the eye can you!' Joe challenged.

Bunton's face flickered. Or was it just the candlelight? Either way, he turned his back, avoided testing his will and busied himself trying the strength of the hinges and locks on the hatch next to him.

'Come on, Alan,' Raines barked, as if they were setting out on a jolly hike.

Bunton paused to take off his anorak and stooped to pull together the one Lily was wrapped in and zip her up like a precious parcel. Then, arms outstretched and head half-turned away as if she were a stinking corpse, he lifted her upper body awkwardly. But at this distance even her slight weight's leverage was too much for feeble muscles further weakened by even feebler resolve and she slipped to the floor with a muffled thud. Hands bound behind her, the shiny black parka like a puffy carapace, she struggled like a beetle on its back to get up. Unwilling or unable to touch her, Bunton seized the nylon fur edging the hood and hauled her to a sitting position before crawling after Raines, over Joe and through the hatch at the end. The clunk and rattle of the padlocks' hasps slotting into place for a moment evoked memories of good times in this private priest hole – and of the not so good ones in Joe's days as a runaway. Then suddenly they didn't sound so pleasant. In fact they sounded horribly final.

They talked. Sort of. But with hands tied and facial expressions all but invisible, the words weren't working. Worse than that, the silences between them that usually said so much had dropped their signals like mobile phones on the tube – in another tube. *Maybe telepathy only works above ground, like phones and radio,* Joe mused during a brief interlude in which he allowed his mind to stray from Lily and their ordeal. *Maybe that's why dead bodies have always been buried. Shit. We've been buried. They're not coming back. We're dead.*

It was as if the two men had sucked the air out of the tunnel when they left; like they hated everything vital so much that life and love withered as they walked over it, trampled it and left it all for dead. Like they were leaving Joe and Lily. Nothing could be transmitted through a vacuum. No sound. Nothing. Only light – and there was precious little of that left.

It had been several hours – as far as he could work out. Those bog standard Woolworths' candles used to last five hours. He remembered that from Nelly's careful experiments inspired by precise cost-benefit calculations based on the relative investment in lighting set against the cider, cigarettes and top-shelf soft porn from which they could eke out optimum enjoyment from their limited funds. Not that he needed that wisdom now. The candle, the light in their tunnel, was about to fizzle out any second. And with it hope.

Lily's whimpering sob somehow reached his ears before the darkness hit his eyes. The speed of sound accelerated by love to that of light – or even exceeding it, their relationship, being their universe, was overpowering relativity; the primal energy of procreation making its own laws inside their timeless black hole.

'Don't cry Lily,' he murmured, failing to sound very reassuring.

'Why the fuck not!' came her sniffy, snotty reply, which nevertheless sent a watery smile to him through the gloom.

He smiled back and hoped the beam reached her.

'Yeah. Why not!' he said bravely, and cursing the semi-sob that rent the last syllable.

'I'll think of something,' he ventured.

No reply.

'Can you move?'

'The thing on my ankle's tied to something on the floor.'

'Same here.'

Joe tested the binding. It didn't give. But an eerie creak told him something did. There was a definite flexing somewhere below him.

'Nelly's pipes!' he exclaimed as realisation dawned.

'What?' Lily asked.

'Drainage. They run along the tunnel under the boards.'

'So?'

'If we tilt the boards a bit we can slide the cable ties along.'

Her silence said she was baffled.

'So we can at least be touching each other,' he explained.

'Oh. Yes. Good,' she mumbled.

Heartened by having a mission, however useless, Joe began rocking from side to side. The boards beneath him shifted – but not enough.

'Feel around by your feet, next to the wall. See if you can get your fingers into the gap.'

After a lot of scrabbling and grunting she replied.

'Got it!'

'Right. Keep them clear for a minute. I'll shift all my weight onto the far end and with a bit of luck your end will rise.'

'Then what?'

'Slide your ankles along bit by bit towards me.'

Uncomprehending silence again.

'Then shift your bum, then your ankles again.'

Her laboured breath drew closer and closer but still it seemed it took her an hour to shuffle and nudge her way across the three or so metres between them. When finally her head nestled into his shoulder and he raised his bound arms over her in an awkward embrace the idea of escape suddenly didn't seem so urgent. Joe grinned.

'All that sneaking about so your dad wouldn't find out and now he's the one who's forced us to spend the night together!'

'Mmmmm,' Lily purred as she snuggled.

'I'd suggest we made the most of sleeping together but...'

'But what?'

'I'm afraid my hands are tied!' he chuckled.

'I'd slap you for that if mine weren't,' she teased.

28

Daisy on the Job

Chalfont was a more than considerate employer. Daisy was to work whatever hours suited her – and he was happy for her to work at home if she found what she called his 'Batcave' too oppressive. She did – and she did. Nevertheless, her employer was adamant about one thing: the customer files were never to leave the secure room in any circumstances. That wasn't too much of a problem; her work was mainly about new business, so as long as she checked whether or not the new prospects she trawled from her own network of contacts already appeared in Chalfont's database she would hardly need to venture into the Batcave.

For now though, the boss wanted her to immerse herself in the minutiae of his business; become as familiar as he was with its esoteric *modus operandi* and clandestine customer communications systems.

'You need to have this business in your blood as well as your brain!' Roland had insisted. 'I shan't be expecting any results from you for at least a month – so I'd like you to use the first couple of weeks to get yourself up to speed.

Daisy had taken him at his word and after six hours in the Batcave with a sizeable bag of amphetamines and a bottle of JD she was exceptionally up to speed. With every line of sulphate her progress through the vast database accelerated, even if the acuity of her focus was blurred. At first she'd been reading each file with conscientious absorption but by now she was skittering through names, regions, countries and personal peccadilloes with little more thought than a hamster on a wheel until one name sent her mouse scurrying round its mat more feverishly than ever:

RAINES. L. (?)

BARCELONA, PORT OLYMPIC.

DAISY CHAIN (yacht). BERTH NO: UNDISCLOSED

TEL: NOT DISCLOSED

LANDLINE. NOT DISCLOSED

MOBILE: NOT DISCLOSED

EMAIL: NOT DISCLOSED.

OTHER CONTACT DETAILS: see Premium Security Client code list.

CUSTOMER PROFILE:

GBM. V. SM. GRP.MSX

Daisy opened another window on the PC and scrolled to the glossary.

GBM meant Gay/Bisexual Male. V meant Voyeur. SM − well we all know what that means, and GRP meant the client was up for an orgy (or presumably just watching one, in view of the 'V'); MSX that he wasn't fussy which gender was involved.

'Wotcha big brother,' she breathed. 'Still love your telescopes I see!'

She hit the *ACCOUNT HISTORY* button. So far this had invariably led her to one further page that listed perhaps ten or so transactions over a similar number of years: a hidden camera, a bugging device... Then a couple of years later something more sophisticated. More often than not, the account history showed a series of a new type of transaction, beginning a couple of years back when Chalfont had introduced his 'premium services'. Many of the customers whose pleasures had initially been vicarious had availed themselves on more than one occasion of the services of sub-contracted 'escorts' and 'masseurs' and 'masseuses'. But her brother's account history was an epic of its kind, the billing running to hundreds of thousands of dollars, pounds and euros. Unlike others on the list, he hadn't started in a modest fashion. No shrinking violet, her Pansy. The first order, as far as Daisy could make out from the impenetrable list of technical specifications, was for a monster telescope, custom built, computerised, networked and built into a vast luxury yacht. This last nugget of information she gleaned from the attached plans for the vessel. *Fit for a queen!* she thought with a sour smile.

Later, other similar devices had been added to the list – a couple augmenting his ship's bristling array of lenses, microphones, radar and an incredible volume of broadband capacity. Daisy was no computer nerd – but she remembered the analogy her local cable guy had used to sell her a broadband account: 'Think of the cable as a water pipe. There's only so much water you can squeeze through it. Get a wider pipe and the volume of water, or in this case information, you can get is multiplied massively.'

'So you can pump more of your stuff into me much faster?' had been Daisy's disingenuous reply. To which the disconcerted, but decidedly and visibly aroused, cable guy had replied,

'Well yes, that's about the size of it.'

Daisy smirked at the memory – then smirked much more when she deciphered the jumble of numbers on the screen. If the internet access she paid twenty-five quid a month for at home was a hose, her brother was sitting at the mouth of a giant sewer pipe. And she didn't doubt for a moment that the analogy would stand up when she found out what was pouring out at his end.

'Wotcha Bart, you dirty little git,' she muttered, at once amused and disturbed.

29

Darkness Visible

Darkness visible. Milton's oxymoron had only ever made a sort of intellectual sense before, in the classroom; in a lacklustre essay on *Paradise Lost.* Now there was nothing oxymoronic about it. The almost grainy blackness had a solidity about it that felt like it was oozing slow as graphite into the black of Joe's pupils and dying him the colour of death.

For a precious time, which seemed fleetingly brief now, they really had made the most of their enforced but nevertheless strangely welcome time alone together. In fact they were experiencing something the likes of Roland Chalfont might have paid for handsomely. Just touching was enough of an adventure. Love was enough, really. Or it would have been had their hands and legs not been tied. You could hardly call it luck – but it was some consolation that Lily was naked underneath the loose wrapping of her father's coats. And while Joe manoeuvred his hungry mouth under their folds, she giggled and sighed and unbuttoned his shirt and jeans with her mouth. If they'd been jaded enough to have explored the darker side of sexuality the frustration of their shackles might have been exciting. Maybe in some way it was. But actually it was just a pain in the arse. And neck. And back. And try as she might, there was no way Lily could button *up* anything using only her mouth – especially in this bitch black. Not that it mattered. Only the creeping shivers reminded Joe to pull his shirt together as much as he could.

At least Lily was sleeping now, albeit fitfully. The susurration of her delicate snores was the only measure of time and Joe counted them into several hundreds, determined to stave off sleep and watch over her. And despite their incarceration, her unbearable ordeal and whatever her father and the hateful Raines had in store for them, as he lowered his face into her hair and breathed deep, he smiled at the prettiness of Lily's scent. Not the perfume she put on the moment her father's back was turned. Certainly not her parka-anorak combo's *eau de wet dog*. It was the infinitesimal but still discernible trace of the softest of soaps – some traditional brand that still conjured up images of cherubic, rosy-cheeked infants or well-scrubbed and wholesome girls, even to Joe's generation. It was the essence of blossoming Lily. So his smile slowly spread, warmed and widened to a grin, then a yawn, as he slipped into sleep.

★   ★   ★

Chalfont was more than impressed with Daisy. He'd hoped that she'd take seriously his suggestion that she spent her first few weeks familiarising herself with the ins and out of the business – and he'd been steeling himself for what he thought was the inevitable confrontation when she took advantage of his reluctance to come on like the boss man. He couldn't have been more wrong. If he now saw any need to have a disciplinary word with his new employee it would be to warn her against overworking; to keep in mind the importance of the work/life balance with which the zeitgeist kept on haunting small employers – rightly in Chalfont's view, which was surprisingly temperate for one so keen on certain extremes of behaviour. Or perhaps his untiring tolerance of others was a product of his proclivities – and the 'normal' people's intolerance of them. Roland couldn't help indulging in this sort of self-analysis. It was how he policed himself and guarded the borderline between what was ethical and what wasn't, in his own behaviour and that of his 'clients' – certain of whose files he'd marked with a '?', which denoted those he'd come to regard as questionable. The idea was that he'd occasionally review the client list and invest some serious time in investigating the activities of the people thus highlighted. If he found any suggestion of real exploitation or lack of consent or anything involving kids, he meant to close down that person's account, purge all records from his systems, electronic and manual and refuse to communicate with them except for a final tersely and officiously worded email that alluded to unacceptable practices and carried in its subtext the threat of police involvement.

In practice, he wouldn't report anyone. His premium prices guaranteed anonymity and total privacy. To break that strict contract would be unforgivable as far as the rest of his clientele was concerned. It would also be the end of the business, based as it was on that guarantee of the utmost discretion. But so far that dilemma hadn't arisen – mainly because Chalfont hadn't had the time to conduct those investigations. Nor had he possessed the dedication, determination, perspicacity and sagacity the task would require. Now, sitting in the shop, watching Daisy downstairs on the webcam, absorbed in her work, surfing the database with almost robotic speed, he knew that he had the partner he needed. Not just to manage and magnify the effectiveness of the enterprise – but also to put those high-minded ideals into practice. He smiled to himself. *I've got a friend as well as a business partner!* he thought. *More than a friend maybe,* he allowed himself to hope.

If he hadn't happened to be gay, he'd have fallen in love with her, this epitome of the cliché of the tart with the heart of gold. Maybe he was in love with her. After all, real love doesn't need to be about sex, does it? At least the two of them shared that certain knowledge, having spent their adult lives engaging in sexual transactions that had no relationship to love, except for rare intrusions of its distant cousin, affection, which always gooseberried on the coupling of filthy lust and lucre. In the little square box on his PC screen, Daisy suddenly swivelled on her seat and blew him a kiss, lasciviously, as if she knew he was thinking about her. He blew one back and waved – then stopped when he saw how camp he looked on the tiny image of his image on her screen, bounced back to his screen, and again and again and infinitely onward. *How many images of her and me are there now?* he wondered, *bouncing back and forth like electronic reflections, till they're too small to see.* If, as people who'd never had contact with the developed world's technology apparently believed, those pictures stole your soul, how soulless can we be? he wondered. The answer, of course, was infinitely.

Bless him! Daisy thought, then giggled as she realised she'd said it out loud. The silence, the speed and the isolation of the Batcave were obviously getting to her. But she was enjoying this. Partly, she acknowledged to herself, because she was such a nosey cow. Although she had no intention of breaching the sacrosanct code of silence about Roly's clients, she couldn't help getting a kick out of the latent, if unusable, power she was tapping into with every hit of the *Return* key. The things she now knew about all these thousands of people. Things that probably only an experienced hooker could infer from the discreetly presented bare facts of these accounts. What she'd found out about her brother so far wasn't overly surprising – except that she'd had no real understanding of the magnitude of his wealth. Already aware of the kind of thing that turned him on, she'd found little she'd consider outrageous. What was definitely obscene was the amount of money the greedy little Pansy had amassed. But then, this was the only connection she had with her brother now. So why, she asked herself, was she wasting time on just one of the thousands of files on the database? *Move on to another client,* she told herself. So she did. Daisy scrolled to the alphabetised menu and hit at random another page of twenty names under the PQRS category.

'Fucking hell!' she said, as the next screen popped up with RAINES, ERICH (???).

'Wotcha Dad – you dirty old fucker!' she exclaimed gleefully for an instant before the chuckled choked in her throat as she frowned, suddenly not sure that she really wanted to know what her father had been up to. *Can of worms* was the phrase that came to mind.

She waved at Chalfont's image in its little box at the top right corner of the screen. He peered back at the webcam, mouthing, What?

What do the question marks next to a client name mean? she typed. In stilted, stop-go animation she watched Chalfont tap out his reply.

Ah – been meaning to talk to you about that. Means I'm worried about their activities.

In what way? She typed a lot more rapidly and sat back to wait for a response. Chalfont bent to his keyboard, started typing, then hesitated.

Been meaning to explain that...

What? she typed and glared impatiently at the webcam, galvanising an indecisive Chalfont.

? means I'm a bit worried whether the client is doing something questionable morally. ?? means I'm more worried. ??? means I'm thinking I should check them out and maybe refuse to deal with them.

Oh fuck, Daisy typed.

Why? came the reply.

Oh for fuck's sake, why are we typing messages? I'm coming up.

★   ★   ★

The new reality; the awakening for Joe was a flash of light followed by a boot stamping on his face. Literally. And it really hurt.

'Get your filthy hands off her!' an old man's voice wheezed out of the darkness as the steely light pouring through the open hatch was eclipsed by a slab-like silhouette, which folded as it entered the hole, let in a monotone snapshot then blotted it out again.

'Shut up Alan,' a deeper, darker voice issued as if the soundwaves it made were woven out of the horribly solid black that the infiltration of day couldn't dilute.

Intermittently dazzled, then blinded, and in both states eyeless and fearful, Joe could tell them apart only by their voices: Bunton's tremulous, taking out his shame on a shackled target; Raines's sonorous, booming in the cavernous halls of his self-righteousness.

'Get her back up there,' Raines barked at Bunton, who scuttled to his quivering daughter's side and began fiddling with her bonds.

'Be brave sweetheart,' he mumbled as his movement admitted a shaft of light. 'Won't be long.'

But she spat in his face. Wiping the spittle from a tearful eye, unseen by Lily or anyone else, he shivered and grabbed her ankles a little more roughly than he'd intended. And as the plastic ties bit into her ankles she yelped and kicked out with both feet, catching him full on the nose. The darkness denied the prisoners the satisfaction of seeing it bleed as he dragged Lily's ankles, inch by shuffling inch, away from her lover. Raines did the same to Joe with a lot less finesse, his repeated kicks on Joe's ankles forcing him to co-operate and shuffle along the pipe till he was tantalisingly close to the tunnel's entrance. There, sounds came rushing in in waves behind the light: the drone of traffic, the cackle of gulls, a distant police car laughing at his helplessness: *ner* ner, *ner* ner – *whooooooooo!* Ner ner, ner ner – *whooooooo!*

'You're not here to enjoy your sordid little affair,' Raines grunted as he bound Joe's legs to a floor plank at right angles to the pipes to ensure that he couldn't get close to Lily again.

Joe kept his mouth shut. No point giving the bastard an excuse to lash out. He'd only enjoy it.

'Alan. You done?' Raines demanded with a nod, satisfied with his handiwork.

'Think so,' came the quavering reply.

Bunton tried to take his daughter's hands in his, was batted away like a fly and beetled along the boards towards his mentor.

'Lily. I know you're upset – but you must go through this. It's only forty hours. Not long now,' he reiterated pointlessly.

Nothing. Then darkness as the two figures crouched through the opening, then a cruel flash of day before the hatch folded in, squeezing the last drops of light from the tunnel and compressing the darkness into that near-solidity again.

'Fuck,' said Joe as the muffled thump of their footsteps faded and the horribly dense emptiness of silence filled their little tube so that there was so space left for time.

★　　★　　★

'It wasn't the fact that my name's really Daisy that surprised you, was it.'

It wasn't a question so much as a challenge.

'No,' Chalfont admitted.

Daisy's crossed arms and raised eyebrows achieved several hours' worth of interrogation in the minute it took to dissolve his resolve.

'You were right – what you were thinking...'

He said nothing.

'You're wondering if I'm related to a Raines on your list.'

A barely perceptible nod said yes.

'Well I am. One's my dad. The other's my brother.'

'Thought so,' Roland sighed, his relief visible if not quite palpable.

'And both have question marks against their accounts.'

He nodded.

'Which means that you – you of all people – are worried about what they're up to.'

Another nod.

'And you're not exactly the most shockable bloke in the world.'

Roland shook his head.

'So...'

He nodded.

'Daisy, yes, you're right. I think they're up to no good.'

'By which you mean something really bad,' she said, 'and if you do that sheepish nod again I'll punch you.'

'Yes,' he said, realising too late that he'd also nodded and trying to dodge Daisy's swipe, which she slowed and converted into a chummy chuck under the chin.

'You old softy,' she grinned. 'It's all right. There's nothing about them that's gonna upset me.'

'You sure?'

'Think so.'

'Shall we check them out then?'

Daisy nodded, took his hand and led him towards the stairs. He halted her and disappeared into the back room, then emerged with a two bottles of wine. She smiled. It was going to be a long night. Enjoyable, she hoped, because of the renewed sense of camaraderie. Scary, though, because she wondered whether her father and brother had delved deeper into darkness than she had, or than she could imagine.

'Is this going to be bad?' she asked, squeezing Roland's hand as they negotiated the dark downward stairwell as if it led to hell.

'I'm not sure,' he answered. 'I hope not.'

Once they were ensconced in the Batcave, Roland poured out generous glassfuls of wine. Daisy reciprocated rapidly - with speed. Which he turned his nose up at first – the poor man's cocaine – but finally relented and suffered the caustic nasal scrape and chemical stench just to be able to keep up. And while Daisy Googled every hint she found on the two sets of Raines records and they both goggled at what they found, Roland talked. And talked and talked. He explained how he'd always meant to instigate some sort of monitoring system and to police the people he dealt with, however remotely, so that he could be certain that he wasn't abetting anything that he considered beyond the pale. She teased him about his so-called principles – and more about his failure to get round to implementing these well-intentioned plans. He pleaded guilty to the charge of failing to carry through those ideas but, in mitigation, pointed out that he'd been hoping to find a business partner worthy of his trust, who'd be willing – and capable enough – to take on that very task. It would, he was at pains to explain, have to be someone to whom he could feel genuinely close, the nature of the beast being so personal, so much to so with what he was, what his clients were. In short, he'd been hoping for a very long time now to find this combination of business partner and soul mate...

'And,' Roland concluded shyly, 'I've come to believe that you're that person.'

Not the kind of thing you should say when perched on a backwards swivelly chair on wheels. Daisy launched herself on her own similar chair across six feet of floor and before Roland could react flung herself bodily at him. And just as her big lips enclosed his less kissable ones, his chair keeled over

'Know what? In my whole life you're only the second bloke I've felt safe with and close to.'

'What happened to the first one, or shouldn't I ask?'

'He couldn't handle me,' she grinned ruefully. 'Check this out.'

Scooting back to her desk on her chair like it was a chariot, she Googled a name but before she hit the *SEARCH* button. Roland trundled over and squinted at the screen. Daisy searched his face for a response. It was blank. Then understanding dawned.

'What's *1984* got to do with anything?'

'Nothing. This is the name of the other man I was close to,' she explained.

'A fictional character?'

'No. Well yes. But, Winston Smith is also a rock star. Called 'Stone' for short. You must've heard of Airstrip One – he was the lead singer, writer.... Massively famous – well, not so much now but...'

Roland shrugged.

'I'm not exactly *au fait* with the Hit Parade.'

'Clearly,' she snorted. 'Hit Parade! What are you like!'

She hit the *SEARCH* button and pointed at a figure at the bottom of the web page. Then Daisy giggled as, again, Roland goggled at the Google.

'Fifty-seven thousand results. Flipping heck he really is famous isn't he.'

'Was,' she corrected.

Another click of the mouse pulled up a ten-year-old photograph of Stone in his heyday.

'Nice,' Roland commented. 'So you and he were...'

'No we weren't. Not really. I thought once we might but, you know...'

I probably do, Roland thought.

'Anyway,' Daisy said, switching to business mode.

'Hang on. I'd like to see a bit more about this bloke – that is, if it's not too....'

'Whatever. Let's see. Here we go.'

She clicked on a link to a BBC page:

WINSTON SMITH ALBUM LAUNCH. LIVE WEBCAST.

'Blimey, the old git's making a comeback!' she muttered, and leaned back to wait for the Real Player window to buffer the live video stream.

Smith's face, a lot less heroic than in the picture Roland had just seen, filled the screen. His mouth began to move but then his features froze while the PC strained to catch up. After a couple of minutes, like a cistern filling, then finally flushing, the screen poured forth a stream of stills and video clips: a bullet point history of a rock star's rise and fall. A callow spiky-haired youth filled out into a commanding presence swaggering on stadium stages, then less heroic images cut him down to size: paparazzi shots of the wild and wasted rocker falling out of cabs with wired and wiry models and silicon-titted soap stars and children's TV presenters with expensive habits and too-white smiles. A particularly drug and drink addled appearance on an insipid smug-on-a-sofa daytime show was gleefully presented in slow motion, which accelerated nauseatingly to the point when Stone told the leader of the opposition very emphatically that he'd 'See You Next Tuesday!'

The putative next Prime Minister didn't get it.

'I rather think not. I shall be in the house next Tuesday,' he blathered.

But the audience did: *C.U.N.T.* And Winston Smith took a winsome bow with a winning smile. And then fell over.

Roland leaned forward, his curiosity piqued as an orange-tanned, big-haired American TV evangelist's shiny face smeared itself over the screen followed by a nauseating ooze of unction. This Winston chap lurched into shot, leered like Johnny Rotten and whispered 'Wanker!'

right into the camera, jerking a curled fist evangelist-ward. The preacher's smug composure dissolved into a snarl and headsetted, dark-suited minders poured into view issuing terse warnings to the grinning rock star. As they loomed close and a flattened hand obscured the lens, the screen went black for an instant. When transmission was restored seconds later, it was to reveal Stone wrenching himself free of the suits, leaping across the set and headbutting the evangelist full in the face. The explosion of blood blossomed satisfyingly down his pristine white suit and shirt before the clip was cut savagely to black, over which a glibly solemn voice-over intoned standard rock commentary words in what sounded like a shopping list: hell-raiser, bad boy of rock, the spirit of rock, rehab, dry spell, difficult third album, musical differences and, most damningly, a rebel without applause...

Daisy's hair crackled like static against Roland's cheek and for an instant her head dipped to rest against his before she dismissed whatever form of warmth was melting her and with a visible shiver resumed her cold steely irony.

'Oh man what a hero. What a rock god! What a wanker!' she sniped without much conviction.

'Actually, I'm rather impressed,' Roland began.

'Oh bollocks, he's just...'

But she was silenced by a series of images that juxtapositioned the apex and the nadir: Stone, cold and cadaverish in the gutter. Stone strapped into a stretcher and carted off to A&E – a night-time shot full of un-special effects like a Hammer Horror; the flicker and flak of lightning, generously supplied by the photographic vampires. White and marbly skinned, the former punk who'd railed against the pallid posing of the Goths who'd sucked the blood out of punk's heart had inadvertently joined their ranks. Bloodless, ashen and drained and doomed. Stone broke and broken.

'Jesus,' Daisy said, somewhere between a whisper and a whimper.

Roland put a hand lightly on her shoulder.

'I didn't know he was in that state,' she mumbled. 'I thought...'

'What?' Roland coaxed.

'Nothing.'

The montage finally ended, cutting to a roiling mass of TV crews, photographers and reporters, cruel-faced like a lynch mob. Some faces were already familiar from the earlier scenes. It was a bar — somewhere so excruciatingly hip it didn't even bother to look it. All organic curves, polished wood and subverted grandeur. The cameras zoomed, their motion stilted by the poor streaming, onto Winston Smith's face. Not a happy face. Nor a sober one.

Then they panned out. And suddenly Daisy burst into tears, then great heaving guttural sobs. And Roland had no idea why. She just pointed at the screen. Again and again at the doubly pixellated image on the wall behind him, filtered through PhotoShop and posterisation effects and printing, then cameras and computer compression, of a young, lost-looking boy in stark monochrome.

'Tell me Daisy, please,' Roland coaxed, now stroking her electric hair.

'That's my son.'

'Winston Smith?'

'No you fuckwit. That's his dad.'

★   ★   ★

It was hard to tell whether it had been hours or days. But Joe was pretty sure that another night had fallen by now if the grey dawnish light that had leaked in behind their captors at their last visit was anything to go by. Then again maybe it was another day. He dismissed the thought. If it were daylight out there, at least there'd be some glint of hope through the hatches at either end of the tunnel. Wouldn't there? Surely even Nelly's expert handiwork couldn't have been so precise that it excluded light completely. Galvanised by a flash of inspiration, he jumped up - and winced as the cable ties bit into his ankles.

'Nelly's periscope!' he shouted.

Lily stirred.

'What?' she croaked sleepily and it was easy to imagine her rubbing her eyes and stretching – although he knew she couldn't be.

'Nelly's periscope!'

'You're having a bad dream, Joe. You're OK. I'm here,' she whispered, assuming the reassuring tone her mum used to use, then faltering as she remembered how empty its promise had proved.

'A nightmare you mean,' Joe came back, surprisingly chirpy all of a sudden.

'You're babbling,' she pointed out, mock-cheerfully mocking.

'No I'm not,' came the excitable voice she loved so much from the other end of her cylindrical universe. 'I mean, I am, sort of... But Nelly's periscope you see...'

Her baffled silence silenced him.

'I'd better explain what I mean,' he said, more levelly.

'Might be an idea,' Lily shot back, striving to keep her voice shake-free.

So Joe launched into the long and detailed story of how he and Nelly and Sweater and Dogshit had laboured to build the tubular refuge that was now their prison (tomb was the word that crossed his mind but he spared her that). At first, Lily was impatient for him to get to the point, but the boyish enthusiasm that these memories infused in him was what most made her love him. She felt she might hurt him if she tried to halt his excitable flow. She even laughed, as he did, when he planted in her imagination the sight of his friends charging about with brick-laden wheelbarrows while this mad scientist type; the archetypal ginger geek kid; the man with the plan, issued his instructions. She even managed to laugh at the irony of their efforts: the fact that it was Joe's and his friends' ridiculously over the top determination to make this place their impenetrable secret fortress that had made it their inescapably secret prison. And maybe their tomb.

Finally Joe got to the point. The one about the periscope – which Lily had forgotten all about.

'...and once we were in here with the hatches battened, no one could find us. We couldn't hear anything and it was pitch dark if we didn't have any candles...' he went on.

'So?'

'Nelly had an idea, as usual. There was a ventilation shaft that came up in the woods where the footpath joins the main road. And you could see light.'

'So it must be night now then.'

'That's just it! I'm not so sure. When your dad and that other fucker came back it was day wasn't it?'

'Well yes. It was light. Yes.'

'But I don't remember any light in here at all before they came in, do you?'

'No – it was dark. But I think I was asleep.'

'There should have been. Just a little shaft of light in the middle – halfway between us.'

'Right where we were?'

'Yes – right at the middle. And there wasn't.'

'And that's a *good* thing is it?' Lily replied, now unable to hide the hint of petulance.

'It might be if the thing blocking the hole is Nelly's periscope! It's a piece of pipe with angled mirrors either end that you...'

'I do know what a periscope is!'

'Sorry.'

'So you stuffed this Blue Peter periscope, made of Fairy Liquid bottles and Mummy's make-up mirrors up the pipe and when you wanted to look outside you all pretended to you were in some old war film and said, "Up periscope!".'

'Something like that,' Joe bleated back, glad she couldn't see the flush that was warming his cheeks.

'Bless!' she cooed. 'But I still don't see what good it does us.'

He had to think about that. In his excitement he hadn't stopped to consider exactly how it helped; he just thought it could.

'Well, if we got it out at least we'd have some light,' he offered feebly.

'True. But we can't even reach high enough to try,' she said, then, with an effort, brightened. 'Anyway, you heard them. It's just forty hours. It's symbolic. It can't be far off that now.'

'It's bollocks. Surely you realise that by now!'

The moment Joe said it he wished he hadn't. Lily's only reply was a stifled sob. If she'd believed it before, she certainly didn't now.

★   ★   ★

Their longest silence in the history of the longest, most passionate relationship either of them had experienced probably didn't last very long at all. But it seemed like weeks. And measured by the rule of two teenagers who'd never before been out with anyone for more than a couple of months it was an eternity. Without the eye contact or sheepish smiles that radiated the form of gravity that kept them in orbit around one another, the invisible space between them seemed to stretch.

Finally, it was Lily who fired out a probe.

'Surely if we shout loud enough, someone will hear us,' she ventured.

Joe smiled. Communication re-established. Thank God!

'Egg cartons,' he replied ruefully, shaking his head, forgetting for a moment that she couldn't see him.

'Let me guess: egg boxes are some obscure scientific invention of your mate Nelly's?'

'Not exactly. They're good for soundproofing and when we all got guitars and…'

'You soundproofed this fucking tunnel?'

'Yep. Sorry.'

'With egg boxes?'

'Yep.'

'Well OK – but we *are* talking *Blue Peter* projects again here aren't we. I mean how effective could it be?'

'Egg boxes, layered on plywood, sandwiching three layers of Rockwool.'

'I'm not even going to ask what that is. So you're saying it works.'

'Oh yes.'

'Certain?'

'Yep. We put a hundred watt Marshall amp in here and got Sweater to play his guitar through it. Couldn't hear a thing outside.'

'That's loud is it?'

'Very.'

'Shit.'

'Shit indeed. Sorry.'

'Stop apologising.'

'Sorry.'

At least we're laughing now, Joe thought, just as he started to cry.

At least she can't see I'm crying, he thought, before the silence so complete you could hear your blood thrumming in your head, in which you could hear a teardrop, gave him away.

'Don't cry. We'll be OK,' Lily's voice crackled through his emotional static. 'Come, on. Nelly's Periscope – how we going to get at it?'

'Shit,' Joe groaned.

★   ★   ★

'It's a long story,' the pixellated rock star was mumbling on the screen, wincing under the barrage of flashlight.

'So tell it,' someone shouted.

Stone shook his head.

'Turn the sound up!' Daisy urged and Roland, understanding the import of this strange transmission, complied quickly.

'...not the time to go into it, because I...' was all they caught of the sentence before it was drowned by a groan of disapproval.

'What's happened? Talk you idiot!' Daisy snapped at the discombobulated ex-rock god.

As if at her bidding, a middle-aged man in an ill-advised biker leather, shirt and tie combo shoved his pasty mug into shot.

'I think I can speak for Stone here. This a difficult time as I'm sure you all understand...'

He nudged Stone, who oozed slowly but with practised efficiency into the adjacent chair that his agent had just vacated.

'This press conference was initially called to announce the launch of Winston Smith's first release since the split of Airstrip One – and the release of a brand new recording of *Bring It On*, which will be released as part of this year's *Children In Need*.'

Jimmy waited for the tide of cackles and sneers to ebb.

'But, events have overtaken us. And both Stone and I feel that it's more important to use this forum to make an appeal for information about his missing son.'

He raised a hand to forestall the anticipated questions.

'Bear with me, please. Yes – Winston Smith, Stone, has a son, whom he has never met. In fact the boy doesn't even know who his father is.'

A rumble of disapproval.

'Before you start writing your headlines, please listen. Please.'

Incredibly, they listened.

'He's good, this chap,' Roland murmured.

Daisy just shrugged impatiently.

'Winston was not in a relationship with the child's mother and she never informed him that he was a father. When, years later, he became aware of the child's existence, he set up a trust fund to pay for his education. And that's as far as Stone's been involved. Of course, the boy's disappearance changes all that – and we're appealing for everyone

watching to think hard. Have you seen this face? Do you have any
information that might help the police to find him? Winston, would
you like to...'

30

Skimming Stone

'Coincidence? Do you really believe in them – I mean in the context of what you and I get involved in...' Daisy's murmur was almost lost in the computers' insistent whirring.

Roland nodded.

'The same characters keep turning up don't they. The really shitty ones; the ones we don't ever want to see again.'

He nodded again.

'Scum rises to the surface.'

'I rest my case,' Daisy stated without any pleasure. 'Do you mind if I do a bit of rummaging about on your time?'

'If I did I'd be a bastard,' he began.

'And you're not!'

'Hope not – but my point is that this is part of the job. OK we can't exactly shop them – but we can do something... Actually I don't know really know what but still...'

Daisy was way ahead of him and was already watching archive news stories she'd trawled up with a net search for teen runaways who were still missing. The hit list ran to thousands in the UK alone. Over 200,000 missing people of all ages each year.

Daisy typed *Hartham-on-Sea* into the database.

'Here's a local one – from my home town,' she murmured as the face of one Stephen Duxford appeared, with his dog Brandy. 'Christ, he lived just up the road from our place. Disappeared November 6th 1976. Last seen at about eleven at night.'

Eyes closed, she held her witchy finger on the mouse and let it scroll and then released it at random. The smiling face of a girl in her early teens appeared. Cross-legged on a carpet, she was beaming with a goofy grin. The next thumbnail expanded to show why. She was holding a tiny black puppy. Behind her was a banner: *HAPPY BIRTHDAY SUSAN*.

Roland leaned in and squinted at the screen.

'Lost on the beach at Brancaster, Norfolk on Sunday 29th June 1969. Presumed drowned by treacherous tides,' he read out. Brother Simon plucked from the sea by the lifeboat. 'So?'

'The family still refuses to accept that,' Daisy pointed out, her fingernail tapping on the screen.

'Well, that's understandable but, you know. A young kid, paddling, gets out of her depth...'

'I know Brancaster beach though. We used to go there in Dad's crappy old caravan – when it wasn't his even crappier old beach hut down the road somewhere. I never could understand why he rented a beach hut in Norfolk, when we only lived a hundred yards from the beach at home. Know what – I've got this vague idea that I once heard a girl my age crying in there. Dad wouldn't let me in. Mum and Bart and I had to wait outside in the rain while he made sure it was all locked up...'

Daisy shivered, shaking off her father and her childhood.

'Anyway,' she went on, 'he was too tight to stump up for a camp site so we had to sit in this windswept gravel car park and wait till everyone else had fucked off before we could get the awning out in case we got kicked out.'

'Sounds idyllic,' Roland sympathised. 'At what age was...'

'Age – I dunno. Nine? Eight? Me and my arsehole brother huddling under a leaky tarpaulin on camp beds and the parents shouting and screaming inside a tin can on wheels!'

'Oh,' Roland murmured, dismissing an image of his more fortunate eleven-year-old self, snorkelling off the beach at St. Raphael at about the same time, and letting a companionable silence settle between them.

A good move, it seemed, because Daisy turned from the screen and softened as she fixed her gaze on his face.

'It was shit. It really was but... There were bits, you know, that...'

'Weren't so shitty?' he smiled encouragingly.

She nodded.

'Bart and I used to talk then. Sometimes, anyway. He was, is, two years older than me...'

'A lot of years at that age.'

She nodded.

'A lot, yes. He was such a fuck up. But that year he finally had a friend – or the closest thing to one he'd ever had. Actually, more of a hero than a mate,' the interrogative inflection of the last sentence suggested a response was required. So Roland complied – and for once he could do so with a confidence that came from empathy with this brother of hers.

'A protector. A good guy to defend him against the bullies. But not a friend exactly. Just a boy with a conscience.'

Daisy's slight nod and smile said 'go on'. So he did.

'And your brother idolised this boy – tried to emulate him but couldn't. Wanted to be him but couldn't. Then realised that you could only be true friends if there was some kind of parity, which there wasn't...'

'You know you've just told me more about yourself than you ever have before don't you,' she whispered, the intended teasing tone slipping away into dangerous sincerity.

'Suppose I have.'

For once Daisy forgot to take the piss and instead went on remembering.

'It was Stone... Winston Smith.'

'The pop singer?'

'Yeah!' she cackled, 'but I doubt he'd like that job description. Seriously though, he was a nice bloke. Maybe he still is. Really looked after my brother at school...'

'He beat off the bullies?'

'No Bart used to beat them off. Stone beat them up!'

'Very funny.'

'Not really. But true. But it wasn't just the knight in shining armour stuff. Richard – that's Stone, or Winston Smith's, real name - used to try and train Bart to protect himself. Not just fighting – for a while he almost made my mad brother normal.'

'And in what way is normal good?' Roland suddenly challenged in spite of himself.

'All sorts of ways when you're the school weirdo and you're getting the shit kicked out of you at home and at school. Richard was mad about all those Arthur Ransome books – *Swallows and Amazons and...*'

'I take it you mean the children's books and not the movie entitled *Amazons Swallow?*'

After withering him with a glare raid, Daisy went on.

'He used to teach Bart about stuff like tides and how to sail and how to light a fire and build a shelter and.'

'So the big pop – sorry *rock* – star was a flipping boy scout!'

'He was a *fucking* boy scout when I met him,' Daisy countered with a smirk that managed to be reproving as well as lewd.

'OK. I'll shut up.'

'And my brother and I hid under the sleeping bags and read *Swallows and Amazons* together by the light of a torch. Which was great...'

'Wildcat Island! Captain Flint!' Roland interjected with sudden glee. '*Picts and Martyrs! Coot Club, We Didn't Mean to Go To Sea!*'

'Christ, not you too! But yeah. And the funny thing was that when Dad caught him he wasn't annoyed. In fact that Christmas, he gave Bart this ancient copy of *Swallows and Amazons* – a first edition. We had no idea the bastard had ever read anything but The Bible. Anyway, Pansy boy would go on and on about all this stuff he'd got from his hero, and now from our dad – tides and marine etiquette and Morse Code and Semaphore and mad ideas about treasure hunts and pirates and all that swashbuckling boy stuff. It was the closest him and The Reich ever got to talking....'

'The what?'

'Reich – as in third. Believe it or not, his dad and his dad's dad were both called Erich – no narcissism there clearly!'

'Oh.'

'It's an anagram of Erich.'

'Thank you so much for explaining that to me,' Roland bitched.

'Sorry. Used to talking to fuckwits. Anyway, it's fucking apt.'

'Apology accepted.'

'Anywhere we went on holiday - in shitholes like Hunstanton - the Reich and the Pansy used to call the locals 'natives' – *in front of them!*'

Roland nodded. He remembered that from the book, the Blyton-esque Blighty whitey arrogance.

'Can you imagine the embarrassment! Anyway, there was a shipwreck that was exposed at low tide. So of course Bart was desperate to walk out about a million miles and explore it and finally one night he got me to go with him after Mum and Dad were asleep. In fact, it must've been almost morning because the sun was coming up by the time we reached the ship. Not that there was much to see – just a pile of rusting metal – but he was a pirate you see. With the eyepatch. Only way he could look cool – later on, Adam Ant was such a blessing for our Bart. Oh, but I haven't told you about that yet.'

One Chalfont eyebrow quivered with a half-formed question – but he decided to let her go on uninterrupted.

'Anyway, the tide was coming in really fast. Scarily fast. One minute we were on hard damp sand – you know the sort that kind of blushes all silvery underfoot? Next thing the water was up to our ankles. Dad had gone on and on at us about the dangerous tides there – how they'd sweep you away before you even saw the waves coming in. "Children are lost to the tides the moment careless parents allow them to stray", he used to say. Or "time and tide wait for no man" or some other cod-philosophical shit like that. Sorry - I'm really going on about it aren't I. But just thinking about the old bastard, he gets right on my tits!'

'So get it off your chest, love!' Roland cooed with an encouraging grin.

Daisy's cat's arse pucker slackened to a smile as she kissed him warmly on the cheek.

'You asked for it darling! So, anyway,' she continued, ignoring Roland lolling back and feigning sleep, 'every time we drove along the lane through the salt marshes he pointed at the warning signs. If we weren't in the car park by six in the evening the road would be flooded. And once we were there, there was no escape till low tide. So I was crying my eyes out – but Bart wasn't bothered. He was laughing at me. Nothing unusual about that – except that he put his arm round me and said, "Dad doesn't know but I do cos Richard told me! It's true we need to hurry back – but the beach is so wide and flat it wouldn't be that deep even if the tide was in. The warnings are only talking about the spring tide...'

'At new moon and full moon,' Roland breathed.

'Yes!'

'So do you mean your dad was lying to make sure you didn't go anywhere? Or that he didn't understand or...'

'I don't know. Don't care any more. It's just that I can't see how this girl could've been swept away there.'

'Why not? I mean, if the parents let a child go out far enough and the tide came in...'

'OK – it's possible. Yeah, perfectly possible. But on that beach you're not talking about Mummy and Daddy being distracted for five minutes – we're talking about letting a kid wander off for a half-hour walk.'

'So?'

'You're not a dad.'

'And you're not a... Sorry.'

'I am one in my head you know.'

'Sorry.'

'Fuck, so am I.'

Another silence hummed between them.

'Where else did you go on holiday?'

'Walton on the Naze... Hunstanton, as I said, Ilfracombe... Some shithole in Wales...'

'That *is* what you're thinking?'

She shook her head. Then nodded.

'I suppose. That's terrible of me isn't it.'

'I hope so,' Roland half-smiled. 'Shall I... Or would you rather...'

'You type – I'll tell,' she mumbled.

★   ★   ★

Between Nelly with his Heath Robinson gadgets and inventions, Joe's Arthur Ransome-inspired enthusiasm for the 'great outdoors' and Dogshit's brief career as a Patrol Leader in the Scouts (before his ignominious obligatory resignation after he and his patrol were caught smoking and drinking pale ale outside the local off-licence while ostensibly on a night orienteering expedition), they'd been quite a resourceful little gang. OK, so their ingenuity was applied to unconventional missions - such as the acquisition and safe storage of porn mags, fags, dope and Woodpecker cider. Nevertheless, Baden-Powell would have been proud – as long as he only saw the means and not the ends (or maybe even then).

Joe had been passing the time by regaling Lily with his reminiscences. And as much as she loved him; as much as she needed the distraction, in the end her gentle snores admitted her boredom. Joe was unfazed though. Lily's snores were kittenish purrs to him. More important was the contrast between them and Dogshit's equivalent, which were more like a chainsaw recorded, slowed to half pitch and amplified through that Marshall 100 watt job they used to have down there. Joe knew this because Nelly had taped a microphone to Dogshit's face, plugged it in and cranked up the volume till the sleeper awoke and, the others all agreed despite his denials in the face of irrefutable nasal testimony,

269

actually shat himself.

In that confined space, it didn't smell good. So, at Nelly's suggestion, a Zippo was produced and several candles lit to burn off the methane. Since the tunnel didn't actually go off like a giant single bore shotgun, they decided that as a matter of policy they would replenish the candles every time they could afford to – and leave a Zippo lighter, with plenty of lighter fluid in a little niche behind a loose brick right at the far end.

'Lily!' Joe shouted, the exclamation resounding like a firecracker off walls that had long ago lost the knack of absorbing sounds.

31

Trawling

'Ilfracombe. 1973.'

Roland tapped the information into the various search engines.

'No one went missing there in '73.'

'1972?'

'Hang on. Yes. A boy called Colin Chesterfield.'

'Walton-on-the-Naze?'

'Year?'

'Dunno. Earlier. I think.'

Daisy spun on her chair and scooted across the floor to where her handbag hung on the back of another seat. A hefty line of speed sent her rocketing past Roland down one of the aisles of files and stared at this information overload like she was looking out of a window at a car crash.

'Walton – yes,' Roland called out over his shoulder. '1971. July. That fit?'

'Oh shit. Oh shit. Oh shit yes I think so,' she near-sobbed.

'Oh shit indeed,' he replied quietly. 'Come here.'

Such was their new complicity or empathy or maybe even friendship or love that he didn't need to look round at her. A big snotty sniff was followed by a quivering, quaking sigh that jet-propelled her on her wheels to his side, where she cried like a hard-bitten, non-crying, hard-arsed high-class hooker with a quicksilver brain and a clichéd, and therefore true, heart of gold.

'Flipping heck,' Daisy finally managed to whisper.

'Fucking hell,' Roland replied and hugged her for a very long time.

Roland had entered every approximate date of every Raines family holiday into an Excel spreadsheet. He'd done the same with the dates of numerous kids' disappearances. The number of matches, though far from complete, showed a correlation that any statistician would find hard to dismiss as a standard deviation. But then no deviation, in Daisy's experience, was standard when it came to her family's fucked-up history.

The Third Reich, it seemed, was not so much the 'Fisher of Men' as a trawler for children.

'It could just be coincidence,' Roland suggested without much conviction.

'Yeah right.'

'Well let's check some more then,' he said, his tacit agreement bringing tears to his eyes and hers.

'How?'

'Well,' he began tentatively, 'in my experience, the ones that make some sort of religion out of their, er, habits, tend to give themselves away...'

Daisy blew her nose loudly, but raised an enquiring eyebrow as she snuffled.

'They turn it all into ritual. They can't admit to themselves that it's just about sex. And if there are rituals, there must be routines; there must be a pattern.'

'Nice one, Sherlock. So where does that leave us?'

'Elementary, my dear Daisy. We look into your father's 'flock'. What's his "church" called?'

'The Fishers of Men,' she replied with a hollow laugh.

'Website?'

'Fuck knows.'

'So get Googling!'

At this, she brightened.

'OK – you take this one,' she indicated the PC, 'and I'll get the laptop!'

And they Googled and Googled and Googled in tandem through the night, calling one another over to check out the results of the latest trawl of the net for the 'Fishers of Men' and by turns goggling and sobbing at their catch. Hour by hour, the inconsistencies in their spreadsheets were eliminated and replaced with concrete correlations. The deviations that had been the norm were now rarities.

Where the dates of disappearances – or at least the dates of their first mentions in the press – didn't match up with Daisy's admittedly approximate memories of childhood holidays, they looked like they might match with one of her father's frequent 'walking expeditions'. What was more disturbing was the almost unerring accuracy of their correlation with the Fishers of Men's monthly 'walks in the wilderness', of which Daisy had been unaware till now.

The two of them had had a few moments of semi-hysterical hilarity when they'd first hit on the 'FOM' website. The appalling childlike grammar and even worse spelling made it hard to take seriously the fire and brimstone and blood and thunder it purported to convey. So staggering was the hypocrisy; so mean-spirited and so ignorant of what The Bible actually said, that it would have been easy to dismiss this 'church' as a bunch of in-bred halfwits, full of shit and in the end fairly harmless.

'Wotcha, Daddy!' Daisy sneered at the screen, then to Roland, 'Tell you what, if I'd seen all this crap when I was a kid it would've been hard to be intimidated by him.'

'Well there was no internet when you were a kid,' Roland murmured.

'No, but I bet there was a network.'

After several more hours of searching, Daisy beckoned Roland. He knelt next to her and stared at her screen – which displayed a grid of dates and times like a railway timetable.

'Tide charts,' she explained grimly, handing him a sheet of paper on which she'd printed a list of the dates of her childhood holidays and the Fishers of Men's 'wilderness walks' in chronological order. 'Check out the dates,' she continued grimly.

Roland glanced repeatedly from screen to paper, trailing down the list with his finger.

'Flipping heck!' he breathed.

'Fucking hell indeed,' she agreed.

'Daisy, I'm so sorry.'

'You agree then? It's him?'

'Looks like it.'

'The werewolf!'

'You what?'

'All the kids round our way used to call Dad "The Werewolf". I never understood why until the first time he left me at my nan's when he went away. I went home to get something and the dogs were howling the place down. It was awful. Heartbreaking. The bastard didn't leave any food out for the dogs; didn't get anyone to look after them. They just howled and howled and pissed and shat everywhere till the evil cunt came home to give them a bowl of food and good hard kicking.'

Roland hugged her and tears flooded out of her eyes as if under the pressure of his comforting squeeze.

'So, how does that…'

'Look at the dates! Every one of them was a full moon. That's why he was the Werewolf – because the howling only happened at full moon.'

'And that's when you get a Spring tide…' Roland completed.

Daisy nodded.

'I've got to help Stone find Joe.'

'Of course we will.'

'You'll help?'

'Just try and stop me. Now, where's this Babington place?'

★   ★   ★

'Hello babe!'

I swam up out of a deep sleep full of unfathomable and frightening nightmares and opened my crusty eyes to see four familiar words in Gothic type floating around in front on me: *I'M MEAT EAT ME.*

And like the last time, they were accompanied by a certain sort of pressure on my groin – which I identified as the pleasantly shifting, warm and welcome weight of a woman straddling me.

'What the fuck are you doing here?' was my gentlemanly greeting to the errant mother of my missing child.

'Lovely to see you too darling!' she pouted, pulling down her black crop top and dismounting. A middle-aged man in an expensive but very old-fashioned suit hovered by the door, shifting uneasily from one foot to the other.

'Rich, this is Roland.'

I sat up and nodded. He nodded back shyly.

'We saw you on the web – on telly too. We've come to help find Joe! Come on – see you in the breakfast room and we'll draw up a plan of action!' Daisy Enid Blytoned.

I grunted. The guy in the doorway shrugged sheepishly at me. He obviously knew her pretty well. I winked at him. He blushed.

'Come on Roly,' Daisy ordered as she sailed out of the door. 'Full English for you Rich, yeah?'

'Whatever,' I groaned as the door slammed after them.

Daisy! Always did make a big entrance.

★   ★   ★

It took a while, but Lily managed to wedge her legs into a rut between the planks enough to get some purchase and begin to strain her body up and out to form an angelic arch from the wobbling floor to a point three feet up the tunnel's concave wall. Anchored at the top only by the friction of her hair against coarse damp brickwork, she edged painfully upward, inch by inch.

Joe could only make out a dim outline curve of white goosepimpled and frozen delectable flesh, picked out by some indiscernible pinprick of moonlight or sunlight or streetlight. The glimpse struck him as beautiful – but her gasps of pain chastened him.

'You OK?' he whispered.

'Six, seven, eight… Nearly there,' she grunted as her fingers scrabbled behind her, reading the lines of mortar like braille.

'Ten rows up, I'm sure of it,' Joe urged.

'Nine… Oh God I can't. I can't Joe,' she began to sob.

'One more brick Lily. One more,' he breathed, torn between love and what had to be done. But the sound of her bare bum slapping the planks told him she couldn't make it.

'Never mind. Doesn't matter. You OK?' he murmured, every molecule of his body screaming silently to cross the uncrossable few feet that separated them.

'Yes. Just about,' she gasped. 'My fucking coat's fallen off now though!'

'Oh no. You must be so cold. I'm sorry. I shouldn't have asked you to…'

And then there was light! Heavenly, warm, orangey flickering light. Doubly heavenly because what it lit was Lily's naked form, gentle curves shimmering in the hesitant lick of a Zippo.

'Da *daaaa!*' Lily giggled, hugging her knees and holding up the lighter towards Joe as if he could catch its warmth.

'Fucking hell!'

'It was the eighth brick you fuckwit!' she laughed as she melted the ties on her ankles.

'Never was much good at maths,' he beamed as she crawled up to him and held the flame to his own ties.

The best hug in the history of hugs had to be cut short though.

'Candles!' Joe ejaculated verbally, just in time.

Lily lifted her face to gaze searchingly into his.

'You what?'

'Were there any candles behind the brick?'

'Call me old fashioned but since I had my hands tied I didn't hang about to rummage around!'

Freed, Joe jumped up. Then fell down, having smacked his head on the tunnel's top. Recovering, he crawled to where Lily had been and felt his way up the brick layers to the hole.

'Yes!' he shouted, pulling out a pack of candles.

'I think "Eureka" is the word,' Lily beamed.

'Yep,' Joe agreed. 'And now I can start doing something about getting us out of here.'

He tried the locks and the strength of the doors at one end to no avail, then the same at the other end. He shoved a tentative arm up the vent pipe and pushed – but if it was the periscope that blocked it, it was jammed solid.

'Bloody Nelly – too good for his own good!'

'For our good!' she corrected.

Joe nodded. Lily lit two candles.

'Better save the rest, eh,' she breathed. 'Come here.'

So he did.

★　　★　　★

I always did love the breakfast at Babington. But I couldn't eat. Not after Daisy and this Roland guy laid out their tide timetables and holiday lists and full moon dates on the table. It took a bit of explaining – and for some childish reason I felt the need to give her a hard time for having my child without bothering to tell me until the day she got busted for 'living off immoral earnings and possession of Class A drugs'. Apparently the social services take a dim view of that sort of thing and Joe was to be put into care.

'I mean, Christ, I know nothing – then, out of the blue I get a call from some social worker telling me the kid I knew nothing about had been put in a children's home. And then that he'd done a runner. Excuse the fuck out of me for being a bit put out!' I moaned bitterly.

Strangely, she took it in good part.

'Rich, I know I was out of order,' she said matter of factly, 'but I wasn't exactly together at the time and up until the moment the Vice Squad came charging in, I didn't want you to feel lumbered...'

'Funny that, because I felt quite lumbered when I ended up paying the school fees,' I sulked.

'Well that was your own fault for being such a snob,' she countered, with depressing accuracy. 'You could've put him in your old school in the first place! But that would have cramped your style wouldn't it!'

'So does she give *you* this sort of shit all the time Roland,' I joked, swiftly changing the subject.

The guy went red.

'For fuck's sake Rich, he's not my *man* – he's my mate. You always were slow on the uptake – can't you tell he's gay?'

The poor bloke virtually wriggled in embarrassment.

'No, actually. I'm not equipped with your legendary GAYDAR,' I reminded her. 'And anyway, it's none of my business. Eh Roland?'

He nodded with something like sheepish gratitude.

'What we gonna do Rich?' Daisy cut in, reaching out and touching my forearm. I don't think I'd ever seen her so earnest or as vulnerable. I had seen her as beautiful though.

'Find him. Somehow. Got any ideas?' I asked helplessly.

With a screech that scared the shit out of a couple of famous broadcasters, the percussionist from a currently hot acid jazz band and the hungover remnants of yesterday's TV crews, she sent her chair scraping backwards and jumped to her feet.

'Were you actually thinking of fucking doing anyfuckingthing mis terfuckingrockfuckingsuperfuckingstar?'

'Yes I fucking was act-u-fucking-ally!' I lied.

'What?'

I hesitated.

'Thought so.'

'Oh so *you've* got a plan, have you?'

'Yes act–u–fucking–ally,' she mimicked.

'Well not much a plan as an idea,' the gay bloke interjected humbly.

Suddenly I felt for him. Liked him, even. I squeezed his shoulder.

'Don't mind us mate. Daisy and I always had a…' I searched for the right word, '…*confrontational* sort of relationship.'

'Relationship my arse!' Daisy carped.

'See what I mean,' I grinned.

Roland smiled. Bonding complete.

'Seriously, though,' I said. 'What can we do that the cops can't?'

'Most things really,' Daisy joked. 'But we do have an asset they don't.'

I raised a sceptical eyebrow.

'My brother,' she said, defying my scepticism and upping the ante.

'What about him? Not exactly my favourite person your brother.'

It took an hour or so, the long story of what Daisy and Roland had found out – about her dad and her brother.

'But your dad's dead,' I exclaimed.

'Nicely put. So sensitive. And so wrong. What made you think that?'

'Bart told me.'

'And you believe a word the little shit says?'

I shrugged.

'Probably wishful thinking on his part. *I* wish he was dead, believe me,' Daisy went on. 'Now, if you'll shut the fuck up and let me continue…'

Little else of what she had to say surprised me after what Bart had done to me and Georgie – and what he'd told me so proudly about his sordid empire. Daisy confirmed it all – that he was a watcher and a lecher; a professional voyeur who'd turned his fetish into a ludicrously lucrative business based on blackmail. Hardly surprising really, given his upbringing – abused at home, abused at school and even at the age of eleven a serial abuser of insects and small rodents. Always an outsider; always the one without a girlfriend – or a boyfriend – the only sense of sexual excitement he ever had, even back then, was through watching others – in the bushes outside bathroom windows, then later through a series of ever more powerful telescopes. Which was presumably why he'd got his sidekick to seduce Georgie: to pique my jealousy further by showing me how little she cared while he stood there chortling and recording every gynaecological nuance from every angle for future use. For him the victory was empty unless the watcher got to watch me suffer.

I said as much to Daisy. She shook her head.

'God. I'm sorry Rich. Why would he do that to you – of all people?'

I shrugged.

'Well, for what it's worth, he seems to have got past his voyeur phase. In fact he's got a seriously tasty babe in tow these days. Which is weird cos I was sure he was gay.'

'Well he probably pays his little buddies to service her,' I said bitterly. 'In fact I know he does.'

She shrugged, unsurprisable; unshockable.

'You're not going to like this Rich,' Daisy warned, the sincerity she so rarely revealed chilling me instantly as she pulled a laptop out of her bag and put it on the table between us.

'Oh fuck,' I said. Not so much surprised as disappointed at the scan of an article in *HEAT* shouted *WINSTON'S WINSOME WOMAN IN THE ARMS OF INTERNET TYCOON!*

'Looking George-ish as always,' I mumbled.

'You didn't know?' Daisy stated.

I shook my head.

'I assumed she screwed that arsehole Burroughs just to get at me – and then fucked off with some billionaire she picked up in Cannes.'

'Looks like you weren't far wrong. Just that the stinking rich bastard happens to be my brother. Sorry,' she added and put a hand over mine. Roland nodded agreement.

'Thanks,' I said, meaning it. 'But it's obvious she was only with me for one thing — and it wasn't my body. Or my mind.'

'Can't say I blame her,' Daisy laughed.

'Yeah, thanks love!' I feigned hurt. 'Tell you for a fact, if she's with your brother it's only because he said he'd finance her fucking film.'

'Whatever. Thing is, Bart can help us find Joe — if we're right about my dad.'

'Why would he though? He hates me. And I hate him now for stealing my Georgie!'

'Because, a) he doesn't hate you. Not really. You're just a symbol of all the shit in his childhood. He loves you. I know he does…'

I laughed.

'Yeah right,' I Yanked. 'That's why he humiliated me, had me beaten up and fucked up and screwed me over. So let's hear "B" just for a laugh.'

'"B" is the fact that he hates Dad. More than he hates anything or anyone. More than he *loves* anything or anyone. We give him the chance to get revenge on The Reich and we've got all his millions and his army of henchmen on our side.'

'I'll think about it.'

'There's no time to think Rich. Tomorrow's full moon!'

'What's that got to do with anything?'

Roland pulled out their sheafs of charts and lists from under the laptop and waved them under my nose.

'Mr Smith, she's right. We really have no time to lose.'

'Call me Rich,' I said. 'Come on, you two obviously have some sort of plan, so let's hear it!'

32

Hurt 'Em on Sea

The plan was that we went back to my hometown — and Joe's, Daisy's and her family's. Hartham-on-Sea. Unaffectionately known as Hurt 'em. I couldn't argue with their reasoning. Every bit of evidence we had and all our shared history had its roots there - it was the shithole from which all this shit flowed. Surely that was where we should start looking. That was fine with me. Made sense. It might also give me a chance to get my own back on Raines and Burroughs, though I wasn't quite sure how.

The bit I wasn't so keen on was the bit where we came face to face with Bart and Georgie — first on a videoconference, then in the flesh. I dreaded it. So it was with more than a little trepidation that I composed myself in front of the video camera in Roland's much-bigger-than-mine-and-with-mezzanine-too Babington room ready to see Georgie again — presumably in the arms of the appalling Raines. It wasn't so much jealousy as humiliation at the discovery that I was worth nothing more than my rock star stock, whose share price had evidently dropped through the floor as far as Bart's new trophy was concerned. I felt cheated. I felt used.

Oh, who am I kidding? I was just jealous. I needed some serious arm candy to make me feel better about this — and to trump Bart's inevitably triumphant crowing. But there I went again doing the egomaniac rock star thing. This wasn't about me any longer. It was about finding the kid. Or was it? I hadn't yet shed a tear for my son, who was dead for all I knew, or about to be or being subjected to some hideous paedophile ritual. I didn't even know him. I should have known him. I should have insisted on protecting him. I should have grown up a long time ago. I should not have let a casual shag lead to a life without being there to nurture it. Him. Nurture him. Be a father. Stop this happening. I thought I'd been careful. Could have sworn. But then, there was the drink and the drugs and Daisy's all-pervasive and persuasive ways… I didn't really remember what happened. But I did remember that rambling rant with Ralph – and that he'd pointed out that if we found the kid I could make a chance to start afresh. I hoped so. At least I think I hoped so.

Lying goggled on a sun bed in the Cowshed, which housed Babington's spa and super-cool yet well-heated swimming pool and which was the hippest barn in the world, I phoned Ralph to tell some truth.

'Hello mate. Remember I told you about Daisy?'

'Yes of course,' he said, and I loved him for that utter lack of the power-trip-pretend-pause-for-recall I was so used to in the music biz.

'She's turned up here.'

'Because of Joe?'

'Yep.'

'That's great,' he enthused, then stalled. 'Isn't it?'

'Yes I think it probably is. She thinks she knows something. We're going to try and find him… But would you come with us? If you don't…'

'Of course mate. If I can help I'd love to!'

'So, you wanna come…'

'Be there in ten minutes!' he gung ho'd.

Jesus I loved that guy. Sorry Jesus. Ralph wouldn't approve of my taking your name in vain – but in my defence, in reference to that saintly man, I'm not sure it qualifies as 'in vain'. I think he's one of you. One of the real ones. One of the good guys. One of the Desmond Tutus. Not the Ian Paisleys or Popes. I wish I could join that club but there's no way I'm wearing sandals.

And while I'm on the subject, I was also reminded how I'd loved Daisy. I'd forgotten how kind and gentle she could be. It was so easy to take her at her hard-faced price and forget her values. She'd teased me about my frantic workout, sun bed and swimming session in preparation for this remote control confrontation with my lost love and my ex-friend, pointing out my pathetic need to live up to the crappy image that had been constructed for me over the years. I'd been hurt. Because I knew she was right. But then she'd turned up and turned out in full-on rock goddess mode hanging onto my arm and my every word as if she were my long-standing and loving wife. More importantly, she was the serious arm candy armour or Karma I needed to face my lost *amour*. And she knew it, bless her. A friend in need and all that.

Just as I made a mental note to ask Ralph to bless her properly – canonise her if possible – the rocking Reverend himself tipped up. I'd correctly identified the growl, fart and pop of his ancient BSA Bantam coming up the elegant tree-lined drive long before his tentative knock at the door of Roland's coach house suite.

'That'll be Ralph,' I said, opening the door to reveal a vision in black biker leathers.

'This is Ralph,' I updated, ushering in the hesitant clergyman and clocking Roland's unequivocally enthusiastic reaction.

'Ralph – this is Daisy. My long lost and now found friend,' I said, now pumped and pompously full of the import of what we were trying to do. Amazingly, Daisy didn't laugh at me. She held out a black taloned hand as if for him to kiss. Ralph took her fingers gently and shook them in a strange approximation of a handshake.

'Pleased to meet you,' he said shyly as he started wriggling out of his brand new and overly stiff leathers.

'And this,' I went on, 'is Daisy's good friend Roland.'

Roland flushed stood and held out a gentlemanly hand, which I'm sure quivered a little as Ralph's dog collar showed itself.

'Any friend of Rich...' Roland began.

'Ooh, a dog collar. I used to wear one of those – only professionally you understand,' Daisy interrupted in a doomed effort to put everyone at ease.

Roland and Ralph blushed in what I'd swear was unison.

'Same here,' Ralph mumbled.

'Different profession I think,' Daisy breezed back and a riffle of laughter shooed away the shyness.

The upshot was all four of us in shot for the conference call. As a team. And I liked it. At the appointed time I clicked the mouse and composed myself for the cam. And Georgie's gorgeousness swam into focus in the dappled, rippling sunlight of whatever glamorous marina Raines Jnr's yacht was moored in.

'Hello Georgie. Long time no see,' I said sullenly.

'Hello Rich. I'm sorry it's worked out this way but if you'd bothered to talk…'

'This isn't about us,' I cut her short, more curtly than I'd intended. 'Daisy says Bart can help us find Joe. So let's hear it.'

'Ahoy there matey!' chirped my erstwhile friend, shoving his stupid piratical eye patch into view.

'Don't "mate" me you…' I began to growl before Daisy piped up with a hasty interruption,

'Ooh look it's a pirate without an "I". Or an "E".'

'I think he might have had an "E" I chipped in.'

'Funny you should say that,' he grinned.

'Shall we get to the point?' I snapped.

'Certainly old boy. I gather you need someone who's good at finding young boys! Well I'm your man!'

Having no hackles to rise, I clenched my fists and looked to Daisy for help. If I rose to the bait, I'd blow the whole idea of getting him to co-operate.

'Brother dear,' she simpered, oozing even more unction than her oleaginous brother could manage, 'I know we haven't been the closest of siblings but now Rich needs you. And I need you — and so does our son. We know all about what you do — and we know you have the power to help us.'

'Do you like my ship sister dear? Named her after you!'

Now Daisy began to lose her cool.

'Yes it's fucking lovely. Bart – just shit or get off the pot will you!'

'Thing is, I wonder whether you've misunderstood the brand name. It's a Sunseeker – spelt S.U.N, not S.O.N. It has no special facilities for tracing missing sons.'

Daisy reached out and clasped my hand tightly to pre-empt an outburst. Amazingly, I restrained myself. Much more amazingly the Reverend Ralph didn't. Daisy and I were seated in the middle of the row of four chairs in shot, like the bride and groom at a wedding. Ralph was on the left, his vicarishness adding to the nuptial vibe - until he lunged across me and grabbed the camera with both hands. We found ourselves watching on the monitor - so much more real than real life - as our co-conferencers were treated to random panning shots of the room's décor from polished floorboards to art deco lamps before finally Ralph got his mug into the picture.

'Now listen you... This is no time for joking. Rich has told me about you and I don't like it one bit. But you have a chance to do something decent and I bloody well think you should shut up and listen to what Daisy, Rich and Roland here have to say to you... You, you, you... self-satisfied *cunt!*' he blathered, then shrank back from the cam.

Silence at the other end. Silence our end, broken after seconds by Daisy's titter. Then mine.

'Talk about an icebreaker,' Raines's startled voice bleated back. 'Are vicars allowed to say "cunt"?'

'To you they are,' I grinned.

'Heavens above, Ralph!' Daisy murmured.

A sheepish Ralph peeped into the periphery of the frame.

'Sorry everyone. But it's Stone's fault. Just had some of his charlie. Again. Can't seem to shut up. You should've heard my sermon this morning. No you shouldn't. Oh dear.'

It was funny. It also worked. If you can't get God, at least have a vicar on your side - even if he's a shitfaced one.

'All right,' Raines sighed. 'What is it you want, sister dear?'

'We think it's Dad.'

'Dad?'

'Yes. I mean it's not just us he's done things to.'

'Shit.'

'Yes, shit. Really shit.'

'All right. I'm listening.'

Daisy and Roland were a great double act. While she read from her bullet-pointed list of the key bits of evidence they'd compiled, Roland methodically fired off PDF documents from his laptop, which Raines received on his super-broadband wireless connection and scanned with his built-in one as he listened. As each screen of information wiped to the next, it wiped away another stratum of his sardonic perma-smirk.

'All our holidays. All his bible basher trips?' Raines mumbled.

Daisy nodded.

'And you see the way full moons and spring tides hook up with those dates?'

Now *he* nodded.

'Yes. It fits doesn't it. So you think the Reich's been kidnapping kids all our lives?'

'Looks like it. And maybe even killing them – and God knows what else in between.'

'Shit. That is terrible,' he said, 'but I don't see how I can help. For a start, I'm in the Med – and you're all in Blighty so...'

'So you get your chopper or your jet out and get your arse over here!'

Raines's blinkable eye displayed his discomfiture - and the hidden one made his eye patch writhe in its attempt to follow suit.

'I don't really see what the point is...'

'How about the fact that Roland here has all the dirt on all your nasty little activities?' Daisy bluffed.

'Roland?'

Daisy manoeuvred the camera to get Chalfont into shot.

'Hello Mr Raines. You might know me better as the proprietor of Chalfont's of St Giles.'

'Oh,' Raines breathed in dismay, then rallied. 'As a client, I'm guaranteed absolute discretion - that's the deal. Are you telling me…'

'Yes, I'm telling you,' Roland interrupted, 'that all that changed when coincidentally I employed your sister. She's in charge now – and she's a lot more ruthless than I.'

'You blackmailing me? You're reneging on the fundamental points of the agreement?'

'We prefer to call it "extortion" – so much more professional, we feel,' I interjected with vengeful glee.

'But, basically, yes,' Roland added.

I shook his hand.

'All right. What is it you want from me?' Raines sighed.

Suddenly he was the mocked and beaten, used and abused freaky geek I'd befriended all those years ago. So I softened.

'Nothing you wouldn't want to do. Not really. Just help us find the kid – and if it really is him that's done this, get your own back on your dad,' I coaxed.

Daisy hugged me. I tried not to cry. Because if I did, I knew it wouldn't be for the boy. Not really. It would be the pure self-pity of the fucked up and faded rock star that I was. If the kid were found dead somewhere I'd probably get a maudlin top ten hit out of it.

'Bart, it's my son. It's our dad we think's got him. He's your… *nephew* for fuck's sake. Or don't you care at all?' Daisy cajoled.

I cringed as Georgie's pixellated image leaned over and embraced Raines. Then the camera zoomed in on his podgy, bloated face. He was crying. And although he now filled the screen, he'd shrunk.

'OK. What do I do,' he wheezed, hyperventilating now; the puffed up fucker was being deflated.

A familiar pair of spade-sized hands passed him an inhaler.

'Roland – get the list out!' Daisy sergeant-majored, then came over all Playschool, 'You sitting comfortably? Then I'll begin.'

We had it all worked out – just in case he co-operated.

'Mr Raines,' Roland began. 'As you know, my company has all the surveillance kit we need. But where you come in is in monitoring internet, email, mobile phone, landline and police and emergency services traffic. I know you have that capability.'

Raines nodded.

'And more,' he added.

'And we want some money,' Daisy added. 'Just to cover costs.'

He nodded again.

'Ten grand paid into the bank account Roland's emailing now – straight away.'

'All right.'

Daisy winked at me. This was going a lot better than expected.

'A chopper on the back lawns of Babington House to get us to Hartham-on-Sea.'

'Back to old Hurt 'em, eh. OK. What time? Give me the exact map reference for my pilot.'

Roland nodded and resumed his laptop tapping.

'Anything else?' Raines enquired with a sincerity I hadn't seen since school. 'Want any of my cigarettes, Richard?'

'We'll let you know,' Daisy said, ignoring his dig at me, 'but for now, we just need you to pass on anything at all pertaining to Joe – or to Dad. You've got people to collate and analyse that kind of stuff yeah?'

'Oh yes. Fine. Send me everything you can get and I'll get them on it… I'll look into…'

But Georgie's face replaced Raines's.

'Rich, I…'

'Fuck off, Georgie.'

★   ★   ★

'I can't believe the arrogant bastard can talk to me like that. He never used to!' Georgie griped, calling up the gangway to Bart, who was sunning himself on the foredeck.

'Well that was before you came to your senses and hooked up with the Daisy Chain,' he crowed.

'Only because the bastard cut me dead for no reason. Jesus, I don't know what I ever saw in him!'

'Well my dear, if a man can't allow his woman to enjoy the odd evening out with civilised company, he's not a gentleman. You're better off without him.'

'You got that right!' she spat with a vehemence she didn't quite feel. 'Know what? I think I just might change the ending of *Rock 'n' Droll*. He comes off pretty good as it stands – but now...'

'We haven't got to the ending yet though,' came Bart's languid reply.

'Course we have – it's all written.'

'As a first draft, of course. But I'll be writing the *actual* end,' he said, stepping lazily down into the stateroom.

'What d'you mean the "actual" end? This is my story – well, the story of me and Stone.'

'Exactly darling. And I've arranged for a conclusion that's dramatic, tragic and moving.'

'You've arranged? What the fuck are you talking about. This is a true story. It's *my* story.'

'Yes I know that. Of course I know that. Which is why I've made the true story a tad more exciting. Just wait and see – and then you can re-write the ending the way it really happens. Trust me, it'll be a tear-jerker.'

Now it dawned on Georgie how she'd been used

Anyone capable of blinking might have missed the glass ashtray missile and been hit. The one good thing about Raines's blink deficiency was that he missed nothing – which is why the missile missed him. So Georgie went into blitzkrieg mode and hailed him with bottles, glasses, laptop computers and everything else that wasn't fixed to anything in the few seconds before Burroughs materialised and manhandled her up to the deck, down the gangplank and threw her to the hot decking of the harbour in front of a score of wolf-whistling yahoos.

The Daisy Chain's engines gurgled then roared into life, as if deliberately to drown Georgie's tirade of righteous abuse. Burroughs appeared at the bow, slackening off the moorings with one hand and casually tossing a sneer and a suitcase her way.

'Cast off!' came Raines's naval command and the ship surged at an arrogantly illegal speed towards the harbour's portals to a chorus of protest from a hundred indignant, teetering, aperitif-spilling yacht-people on the decks of lesser vessels, which rocked sickeningly in the Daisy Chain's wake.

The suitcase cracked open on impact, scattering everything Georgie owned across the immaculate paving for the cackling crowds on the harbourside restaurant terraces to examine and ridicule. It wasn't even her suitcase! What was worse was that the bastards had picked a time when she was naked save for a thong – although admittedly that could have been almost any time.

Presumably on the Raines payroll, the wind joined in the fun and wafted her most delicate and private items of clothing inshore, where orange-tanned Essex boys whooped and hollered as they chased them like puppies chasing leaves in the breeze. Weighed down by way too much gold, all but one failed to catch any of the diaphanous but incredibly expensive flimsies – but at least the one who succeeded turned out to be a success.

'Yours, I believe,' the four-foot wide slab of a man said, not half as lewdly and twice as gently as she'd expected as he handed her a bikini top, which was exactly what she needed. 'You might wanna cover yourself, love. That lot,' he tilted his head at the nearest bar. 'They're a bit... You know...'

'Thanks... Thanks very much,' Georgie gasped, struggling to cover herself and regain something like composure.

'Name's PJ,' he said, holding out a hand, which she took and converted a lift upright to a handshake and rounded off with a winning smile.

'Wanna come to my boat and get sorted?' he suggested, indicating a gleaming swan of a ship not fifty yards along the quay.

'That's a ship, not a boat!' she replied.

'So I'm told,' he laughed, scooping up the splayed suitcase and stuffing everything inside.

★   ★   ★

Hurriedly getting my stuff together in my room, I couldn't help feeling excited. Just getting Raines to do what we demanded was a kind of revenge. The prospect of the private helicopter took me back to my real rock star days – and I had to keep reminding myself that this wasn't a gig; it was a life or death mission. Even that filled me with self-importance, though. Where was Ralph with his humility when I needed him to shame me?

The phone rang. Guy on the front desk.

'Wassup, Guy?' I rock starred and cringed simultaneously.

'Apparently there'll be a chopper on the lawn waiting for you and your party in about ten minutes. Courtesy of a Mr Raines?'

'Fuck me, that was quick!' (It had only been a couple of hours). 'Could you call Daisy, Roland and Ralph and let them know too please?' I replied excitedly.

'Already have. They said to meet in the bar in five.'

Grabbing my holdall, I flung myself down three sets of stairs and through the corridor to the bar with its high Regency ceilings and sash windows, outside which there were steps so you could toddle out onto the lawn – and that's what I did, to find the other three craning their necks at the sky. A few low-slung and drunk hipsters and minor celebs hovered at the windows – even they, even here, were impressed by a private chopper.

'Jolly quiet helicopter, I must say,' Roland breathed.

We waited a few more minutes. Nothing.

'I'll get us some drinks shall I?' I suggested, impatient now. I skipped up the steps, catching the barman's eye on the way.

'Four Bloody Maries, when you've got a minute, *mon ami!*' I called cheerily, almost my old self again as I hauled myself onto a stool to watch his expert alcoholic alchemy. Massive Attack was on the surround-sound. Those Wild Bunch guys seemed to be following me around.

'Turn it up Francois, *s'il vous plait,*' I jollied and as that lovely fat warm bass filled my ears and my guts something in its sibilant top end whispered 'Charlie' to me and in an instant nose-jerk reaction I toddled off toilet-ward. Which was where I got chatting to a pair of newly-weds, their best man, bridesmaids and someone's uncle ceremoniously cutting the wedding coke, camera, speeches and all. It was also where Daisy's unerring nose led her a few minutes later.

'You wanna lay off that stuff a bit. Apparently it's addictive,' her knowing voice oozed under the cubicle door.

I opened it.

'Want a line?'

'Seriously though...' she said, stepping in, cutting mine in half and snaffling hers in one efficient movement.

'It's not the drug I'm hooked on,' I wheezed, mid snort.

'What then?'

'The optimism.'

She nodded.

'Come on. You're gonna need it,' she murmured, tugging my sleeve and leading me back out to the lawns. 'Chopper's outside.'

Of course, I hadn't heard it approaching over the wall-to-wall sonic boom of the poignantly apposite *Safe From Harm*. And there it was, glinting regally in the sunlight and strangely vulgar against the muted elegance of the house. Its sumptuous seat wasn't leather though – just cheap sponge and vinyl. The paintwork gleamed in racing red and its weight bounced gently on its sophisticated suspension system like this transport of delight would any second take flight all on its own. But it was the ape-hanger handlebars and crossbar gearshift that made a Raleigh Chopper the 1970s bicycle the kid in me had always craved. And Bart Raines knew it. A gift tag on the right handgrip told me so: *Here's your Chopper matey. I know you always wanted one!*

33

Spring Tide

'On yer bike Nelly!' the jumped-up new manager of the newly streamlined sorting office chipped in his crappy one-of-the-lads mockney.

'Cunt!' Neil snorted to himself as he stood up on the pedals and wobbled off on his laden red and white postie's bicycle into the relentless rain that had soaked him every day that miserable week. It was only once he'd escaped the soulless, witless expanse of the sorting office that he began to enjoy his job, rain or shine. Long ago he'd stopped being bothered by his parents, pushy uncles and arsey aunts and non-friends' disapproval; their insistence that with four scientific GCSE A's he was wasting himself as a postman when he should be in the sixth form preparing for Oxbridge exams. What they didn't get was what the job gave him. It wasn't exactly his *métier*. But it was his meditation and, in a way, his medication. Prone to asthma and to panic attacks and to extended bouts of the disease they all called 'cleverness', he'd found that his post round alleviated his perennial nervousness while providing what he needed to live on. Which wasn't much: a job lot of baked beans and sausages, some beers, an eighth of weed and some Rizlas were all he needed to get by quite happily each week. Most importantly, the job gave him thinking time: he could cover his daily cycle on a sort of autopilot while his mind carried on working away at his inventions. His subconscious worked through the ideas that would one day be patents and bring royalties and recognition – so he was already on the road to being what he wanted to be. And in the meantime, being on the road as a postman was not too bad at all.

But today he couldn't quite get his head round the final nagging problem with the telecine fault-correction device that had deprived him of sleep for the last two nights. Worse still, last night's news about Joe's disappearance was getting in the way. He hadn't seen Joe for a while – or heard from him. But then, Neil wasn't much of an emailer, let alone letter writer. You'd think a postie would value the notion of old fashioned mail. But he didn't. Neil did equations and coding, solder and circuits – not words.

Of course they all talked about last time Joe had gone AWOL. But he'd been a kid then. They all had. Joe wouldn't have gone back to the tunnel now, surely. And even if he had, it wasn't likely to be intact after all the scumbags who'd found out about it.

He freewheeled, legs akimbo to avoid the spray, through the super-puddles and mini-rapids that had overwhelmed the path past the Werewolf House. He was used to the rain but this was ridiculous – no let-up for days. Swerving to a halt to shelter under the comfortingly familiar conker tree, he leant his bike against the little bridge's rusty handrail. *Since I'm here,* he thought. *Just to be sure.* Ducking through the hole in the fence with a furtive glance over his shoulder, he fought through swathes of nettles and cow parsley, which set him sneezing, and pushed the foliage aside to get a look at the doors and locks he'd been so proud of a few years back. He pulled at one of the padlocks: it was shiny and new. So were the other two. None were his. Evidently someone else had taken it over. *Probably the Water Board or someone,* he thought. *Someone official anyway.*

'Joe?' he mumbled tentatively, then laughed at himself. As if anyone could be heard like that. He looked up through the leaves: no one about.

'JOE!' he shouted.

Nothing.

He took out his Rizlas, rolled a fag and took a few minutes to reminisce.

‪*‬   ‪*‬   ‪*‬

'Did you hear something?' Joe whispered.

'No,' Lily replied.

'Thought I heard my name.'

'Wishful thinking.'

'Suppose so.'

'Don't worry. My dad will come for me in the end.'

Joe couldn't reply. Couldn't tell her what he thought: that they'd been left to die and that her father was in thrall to Raines's screwed up version of Christianity. So he hugged her so tightly they'd either become one or die. Become one or die. Or die and only then their remains become one. In a tunnel. Underground. In a grave.

‪*‬   ‪*‬   ‪*‬

Fuck the Post Office, Neil thought, finishing his roll-up and pulling out his baccy tin to build a spliff. Might as well have a quiet break for some serious thinking. He was about to sit himself down to the right of the tunnel entrance – but stopped when his arse met water.

'Shit,' he blurted.

The stream's water level had risen visibly in the short time he'd been there. But of course, he was upstream. The tunnel was designed to drain away excess rainfall from the streets – and of course Neil had interfered with it. Although he'd laid pipes underneath the tunnel's floor, there was bound to be a bit of a back-up. But it would drain away soon enough. He shifted his arse up the muddy bank a bit and finished rolling his joint.

‪*‬   ‪*‬   ‪*‬

'Joe! JOE!' Lily was shaking him awake, her face eerily uplit by the candle she'd set down between them. Suddenly it was even colder – if that were possible. Lily shuffled closer, eyes wide with a whole new level of fear – and as she moved he heard the swoosh of water, as if she were wading. She was. And she had a hand clamped tight over nose and mouth as if she were about to throw up. She was.

'Oh my God,' he stammered through jackhammer teeth, and retched as the stench reached his nostrils.

'I think it's sewage Joe. And it's still rising.'

He lifted the candle. The black and suspiciously viscous liquid was lapping against the mortar lining the top of the first layer of bricks. With a supreme effort of will, Joe flashed what he hoped was an encouraging grin at her.

'First things first – is the Zippo dry?'

She nodded gravely.

'I put it back behind the brick. At least it'll be safe there, eight bricks up. Won't it?'

'Course it will,' he murmured.

'Oh my God,' she panicked. 'You don't think it could get that high do you?'

'No. No way. It'll soon go down once the rain stops.'

'But look, it's not just coming from upstream!' She pointed to the barricaded doorway at the tunnel's seaward end. Water was spurting and dribbling through its frame like the sluices of a dam. Joe shuffled a few metres towards it. The odour was definitely different down there.

'It's seawater,' he reported grimly.

'You mean the sea's risen up above the tunnel? It can't have – can it?'

'You know what, I think it can. I think it's spring tide.'

★   ★   ★

Neil had been having quite a pleasant dream, involving a harem of women who were inexplicably turned on by ginger-haired genius inventors to the extent that they wanted desperately to massage his nether regions with ice cream. And he wasn't complaining.

'Ohh yes!' he purred as icy cold but gentle fingers probed into his most private places.

'Oh shit!' he croaked as he woke up and found the stream had turned into a river and icy and unpleasantly murky water had crept into every crevice of his stoned and soaked lower half.

'Oh SHIT!' he screamed as a giant turd floated towards the harbour of his crotch on its dainty boat of toilet paper. Scrambling up the slimy bank, slipping and smearing raw sewage down his jeans he retched and puked – more effluent for the swelling flood. Back atop the little bridge he stared down with a kind of morbid fascination at the swirling eddies of slurry, now inches from footpath level. He scrabbled his way through the undergrowth to the wooded peak of the little mound that housed the tunnel. Straight ahead, he could see the waves crashing over the sea wall the other side of the coast road. Behind, the brown flood was creeping into Mimram Crescent, and pooling up at the front of the Werewolf House, rainwater running down from above to mingle with sewage from below and make an oxbow lake. *Good job Joe's not down there!* Neil thought, listening to the insistent tap and clink of the streetlights' internal wiring as they flexed in the heavy gusts of wet wind – just like the sound of the yacht masts in Hartham's half a harbour. It was almost tuneful.

★   ★   ★

Terrible waste of a classic bicycle really – especially one that's a seventies icon. Specially since the evil bastard knew I'd always wanted one and that my mum and dad wouldn't allow it because they were allegedly dangerous. Although I think dangerously flash was really the problem: the pre-teen Ford Escort.

They were all horrified when I picked up the brand new bike and hurled it into Babington's small lake. The mallards quacked up a frenzy and the no longer mute swans hissed haughtily. And I suppose they were right. But I wasn't going humble myself by diving in and retrieving it in front of this audience of the hip and happening. And they, in their Prada and Paul Smith and D&G certainly weren't about to go wading. Once we found Joe; once everything was sorted – then I'd come back, under cover of darkness, in a wetsuit and retrieve it. Or pay someone else to.

Anyway, while I was frightening waterfowl and chucking chairs about, a real chopper turned up. I was so busy shouting abuse at the sky as if Raines were God that I didn't even hear it.

We did that ducking thing you have to do when boarding a helicopter in case you get your head chopped off, then settled in our sumptuous leather seats and took flight. After circling the estate, we set down again so that some idiot could run to his room to get his drugs. Yes, it was me. At least it was me who'd left my baggie behind. It was Ralph who kindly volunteered to go and get it.

The great thing about choppers is they're noisy: you can't hear people moaning and tutting. So the flight flew past, as flights ought to, and in no time we were nearing my horrid home town. The atmosphere was awful. And I'm not talking about the vibe. It had been drizzling all the way but the clouds were happy to slip aside for us to see the patchwork quilted farmland below, leaving wispy trails as if a giant farmer was having a swift contented puff on a Brobdingnagian cigar. But in the final approach it was as if Thor were standing in for God on border control. If he was, he was telling us to fuck right off. Only time I'd seen rain as heavy was in the Caribbean – that welcome soft and warm nighttime rain that's like a power shower from Heaven. This wasn't like that – it was cold and hard rain from hell. Although I suppose rain from hell would be hot – but you know what I mean.

The wind batted us about like the chopper was a shuttlecock and the lightning was all too keen to show us the quick way to the ground.

Which, amazingly, our heroic pilot found in an amazingly gentle, if dizzyingly swaying, way as we all sat in terrified silence. I was on one side, Daisy to my left. I don't know at what point she grabbed my hand or she grabbed mine. All I know is we were holding one another's hands for dear life – someone's dear life, whether it was mine, hers or our son's. Next to Daisy was Roland, who was clutching her other hand. The Reverend Ralph, who'd been very quiet since his television appearance, was looking intently out of the window at a blank wall of cloud like he was expecting to see God sitting on it. Actually he wasn't just looking out there, his whole body was twisted outward against his seatbelt's explicit wishes and his left hand busily drummed on his omnipresent Bible. His right hand, however, clearly didn't speak Ralph's body language and nestled very happily in Roland's.

★   ★   ★

Four bricks high. Four till it reaches the Zippo. Another four and we're fucked, thought Joe, eyeing the brown scum lapping at the walls and hoping Lily hadn't noticed him watching.

'Four bricks. Eight to go,' came her brave but wavering voice.

Shit.

'You know what's ironic?' she said as brightly as she could.

'That my little hidey-hole has turned into a tomb?' he replied and instantly regretted it.

'Cheer me up why don't you!'

'Sorry.'

'No – what's ironic is I've been dying for the toilet for hours.'

'So have I actually. Didn't want to…'

'Do it in front of me?'

He nodded. Lit a new candle from the dying flame of the last.

'Hardly matters now does it,' she laughed.

'Nope,' he agreed, managing a half-hearted chuckle. 'Every little helps...'

'Said the old lady as she wee'd in ocean of shit and piss,' Lily completed. 'My granny used to say that every time we went down to the beach. Well, not quite that...'

'So did mine. I think it's compulsory – an agreement they make when they sign up for their bus passes to trot out some old shite at every opportunity.'

'Like "don't shit on your own doorstep", for example.'

'Yeah. And I've got a new one: at some point after falling in love you both have to admit that you have to piss and shit,' he added wryly.

'Usually when you get to move in together.'

'As opposed to setting up home in a tunnel full of sewage.'

'Not ideal is it.'

'No. But you can't say I'm not romantic. It's beautifully candlelit – what more could a girl want?'

'Oh God Joe I'm so cold and I'm so scared. My dad's not coming to get us is he!'

The brittle levity had to snap. And it was Lily's heartbreaking sob that broke it – and Joe's heart, if not quite his resolve.

'Sit on my lap. Put the anoraks under you.'

She complied, and perched shudderingly on his thighs, her every molecule oscillating as if her body was trying to run away in a billion separate pieces. Joe flexed his leg muscles to raise himself to a squatting position and raise Lily above the water. But his blood had abandoned his muscles and retreated inwards to preserve his warmth. It didn't know its primary mission was to preserve hers. The slight frame that was usually so light now weighed almost unbearably heavily in the hyper-gravity of their situation; of their black hole. Joe gritted his teeth, squeezed his eyes shut and held Lily tight, his cramped, bloodless limbs wobbling under him until finally they gave way and they both subsided into the icy muck.

'I'm sorry Lily, I'm sorry, my legs just went...' Joe cried.

And now Lily kneeled, impervious suddenly to the deathly filth swirling round her thighs, and cradled his sobbing face in her arms.

Now *she* counted the bricks. Six bricks down. Six to go.

★   ★   ★

There's only one hotel in Hartham-on-Sea. Apart from the B&Bs that is – and trust me you wouldn't want to go to any of them. In fact I can't imagine anyone ever did. So we found ourselves in the one Daisy and I spent a fateful night in years before. Roland had booked it – well, he wasn't to know. He also wasn't to know that it was customary for rock stars to book into hotels under an assumed name. Come to that, he wasn't to know I was supposed to be famous. Anywhere but here, I hardly am these days, I reminded myself ruefully as I gazed out of the salt-scoured windows at the roiling brown waters battering what passed for a promenade. On a day just like this more than thirty years ago, my dad had braved the weather at my insistence and brought me down there for the maiden voyage of the inflatable dinghy he'd bought for my birthday. I've still got the photo somewhere: yours truly beaming in glee in a captain's hat, water wings and lifejacket while Dad held fast the ten-foot painter that moored me to him. It was high tide, then as now – and at least according to my childish memory, the waves were frighteningly high. It was a hell of a long way from Cannes.

My mobile rang. *DAISY,* the display said.

'Come down here, it's great!' she enthused.

'Where?'

'Look to your left. Opposite the chippie. On the prom, prom, prom.'

'Tiddly om pom pom,' I completed, spotting her incongruous waving figure next to two other equally out-of-place ones. 'On my way!'

'Don't come out the front way – there's an army of press waiting to

303

ambush you Mister Rock Superstar.'

'Ha ha.'

'No really!'

For a moment I was chuffed. I was still a player! But then it struck me - of course, they just wanted to know about Joe. Dig some dirt on the human interest story. The rock star, the whore and the runaway boy. Humming the Stray Cats tune of that name (the Runaway Boys bit, I mean), I slipped out of a fire exit into the vinegar and candyfloss, seaweed and salty blast and joined the others watching a lone fishing boat battling heroically against the onshore wind towards a blurred horizon.

'Wouldn't like to be out there,' I commented.

'It's getting pretty dodgy on dry land,' Ralph said, pointing down and to the right where, about half a mile away, a few beach huts squatted as if shrinking from the onslaught of the waves that crashed intermittently over the seawall

'Don't think I've ever seen it as wild,' I shouted. 'Or as high.'

'Spring tide!' Roland yelled back grimly, pointing up at the dusk sky, where a giant waxen full moon smirked mockingly through its veil of clouds.

All four of us peered over the wall. Ten feet or so below, another, narrower, walkway paralleled the promenade – not so much for bucket and spaders as to provide access to the arches that summer traders used as lock-ups. Now all that you could see above the waters were the signs crowning each arched entrance. The faded red and white lifebelt station was underwater too – as was the iron-grilled drainage tunnel through which I used to creep as a kid. There was a series of these, conduits for the rainwater and sewage overflow from the town's hilly hinterland and keeping the paved, playgrounded and crazy-golfed, low-lying salt marshes from returning to their natural state – something they tried hard to do every time it rained heavily.

'Rich.' Daisy tugged at my sleeve and I followed her gaze to the hotel entrance, where a *Sky News* outside broadcast van was pulling in.

'Shit.'

'I don't know, Richard,' Roland mused. Do you not think we might use the media to flush this Raines chap out, as it were?'

'Hark at him, all media savvy!' Daisy crowed.

'But IF it's him, and IF he's got the lad – they're both very big ifs, don't forget – we'll lose the element of surprise,' Ralph pointed out.

'Don't think we've got a lot of choice in the matter,' Daisy interjected, nudging me urgently. 'Anyway, the Reich won't be watching telly – doesn't approve. He's like the Amish.'

I turned to face a gaggle of reporters.

'Mr Smith, have you come home to Hartham to search for your lost son?' a callow and cagouled cub reporter pressed.

'What do you think?' I replied tersely, then relented. 'I don't really know *why* I'm here, to be perfectly frank, guys,' I began, pausing as several more notebook and camera-touting figures scurried across the road to join us. Once they were all within earshot, I resumed, careful to avoid specifics or any hint that we thought we were onto something. 'I guess I felt a need to be in my hometown; to be close to where Joe disappeared. At least I'm here if he needs me.'

A TV reporter stepped forward.

'Is there anything you'd like to say to your son? Or to the public? Mr Smith?'

'Thanks. Yes,' I said and squared up to the camera with practised ease.

'Joe, if you're watching, please get in touch. I know you've never known me but I hope to put that right as soon as we find you.' I grabbed the sleeve of Daisy's long leather coat and tugged her into shot. 'I've got your mum with me and we're very, very worried.'

'What's your name love?' someone at the back of the still-growing huddle called out.

Daisy was uncharacteristically shy. I put my arm round her, conscious that this looked like the staged show of unity that disgraced MPs put on for the press to elicit sympathy, but also aware it was real.

She was crying.

'Her name's Daisy Raines and it's not her fault she was never a real mother to him,' I replied for her, alluding to the less-than-sympathetic press accounts of Daisy's 'career'.

'So whose fault is it?' a young woman sneered. 'Ms Raines has hardly been a paragon of virtue… Come to that neither have you Mr Smith!'

'Ask the fucking cops! And who do you think you are, standing in judgement of a woman you know nothing about… Fuck off!' I Geldoffed.

'Charming,' the wannabe red-top writer smirked, scribbling in her pad with great satisfaction.

'And if someone's holding my son… I'll…' I blurted. But now I was crying too.

I thanked God that the rest of these local hacks lacked the paparazzi ruthlessness I'd once been used to. They fell silent - respectful even - and shrank quietly away. The four of us just stood there, shivering, and watched the sea sink back, flex its muscles and lunge at us again and again and again.

A bleep broke through the noisy silence as if Daisy's phone had been waiting for a lull before piping up.

COPS HAVE LINKED JOE TO GIRL CALLED LILY BUNTON. FATHER ALAN. LIVES HRTHM. GIRL ALSO MISSING said her brother's text message as a gust spat spume at us off the crust of a dirty wave

'It's gonna be dark soon. Another day lost. Let's get back and get cracking before we drown,' Daisy sniffed.

34

Scum Rising

The scum was fizzing and sloshing at the seventh layer of brick and, shivering uncontrollably, Lily and Joe were now made to stand, the arch of the tunnel's walls forcing them to stoop and stare this shitty death in the face. Lily ground her teeth, maddened by Joe's insistent, rhythmic clink, clink, clanking of the Zippo against the rusted mouth of the vent pipe. Having failed to extract Nelly's periscope, he still had no idea whether it was night or day or how many days and nights had passed. The waves' steady battering and the vile tide's slow but inexorable rise against sodden bricks and mortar was the only measure of time.

'Please God save us,' Lily wept, pressing her numbed palms together.

'No point praying to him,' Joe muttered. 'He's on their side.'

With every breaker, the sea was hurling itself against the seaward hatch with ever increasing force, each terrifying crash followed by the hissing and clattering applause of tumbling pebbles, as if the beach were cheering on the assault.

Lily held the candle up to her face.

'Well have you got any better ideas?' she shouted angrily.

He shrugged.

'And will you stop that fucking tapping! It's driving me mad.'

He stopped. But not for long. Lily was too weary to press the point – and anyway, the tiresome tune soon became inaudible. Like the unheard tick of a familiar clock.

                    ★   ★   ★

'Right, let's check out this Bunton bloke,' Daisy said, blinking back
the tears. After a shit, shave, shower and snort break, we'd reconvened in
Daisy's hotel room – ever the gent, Roland had booked her the best the
Hartham Arms had to offer: chintz city, pretty in pink with tea-making
facilities.

'Already started,' Roland said, stiffly perched on a chair and tapping
away on his laptop.

Ralph was pacing up and down anxiously.

'What's up mate,' I asked, surprising myself with my tenderness of
tone.

'I feel I should be doing something – but for the life of me I can't
think how I can help.'

'I can,' Daisy said, reaching up to take him by the trembling
shoulders and gently sit him down on the edge of her bed.

'You're a vicar. So go to church,' she urged, searching his eyes for
the cloud of utter bafflement to disperse.

'You've lost me,' he admitted after some thought, scratching
the aquiline nose that made him so crow-like when in his priestly
vestments.

She looked to me. I shrugged.

'You've got me too.'

'Oh you fuckwits!' she sighed. 'Look, it's all very well waiting for
Bart to come up with something – but we know the fucker can't be
trusted. And we can do our best getting information off the net – but
my dad's a religious nutter. And so's Ralph!'

'Is that what you…' Ralph began, horrified.

'Shit, no! Sorry – religious. Not nutter. Sorry, sorry, sorry.'

'Oh OK,' he beamed.

'What I mean is that you could talk to the local vicars, churchey
people… They must know something about Dad's "Fishers of Men"
rabble. And I bet they don't like them.'

Ralph jumped to his feet.

'Yes! Of course. The local vicar or priest would certainly have some insight!' he exclaimed, suddenly flushed with enthusiasm.

'And you're the guy they'll talk to!' Daisy smiled.

'Where's the phone book? I'll go and see some people straight away!'

'You might want to get changed first,' I pointed out with a smile.

He looked down at his black-leather-clad gangly body and grinned sheepishly.

'Yes, see what you mean. Dog collar and tweed jacket it is!' he beamed and beetled off on his mission.

★　　★　　★

'Father Moncrieff, thank you so much for agreeing to see me,' said Ralph as he stepped through the gloomy portals of the church, dazzled by the gleam of candlelit gilt.

'Well you sounded desperate Mr… Pembroke, was it?' the priest said over his shoulder as he lit a candle, which showed Ralph a face that looked even older than his venerable church. So, he was about fifty, tops. Although its interior décor was definitely traditionally inspired along the theme of martyrdom and purity and lots of gold and guilt, the building itself looked like someone picked up the wrong set of plans and built a hybrid comprising half a bungalow with half a multi-storey car park.

'Pemberton actually,' Ralph replied humbly, as if it were his fault that his name wasn't Pembroke. 'And yes, I really do think this is a matter of life and death.'

'So I'll do my very best to help you if I can, Vicar,' the priest said in his kindly, practised priestly tones.

'Well it's a long story,' Ralph began hesitantly. 'I'm not sure where to start really.'

'Fancy telling me over a pint?'

In a dingy pub full of reverent locals, a few steps from the concrete church, Ralph gave Father Moncrieff the low-down over several pints of the local ale.

'Bitter and twisted, like the scum that live here,' was the priest's opinion of the local brewery's finest. 'But it's fecking cheap!'

Little of what Ralph had to say appeared to ring any bells — until he mentioned Lily and her connection with Joe.

'Lily Bunton?' the now decidedly pissed cleric slurred.

Ralph nodded.

Moncrieff suddenly sat up and shuddered, as if shaking off the alcohol's effects.

'There is something. But it was something I heard in the confessional.'

'Ah.' Ralph murmured. 'Then, clearly, you can't tell me.'

'No,' he replied, his eyes rolling back in their sockets as his head lolled tableward.

Despair welled up in the Reverend Pemberton. He couldn't ask the father to breach the sanctity of the confessional. Could he? Anyway, it was a moot point because the old guy was clearly going to pass out any minute. Suddenly the priest shook himself.

'Call of nature!' he slurred as he swayed towards the gents.

'Forgive me Lord,' Ralph murmured as he fumbled for a little polythene sachet in his jacket pocket, found it, ripped open its prim lips and, after a furtive 360 degree scan, sprinkled its contents into Father Moncrieff's half-drunk pint.

'God forgive me,' he mumbled and as he sat back to wait for the coke to take effect he re-ran his stoked conversation with Stone: cocaine, the secular confessional. *First I become a drug user. Now I'm a drug dealer. What on Earth is happening to me?*

An hour later the old buffer still wouldn't shut up but, among the intimations of shaky faith and shakier hands at Communion after a night on the booze, Ralph managed to glean some information about Raines.

'Fishers of Men my fecking arse,' the priest growled at the first mention of Raines's name. Feckers of Minors, more like – that evil fecker's a greater disgrace to the Christian faith than… For a moment he was at a loss for a greater treachery… Than those paedophile priests in America that got off scot free thanks to his feckin' Holiness and his Papal bull!'

'But Father, you *are* a Catholic minister, are you not?' Ralph asked, now very confused.

'Sure I am – but that's not to say I can't criticise it. And you're an Anglicanostic, I take it?'

Ralph laughed.

'Yes. Anglican, but believe it or not I really do believe in God! Look Father, if you think this Raines has been up to no good it's your duty to help us stop him. My friends have been checking up on him – and something terrible happens to a child, somewhere in this country, every time it's a spring tide.'

The priest nodded, frowning.

'At full moon, you mean. Lord preserve us – did you know all the kids call him the werewolf? Because the dogs howl at full moon in his house?'

Ralph nodded.

'What did Lily Bunton's mother tell you, Father?'

The priest took another big swig of his souped-up beer and Ralph couldn't resist a grin. That would do the trick.

'Day before yesterday, she came in. Waited for everyone else to disappear before she came into the box – always know it's going to be a big fat juicy sin when they do that!' he grinned, then put his hand on Ralph's. 'This goes no further – just between clergymen, you understand?'

'Yes. I'll be ecumenical with the truth, as it were – but you appreciate I must act on the information?'

The priest smiled at Ralph's quip and shrugged agreement.

'Mary was in a terrible state. Sobbing. I remember I passed her a handkerchief. She suspects – no, actually I think in her heart of hearts she *knows* – that Raines and his fecking flock are involved in ritual abuse of children.'

Ralph went white. Not that he was surprised – but to hear corroboration of Daisy and Roland's theory from a priest, no less, was unexpectedly distressing.

'Oh good Lord.'

'It gets worse. Her husband, Alan, is part of it. She doesn't think he's actually been part of the abuse but he's apparently in thrall to Raines. Have you seen the man?'

Ralph shook his head.

'The epitome of evil in my book – a scruffy, smelly old fecker – mid-sixties I'd guess. Greases his hair back like someone from the forties, like one of those repulsive American TV evangelists without the suntan - or the money.'

'But why was Mary telling you – not the police?'

'Because she's part of it all, albeit in a passive way. And she's terrified – not so much of her husband; he's a spineless little shite of a man, but of Raines. And of course, she knows she's culpable…'

'Hence the confession,' Ralph concurred.

Father Moncrieff paused for a gulp of beer.

'You ready for this?' he burped, crossing himself robotically.

'She's sure Raines routinely rapes a virgin girl at each of his so-called church meetings. And last week it was Lily's turn.'

'Oh my God. Where…'

'They hire the grammar school's old sports pavilion once a month – why the school allows it I don't know. I've asked them time and time again to blacklist them but they won't. I don't know why. Maybe someone there's part of it.'

'She's sure Lily was raped?'

'Not a hundred percent – all she knows is they locked Lily in the pavilion alone. Some sick ceremonial shite of theirs. Apparently after he's had his way with the girls, he imprisons them for a day or so. Raines confiscated her mobile phone – but Mary managed to steal it back and leave it in the girl's bag, thinking then she could at least know she was all right. But Lily never called – and she hasn't been seen since. Neither has her boyfriend – a young tearaway called Joe.'

'That's the lad we're looking for. My friends, they're his parents.'

'Ah the rock star and the whore! What a start in life that lad had!'

Ralph looked startled.

'Did you not see the six o'clock news?'

Ralph shook his head.

'They're friends. They're good people – really,' he murmured.

'I don't doubt it – Christ, anyone looks like a saint compared with that bastard Raines!'

'Have *you* not been to the police?'

'Oh yes – but I had no evidence. Just a gut feeling. They wouldn't even put him under surveillance. Of course, that was months ago – before poor Mary came to see me.'

The import of Ralph's mission seemed to have sobered him – that or the covert cocaine, or both.

'So you think Raines has got both kids?'

'Yes. Have you any idea where he might hide them?'

The priest shrugged.

'I'd have suggested the pavilion – it's hardly ever used these days. But Mary said she'd been up there. Looked like someone had broken in, windows smashed and door wide open – so she had a good look round but found nothing.'

'What about her husband then?'

'He's claiming the boy's abducted her – reported as much to the police.'

'And they believe him?'

'Why wouldn't they? He's known as a tearaway – a wayward kid from a care home – and of course he's gone missing before.'

'Thank you very much Father – excuse me a minute would you? I must phone the others and let them know.'

★   ★   ★

Being famous definitely has its advantages – even when you're on the wane. The hotel offered us use of their dingy 'conference suite' as a sort of 'incident unit', complete with a couple of PCs, broadband wireless net access and a phone. They even kept us supplied with coffees and sandwiches – and seemed a little hurt that none of us had the slightest appetite.

I suppose Ralph's breathless report should have been encouraging in a way – at least it proved that all our suppositions had been right on the money. But it was also chilling for exactly the same reason. Worse still, we now knew we had *two* kids to find.
'Where's this Mary live?' I asked Ralph.
'The Father didn't know – but in the town somewhere.'
'Surname?' Roland called from his workstation, already clicking on the local directories.
'Bunton. She's called Mary, as I said. Husband's Alan.'
'Ex-directory,' Roland said after a few seconds' tapping.
'Get Bart on it!'
Roland swivelled in his chair to face his seriously whizz-bang laptop and with a brush of the track pad the G5 Powerbook lit up and almost instantly Raines's smug mug filled the screen.
'Hello chaps!' he smirked, his levity annoyingly immune to the gravity of the situation. 'What can I do for you?'
Daisy hurtled past me on her wheeled studio chair like it was a chariot, determined to pre-empt a breakdown in co-operation caused by my undiplomatic frame of mind.
'Mary and Alan Bunton – parents of Lily Bunton. Reported

missing two days ago. The husband's one of dad's Bible bashers. They're ex-directory. We need their address, phone, email - any info you can get. And fucking quick!"

'Consider it done, sister dear.'

'Can you send it direct through the wireless connection?'

'I can do better than that – pop over here and see me! Look out the window! I'll give you a toot!'

Exchanging suspicious glances, all four of us stood and peered out over the half-flooded coast road to the harbour.

A foghorn blurted out, clearly audible above the howling wind and through the rattling window, and a sleek, white ship, blazing with lights like a birthday cake, nosed into the harbour entrance. The *Daisy Chain*.

'Well get your arse over here then!' Daisy said.

'Ah, bit of a problem there,' Raines voice chortled from behind us. 'Small matter of an arrest warrant for serious fraud if I set foot in old Blighty – so I think I'll stay put if it's all the same to you.'

'No it isn't,' Daisy replied, glaring at the screen.

'Flash fucker!' I growled.

'I heard that!'

'Just get cracking and send everything across as you get it. You never know what might help.'

'All right, all right, Bunny and I are on the case! Have they got CCTV in this dump yet?

We all shrugged.

'I'll check – if they have we can get into it and get my team to run it through my facial recognition systems. I'll soon tell you if the kids – or my darling daddy and his buddy are around.'

'Bloody hell,' I marvelled, and kicked myself for letting him see I was impressed. 'What team? Where?'

'I've got about a hundred little techies on the payroll dear boy – all sitting in front of their PCs all over the world. "Where" doesn't come into it in cyberspace!'

'Yes, we're all ever so impressed – but how about you getting off your arse and actually helping. In person. Dunno if you're familiar with that concept,' Daisy carped.

'And get arrested?'

'The cops are too busy looking for Lily to worry about the likes of you. And anyway, don't you think saving two lives is a bit more important than saving your fat arse?'

'All right, all right,' he surrendered. 'Tell you what, I'll take a drive down to the old homestead – see if Daddy's home.'

Daisy winced at the very thought but nodded.

'Worth a try. But if he's there – which I doubt, since it's full moon – he's hardly likely to keep them there!'

'He might find something out though,' Roland pointed out.

'Get your lardy arse over here pronto then,' Daisy ordered.

'Wouldn't you like to come and see Daddy too?' he smirked.

Daisy shuddered and shook her head emphatically.

'Just get here,' she said flatly.

35

Dark Side of the Moon

Star Trek: *The Next Generation*. Why couldn't they do a new series? Although Neil had Patrick Stewart down as the definitive Federation Captain, Shatner aside, even he had *TNG* fatigue, having seen every single episode a hundred times. At least it felt like it. *DS9* was on Sci-Fi but that was crap. Specially when you weren't very stoned. So he flicked through the channels and stopped at VH1. A Pink Floyd documentary. He tutted at their crassness. Hardly a mention of *Atom Heart Mother*. No more than a passing reference to the insane genius of Syd Barrett. Just a whisperingly reverent review of *Dark Side of the Moon* - of the bleeding obvious. That once-loved, now tediously familiar cash-register click and kerching on the intro that formed the root groove of *Money*. The song that had been playing on endless repeat in the iPod of his mind and driving him nuts for no reason he could think of all day long. He didn't even like the tune – the closest the Floyd came to a pop single. Apart from *Brick in the Wall*. The one Joe always used to tease him about because he was so punkier than thou. Because he had this 'Never Trust a Hippy' thing he'd picked up from some sad old punk rocker somewhere, sometime.

In spite of himself, Neil grinned at the memory and lit a celebratory spliff. Back at school, the deal had been that you tapped out the *Money* groove on the pipes if old Patel was approaching. But Joe always had to wind Nelly up (it was always 'Nelly' in those days) by tapping that bloody rhythm out on the pipes every time he knew a spliff or a tailor-made was about to be sparked up. The little bastard! Neil took a deep tug on the fat joint he'd rolled. This was no crappy hash; it was his special homegrown grass and as that uncontrollable full-face beatific beam took over, he snuggled contentedly on his beanbag and sang under his breath:

Money, it's a crime. Share it fairly but don't take a slice of my pie!
Money, it's a hit. Don't give me that do goody good bullshit,
But if you ask for a rise it's...

Neil sat up like he'd been electrocuted. He'd been tapping out that insistent rhythm on the top of the TV, using the remote as a drumstick.

'Shit!' he shouted yet again as he realised why that song had been in his head all day. It was what the streetlights had been clicking in the wind. Or what he'd assumed was the sound of the streetlights - and it was still that groove in which he tapped three numbers on the remote to get the news channel.

'*...waves crash over the sea wall, Hartham-on-Sea is facing a battle against the elements − and against time. Hell raising rock star Stone, formerly of the legendary Airstrip One rock group has arrived in town in search of the missing son he's never known, accompanied by the runaway's mother, a former prostitute...*'

The reporter was standing outside the Hartham Arms. There was nowhere else round there that a famous person could possibly be staying.

'Shit!' Neil shouted at the walls of his bedsit.

'Got to stop shouting "shit",' he shouted to himself.

'Got to stop shouting to myself,' he whispered as he ran out of the door, ducked back for his tin of gear and hurled himself out into the elements.

36

Shit and Fans

It was hardly a minute before Roland's printer wheezed and whirred into life, spewing out information on the Buntons. Ripping out the first sheet the moment the print carriage slid back on its final pass, I came on all leaderish.

'Right, Roland, get Reception to get us a cab to this address,' I commanded, waving the paper at him. 'Daisy, maybe you should phone this Mary – better coming from a woman, another mum… Tell her we're picking her up and bringing her back here via that sports pavilion.'

'Where's that?' she asked, already on the phone.

'Oh I know that place all too well!' I replied, hauling on my coat.

'Rich, hang on a minute,' Ralph piped up. 'Don't you think we should talk to the police?'

'I'm not sure we have time, Ralph,' said Roland. 'I mean it's not as if we have anything but hearsay.'

'But still – surely the more people searching, the more chance we have of…'

'Tell you what,' Daisy interjected. 'How about Ralph goes to the cop shop with everything we've got? They're a lot more likely to listen to a vicar than a hooker or a pop singer!'

'Rock singer,' my ego corrected.

'Yeah whatever, love!'

'That sounds like a plan. Let's go,' I hooted, already halfway out of the door.

'Rich – hang on,' Daisy called out. 'Guess what – I got her mobile.

Mary Bunton's, I mean. She'll be here in a minute.'

'Tell them to send her straight up,' I said, taking off my coat just as Ralph was putting his on.

'Rich. You can't...' Ralph started.

'I know. I won't let on about the confession. Well, I'll do my best. But you know, once you've had some of MY Charlie, who knows what you'll confess to!' I teased.

'Please,' he pleaded.

'Don't worry mate,' I relented, feeling a bit ashamed of myself. 'Do what you can with the cops and give us a shout soon as you get a chance.'

He nodded and ducked out, hunching his lanky frame the way the too-tall do when they want to look inconspicuous and failing dismally. In fact, with his aquiline nose and long angular face, he just looked like a vulture instead of his usual crow, when he should have been a dove. Which is presumably why a timorous Mary Bunton nearly shat herself when she literally bumped into him as she exited the lift as he hurriedly tried to enter. Peering out of the door down the flock-walled hallway, my heart went out to both of them – for not entirely different reasons. To him because he really was the truly gentle soul everyone talks about but nobody's ever met. And to her because she was going through an ordeal whose horror I was only beginning to comprehend. She was a mother – a real and proper one as far as I knew, to whom the loss or abuse of her daughter must be the most unbearable of tortures, especially if, as we thought, her own husband was complicit in her abduction and God knew what else. I hadn't even found out what it was to be a father. So how could I feel the pain she was feeling? I couldn't. But maybe I was learning to. There was definitely a dull, sick feeling deep in my guts – a bit like the one you get when you fall in love. But not that weirdly welcome pain – something much more ominous. More like the aftermath of a well aimed kick in the balls actually – or of love lost. Maybe there's a reason for that – the attack on your testicles signifying the death of hypothetical offspring and this new version of the same dub-bass-deep ache portending the demise of offspring whose existence had till now been hypothetical – to me anyway – and was now agonisingly real. I wasn't sure whether I wanted to know what it is to be a father or not. I certainly could do without this pain, this fear, this giving a shit. Not giving a flying one had always been a reliably prophylactic worldview for me. More reliable than any other prophylactics anyway – because Trojans or Durex or Mates had failed to insulate me like they'd promised, from love or from a world of pain.

'Mr Stone?'

Mary Bunton's reedy, quailing voice was like chalk on a blackboard. Pain was what it wrote in its scratchy italics. I jumped up and accidentally assaulted her in an attempt to help her with her coat.

'It's Rich, actually – or Winston. I mean not "mister". I mean, "Winston" – or Stone. It's like "Sting". Just a name I…'

'Shut up Rich,' Daisy said, quite kindly and with a smile. 'Mrs Bunton, thanks for coming.'

Roland jumped up and joined in with Daisy's clucking and fussing around the new arrival.

'Cup of tea? Coffee? Sandwiches?'

Mary shook her head politely to all their mumsy offers and perched on the edge of the sofa in the corner of the room, as far away from us as was possible without slipping through the walls like a ghost. And she was wraith-like; a haggard refraction of her daughter through the dirty prism of two decades; an image of the daughter who might soon be dead, if she wasn't already; the girl I'd seen in the police photos and in every image Raines had dredged off the net – school netball team shots, the local paper's cheesy picture of her receiving some school prize, that sort of thing. Mary was about my age but so much older. Like one of the prematurely aged pram-pushing babymammas I used to see carting their bawling brats through my home town's shitty streets like advertisements for contraceptives on wheels – the ones you knew at primary school but who'll never pop up on Friends Reunited because betting-shop-bound hubby won't let them have a computer. Or a life. The ones who made me feel a little bit better about myself because I hadn't done that to anyone. Well not exactly. Not quite. I oppressed women in far more creative ways. I mean at least they had a sporting chance. And at least I usually came off worse.

If she could smile now, I imagined, we'd see her daughter's unsullied smile in hers, identical apart from a wrinkle or two. But of course smiling wasn't going happen anytime soon. So I tried to do it for her and amazingly elicited the faintest trace of the infinitesimal DNA of a thing called hope that her face had almost forgotten how to recreate.

'Mary, thank you so much for coming. Seems your daughter and my son – *our son*,' I corrected, indicating Daisy, 'are very close.'

She nodded, her face rigid, hands clenched in her lap.

'You don't remember me do you,' she said, stating a fact, not asking a question.

My music muscle put its stylus straight in the groove of that bloody Hot Chocolate song again, complete with vinyl scratch effects: Errol Brown's histrionic, You don't remember me do you! You don't remember me do you!

And suddenly I did remember her. Aged five or six or seven, I'd cried when she didn't turn up to my birthday party. A white-skinned pixie with the blondest curls I ever saw and limpid pale blue eyes and so timid no one ever really heard her speak. Too beautiful to be shy – it was her name that made her that way. Mary Bumstead. AKA Bumface. AKA Arsehead. The pretty girl the other girls bullied:

Mary, Mary quite contrary
She's so ugly she looks scary
Mary Bumstead, from our class
Cos her head looks like her arse
Mary Bumstead go home now
Cos you are an ugly cow

Thirty-five odd years on it had taken the echo of that cruel singsong ditty to tell me why I'd been crying at that birthday party. It wasn't just because she hadn't turned up. It was because it was my own fault she hadn't turned up; because I'd been a coward and a bully and joined in with the rest of them. Like a Nazi in fact – I was just acting on the orders of my peers.

'God, yes I remember you, Mary. Sorry – I didn't at first… How are you?' I blathered. How dumb can one man be? 'Sorry. Stupid question,' I apologised.

'It's all right,' she replied, and a watery smile almost broke through her clouded face.

It took Daisy to break the awkward silence. Bless her.

'Seems like people going missing is bringing a lot of us back together,' she said with a forced breeziness whose warmth was cancelled out by a particularly ominous blast of wind rattling the windows like an order to get things moving. So we got things moving.

'Mrs Bunton,' Daisy said, 'we've got a lot of information to show you – and you're not going to like it. But we haven't got time to go through it all… Or to spare your feelings…'

Mary closed her eyes.

'Just tell me what you know,' she said through gritted teeth.

So we told her. And she sighed. And cried. And then she leapt to her feet.

'I'll fucking kill him!'

We jumped to our feet – all three of us.

'Mary, we're not saying your husband's the one…'

'Oh yes he is. He does anything that sanctimonious fucker tells him. I can't believe I've…'

Suddenly she wasn't on her feet. She'd fallen to the floor. I picked her up and set her down on the sofa; she was surprisingly light, considering what she had to bear. I brushed a tress of her brittle blonde hair out of her red-rimmed eyes and gently tucked it behind her ear. Then I took both her ruddy, scaly hands that did dishes in mine that didn't and said,

'We're going to find them. It's going to be all right.'

As I hugged Mary as if my diluted newbie paternal concern had the right to empathise with her high-octane, long-term maternal anguish,

Daisy smiled at me. I think it was with approval.

'Have you any idea at all where your husband could be?' I coaxed gently.

'If I did I'd be on my way wouldn't I!' Mary snapped, not unreasonably. 'Raines's place maybe.'

'My brother's going to check it out soon as he gets ashore – he'll be here any minute. Roland, phone Bart and tell him he's taking Mary with him.'

Headsetted and efficient like NASA Mission Control, Roland nodded.

'Come on,' Daisy chivvied. 'Let's get going. We'll all go mad otherwise. Any other ideas, Mary?'

Mary and I stood up, together, releasing each other with a frisson of reluctance.

'Well I know they had Lily locked in the pavilion – she's not there now. I looked. But maybe I missed something, she said, brushing off despair with a flick of her hand that simultaneously seemed to wipe on a faint flush of hope.

'As good a place to start as anywhere,' I said.

So the hooker, the rock star and the bereft and betrayed mother left Roland at Mission Control and walked hand in hand out of the conference room, down the stairs, past the lingering press diehards and the depressingly glamourless Airstrip One fans. Daisy and I to a waiting cab and Mary to Bart's big black beast of a hired SUV, which growled and glowered at the kerb.

'Winston – I need to talk to you. It's important!' shouted a carrot-topped geeky type, a lot younger than the usual rabble.

Usually, most times, in my post-supernova, white dwarf stellar life my Joe Strummer conscience had ordered me to spend time with anyone who cared enough about my music to hang around waiting to meet me. I'd obeyed nearly all the time. But not tonight.

'Not now mate! Sorry!' I called out with an unctuous grin that had become automatic for the people over the years.

$\star$ $\star$ $\star$

In hindsight, the blacked-out windows had been a mistake. He'd thought he was being discreet in hiring a run-of-the-mill 4WD job instead of a Limo. But as Bart Raines and Mary were driven sedately along the esplanade Bart hadn't seen or thought about for twenty years, they were suddenly the focus of attention.

'Oh for fuck's sake,' he carped when, oblivious to the breakers swashing onto the seaward side of the road, a bunch of pierced and tattooed girls in Airstrip One regalia pressed up against the car screaming 'Stone!! We know it's you!!'

'Get me the fuck out of here!' he snapped at the driver. 'Mimram Crescent — it's only a few yards back from the seafront. Let's get round there before the whole fucking shithole gets washed away.'

'Not the werewolf house of hell?' the driver joked.

'Obviously a local boy then,' Bart replied with a dry chuckle. 'Yes chummy, the werewolf house!'

The driver fell silent for a moment. Then, in an effort to undig his hole,

'You know the people there then?'

'I *am* them, mate.'

That shut up the driver — at least for the couple of minutes' drive to the town side of Mimram Crescent, when the opening car window admitted a stomach-turning stench.

'Far as I can go, mate, look,' the driver said, clamping a handkerchief over his mouth, gagging and gesticulating at the swirling gunge that was congealing round his tyres.

'Jesus — what's going on?' Bart gasped, equally nauseated.

'Fucking sewers are flooding — what with the rain and the high tide. Nowhere for the crap to run off to,' the driver replied philosophically. 'Sorry mate, but if you wanna get down there you're gonna have to wade through a sea of shit!'

'Think I'll pass actually. Take us back to the harbour please,' Bart replied very quickly, relieved to turn away from his father's houseful of bad memories. Mary, though, seemed immune, or maybe inured, to the overwhelming stench and turned to gaze fixedly out of the rear window through eyes like rifle sights, watching the black, lifeless windows of the werewolf house recede as the taxi gathered speed.

As they rounded the corner, the crescent was lit as a door opened and a horribly familiar tall, square-shouldered figure appeared, silhouetted by the hall light, to let in a smaller, hunched figure in cagoule and Wellington boots.

'Stop!' Mary shouted and the driver emergency stopped like he was on a driving test. 'Let me out. You go. You go. I'll stay and check,' she rasped breathlessly as she fumbled with the door catch and without hesitating slipped her nyloned legs into the sill-deep slurry and stood, waving them impatiently away.

Recovering from a smack on the head from the seat in front, Bart blinked with one eye and stared with the other.

'OK!' he said. 'If you say so. Home James – or whatever your name is!'

The driver didn't need telling twice and the 4WD spun its tractor-size tyres, skidding in slurry and showering Mary with shit as it sped enthusiastically away.

★   ★   ★

'Fuck you,' Neil called half-heartedly after the rock star as Winston Smith and his hooker jumped into the waiting cab, eyes down to avoid the gaze of a hundred cameras and a lot more pairs of eyes.

'Looks like it's down to me, Joe, my old mate,' he said to himself grimly as he hurried across the road to a payphone and turned back unsurprised when he saw the frayed, phoneless leads dangling out of its splayed guts.

Eyes screwed up against the wet sandpaper wind, he mounted his postie bike, hunched over the handlebars and wobbled off along the puddled prom towards the tunnel, frantically ringing his bell to clear a path through the rabble of press and rubberneckers. Slowing as the road curved inland, leaving the tunnel's seaward mouth behind, he was horrified to find that the roiling water was little short of a foot from the top of the heavily barricaded hatch – and that the concreted tract that once carried its outflow to sea had recently been masked by a heavy iron fence, spiked at the top and curved outward to make it impossible to scale. Wheezing now, he flung the bike from side to side, using his weight to help his leaden legs speed him up.

37

Mary Not So Meek and Mild

The back door of Raines' house was usually left ajar so that his 'hell hounds', as Alan once described them in a rare respite from his obsequious grovelling, could go in and out freely to shit and piss – so the cracked concrete yard with its ramshackle shed and outside lavatory stunk almost as horribly as did the inside. Cleanliness clearly wasn't next to Godliness in Raines's book. Tonight though, the place's miasma of corruption was subsumed by the all-pervading sewer stench. Mary skidded on a well-trodden faecal smear, catching hold of a drainpipe to stop herself falling. Its rattle set off a salvo of angry barking. Straightening up, Mary flattened herself against the wall, as if that could make her invisible should the householder come out to investigate. He didn't. He was too busy ranting – and simply silenced one of the mutts with a vicious kick that sent it whimpering in terror to its basket. Mary edged closer. The uncurtained window filtered a bare lightbulb's harsh light through a film of ancient grime, so that the two figures within were somehow otherworldly, removed from this reality.

Her husband was slumped in a threadbare armchair facing the window. Raines, his back to Mary, was pacing to and fro, gesticulating wildly just like he did in his crappy home-made 'pulpit'. Presumably he was running through a 'dress rehearsal' of his latest sermon with the ever-biddable Bunton as his congregation. But if Raines was unsurprisingly animated, her husband was strangely inert. Even through the window panes' semi-opacity, she could see that his eyes were glazed, watching, unblinkingly fixed on his hero as if his lids were pinned back. Trying and failing to calm a heartbeat she felt sure must be audible, she held her breath and slid silently through the door into the musty porch full of Wellington boots, assorted hammers, drills, braces and bits, damp clothing and a scattering of bowls containing remnants of dogs' dinners in varying stages of decomposition. Mary almost preferred the reek of sewage outside but at least now she could hear them, or to be more accurate, hear Raines, because she couldn't make out anything more than a pathetic beastly whine from her cowed and sickeningly craven worse half.

'You must understand, Brother Bunton, that the Lord's work has to be our priority here – the good of all the congregation and of the people yet to open their hearts and minds to His glory!' Raines boomed as Mary squinted through the chink between the inner door's frame and hinges.

Alan's only reaction was an almost imperceptible shake of the head and a guttural gurgling in the back of his chicken throat. That was a first, she thought, her curiosity piqued by her yes-man husband's evident attempt to say no. *Must have been a struggle. He's never said no to the bastard before!* she thought grimly.

'Jesus suffered for us. And we must suffer for him. I'm terribly sorry that it has to be you, of all people, my most loyal disciple, and of course Mary, who will of course be stricken…'

Again Alan's head shook very slightly, as if it were held in a loose clamp. Mary shrank back from the door as Raines turned towards her. But he stopped to the left of the jamb.

'Another Guinness? Make you feel better!'

There was no reply – nevertheless a new can clicked and hissed open. Keeping his back to Alan, Raines poured it carefully into a pint glass, then fumbled in a pocket and pulled out a small brown glass bottle with a rubber teat-like dropper - like the ones eardrops used to come in. He shook it over the glass, then impatiently unscrewed the cap and tipped in a clear liquid before turning back to Bunton, placing the glass in his limp hand and folding his number one fan's fingers round it as if he were a puppet.

'There you go old son. Drink up!' he breezed with forced joviality and raised his own glass of stout.

'To the Lord and the future of the Fishers of Men – and to the noble sacrifice you, your wife and, of course your lovely daughter, are about to make in the name of God,' he went on, kneeling at Bunton's feet, and trying without much success to tip Guinness into his slack mouth. Suddenly losing his patience, he heaved himself creaking to his feet with a groan and lumbered towards Mary who hastily stepped out of the back door, just as the inner door scuffed across sticky carpet and Raines's frame filled the door's. He took another little dropper bottle from a carton on top of an ancient top-loader washing machine next to a pile of several mobile phones and an assortment of SIM cards and strode back to Bunton's side, half-closing the inner door behind him. Once he was safely seated again, Mary popped up a meerkat head to check out the carton: CHALFONTS OF ST GILES, the logo said – and in rubber-stamped lettering beneath, 'Gammahydroxybutyrate – 48 x 10cl'.

So that's how he gets the girls to be so compliant, Mary thought with a fresh rush of intense hatred coursing through her veins like several shots of adrenaline. And evidently it was how he'd further subdued her spineless husband. GHB, otherwise known as liquid ecstasy – a date rape drug like Rohypnol. Takes between ten minutes and an hour to take effect. Small doses make you feel like you've drunk too much; bigger doses leave you incapacitated and unable to remember what's happened to you – or more to the point what's been done to you. She'd read about it in one of the pamphlets the school drugs counsellor doled out – before Alan had torn them up and burnt them because their Lily would never ever…

'Sacrifice,' Raines had said. Did he mean his ritual deflowering of her daughter, just the latest in a long list of violations of innocents, but the one to which she'd been a party; that she'd been too timid to prevent? But that had been three days ago now. He couldn't be talking about something more, could he? An even greater sacrifice? Replaying in her mind the unctuous sermonising that had become so depressingly familiar over the last few years, Mary shivered in horror: 'the noble sacrifice you, your wife and, of course your lovely daughter, are about to make in the name of God'. That was what he'd said.

'Oh my God he's going to kill her!' she muttered to herself.

As if echoing her words, Alan emitted a feeble whine, his Plasticine mouth struggling to form words, 'Forty hours you said – and then she'd be free. You lied...'

'That was before the boy complicated matters – but then it was true. Obviously we can't release him now – he'd ruin everything the FOM has worked for. And, because of him, so would your little Lily. So you must understand that it's for the best – that we must leave the forces of nature to take them gently away.

Bunton writhed in impotent and virtually paralysed rage.

'Fgging drownm you mean you fggging mdrer,' he groaned, his drooling lips and spastic tongue now flapping helplessly at the consonants as the drug took hold. The saliva dribble ran red as Raines's left hand almost casually, but very effectively, jabbed at his jaw.

Rubbing his hand, Raines fixed Bunton with a wounded look born of his stunning arrogance.

'That is a terrible thing to say, Brother Bunton. You know full well that I regret this, um, tragic, turn of events as much as you. But I'm left with no other choice.'

Mary watched with a mixture of nausea, loathing and morbid fascination as her husband's nerves fitfully and ineffectually twitched his uncooperative muscles.

Now he wants to stand up for himself! she thought bitterly. *Always the same. Too little. Too late.* To think she once loved him. To think he'd fathered her only child. And now to think he was instrumental in her murder.

Raines grunted to his feet, scrabbled in a carrier bag he'd left next to the armchair and produced a handful of cable ties. Bunton's eyeballs now seemed to be the only bit of him still answering his brain's commands

– and they oscillated like windscreen wipers in their wide-open sockets as Raines secured his wrists and ankles and, with an efficiency born of years of experience in the arts of kidnapping and rape, slapped a length of duct tape over his mouth.

Oh my God, Lily's going to die, said the voice in Mary's head.

'I'll say again – I'm sorry to have to do this. But I have a service to celebrate – and I don't feel that you're to be trusted any longer. I'll leave you now but I'll be back to let you go when the Lord's work is done. In the meantime, I suggest you pray for Lily. The spring tide will raise her up, cleanse and baptise her before it carries her to Heaven. Pray for her soul – and pray more for the boy's if you have it in your heart, because he's headed for Hell!'

Bunton's eyes looked like they were going to burst out of his head.

My Lily's going to die, insisted the mantra in Mary's head

'Calm yourself, Alan, please. I'm going to…'

Until the claw hammer glanced off Raines's skull and the skein of blood crept out of his slicked hair, black against his grey, cratered forehead, Mary had never hit anyone – apart from the odd, barely punitive slap across the back of primary school Lily's legs. She'd hardly ever raised her voice. Let alone a weapon. She'd never told her husband what she thought of him. Never broken the speed limit. Never left the country, except on one school day trip to France. Never been on an aeroplane. But now she'd somehow flown across the room with a supersonic scream and supernatural speed.

It was if his head were made of rock. As the rounded end of the hammer's head hit bone, the impact twisted the handle in her hand and it slid ineffectually off Raines's Pluko-slick hair. He reeled and wheeled, as much surprised as stunned, and as his legs buckled under him he slumped to his knees as if to pray. In the slow-motion follow-though, the hammer's weight took on a life of its own, spinning Mary through a full orbit before rocketing out of her grasp and crashing through the window, and as the centripetal effect sent her tumbling Raines's giant hand caught hold of her, lasciviously, painfully, by the groin and his immense weight bore her down till she was pinned to the floor. He knelt over her, arm up her skirt, middle finger and thumb penetrating her in two places, grasping her rapist-tight like a bowling ball and the rhythmic flexing and release, flex and release, of his taut, scaly, vein-cabled forearm rocked her back and forth in time with her molecule-deep spasms of fear.

'Hello Mary. Gave me a bit of a fright there!' he grimaced, dabbing tentatively at his bloody temple with his free hand.

'Where's Lily you fu...' she began — the F-word another first for her. Or was it a second? But he pressed his free index and middle fingers against her lips.

'Shhhhhhsh,' he lullabied as the bitter metallic taste of his blood seeped sickenly from his fingers into her mouth. 'Another word and I'll tear these two vile holes into one you evil bitch,' he went on as equably as if he were talking about the weather. Then he trailed those two fingers teasingly from her fear-zipped lips over the tip of her nose to its bridge and let them rest for a few terrifying seconds on the centre of her forehead, just where a Hindu would have a Bhindi spot. And there, as she tried and failed to wriggle away, he painted a cross with smears of the blood she'd drawn and muttered, 'In the name of the Father and of the Son and of the Holy Spirit...'

'Oh you're John the Baptist now are you? Been demoted from Jesus fucking Christ have you?' Mary snarled, outrage overcoming terror in her second — or was it third - use of the word 'fuck' in her entire life. 'Where's Lily? What've you done with her?'

'I'm afraid she's gone now; she's with God,' he said blithely, thinking it was a lie, unaware that the day-long downpour was filling the tunnel ahead of the tide chart's schedule and about to make it truth any minute.

Pre-empting her reaction, his free hand found its habitual way to a secure grip on her throat while he took his torturous time in slowly withdrawing his invasive thumb from what felt like somewhere near her womb and the finger from halfway up her colon – producing a fart from her rectum to add insult to injury. Another F-word first for Mary, at least, with an audience.

'Not very ladylike!' Raines smirked, holding up a soiled and glistening finger with ostensible distaste – as if Mary had smeared her shit on it herself – and then wiping it with unnecessary thoroughness on her hair.

'Where is she you…'

He choked her words with an easy squeeze of his hand.

'I'm sorry my dear but if she's not left us yet, she certainly will do soon. It's God's will. There's nothing you can do about it but pray for her soul,' he oozed, releasing his garrotte grip.

As Mary splutteringly guppied for air, Raines reached for his plastic bag and whipped out his far tougher plastic bindings.

'Where is…' Mary gasped again as the grip tightened again round her throat and she felt him lashing her ankles tightly together with the speed and efficiency of a storm-lashing sailor.

'I told you. She's in Heaven. Or nearly,' Raines gloated as he quickly bound her wrists, turned away and stepped into the porch. In an instant he was back, triumphantly touting one of those nasty little bottles.

'And you'll be joining her soon, one way or the other,' he continued, JCB hands spreading and closing in on her face, blotting out the light. One hand seized her utterly irresistibly by the chin as the other pinched her nose. Mary saw blue lights, then red, then pictures of Lily before every self-defeating, survival-programmed gene of every cell in her body overrode her will and opened her mouth for air. It was only because Raines was fumbling with the vial's cap, trying to unscrew it with the same hand that was clamping her nostrils shut, that Mary got to inhale air rather than GHB. And while he fiddled, she breathed in big gusts, like these were the last breaths she'd ever get – which they very probably were. As she knew he would, Raines poured the clear liquid into her mouth. As she knew she would, she gagged on the salty taste and her mind filled with unbidden memories of childhood seaside holidays with beach huts and sandcastles and windbreaks and lilos and a horrible man who'd made her gag on his horrible thing with its salty stuff and… Then she heard again the rip of that heavy tape and one of those great big awful hands clamped over her face and left her mouth sealed.

Nostrils flaring and hysteria strobing in her eyes, Mary rallied every atom of her being to slow her pulse and steady her breathing. Tilting her head to the right, she pooled the briny chemical in her cheek and rocked forward to get it off her tongue; to gag the gag reflex. Raines had left the room but the gush of taps, clanking of an archaic immersion heater and the flushing of the lavatory told her he was upstairs. She wondered whether Alan was conscious – not that she cared about him any more. All she wanted from the sycophantic fuck was some hope or help or hint of a way of saving their daughter's life. But if she turned her head to look, the vile stuff would trickle down her throat and she'd have no control. As it was, it was inside her – but not part of her – like Raines's finger and thumb had been: a successful invasion falling short of surrender. Like a rapist, like Raines, the drug couldn't get what it wanted just by being in you. It had to go deeper. And Mary wasn't going to let that happen. Even Alan had never got that deep – and he certainly never would again, whether she lived or died.

At first it was a mouthful of seawater. Then it was like a too-hot curry. And then it started to burn her face from the inside out.

<h1 style="text-align:center">38</h1>

Papa Don't Preach

'This isn't going to work,' Daisy said as the cab pulled up in a lay-by next to the school sports field. 'That's no prayer meeting – it's a rave!'

'Well we're here now. Let's check it out,' I said, paying the cabbie.

'Suppose we might as well. If there's nothing, we can walk to Dad's – it's only a couple of minutes down…'

'I know.' I interrupted.

'Sorry. Course you do.'

Her phone bleeped.

'It's my darling brother. Text. No one there, he says. Gone back to his fucking boat, surprise surprise.'

'It's a ship, apparently,' I quipped, suddenly wondering if Georgie was on board. 'Anyway, what about Mary?'

'He didn't say. Guess she's with him.'

I shrugged.

'Well he can bring her here if we find anything.'

We were nearing the pavilion now. The damp grass muffled our footsteps and the breakbeat and bass boom throbbing out of the pavilion meant there was no need to hush. But we did anyway.

'Like this tune!' Daisy murmured *à propos* of nothing.

I was about to agree, when I recognised it. It was *me.*

Bring it on, bring it in

This is the sound

Of ageless sin…

To be precise, it was my tune without me singing. Some instrumental remix or other. But what was uncanny was the vocal track. No one but me, the denizens of Babington House, Ralph and his choir had heard my new choral version of Bring It On. No one but me had a copy. So how the fuck could a choir of children be singing my song on the playing field of my old school at ten in the evening? I reached out a hand blindly to stop Daisy and steer her off our beeline towards the cover of bushes lining the perimeter. But she'd frozen like she'd seen a ghost. And there it was: the frame of her father striding across the moonlit turf with a self-satisfied smile like a fresh-dug grave with tombstone teeth in a grey pockmarked face hewn out of moon rock. As we shrank into the shadows, the pavilion doors opened, pouring light and music, *my music,* out. A phalanx of cherubic kids in ill-fitting white robes filed out. Nauseatingly, they were still singing *Bring It On.* They lined the entrance as the preacher slowed to a stately march, savouring his pompous progress towards his pulpit.

'What a cunt!' Daisy giggled, marshalling her faculties with the alacrity of the super-streetwise.

'But if he's here…'

'Where are the kids!' she cut in, instantly catching my drift. 'He cut diagonally across the field, Rich. He must've come straight from home.'

Daisy put two fingers in her mouth at the resonant boom of her dad's amplified warm-up to a simmering sermon that promised to boil over with fire and brimstone. Like the sick button needed any help.

'Let's go,' I agreed, hastily, looking up at the rugby goals' giant aitches and remembering with a shiver the crucifixion of Bart Raines.

★   ★   ★

Ten bricks. Two more layers of mortar to mortality. Long ago inured to the seawater and sewage stench that had stymied every breath, now literally up to their necks in shit, they savoured every gasp of air as if it were their last. A sort of numbed acceptance had taken hold of them both. No feeling left in their skin, their limbs were rubberised and useless like their very bones were waterlogged, only their buoyancy in the icily viscous liquid keeping their heads out of the water and in the fast-shrinking pocket of air. Joe had finally stopped that infuriating tapping. But Lily was beginning to think it was preferable to this deadly silence in which every breath was an unwelcome digit in the agonising countdown to death (it had been hours since she'd last been able to convince herself that her father was ever coming back to get her).

'We're dying aren't we,' she'd whispered. Joe's ominous silence was all the answer she needed.

'Drowned in shit and piss,' she whimpered, the full enormity of their fate ballooning from the pit of her stomach to the back of her mouth.

'Actually, I think we're more likely to die of the cold. Better, I think...'

Silence again. Her hand was in his, under the water but she could no longer feel it. And then that bloody clink, clink, clink started up again. Lily tried and tried to tolerate it but finally she'd had enough.

'If you must keep doing that, try a different tune will you!'

She felt a ripple lap against her chin as Joe stirred.

'What? I'm not!'

'That's not funny.'

'Shhhhsssh!' Joe hissed, suddenly animated. 'Listen!'

'Yes, very good. *Money* by Pink fucking Floyd!' she snapped.

'Exactly – and it's not me!'

He held the candle between them: two hands and still the clinking continued.

'How the...'

'It's Nelly – it's got to be Nelly! We're going to get out of here Lily. It's Nelly I just know it is,' he babbled as he began banging the Zippo against the pipe rim with renewed zeal.

39

Remorse Revisited

Maybe it was a good thing Winston Smith had blanked him. He'd have looked such a fool – a nutter even – if he'd dragged them all up here, the police and fire brigade and everything all for nothing. Probably would have been arrested for wasting police time. Sitting atop the mound, he defied the wind and rain to stop him rolling a spliff. So much for Zippos always lighting in the wind! He curled himself protectively around the vent pipe's lip, lowered the lighter inside and finally managed to get a light.

And then he heard it. The insistent clinking of *Money.* He put his mouth into the top of the pipe.

'JOOOOOOOOE!' he bellowed as hard as he could.

He placed an ear in the pipe. Was that his name he heard, shouted from a million miles down? Or was it just the fluting wind?

He lit a match and dropped it down as it flared – but it stopped just a couple of feet deep, igniting some leaves then fizzling out. So the pipe was blocked. No wonder he couldn't hear.

Nothing. Then a new clinking rhythm. He frowned. Then grinned with sudden recognition: remorse code. The old school tradition!!

'Fuck me. He's really in there!' he said to himself, rummaging in pockets for paper and pen.

--- ...- --.. -. .-- .--. .-. .--. -... .-- .. -..-..-.

-.-

(OV ZNW PR PB WIMDNR NT – ME AND LILY DROWNING) was what Joe was saying.

339

'Shit,' Neil shouted, trying desperately to write the alphabet on a wet Rizla, finally succeeding and using it to turn Morse to Remorse.

‾.. .‾. .‾‾. .‾‾. ‾ ...‾ ‾‾. ... ...‾ .‾‾. .‾...‾.‾.‾ ... ‾‾.. ‾. ‾ ‾ ‾‾ ‾.

(DRPP TVG SVPL. SZNT MN – WILL GET HELP – HANG ON)

Message sent, he stood on the hillock on which he'd so often done his lonely 'King of the Castle' thing, not to mention his dirty rascal thing, and cast his eyes around. He already knew the sea had claimed its own end of the tunnel. And he wasn't hopeful about this side – the flood must be too deep by now – and even if he could dive down and stay under long enough, he couldn't get through the hatch. He'd built it like a fortress. And now there was also the formidably impenetrable steel fence the council or the water board or someone had put there to keep kids out.

It was too dark down in the gully to make anything out but he peered down there anyway and suddenly a light appeared a couple of hundred yards off, filtered through the bare trees. Neil pulled out the miniature telescope he used for incidental bird watching on his postal round and twiddled the focus until three figures coalesced in his lens, silhouetted by the light from the werewolf house front door. One of them was instantly recognisable. As much as he publicly insisted that Airstrip One and their main man Winston Smith were a spent force, rock dinosaurs, boring old farts, he'd actually bought every CD and watched every live video. That was the rock star whom, unbelievably, had turned out to be his former best friend's dad. He half-ran, half-fell, down the land side of the mound and sloshed through the murky and stinking flood towards that horrid house. Winston Smith would have a phone – and he'd have people to help. He could make anything happen. Surely he could.

★　　　★　　　★

As we bent into the wind and almost right-angled rain and trudged through the slurry towards the Werewolf House, Daisy's mobile cheeped.

'Ralph. He's at the police station. They're going to check out Dad. About time!'

She reluctantly fell in behind me as I stepped up the pace. I think the idea of revisiting that house was more frightening for her than I'd realised. So I stopped, turned and held out both hands. She took them, without a word of sarcasm, and I hugged her shivering and suddenly frail frame.

'You OK?' I murmured in her ear.

She pulled her head back to look into my eyes. Hers were brimming with tears that weren't simply down to the wind. She nodded bravely, and tipped out a teardrop that rolled easily down her cheek as if eager to escape. We walked on determinedly, hand in hand, an old song crackling in my head like a 78 record:

Daisy, Daisy, I don't care where you've been,
I'm so crazy over your eyes of green.
Our love is where we're going, I don't mind where you've been,
we'll get married and...

At number 16 Mimram Crescent, the back door was ajar. But as we'd expected, the lights were off and no one seemed to be at home. Nevertheless Daisy was quaking with reawakened fear now that we were standing hesitantly on the threshold, afraid of what we might find. Stepping into the porch, I gagged as the high-pitched, needling ammoniacal stink of urine invaded my nose and throat. Daisy's gag reflex was far more controlled, I noticed, then recoiled from my mental picture of the reason why as she bravely dismissed her fear with an involuntary shudder and squeezed past me to take the lead. As she pushed open the inner door, there was an animal whimper from within. We froze.

'Dad's mutts,' she mouthed, and I shrank back, anticipating an ambush by a slavering dog – or a werewolf.

Then Daisy hit the light switch and I was assaulted by a sight much worse. Mary Bunton sprawled hogtied and helpless on a swampy carpet – and behind her a corpse, trussed like a turkey, eyes fixed and unblinking; pupils fixed and dilated, as they say on pronouncing death in all the hospital soaps.

'Jesus Christ,' I blurted, kneeling and fumbling with Mary's plastic shackles as she grunted unintelligibly.

'Take the fucking tape off first you idiot,' Daisy called from the doorway, where she hovered as if there were a force field preventing her entering the room.

Strangely hamsterish, with one cheek ballooned for some reason, Mary frantically nodded agreement and Daisy broke her invisible barrier, leapt to my side and held a lighter to the cable ties on her wrists and ankles as I scrabbled with my bitten nails to get hold of a corner of the strip of the Gaffer tape that my roadies always used. Finally I got a bit of purchase and, with a quick, 'Ready? One, two, three,' I ripped it off. Simultaneously the plastic ties melted and fell away and Mary jumped up, swivelled and fell on the dead man, tearing off with pointless urgency the tape that equally pointlessly gagged a terminally silent mouth.

And then she kissed him.

I caught Daisy's eye.

'This'll be her husband then?' she ventured.

I nodded.

But the man wasn't quite dead. And the kiss wasn't a tenderly lingering final goodbye. It was an open mouthed, deep, saliva-swapping snog, during which the man's eyes flickered, at first with gratitude, then with horror as he gagged, struggled and finally swallowed, succumbing to the final oral administration of chemical with something that looked like relief.

Slowly, Mary hauled herself off the inert body of her husband, his eyes now as unflinchingly fixed as Bart's lidless one. She turned to us, ashen-faced, her face sallow and hollow–cheeked again as a half-smile flickered and died.

'That's my husband,' she stated dully – and then turned back to what was clearly now a cadaver and kicked it full in the face. The head just lolled lazily to the left under the impact, its slack jaw dropping into a macabre grin.

'Sorry – my *late* husband, I should say,' she went on simply.

'My dad did this?' Daisy breathed.

'He started it. I finished it. Your dad's got my Lily and your Joe somewhere,' Mary intoned, avoiding the question and Daisy's eyes. 'And they're going to die – if they're not dead already.'

'Oh fuck,' I said.

'Oh fuck,' said Daisy. 'You don't know where? Or how?'

Mary shook her head.

'I listened outside – till I lost my rag and went for him with a hammer. All I could make out was something about the forces of nature. Then Alan tried to say something but I couldn't make it out – Raines had pumped him full of that liquid ecstasy stuff. I think he was saying they were going to...'

A sob like a death rattle swallowed her words as Daisy and I stood helplessly either side of her, propping her up and silently beseeching her to finish the sentence – then wishing she hadn't.

'...Drown,' she gasped, finally.

'Oh my God,' I said quietly. 'I'm so sorry about your husband,' I commiserated.

'Don't be. I'm not,' she almost spat.

'Come on, think,' Daisy urged. 'Where could they be? It has to be near here – doesn't it?'

'Not necessarily,' I replied. 'He could have driven them anywhere.'

'I don't think so though,' Mary said quietly, coldly surveying her husband's corpse. 'Alan was part of it – more than I knew. But they didn't go anywhere - there wasn't time. It happened here somewhere, I know it.'

'Ralph will have told the police by now – but they don't know what you know. I think we should call them.'

'No!' Mary shouted.

'Do you want to find your girl alive or not?' Daisy interjected angrily. 'Because we wouldn't mind finding our boy!'

'Yes, yes, of course… It's just…' she stuttered through great heaving sobs.

'What?' Daisy insisted.

'I just killed my fucking husband, that's what! With the help of someone called Chalfont,' she announced though gritted teeth, nodding at the brown cardboard carton.

Bemused, Daisy followed her gaze. So did I. *CHALFONTS OF ST GILES*, it said on the side of a cardboard package.

'So?' I said. 'What's that — a job lot of haemorrhoid cream?'

'Well it *is* for arseholes!' Daisy murmured. 'That's Roland's company. My dad and Bart are both customers. It's GBH you idiot. That's what killed him,' she tilted her head in the late Alan Bunton's direction. Call the cops and Roland and Bart are fucked — as well as Mary.

'Well we'll just ditch the stuff,' I said.

'And what about what's inside his body?' Daisy snapped. 'It won't take them long to find out where it came from once they start tracing all my dad's contacts.'

'No time to worry about that now,' I said, making for the door and leaving the stuff where it was.

As we walked out of the house and into the overgrown front garden, where the still-rising flood was claiming the many piles of dog turd as its own, it took me a while to process all this new and disturbing information.

'I'm sorry but if you think I'm going to risk two kids' lives because Mary or Roland or your fucking brother don't wanna get nicked, you can fuck right off!' I shouted, whipping out my mobile. 'Shit, shit, shit!' I bellowed as I fumbled and dropped it into the ankle-deep slurry.

'Mr Smith? Winston?'

I'd heard that voice before. Standing knee deep in filth was the geeky kid who'd tried to talk to me outside the hotel.

'Look son, I admire your determination but I'm not doing autographs OK. Not today. I've got a crisis going on if you…'

'I've found Joe!' he shouted. 'I'm a friend of his!'

I waded out towards him into the brown water rapids of Mimram Crescent.

'You what? This better not be a wind-up,' I growled.

'He's gonna drown. Him and a girl. Over there!'

I nodded. His face said it all; an earnest, open one that looked incapable of sophistry. Certainly not one of my fans. Instantly, it seemed, Daisy and Mary were with us and we were sloshing through the shit after him as he told me what he knew between laboured breaths.

The drainage tunnel! The one I'd hid in as a kid. My boy was just like me. And he was just a couple of minutes' walk away. '*My* boy' I'd said, just like a dad. Daisy took my hand and I squeezed hers and suddenly we were no longer the rocker and the hooker. We were a father and a mother overwhelmed with this utterly new kind of agony. Then I remembered the view from the seafront; the waves invading and engulfing the drainage tunnels at the other end; tunnels just like the one my son was in. I started running, dragging Daisy behind me.

'You go on – I'll catch up,' she gasped, almost as breathless as I was.

'OK – get onto Ralph. Tell him to bring the police here now - and the fire brigade I suppose. Divers too – in case I can't get to them.'

'You'll have a job,' Neil called over his shoulder. 'The water's almost at the top of the tunnel entrance this side – and well over it the other.'

'I can swim, can't you?' I wheezed.

'Yeah – but can you hold your breath long enough to break three or four big fuck-off padlocks?'

'Oh,' I panted. 'Shit.'

It didn't sound good.

Ralph had been forced to divulge a lot more of Mary Bunton's confession than he'd suggested to Father Moncrieff.

'The problem is, Reverend Pemberton, that the facts just don't support what you're saying. According to Lily Bunton's father, she's been abducted by her boyfriend. Between you and me, I don't think that's the case. I think they've just run off together. It's a typical case. Girl from a sheltered, religious background falls for local bad boy from the wrong side of the tracks. Parents don't approve so they do a runner. Probably shacked up in some tacky hotel in London by now,' Detective Inspector Masterson said dismissively. It had been a long day and the press attention drawn by the rocker and the hooker's presence in town had made matters considerably worse. 'Anyway, old Father Moncrieff's asked us to investigate Raines and his God-botherers - sorry, no offence - before and we found nothing.'

'Well I sincerely hope you're right. But surely this warrants another look?'

'Tell you what I'll do – I'll talk to your friends, get their version and then we'll see. I need a word with your rock star chum anyway – small matter of doing a runner from a posh hotel.'

'Surely not! His record company would be paying I'm sure.'

'Apparently not. Say they've never heard of him. And he's done a bunk owing five grand and the same thing at some place in the South of France!'

Ralph's phone rang.

'Hello Daisy! Good heavens. No! Oh my gosh! Right away!' Ralph babbled, then turned to Masterson, 'I think this changes everything Inspector.'

Minutes later, Ralph was in the back of a police van racing towards Mimram Crescent, the fire brigade and a team of divers not far behind.

★   ★   ★

Even now, my inner rock star had to make the drama all about me. I'd pictured myself diving heroically into the torrent, yodelling like a lard-arsed Tarzan, wrestling briefly with the locks and then bursting to the surface with my son under one arm and his girlfriend the other to rapturous applause and an explosion of flashbulbs.

Wasn't going to happen.

For a start, the entrance to the tunnel was only just visible now — and the brown bubbling stuff that lapped against it was far from inviting. And it wasn't just the blocked-up tunnel that dammed it. The authorities had become a lot more safety-conscious since my day and the mouth was fenced with spiked metal railings as impregnable as their seaside counterparts. Worse, the scree of fly-tipped rubble, errant shopping trolleys and assorted unidentifiable debris that rolled down one bank now formed an archipelago of spiky little islands, around which the waters roiled and boiled in unshootable rapids.

'See what I mean,' Neil said.

I nodded grimly, willing those divers and firefighters to arrive.

'Let's tell them we're here — find out how bad it is,' he said, turning and scrambling through the bushes. Helplessly, I followed and watched, stricken, as he began tapping away in some code, referring now and then to a scrap of paper. I breathed in and out, deeply and deliberately, just like I always had in the seconds before launching into a song to store up stamina and to settle the volatile cocaine and adrenaline cocktail that always made me shake like a bad Elvis impersonator. Of course the air I breathed was thick with the stink of shit, which was too hard to swallow. Instead the odour tweaked my memory button and first the shitty Mediterranean flashed into my mind, and then the recurring image of being 'bogwashed' in the first week at the grammar school. Then it clicked.

'Bloody hell! That's Remorse Code isn't it!'
Neil nodded, bemused.
'How do you…'
'You went to Hartham Grammar right?'
He nodded again.
'Well our lot invented that – on the pipes?'
'Fucking hell!'
I laughed as Neil carried on tapping…

-.. .-. --. ... -... .. .-- --.. .-- .-.-.- ... .-.. -.. ... .-. -...
-..--..--....-....--..

DRGS BI WZW SLD SRTS DZGVI? (WITH YR DAD. HOW HIGH WATER?)

★   ★   ★

Anxiously pacing up and down in the conference suite, Roland felt helpless – and doubly so when Daisy rang to tell him the latest.

'I'll come to you and help!' he said, already grabbing his coat.

'Don't. Raines killed Bunton with a GHB OD, well, Mary did actually – and guess where Raines got it!'

'Oh flipping heck,' Roland murmured.

'Yeah. There's a big carton of the stuff with your name and address all over it. Sorry – in the shock of it all I didn't think to get rid of it,' she lied.

'The police will be looking for me then.'

'Yep – so get my darling brother to send a boat. They won't be looking out to sea for you!'

'But I want to help… What use will I…'

'A lot actually,' she anticipated. 'Between you and my devious, lying bastard of a brother I'm sure you can cook up a way of pinning the murder on Raines. The fucker deserves it doesn't he – and anyway, Mary only finished off what he'd started.'

348

'Daisy, you're an evil genius!' Roland chuckled. 'Consider it done – and good luck. I'll pray for them.'

'If you think God listens to the likes of you and me!'

★   ★   ★

Eleven bricks – and one to go. Backs pushed against each other and legs braced against the walls, they'd managed to wedge themselves a foot off the floor so that their mouths could stay in the slim arc of air, close to the lip of the pipe, which contained at least a final few litres of life in reserve for the final moments. Joe held his fingers to his face, counting fervently, struggling to interpret the code.

'I think he says my dad's out there. Whoever the fuck that is,' Joe gurned.

'They're too late aren't they,' Lily gurgled and retched as the scum trickled into her moving mouth.

Joe hushed her, straining, hoping for the next transmission.

★   ★   ★

'How bad?' How long?' I urged hopping from one foot to the other. This was unbearable. It took so torturously long to communicate a couple of words – and every tap ticked off another second in the uncountable countdown to my son's death. Neil just shook his head, concentrating.

'Wouldn't it be quicker to just use Morse code?' I pestered.

He shook his head.

'Joe only knows this. Least a bit of it.'

He put a finger to his lips and an ear to the pipe. I joined him.

10 XN

.---- ----- -..--.

'Ten centimetres,' Neil muttered. 'Fuck.'

'Christ. We'll never get help in time!'

I'd never felt panic like this before. I felt sick. If only I could do something – if only I could at least talk to him properly…

'Neil, how come they can hear you tapping but we can't just shout down the pipe?'

'It's blocked,' he replied.

'Well can't we unblock it? Then they'd have some air,' I said, brightening at the thought. But he soon rained on that parade.

'We could try – but why? A clear pipe's no more good to them than a blocked one once the water's at the tunnel's ceiling.'

'Oh,' I replied, deflated. But then I leapt to my feet.

'A hosepipe!' I shouted. 'And a scaffolding pipe!'

Neil stood up, interested. I pointed to a metal tube protruding from the swirling scum a little upstream.

'Bet that's long enough to reach right down to them. We ram it down to clear the pipe and then get a hosepipe… They can use it like a snorkel!'

'Know what?' Neil grinned. 'That might work! I've just remembered what's blocking the pipe!'

I had to cut short Nelly's tale about his periscope, fascinating as it was since it featured my yet-to-be-met son. The main thing was that this Heath Robinson creation of his was probably the main obstruction – the rest would be the leaves, twigs and litter that had accumulated over the couple of years since the boys had occupied the tunnel.

Torch beams strafed the undergrowth. The fire brigade? No – Daisy and Mary.

'Run and get a hosepipe from one of the houses!' I shouted.

Both women looked blank. 'Now!!' I urged. 'They've only got inches - *minutes* - of air left!'

Daisy kicked off her heels and sprinted in stockinged feet after Mary, who'd already disappeared into the undergrowth.

'I'll get the scaffold tube – you tell them to keep away from the

pipe!' I shouted, tripping, rolling and finally plunging up to my chest
into the icy gunge. Stifling a retch as the stink enveloped me, I gave the
slimy metal cylinder a trial tug. It didn't budge. It was wedged through
a buckled shopping trolley and lashed tight with steel hawser-strength
reeds that sliced my hands as I tore away at them one by one till the pipe
came loose and I dragged it with a sickeningly sloppy squelch from the
deep mud bed. I charged uphill with it balanced on my shoulder like a
rocket launcher (if only). Neil wedged a foot under one end and I hauled
it upright, hand over hand.

'Tell them to get clear now!' I bellowed, positioning my ramrod on
the vent pipe's rim.

'Already have,' he saluted army style with a grim grin. 'Three
knocks is the signal.'

I waited.

'From you, I mean - make it loud,' he yelled and I raised it up and
slammed it down hard.

Clang, clang, clang. It sounded horribly like a death knell.

'Fingers crossed!' I shouted, re-positioning the scaffold pole over
the hole and ramming it downward with all my strength. The first
couple of feet was easy — just leaves and brush as I'd thought. But then
I hit something hard.

'Fucking hell, what did you make that thing out of?' I muttered.

'Metal frame, fibreglass housing,' he replied ruefully.

'You better give me a hand then,' I grunted, making like a pile
driver once more to no avail.

Even with two of us it was hard to put enough weight behind the
pipe because ten of its twelve feet were swaying in the air. But finally
we felt an encouraging pliancy, followed by a muffled crack and an
agonising minute or so later we were through. As I knelt to peer down
there, a wraith-like vision burst out of the bushes with a banshee wail.

'Lilyyyyyyyyyyy!' Mary screamed, shoving me out of her way with
surprising strength. And I was still on my knees as we heard the faint,
quavering voice from twelve feet down.

'Mum?'

'Are you all right darling. Oh God I'm so...'

'I'm with Joe. We're...' her words turned to a gurgle.

I nodded to Daisy who'd brought up the rear lugging a vast tangle of green garden hose behind her. She took Mary by the shoulders.

'Come on love. No time to talk now,' she coaxed.

'Joe?' I bellowed into the pipe. 'I'm your dad. I'm feeding down two hosepipes. Get them in your mouths and use them as snorkels till we can get to you!'

There was no reply. I fed them down, fast as I could, with Daisy and Neil on untangling duties.

'Got them?' I called down into the darkness.

I made out a gurgle, which I prayed was a yes. Which I prayed was life.

'It's gonna be hard to breathe through these though,' Neil pointed out.

'Well let's hope it's not for long. Where the fuck are the filth when you need them?'

'This might help,' Daisy volunteered, proffering a foot pump and yet another hose.

Now I was the one looking bemused.

'Run a third pipe down and pump air in!' she explained.

'Who's the plumber now!' I cooed. 'Where did you get all this?'

'Bit of breaking and entering on Mimram Crezz!' she smiled mischievously as she wedged the pump outlet's nozzle into the extra hose and began feeding it down the hole.

'Joe. It's your mum! I'm gonna pump air down the hose that's coming down to you now,' she shouted, pumping away with one foot like there was no tomorrow – for Joe and Lily anyway.

★   ★   ★

As the ridged plastic tubes nosed their way into view, Joe and Lily were taking turns to breathe. Their bloodless deadened limbs reluctant to move, they struggled to tread water long enough to get their mouths into the aperture, now with an elongated, convex bubble of air beneath it barely an inch deep. Like a patient swimming instructor coaching a nervous absolute beginner, Joe coaxed Lily into trusting him and her buoyancy and settling back on the water's thick sludgy crust with her head cradled in his hands, which gently steered her mouth up against the pipe. Lily took one of the hose-ends and with one hand fed it blindly back to Joe and into his mouth. Droplets of water in the cricked tube gurgled in her ear – ominously like a death rattle out of some horror film. Joe, his whole head now submerged, couldn't hear his dad calling. Couldn't hear her praying and sobbing. And only the rasp and gurgle of his laboured breaths through the pipe next to her ear told her he was still alive – that and the gentle fingers that still tenderly stroked her cheeks.

A torch beam dazzled her for an instant the receded to allow her a glimpse of a woman's face far above. Not her mother. Must be Joe's. *People pay for this,* she thought. *Sensory deprivation tanks. Idiots.* She and he were at any minute about to be deprived of their senses forever. *Please God…*

The third hose snaked down towards her hissing rubbery air, which frothed up the scum but did nothing to inflate her tiny bubble of life.

★   ★   ★

'Look I know it's horrible,' Neil was saying, 'but the fact is while the pipe's open at the top, the water will just keep rising. If we plug it, and if it's even half-airtight, the water won't be able to get any higher. It'll buy them some time…'

'No. You can't,' Mary screamed. 'Lily will be terrified. She'll think we've given up on her!'

'Well she can't get much more scared can she,' I observed. 'Do it,

Neil.'

Mary fell on the pipe mouth and shone a torch down. Spot lit in a frame of velvet black opacity was a tiny circular cameo, a delicate ivory face, eyes closed almost serenely as if accepting her death. Daisy knelt and took Mary by the shoulders, gazed searchingly into her eyes, mother to mother, for a moment and drew her gently away as Neil cut off a length of tubing with a penknife on his key ring and deftly weaved it in and out of the hoses in the pipe, lashing them all together in a loose cone.

'Pick up some litter – plastic, paper, anything,' he called out, the closest he could get to an order, as the three of us on looked on bewildered, then dumbly complied. Piling up anything combustible around and on top of the coiled hose, he lit it with his Zippo, then whipped off its sleeve and shook lighter fluid on the flames. It was a short-lived bonfire – but it did the trick. Helped by a bit of deft spatula work from Neil's penknife, the loose plastic cone had shrivelled, melted and fused into an airtight plug. Snorkel pipes apart, the vent pipe was sealed shut. I just hoped it didn't also seal the kids' fate.

We stood, looking down at it in helpless silence. It felt as though one of us ought to utter a prayer but I don't think any of us really knew how. And anyway, that would have made real the tacit suggestion of a watery grave. Where was the rocking Reverend when you needed him? But if we'd all been praying silently, at least we got an answer – the squeal and whoop of sirens, the roar of engines, the blaze of headlights and blues and twos and the squawk and crackle of radios.

'Daisy, Mary, keep pumping!' I ordered unnecessarily, yomping down to greet and brief the wet-suited and wadered cavalry.

40

Who's the Daddy?

'We meet at last Mr Chalfont!' Raines enthused, lacking only a white cat in his lap for the full Bond villain look, as Burroughs helped a queasy Roland from the powerboat onto the ship's aft deck. 'Reckon I must be one of your best customers!'

'You and your father, yes,' Roland admitted.

'We do share a certain nasty streak,' Raines replied cheerfully. But then the glib façade dropped. 'But I'm not in that bastard's league – any way you look at it. Let's stitch him up good and proper!'

'Let's worry about the children first, shall we,' Roland muttered, unable to hide his distaste.

'Of course, of course,' Raines replied, ushering Roland into a stateroom that looked liked the bridge of the Starship Enterprise. 'Welcome to my empire!'

An array of monitors flickered silently covering every TV news channel and several computer screens displayed archived news stories about Joe and Lily and about Winston Smith, mug shot style photos of Raines Senior and even a local press exposé on the activities and subsequent imprisonment of a Madam called Daisy Chains. Raines hit one button among hundreds on a bewilderingly vast console and the invisible speakers positioned around the room squawked into life with the curt, crackling exchanges of police radio. But it was pretty much unintelligible to the uninitiated.

'They're already onto you, Roland,' Bart said as he fiddled with yet another set of buttons and faders. 'That's better, he said as his system homed in on mobile telephone traffic, then isolated that of DI Masterson.

'But I haven't done anything wrong – not really,' Roland said, worried nonetheless.

'That's not how they'll see it – and anyway, once they start going through your client base you won't have a business left will you!'

'Suppose not,' Roland agreed reluctantly, 'but I…'

Raines hushed him with a raised hand.

'…The SOCOs are in the house now. Bunton was tied up and drugged by the looks of it. Raines has to be the prime suspect. Also Mary Bunton – wife of deceased. Maybe they were working together and he found out,' barked Masterson, evidently enjoying himself.

'I'll send a car to the Bunton house. Anything else?' came the reply.

'Yeah – once they get the kids out, I want Richard Smith arrested for obtaining goods by deception. There's been a complaint from two hotels – one in Somerset, the other in Cannes. And while you're at it, give his hotel room at the Hartham Arms a spin - you're bound to find some coke in there somewhere.'

'Who?'

'Mister superstar – Richard, not Winston. Richard Smith's the jumped–up fucker's real name.'

'Yes sir.'

'And while you're at it nick the hooker too – she's absconded from the cushy little holiday camp they put her in. And she's got a list of unpaid fines as long as…'

'The long arm of the law Sir?'

'Shut the fuck up and get on with it! Over and fucking out!'

'Oh Burger King!' breathed Roland. 'I can't believe they're talking about us when they haven't even started getting the children out. There must be something *we* can do!'

'Not really my problem is it – I'm doing my bit aren't I,' Raines muttered distractedly.

'You really don't give a shit about anyone or anything do you!' Roland said, his quiet voice wavering with contempt.

'None of them ever did me any favours. Not Smith. Not Daisy,' he replied petulantly.

'But the boy – he's your nephew for God's sake. Doesn't that make a difference?'

Raines shook his head.

Roland stood up, gazed pensively out of the porthole, then turned deliberately.

'What if I told you Joe was your brother?' he breathed coldly.

Raines chortled incredulously.

'Oh surely even you can do better than that. How can you possibly work that one out?'

'Easy really. You knew your father was abusing Daisy didn't you.'

'Well he didn't exactly go easy on me – and between him and her, they managed to fuck me up good and proper,' he protested.

'You saw what he did?'

'Couldn't exactly turn a blind eye, could I,' he argued, pointing at his scarred and lidless eye. What they did to me meant I had to watch everything, always. Couldn't shut it out...

'So you know he raped her.'

That gave him pause.

'No, I...' he stammered, one eye blinking double time on the other's behalf. 'He didn't actually...'

'He did. Actually. All the time, actually,' Roland stated firmly. 'Your father is also the father of your sister's child!'

'But Smith's the father. That's why I've been stitching him up. That's why...'

'Daisy just needed someone she could love to be Joe's father. So she seduced poor old Rich as insurance – so she could call on him if and when she needed to. And when she was sent to prison, well...'

'But she did a runner years ago. The kid's what, fifteen? He'd be ten years older than that if...'

'She went back. Once – when she had nowhere else, thinking maybe she could, you all could, start again… Your father obviously didn't agree. You can imagine the rest.'

Even Bart's hyper broadband couldn't take this in. It was, after all, verbal, not visual input.

'Oh my God,' he breathed finally.

'Indeed,' Roland agreed, pausing to let the enormity of what he'd divulged sink in. 'This is just between us, you understand?'

Raines nodded blankly.

'And anyway,' Roland pressed, 'what do you mean "stitching him up"? What have you done to Rich – Winston?'

'Ah,' Bart replied, sheepish now. 'You see I'm the new publisher that promised him all that money. It was a lie – revenge. I was going to build him up again, pull the plug on him and watch him go down in flames. Hence the police being after him – I never intended to pay his Babington bill, or the one from MIDEM in Cannes and they must run to thousands by now!'

Now Raines stood and gazed out of the porthole. Roland broke the silence.

'So will you at least try to help now?'

Raines nodded sombrely.

'Yes. I think I've got some penance to pay,' he mumbled and suddenly a smile lit up his face. 'What we need, my friend, is a plan! And evil schemes are what I do best!'

'Evil's not required this time,' Roland pointed out.

★   ★   ★

Things were taking too long. The divers were still checking tanks and wrestling with masks and meters while in the background the local cops, who presumably didn't see a lot of action, were really making a meal of raiding the Raines residence through the front door. When we had finally decided to point them in the right direction with an anonymous tip-off from Ralph, we'd forgotten to mention that the back door was open. I approached the officer in charge in the big van that I assumed was serving as a sort of operational control centre – and although he wasn't the slightest bit surprised to see me, was I astonished to see him, if less than staggered by the realisation that he'd become a copper.

'Dave Masterson!' I exclaimed, not overly pleased to encounter an old school acquaintance but holding out my hand, which he ignored.

'Hello, Smith. Or am I meant to call you *Winston* these days?' he sneered.

'Just Rich, actually.'

'I bet you are.'

I decided to ignore his snide remark so brimming with the resentment he'd clearly been fermenting over the years and rise above it. Nevertheless I also resolved not to mention that open back door. Childish, maybe – but I justified it to myself on the grounds that I wanted nothing to distract him from the rescue.

'Look, my son's drowning in there. Can't you hurry things up?'

'Leave it to the professionals, Smith. OK?' he replied dismissively. 'And make sure you don't get in the way.'

Bloody hell. Hello *David*!' gasped Daisy, hurrying up behind me.

The copper recoiled at the sight of her.

'Remember me, do you? Course you do – how could you forget!' she teased, slyly winking at me.

'And you keep out of the way too, Raines,' he snarled and went on barking orders into his radio.

'It's taking too long,' I said.

She nodded and handed me her mobile phone.

'Rich, it's Roland. You, Daisy and Mary need to get out of there. Masterson's going to arrest all of you the moment the kids are out.'

'I'm not going anywhere till I see they're all right. Or not...' I hissed, agitated. 'Anyway, I haven't done anything wrong!'

'Something about unpaid bills at Babington. And they've raided the hotel and found the rest of your Charlie. So you're in deep trouble – as we all are. Look, Rich, please, will you trust me? No time to explain, but if you all go to the beach, near as you can get to the tunnel's opening, everything's going to be OK,' Roland urged.

I looked dubiously at Daisy. Evidently she'd been more fully briefed. And it was obvious she trusted Roland implicitly. She nodded. Good enough for me.

'Go! I'll get Mary,' she muttered.

I waited to make sure Masterson's back was turned and just as the divers waded in wielding their cutting equipment, I slipped away into the bushes, up and over the mound, halted for a heartbeat and a silent prayer by our plastic stopper, and let gravity take me half-running, half-tumbling down the other side.

★   ★   ★

With Burroughs at the helm and Roland cowering in the gunwales, the launch growled and reared on its haunches as it was unleashed and lunged away from its berth at the Daisy Chain's starboard and knifed shoreward through the waves – more torpedo than boat. Behind it trailed the ship's weighty anchor chain and, as the prow nosed in close to the all but submerged steel palings besieging the tunnel's entrance, Burroughs cut the engine to idling speed.

'Hold her steady as you can!' he shouted to Roland, who lurched to the raked cockpit seat like he was drunk and did his best.

Wet-suited and – Roland couldn't help thinking – rather magnificent, Burroughs squatted, flexed his giant thighs and struggled upright like a champion weightlifter bearing the Daisy Chain's giant anchor above his head. Poised precariously on the tip of the prow, riding the swell like a surfer and wielding the anchor like a harpoon, he waited till the launch rode up on the crest of a wave, hurled his trident through its spume, then tugged hard on its chain before bounding aft to take over the helm.

'Now!' Roland shouted into a radio handset over the tumultuous roar of the engines, the thrashing wind and waves.

Burroughs slammed the drive into reverse and swung the launch out and away from the tunnel just as the chain snapped taut as a cheese wire. Intermittently, when they plunged into a wave's trough, Roland could make out the fairground glare of the Daisy Chain's lights and hear snatches of its deep leonine roar.

★ ★ ★

Splashing ankle-deep across the sea road and vaulting the low fence onto the esplanade, with Daisy and Mary scurrying up several yards behind, I looked down to where the tunnel had been. All I could see of it by what little of the mocking moonlight the clouds disclosed were the spikes of its iron mask, occasionally piercing the froth. Just as the two women appeared breathlessly by my side, we were deafened by the sound of a dinosaur groaning in prolonged agony. All three of us recoiled as one when a metallic clang rent the air and the sea and the twisted remains of the metal fencing sped through the water like a giant rake or the fins of a regimented platoon of sharks. Following its wake, we were momentarily dazzled by the Daisy Chain's receding lights and paralysed in a sort of awe.

'Get in,' someone shouted. And it was only then that we noticed Burroughs balancing balletically on the rocking foredeck of the power launch just a few feet away and closing. I took his outstretched hand and was instantly aboard in a single leap of assisted faith. With my fairly ineffectual help, Burroughs got the girls on board and began unlashing a rigid inflatable that rocked and rolled alongside. By this time I'd worked out what the plan was and as Captain Roland nosed the vessel between the jagged metal claws left by the torn-away barricade, I watched as

Burroughs mimed my mission. Attached by steel karabiners to a hefty steel hawser was an array of thinner metal cables. At the end of each were more clips. Hanging over the gunwales, we flailed each time a wave plummeted us down far enough, trying to hook those clips round the hasps of the padlocks that held Joe and Lily's lives inside the tunnel. With a just-discernible clink, Burroughs secured the first. I missed mine. Agonisingly, we had to wait, not just for the next wave, but for several low-rollers till one high and mighty enough to raise us up and hurl us down low enough came along. With Daisy and Mary hanging on to my ankles, I plunged underwater, succeeded in grabbing hold of a padlock and hooking the karabiner clip onto its hasp before the boat's prow yanked me up and out into the air, spewing water like a gargoyle.

Now Daisy and Mary were in the inflatable, struggling to haul unhelpful lifejackets over their heads. I leapt over the side to join them, missed and floundered in the perilously fast-closing gap between the two hulls, failing to get a grip on the dinghy's slippery sides, which were in any case too high in the water for me to climb aboard unaided.

'Lifejacket!' I screamed and though the storm stole my voice, Daisy read my panicked face, if not lips or mind, and chucked one in my direction. I lunged for it, but missed and it was borne away as much by wind as waves. Burroughs deftly knotted a running bowline in the loose mooring rope and tightened it round his ankle before launching himself like a bungee-jumping pearl diver into the thrashing water between the two vessels. Seizing me under the arms, he rocketed me up and tossed me into the inflatable with depressingly impressive power. Reaching over the backboard to the toggle atop the outboard motor, he yanked, once, twice, three times and the little engine sputtered and coughed into life.

'You're the splashdown team. We're the rocket!' he bellowed as he clambered up back onto the stern of the launch, pushed Roland roughly out of the way and took the wheel. 'So get clear and then steer back in to pick them up!'

I hoped I'd got what he meant as another couple of lifejackets came hurtling my way. Catching them, I shoved Mary aside and took the inflatable's tiller and held us as steady as I could in the backwash as the launch spasmed and bucked and shot off with a lusty roar, the hawsers whipping tight behind it.

In the inflatable, we rode up on a massive swell that threatened to tip us right up onto the road above, then plummeted yet again just as the steel ties tensed like live sinews, strained then hummed and whirred with relief as the padlocks wrenched away the iron straps across the tunnel's hatch. And in that short-lived lull, a stinking cascade of sewage and rainwater spewed out against the sea's onslaught, bearing with it first two small helpless, bedraggled and inanimate bodies, then two more – wet-suited, oxygen-tanked, burly and bewildered. At least they had the wherewithal to survive.

⋆　　⋆　　⋆

The divers had been down in shit creek for several minutes now and DI Masterson was getting agitated. Apart from Bunton's corpse and a stash of GHB, there'd been no great satisfaction at the Raines house – and no clue to its owner's whereabouts. Worse, the whore and the rock star had given him the slip in all the hubbub – confirming Masterson's opinion of them as depraved parasites who deserved everything he and the force of the law could throw at them. And anything outside the law he could get away with, if he was honest, which he rarely was. Still, he had to focus on the main priority: getting the kids out safely. If it wasn't already too late. Failing that, busting Raines and Smith and their partners in crime would be a very acceptable consolation prize. What Masterson really wanted, though, was both trophies. Child saviour on the one hand; crime buster on the other.

Finally the oxyacetylene torches had beaten the outer fencing. Going by the submerged lights that shimmered up from the murk,

Masterson reckoned the divers were now tackling the hinges on the hatch. *Any second now,* he thought, waving over the paramedics and making sure the press and TV contingent caught sight of the gesture and simultaneously instructing his subordinates to hold them back as he waded up to his knees and assumed what he reckoned was an angst-ridden, caring yet authoritative stance for the cameras.

One diver's arm appeared through the scummy froth with a thumbs-up. They were about to open the hatch. But suddenly all the diluted shite flushed away in a toilet tsunami as if God had pulled his lavatory chain. And the diving team was flushed away too, leaving a couple of very startled firefighters writhing in six inches of sewage in their waist-high waders.

★   ★   ★

Copying Burroughs' swashbuckling show of seamanship, I tied the end of the inflatable's mooring rope round my ankle and rolled over the side, sank and then rose, sank then rose. But I couldn't see them – not Joe, not Lily, not the inflatable, not the shore. I flailed pointlessly against the swell in a blind panic but the waves kept effortlessly throwing me down. After all this, they were going to drown. And so was I, unless we were all dashed against the promenade's bulwarks first.

I freed my ankle from the rope and struck out blindly, paddling pointlessly up the convex wall of an overreaching breaker, which broke over me – but as its swell subsided, gathering its strength for the next, I caught sight of Daisy standing unsteadily on the prow, the two extra lifejackets dangling over one arm. Mary's hands grasped her calves ineffectually, failing to steady her. After a too-long time, Daisy spotted me, pointed frantically at somewhere aft of the inflatable and, as I waved back, she dived up and out and disappeared as I sank and swallowed an ocean. By the time I surfaced, I couldn't see Daisy, the boat or the kids. So I swam as hard as my uselessly unused and used-up body would let me, back towards the orange glow of the town's streetlights. Arms and legs suddenly boneless, muscle-less, ears awash, deafened and defeated, I was just a sack of flotsam – and the sea treated me as such, bearing me up with mocking ease, then casually dropping me with a painful bump on the pavement of the prom.

I thought I was dead. Worse than that Joe and Lily must be too. My conviction was confirmed by the hazy vision of a black-clad priest kneeling at my side intoning something that sounded holy. Then, in an instant, I was being reborn. Always knew there was something to reincarnation. But surely they were supposed to slap your arse rather than your face to start your breathing?

'Rich – Daisy's got Joe but we can't see Lily!' Ralph urged, searching my eyes for a sign of life and apologetically slapping me again just to make sure.

I jumped up, staggered and spewed and then together, like Butch Cassidy and the Sundance Kid, we ran like hell and jumped.

★   ★   ★

'I want a chopper and I want it now!' DI Masterson was bellowing into the squawk box.

'Don't we all!' said Raines, eavesdropping from the Daisy Chain.

'No way we can do that sir. It's out chasing a TWOC.'

Bart switched his attention to one of the TV monitors.

'Although the police are making no comment at the moment, there have definitely been dramatic developments in the case of the missing young lovers. The tunnel in which they had been imprisoned has been opened – but not, it seems by the emergency services. The feeling seems to be that they have been washed out to sea – and no one knows whether Joe Smith and Lily Bunton are, or were, alive,' enthused the local TV reporter whose most exciting live to camera piece till now had been the Mayor opening a garden fête.

'And have the police got any idea who abducted them?' the studio anchorman replied, throwing back to the man on the spot.

'Well they're not saying. However, we have observed that they've raided the nearby home of Erich Raines – a lay preacher and father of the prostitute we now know is the missing youth's mother, and who is linked to the controversial rock star Winston Smith. What they've found we don't know. It's clear, though, that Mr Raines is nowhere to be found. For now, over to you in the studio, John.'

'I'll show 'em where to find the evil fucker!' Bart chuckled and started pressing a lot of buttons and typing emails at supergeek speed.

'Oh, Charlie!' he called out on the intercom, almost as an afterthought, 'swing back to shore – not too close. Just be ready to pick up the launch and the inflatable.'

★   ★   ★

Now the Reverend and the rocker were swimming away from the orange lights – into the dark. The sea seemed calmer but still it was hopeless. I could hear Ralph praying under his laboured breaths. Then, so suddenly it was as if by God's command, the wind dropped and Daisy's voice rang out clearly – and very near. And there she was, treading water and cradling our son's waxen white face in a folded lifejacket. I think I felt relief and love for an instant. But I was too numb and too panicked to distinguish one extreme emotion from another. They all blended into one.

'I can't find Lily…' Daisy yelled and whatever else she was saying was drowned by the growl of the inflatable's outboard as it surfed towards them, narrowly missed mincing them and went into automatic orbit as a frantic Mary abandoned the tiller and leapt into the water screaming her daughter's name.

The dinghy's painter trailed after it as it idled in repeated circles. After several tries, I caught it and hauled on it hand over hand till the boat was within reach. And what was impossible before was easy now, in extremis. I threw a leg up and hooked the back of my knee on a rowlock, then levered myself up and in, threw myself at the tiller and gunned the motor, manoeuvring the craft close enough to haul Daisy and Joe aboard.

'He's not breathing!' she stuttered.

'He must be!' I shouted, pumping away at him the way I'd seen on TV till the seawater stopped pumping lazily out and I turned him over and started mouth-to-mouth resuscitation. Kissing my boy for the first time – before we'd even met. Then I stopped.

'Do you know how?'

Daisy nodded and took over with awe-inspiring composure.

'Get the girl,' she said, between puffs.

I hesitated.

'Go – I'll take care of him. Don't worry.'

I think Joe's eyelids twitched then. A flicker of hope. I hoped so.

I smiled. How can you smile at a time like that? I don't know. But I did.

So I teetered on the edge, staring into orange-stained darkness trying to work out in which direction to launch myself and find the girl and/or presumably die. And then I remembered Ralph. I'd assumed he'd haul himself onto the boat after me. But he hadn't. I suppose I was getting used to this kind of stuff – so I just dived with a quick prayer before I winged it.

The amazing thing about leaps of faith is that they seem to work. First a flashing blue light, then a vast, sweeping searchlight turned night into day as the police helicopter buzzed the waves like a dragonfly, winching the two divers to safety. And there in the flickering swipes of radar light I made out a frail-looking and pale, floating waif, looking dead, but presumably alive and not very well because she was clutching one of the lifejackets and holding her head above water – just. But no sign of Ralph. Maybe he'd swum to shore. Maybe not. Either way he'd want me to make the girl safe first. I don't think I'd experienced this kind of clarity since... Well since I was just Richard Smith. My new-found composure sent me surging to her with amazing ease and I buoyed her up and towed her steadily to the inflatable, where Daisy leaned over, took the girl's helpless arms and tugged as I shoved to get her limp form aboard.

Hanging exhausted from the side of the boat, I asked with my eyes about our son.

'He's alright,' Daisy smiled wanly.

The girl coughed and retched and her body jerked like it had been electrocuted. Sick, starved, sullied and abused – but alive.

I did one of those brow-wiping relief things and then remembered.

'No Ralph?'

Daisy shook her head distractedly, struggling to share her concern between our son and the girl he loved, with no part of her heart left to offer.

'Shit! I'll find him!' I spluttered as I dropped back into the water and started swimming frantically away.

'And Mary!' Daisy yelled after me.

The chopper's downdraft seemed to quell or flatten the waves and suddenly I was treading water in a temporarily pond-like expanse of flat water, stippled with micro-waves and ablaze with light. But the private police pond was invaded by the launch sharking in and overwhelming me in the tight arc of its wake and throwing me into shadow. Silhouetted by the searchlights from above, Roland wobbled at the vessel's prow then plunged.

★　　★　　★

Out here, properly at sea, beyond the point where the waves froth and break, the sea was almost calm, the wind riffling across its surface and great fathomless masses of liquid flexing and tensing like muscles under skin. The swimming was easier now; now that Lily was safe there was nothing and no one she needed to save – not even herself. With the town's garish glow dimming into the distance behind her, Mary settled into a languid sidestroke for a while, then rolled onto her back, watched the stars prickle through the dissipating clouds and let the giant moon and its servant tide carry her out and away. Numbed now to the bone-deep, soul-deep cold, she drifted, listening to the swoosh and roar in her ears until her eyes closed and she succumbed.

★   ★   ★

'What the fuck do they think they're doing?' DI Masterson screamed into his headset, his whole body shrinking away from the helicopter's dizzyingly open hatch.

'Getting away, Sir?' the pilot replied dryly.

'They'd fucking well better not!'

'But our mission is to save the children – and it looks like they've done that for us.'

'Save them my arse – they're kidnapping them. We'll get the bastards for that!'

'Sir, they're the parents!'

'Not of the girl. No sign of the mother! Can't you buzz them or something – force them to shore?'

The pilot shook his head emphatically.

'Too dangerous – specially in these conditions.'

Masterson ignored him and grabbed the radio mouthpiece.

'Masterson here. I want these fuckers stopped. Get the coastguard on the case…'

★   ★   ★

Riding at anchor a good mile offshore, The Daisy Chain could be in international waters long before the cops could get close. Although Bart had listened in on Masterson's radio ranting he wasn't concerned. He doubted that even the Coast Guard's fleet had anything to match the quite stupendous power of the custom-built engines he'd had fitted to his pride and joy. Now that Burroughs had whisked Roland off in the launch to join in the fun and games, he could fire her up right now and bugger off to Holland for a bit of high octane perversion in Amsterdam; a short voyage followed by some serious cruising round the red light district… But then he wouldn't just be abandoning them all; he'd be missing his only chance to put right some of his wrongs. *At least then, he thought, I might have some company I don't have to put on a salary.* One of the TV monitors caught his eye. A shot of Smith – as Winston Smith. Then one of his father. He'd also be letting the hypocritical, incestuous old kiddie fiddler off the hook. He'd spent all this time screwing up Smith's life and, he realised now, it was his father he really wanted to hurt. He wanted to do to the old bastard what those mobs of outraged parents did to the paedophiles exposed by the *News of the World's* 'Name and Shame' campaign – tear him limb from limb.

'There's a thought!' he said to himself excitedly as a plan began to coalesce in his mind – one that would allow paediatricians to sleep soundly at night, since it didn't involve the tabloids.

'Charlie!' he shouted excitedly into the intercom. 'Fire her up!

41

Better Drowned Than Duffers. If Not Duffers Won't Drown

Pride comes before a fall, Ralph was thinking as his limbs finally capitulated to the relentless weight of his sodden motorcycle leathers dragging him down. *Pride, proving itself a deadly sin.* If only he hadn't tried to emulate his glamorous new friends. If only he hadn't strayed from his vocation and stayed close to God. If only he hadn't been so vain as to slip back to the hotel to change out of his tweedy vicar gear into something more rock 'n' roll... *Too late now,* he breathed and began a final prayer.

'Our Father, who art in Heaven, Hallowed be his name. Give us this day...'

'Our daily bread,' spluttered Roland, doggy paddling towards him like a big baby, swaddled in a lifejacket and encircled by a red and white striped lifebelt.

Ralph silently thanked the Lord, and then his new saviour.

'Talk about belt and braces, Roland,' Ralph smiled weakly.

'Can't swim,' his rescuer replied. 'Get your arms round the belt and hold on tight.'

Ralph gratefully complied and Roland hollered into the darkness.

'Burroughs? Got him! Go!' and, as if for emphasis, he fumbled with something attached to his lifejacket, tugged it hard and a flare rocketed into the sky. Instantly, Ralph's arms were almost pulled out of their sockets as the invisible Burroughs gunned the equally invisible launch to which the belt was still tethered and the Reverend and the reprobate, clinging on to the ring and each other for dear life and what suddenly felt like love, went hurtling and tumbling through the water at thirty knots like one of those holiday resort 'bananas' without the whoops, squeals, sunshine and smiles.

Then again, maybe two hopeful and shy smiles glimmered around those two pairs of gritted teeth...

★   ★   ★

I couldn't swim any longer. I just had to hope Ralph and Mary had both made it. In his case, somehow I doubted it. Specially since his other putative saviour was the less than manly Roland, who couldn't even swim, as I'd found out after playfully chucking him in the deep end of the Babington pool and nearly drowning him. How brave; how much of a man was that timid, kindly and reticent old queer! He was worth ten, twenty, thirty of Bart Raines, and hundred times Raines's father. If he was dead – if they both were dead – I resolved to write something to commemorate them, do some benefit gigs for something they'd have wanted... Shit, I might even do *Children In Need!*

Pathetically, I didn't have the strength to climb into the dinghy so Daisy, bless her, stripped off the waterproofs she'd donned in my absence and jumped fearlessly again into the icy waters. Floating on her back, she cradled my head in her bosom and manoeuvred us to the inflatable's stern, where Joe, wrapped in blankets, knelt and held out his hand. I took it. *My son's hand.*

'Don't take my hand!' he shouted and, instantly withered by his perfectly justified hatred, I let go and fell back on Daisy.

'Take hold of my wrist – and I'll take yours. Stronger that way!' he bellowed, reaching out desperately to me.

I did, and with surprising strength he hauled me aboard and turned back to help Daisy. His mother. I slumped to the puddled deck next to the tiny waif that must be Lily, mummified and shaking uncontrollably in a foil space blanket, her uncomprehending eyes flickering, her translucent skin frighteningly like a death pallor in the cold moonlight.

Daisy stroked my cheek.

'Thought you were dead,' she said almost casually, a tiny smile telling me that she'd been far from casual about the idea. 'Joe,' she went on as she mumsily tugged a cagoule over my head, 'this is your dad.'

I held out my hand for my second ever handshake with my son. *My son!* He took it solemnly and we shook, and shook and shook. Maybe it was the cold. Or maybe not – either way we were both trembling like washing machines on fast spin. I thought for a temptingly happy moment that the handshake was about to grow into a long overdue embrace. But the boy's face suddenly retreated from mine and he examined me; no, he *analysed* me.

'You're not... I mean you look just like...'

'Yeah, yeah, he's Winston Smith from Airstrip One,' Daisy mocked, poking her tongue out at me.

'You're kidding?' he said, searching Daisy's inscrutable face.

She nodded and her Daisy smile blossomed in spite of the cold and wet.

Cool!' Joe exclaimed, his face wreathed in the goofiest grin imaginable. 'Dad, this is Lily.'

Then I got that hug. Then Daisy joined in and then the three of us nestled round Lily, willing life into her and suffusing her with our warmth, emotional and physical.

★　　★　　★

Now a couple of miles out at sea, Burroughs stopped the launch's engines and started the winch motor, laughing as the odd couple came into view, then hauling them aboard, as they coughed and spluttered and laughed at the fact they'd survived.

'Bunny baby!' crackled the radio.

'Fuck off,' he replied.

373

'This is your fucking Captain speaking – have you got them?'

'Yep.'

'OK – we can see you on the radar. Stay put and I'll come and get them. I've got another little jobbie for you my boy!'

'Oh great. Can't wait!' Burroughs muttered, eyeing the two strangers who now huddled in the shelter of the wheelhouse and wondering if he might get rid of that old queen and get some serious leather-clad vicar action for himself. But the familiar growl of the Daisy Chain roused him from his reverie and he scanned the horizon for her lights. Nothing. The engine noise was suddenly silenced too and all he could hear above the burbling of the launch's idling motor was the slap and slosh of the waves against the hull.

'Wakey wakey,' came Raines's irritating chortle out of nowhere.

'Fuck, where did you come from?' Burroughs snapped, annoyed at being caught out.

'Silent running. Have you never seen any war films?' Raines replied glibly. 'Ah Roland, you found your friend. I'm glad. Help them aboard Bunny!'

As Burroughs guided them up the wobbly gangplank that young Charlie had lowered onto the flat decking aft of the launch's cockpit, Raines greeted them effusively like some Admiral of the Fleet, shaking them by the hand and ushering them into the Star Trek bridge. Burroughs made fast and followed.

'Right Bunny Boy! Here's your mission,' Raines boomed.

Burroughs glowered and was taken aback by his employer's instant chagrin.

'Sorry. I shan't call you that again. Decided not to be a cunt any more. We need to save my sister, Smith and the kids and I need you to do something quite risky…'

Burroughs bristled.

'Look,' Raines went on, 'I've fucked up badly. Do this for them, if not for me, and you're off the hook. I'll pay you off with as much money as you need and you can go where you want – or you can stay if you like.'

Burroughs nodded, bewildered.

'Right. It goes like this,' Raines began.

★   ★   ★

The police helicopter loomed over the tiny inflatable and its bedraggled occupants, eclipsing the moon as it descended.

'You are under arrest. Do not move. Do not do anything till we take you on board,' Masterson's voice barked through his appropriately named bullhorn.

'Like we're going anywhere,' Daisy moaned. 'Shit, shit, shit. I can't go back to prison again.'

'I'll pay your fines – you'll be, er, fine,' I quipped. 'It's going to be a night in the cop shop at worst.'

'You clearly have no idea what sort of shit I'm in and how deep darling! How long did you think my sentence was?'

'Oh shit,' I said.

'Easy to do a runner from open prisons darling!' she said.

'Oh shit,' I repeated.

The chopper settled on its floats and rocked to and fro on the swell as the pilot carefully eased it closer.

'Richard Smith, AKA Winston Smith, AKA Stone,' Masterson announced with all the pomposity he could muster, which was a lot, 'and Daisy Raines, AKA Daisy Chains, I am arresting you for… Fuck!'

From behind us a great angular white hulk hove into view at speed, like a motorised iceberg, slicing off the chopper's tail like… Like a Sunseeker through a helicopter tail really. The crippled aircraft went into a spin – as did DI Masterson.

'I'll have you for this. Destruction of Her Majesty's property, piracy…Ow! AB fucking H… And…'

As the chopper spun faster and faster on its floats and two dizzy divers along with DI Masterson projectile-puked like lawn sprinklers, another vessel approached at terrifying speed, its engines screaming as the propellers thrashed air on every wave-to-wave jump. Then, as the roar dwindled to nothing, a scouring, blinding searchlight ignited. The chopper pilot finally killed his engines. Silence. A stand-off at sea. I could see Masterson stand, just about, and shout and gesticulate inside the craft and shield his eyes from the glare.

The launch idled to a halt abeam of our inflatable. Burroughs and deckhand Charlie diligently helped us all aboard, then hooked up the dinghy to pulleys and winched it up. I offered Burroughs a conciliatory, and grateful, handshake. But he ignored it and instead started issuing orders.

'No time to explain,' he said, quietly but urgently as Charlie, on all fours, slid the inflatable across the deck and let it drop off the port side. 'Lie flat on the deck, and roll across and back into the inflatable.'

'You are fucking kidding,' I protested, suspecting another one of Raines's dirty little tricks but was silenced by the look on Burroughs' face.

'Just get them all in the thing. You'll see why. Anyway, Charlie's going with you.'

The deckhand hopped lightly aboard the inflatable and squatted with arms outstretched as we eased the inert bundle of Lily over the side of the launch and, keeping our heads down, rolled over to join them one by one. The moment we were all in, Burroughs fired the launch's engine and we were scudding out to sea in tandem. It was only as the helicopter's flashing blue light blurred into Hartham's distant orange smear and he began lashing the wheel tight to a couple of cleats that I worked out what he had in mind. After liberally dousing the launch in petrol and pushing the throttle to *FULL,* Burroughs leapt into the dinghy brandishing a fearsome knife, with which he slashed the painters tethering us to the launch. As it torpedoed away from us in a wide arc, wheeling back towards land, Charlie shoved our tiller to starboard and gunned the inflatable in the opposite direction, where the unmistakeable lights of the Daisy Chain flared into life like a faraway fairground. Another distant flash behind us, followed by a thunderous boom, told us that the launch had served its final purpose.

★   ★   ★

'Since we can only assume Mary's dead,' Ralph murmured, not looking very clerical in one of Raines's flashier designer linen outfits in a garish shade of pink, 'I suggest we pray for her.'

'Shhhh!' Daisy, hissed, scanning the room for Lily.

'It's all right, Lily's in her cabin. Bart's medic's looking after her,' I reassured her.

'OK. I think we should wait till she's on her feet before we break the news, yeah?'

Nods all round.

'You're all dead actually,' Bart interjected blithely as we huddled in dry blankets sipping hot soup in his stateroom. 'As far as the police are concerned anyway. So everybody's off the hook!' he went on, clearly pleased with himself. 'No one's getting busted. No one's going to jail.'

'Including our dad!' said Daisy angrily.

'No – he's going to get what's coming to him. For a start, I've forwarded to the police everything Roland gave me plus all the information my team put together.'

'Prison's too good for him,' Joe piped up.

'Indeed,' Bart beamed. 'I haven't been sitting on my arse, you know, while you lot have been messing about in boats! Well, I have,' he corrected himself, 'but I've been busy.'

He pointed a remote at a monitor and *BBC News 24* appeared, the presenter looking unusually grave.

'Troubled rock star Winston Smith has been killed in a tragic boating accident just moments after it is believed he rescued his missing son from unknown captors. Police say that his son, Joe Raines, his mother Daisy

Raines, missing girl Lily Bunton and her mother Mary are also missing, presumed dead after their speedboat exploded off the Suffolk coast. In a bizarre twist, Lily's father, Alan Bunton has been founded dead at the home of Daisy Raines's father – a local lay preacher who is wanted for questioning about the teenagers' abduction. We'll bring you more on….'

Bart muted the monitor.

'Great!' I groaned. 'So much for my dazzling career revival!'

'Ah, well I've been meaning to speak to you about that,' Raines began, unusually ill at ease as he edged away from me. 'You must understand that it was all a misunderstanding… Why I…'

'Why you what? Got your sidekick here,' I shot a killing look at Burroughs, 'to seduce my girlfriend so you could seduce her with your money?'

Roland stood up and diffidently requested our attention.

'You're not going to like this Rich, but – is this OK Bart?'

Raines nodded sheepishly.

'Bart,' Roland continued, 'hasn't been, um, entirely honest with you…'

'Oh for fuck's sake, what he's trying to say is that I'm the publisher that's bought all your rights,' Raines intervened.

It took me a while to assimilate this. Then I nodded. It all made sense. It had all been too good to be true. I shrugged. It didn't seem as important as it would have a few days before.

'And now you've "killed me off" so you can cash in on my "tragic death" I suppose!' I sniped, with a lot less rancour than I'd expected.

'It's worse than that I'm afraid,' apologised Roland as if he were to blame.

'Oh stop beating about the bush you old tart,' Raines interjected and turned to me.

'Look Rich – I've been stitching you up. That's why your Babington bill hasn't been paid. Nor's your Gray D'Albion one. I haven't paid the advance you were promised. You're more broke than you were before in fact. I was setting you up. I was going to fuck you up.'

So I was right. The sudden change in my fortunes had been bullshit, like everything else in my life. Talk about kicking a man when he's down. I felt the blow now, deep in my guts. I clenched my fists and then I clenched my eyelids. Uselessly as it turned out, because I didn't hit him and I did cry. Thank God my son had gone back to his bedside Lily vigil.

'Charming,' I half-said, half-sobbed as Daisy reached out, took my hand and squeezed. I pumped it back, in time with my heartbeat.

'But that's all changed and I'm sorry. Really sorry,' Raines went on.

'I fucking bet you are,' I glared sceptically through the prism of my tears as Ralph appeared and settled on the arm of the sofa I was sunk in. But I let Raines carry on talking, confessing, to me and to the priest - well vicar, anyway - simultaneously, his long, gleefully sadistically drawn-out revenge that had started with the drugging, rape and stealing of Georgie and was to end with my public humiliation – as if I hadn't done that for myself on countless occasions. Once again I drew on my years of experience in condensing complex emotions into catchy, pithy phrases that said it all on a visceral level:

'You fucking cunt,' I Peter Cooked.

Raines nodded.

'Can't argue with that,' he said simply.

'So I've got no money, no record deal, no publisher and you own all my copyrights?'

He nodded again.

'But I'm going to put that right. You'll get the money. Lots of it. And I *will* get your record released and I *will* make sure it's a massive hit – and then we'll both get lots more!'

'Because I'm dead, you mean?'

'Maybe. But not necessarily.'

'So what's brought on this change of heartlessness?'

'Well…' Raines began, clearing his throat as if a revelation of great import was coming.

'Why don't we talk about all this later,' Daisy cut in hastily. 'So cut to the chase, brother dear, and tell us how daddy gets what's coming to him.'

42

Resurrection

I could have stayed dead – and arguably my post mortem record sales would have gone through the roof Kurt Cobain style. But they - Bart, Daisy, Roland and Ralph - gave me the choice - and there was more than one compelling reason to announce my 'resurrection'. One was that I didn't see the point of the money if it meant the end of Winston Smith. Career-wise I'd be a dead man walking. Nowhere to go and nothing to do… Roland and Daisy were happy to stay dead – they both wanted a fresh start. Ralph was tempted to 'die' too, so that he too could reinvent himself in a new, less vicarious life. We'd consult the kids later, once the broken Lily had healed sufficiently for us to break her again with the news that she was an orphan. She was, we all agreed, going to be OK. We were going to make sure of that.

The other reason was revenge. Maybe I should say justice – but I'd be lying. It was revenge, pure and simple, not just for Joe, Lily, Mary, Bart and Daisy, the long lost Susan and Stephen and all the other missing kids Daisy and Roland had cross-referenced and correlated with Erich Raines's movements over the years – but for all the evils men like him had inflicted on the innocent in the name of God. And even Ralph, the meekest, mildest, most consummately, genuinely cheek-turningly Christian man I ever met was in wholehearted agreement. We were a coalition of the good, the bad, the beautiful, the ugly, the arrogant and the meek, united in pursuit of the ugliest of all.

Once I'd phoned my utterly bewildered parents to announce my non-mortality and swear them to secrecy, we gave it a day. Long enough for the world to get the news; long enough for the newspapers and news channels to trot out their obituaries and therefore get maximum impact; long enough for our own version to promulgate and propagate itself throughout the web so that every search engine would make our case the top of every related search. And, of course, long enough for me to revel in the unique privilege of watching the global media's reaction to my own untimely demise.

It was a moving experience. I was moved to tears by the *Independent's* summary of my career, and by that of *The Times,* less so by *The Guardian's* – and moved to make an abusive phone call to the writer of the *Daily Mail's* ill-informed and mean-spirited list of my misdemeanours, which neglected to mention my music. Unsurprisingly, a tirade of death threats from a dead man freaked him out – especially when I told him I was about to be reincarnated so that I could kick the crap out of him in person. I recommended that if he felt the need to talk to a priest, Father Moncrieff of Hartham-on-Sea would be his best bet.

It was a lot of fun phoning poor old Jimmy Gold to inform him that reports of my demise had been premature. He nearly had a heart attack when he heard my voice – although I suspect that was because he'd been counting his chickens and I was worth a lot more to him dead than alive. However, once he recovered his composure (in a nanosecond), he was on board – literally, in fact, because Bart sent a chopper (a real one, not a bicycle) to whisk him out to join the Daisy Chain in international waters somewhere off the Bay of Biscay.

Bart's vast monitoring team assured us that the police had found no evidence that any of us survived – and that they'd heard no radio chatter or email traffic to indicate that Erich Raines's arrest was going to happen any time soon. He'd gone to ground – and since, except by proxy, he eschewed mobile phones, computers and even television, he left no traces. It was quite probable that he didn't even know the whole story yet. We hoped so.

We started with a website, linked to all the Airstrip One and Winston Smith sites, official and unofficial. Bart mobilised his global geek team and millions upon millions of emails reached their destinations with the urgent request that the recipient forward the message to everyone they knew. The same process was repeated with SMS and MMS messages to millions of mobile phones, with another request that they Bluetooth it to every device in the vicinity. Within hours, the millions became billions. Then the press releases went out electronically to every national and local daily paper, every television and radio station in the world. Bart personally emailed every single one of his 'clients', promising them that their 'accounts' would be wound up, that no further payment or favours were required if they used their influence to ensure that our message was screened.

The message was this:
WINSTON SMITH BACK FROM THE DEAD TO SPEAK TO THE WORLD!
Go to www.getraines.com at 18.00 hours GMT and hourly thereafter.

At the appointed time, in the Daisy Chain's stateroom, in front of a dead-eyed camera and a blue-screened back-projection that suggested I was somewhere else, I was seated, sober, suited and booted with an air of composure and professionalism I hadn't managed for at least a decade. Jimmy Gold was ready to do his usual ad glib and everyone else was out of shot and ready to release another deluge of data. Bart's people were monitoring TV and radio transmissions and they confirmed that most, if not all, were building up to the broadcast of my webcast. Most of the media owners had little choice if they didn't want Bart to add their own *in flagrante* footage to what we were about to deliver.

'Three, two, one... Go!' Daisy mouthed at me.

'Hi. I'm Winston Smith,' I recited with well-rehearsed professionalism and a cheesily rueful grin. 'And I'm here to announce that recent reports of my demise were premature. Thank God, I survived. But tragically, my son, the girl he loved, his mother and more friends of mine died in that awful explosion. The irony is that we had just rescued Joe and his girlfriend Lily Bunton. They'd been kidnapped and left to die by a man who is the epitome of evil. A paedophile who poses as a preacher so that he can prey on young people and their parents. We know for a fact that he raped Lily before leaving her to drown and we're pretty sure he's responsible for the disappearance of several other young girls and boys over the last twenty or more years. Personally, I think prison's too good for him – and anyway I don't think the police are going to catch him. But *you* can. *WE* can. Look at this face. Remember it.'

Various renditions of Erich Raines' face paraded slide projector style across the screen, some culled from CCTV, others from Daisy's old family albums.

'Now look at this CCTV footage. This was twelve hours ago in Hartham-on-Sea, Suffolk, England,' I continued.

We screened fuzzy images of Erich Raines scuttling past the Hartham Arms and disappearing furtively down an alleyway.

'We'll be uploading more CCTV constantly as it comes in. We have gained access to systems throughout the UK and as I speak our facial recognition software is scanning for this face – so the website will be automatically tracking this monster wherever he goes... Use your phones. Use your PCs. Use the cameras and Bluetooth on your phones and text us or email us if you see him. We'll be working 24/7 to update the website – so keep watching and you'll be among the first to know where he is. In the meantime, here's his address. He's not likely to go there but it's a starting point. And here is the Hartham Grammar School sports pavilion where his so-called "church" holds its sick so-called "services".'

The pavilion appeared – followed by an aerial shot and a tickertape rolling caption showing its Ordnance Survey map reference, its address and the co-ordinates of Raines's house.

'On this website,' I went on after a dramatic pause, 'you'll find a list of everyone who's part of what he calls the "Fishers of Men", together with their addresses, email addresses, landline and mobile phone numbers. I'm using the net to catch these "Fishers". These people call themselves Christians. They're not. They killed a vicar in all this as well as my son, the girl he loved and God knows how many other children. So crucify them. Crucify *him*.' I ranted

I was turning into my enemy with my own hateful, vengeful tirade. But I didn't care.

'And don't forget, Winston's new single's out soon!' Jimmy squeaked, shoving his face into shot as the ethereal choral intro to *Bring It On* kicked in.

'Fuck off, Jimmy,' I rasped – and apparently those were my closing words before the webcast-cum broadcast went abruptly off air.

'Now all we have to do is wait,' Bart exclaimed, rubbing his hands together. 'Bloody hell!' he shouted. 'Maybe not!'

He pointed at one of the screens, on which his father's fuzzy monochrome image appeared.

'Location?' he barked into the intercom.

'Plotting now. OK. Should be on screen… Now,' one of his geeks reported as a blurred but familiar image coalesced on the screen.

'That's Hartham! He's still here!' I exclaimed, leaping to my feet. 'Are the news people still at the hotel? Can we let them know?'

'I can do a lot better than that,' Bart beamed and in an instant another few million messages told the world, and more importantly the outraged parents of Hartham-on-Sea, the exact location of the man who'd become Public Enemy Number One in a matter of minutes:

Target leaving Hartham sea road on foot, believed heading for sports pavilion, it said, and repeated the Ordnance Survey co-ordinates.

'The old bastard's going to wish he watched telly once in a while,' Daisy murmured in wonder. 'Turn up the news Bart!'

All the news channels were transmitting a shot of a red-nosed, windswept and scowling DI Masterson waiting to say his career-making, promotion-getting piece. Three different reporters began their preambles. We turned the volume up on one of them.

'Following the bombshell revelation just minutes ago that troubled rock star Winston Smith is alive, I repeat, Winston Smith is alive – the police are gravely concerned about his controversial broadcast encouraging the public to take the law into their own hands. Detective Inspector Masterson, what's the police line on this?'

'Our line is that Smith has no business meddling in police matters. It's hardly surprising to see a known drug addict and heavy drinker acting so cynically and irresponsibly – but I urge the public to take no notice of this cynical attempt to cynically exploit their understandable outrage in a cynical attempt to cynically sell records.'

'So are we to take it that you think Winston, or Stone, Smith is cynically exploiting the situation?' the reporter teased.

'Absolutely cynical, yes,' Masterson replied, oblivious. 'Cynical exploitation by a jumped-up, cynical...'

'Thank you Detective Inspector. Well I'm sure the public will cynically take on board the full cynicism of the situation.

Meanwhile, the tickertape at the foot of the screen was efficiently relaying the information on our website to its viewers. A mob was already gathering, waving ill-spelt placards with witty slogans along the lines of KILL PEDOFILES and PEDO SCUM MUST DIE.

DI Masterson's flushed and indignant face filled the screen.

'I would like to take this opportunity to appeal for calm. Please let the police do their job and...'

'Bollocks!' a grinning oaf shouted just as the screen went black and the camera position and the hapless detective were overwhelmed by the herd as it shoved and barged its way across the sea road towards the school sports field and paediatricians the length and breadth of the nation unscrewed their brass plaques and battened down the hatches.

Meanwhile Jimmy and Bart must have been working overtime because *Bring It On* blared out on MTV while the muted THE BOX screen showed the ancient video for the original release featuring a young, thin but much more miserable me.

'Must be fucking Christmas,' I murmured. 'Money time!'

43

Revenge

Immediately after his Sunday 'service' Raines had trudged off along the coastal path, embarking alone on one of his twenty-four-hour 'walks in the wilderness', during which he'd hoped to make the decision whether Bunton was to live or die – that was assuming he'd survived forty-eight hours' bondage and the combined effects of the alcohol, the GHB and the cold. Alive he would be an accessory to murder – and could therefore be replied on to keep his mouth shut. Then again, the craven little sod was sure to break down as soon as the police started grilling him. Bone weary now as he neared Mimram Crescent from the inland end of the footpath, Raines hoped to find him dead and be spared the decision. He'd wait till the floods ebbed away and then deposit the body with those of the kids in the tunnel – then, when they were finally uncovered, the obvious conclusion would be that Bunton had been the kidnapper and that he'd chosen to die alongside his captives.

He halted suddenly, alerted by the crackle of radio. Police. Two cars, sitting outside his house. The lights were on and the front door open. Raines swivelled and stepped into the shadows of the bushes, instinctively heading for the sanctuary of the pavilion, forgetting that only to him and his flock was it anything like a church.

Luckily though, as he stepped into the open sports field, almost bright as day in the reflected radiance of the town and the self-congratula-Tory mock Tudor 'executive homes' that lined its perimeter, there was some major sporting fixture going on. *A floodlit rugger match,* he guessed. *The Lord is with me,* he thought. *I'll mingle with the spectators and slip away with the crowds - when it's all over,* he thought.

It was now!

'That's him!' someone shouted and a two hundred-strong mob turned its heads as one and gave up a monstrous, guttural roar as it bore down on the stricken Raines and engulfed him just as he reached the giant aitch of the rugby goalposts. Suddenly the police seemed like a very attractive proposition – and sure enough here came the cavalry, but at a horribly slow pace.

★   ★   ★

'Hang the fucker from the posts,' Bart shouted hysterically at the screen as Daisy looked on, transfixed in a kind of morbid awe. 'Hang him!'

We glimpsed Raines *père* in an unfamiliar supplicant pose – but the mob was in no mood for mercy and they bore him to the ground. Of course the police had raced to the scene, all blues and twos and sirens wailing, and surrounded the scene. But now they'd arrived, the cordon's mood was more like the police presence at Notting Hill Carnival, smiling, almost kindly and benign – at least recently. Laid-back didn't begin to cover it. The news crews moved close as they dared, zooming in on smiling coppers chatting among themselves and making the odd desultory attempt to calm the crowd. If they'd played a Calypso, I swear they'd have danced along.

★   ★   ★

The last thing Erich Raines saw was the words DYE PEDO SCUM as the unyielding plywood placard descended on his flat and yielding face and immediately made it a lot flatter as he sank into the deathly embrace of the hallowed and waterlogged turf of his own Goalgotha.

'Our Father, who art in Heaven...' he began, but never finished. His Lord obviously hadn't been listening. Or maybe he had.

★   ★   ★

'You ever read *The Crow Road?*' Daisy Raines smirked, rolling on top of me as the Daisy Chain rolled under me.

'Iain Banks, yeah, why?'

'Didn't you just love that bit where she uses Morse code?'

'Oh yes – rude and sexy yet incredibly romantic without being cheesy all at once.'

'Glad you think so,' Daisy breathed as her well-honed pelvic floor muscles squeezed me rhythmically.

.−.   −−− .−.. . ...− ..−.

In the hot and heady afterglow of love and justice, my head resting on her lustrous white nacredness, I murmured, 'I never thought I'd be so happy to be a dad you know. And Joe's so much like me isn't he, don't you think?'

Daisy sat up.

'I've been meaning to talk to you about that,' she said, staring vacantly out of a porthole at the dazzling white glare of Barcelona's Port Olympic.

'What?'

'Oh nothing.'

OVER AND OUT.

Morse Code Alphabet

A	.-	0	-----
B	-...	1	.----
C	-.-.	2	..---
D	-..	3	...--
E	.	4	....-
F	..-.	5	.....
G	--.	6	-....
H	....	7	--...
I	..	8	---..
J	.---	9	----.
K	-.-	Fullstop	.-.-.-
L	.-..	Comma	--..--
M	--	Query	..--..
N	-.		
O	---		
P	.--.		
Q	--.-		
R	.-.		
S	...		
T	-		
U	..-		
V	...-		
W	.--		
X	-..-		
Y	-.--		
Z	--..		